## DEATHSONG

Sykes activated the acoustical monitoring system, a series of strategically placed microphones that relayed the sounds coming from the inside of the nuclear reactor vessel to the control room.

A deafening roar spilled out of the monitor speakers, the sound of coolant water pummeling the core into obedience. Henkel, Jenkel, and Sykes leaned forward, scrutinizing the rumbling wall of noise.

Jenkel was the first to notice. "There," he said. "Do you hear that?"

Henkel and Sykes cocked an ear toward the sound. It hit them within seconds of one another. "Jesus," Sykes whispered, as the fleshy part of his neck prickled with dread.

*It was an eerie barbed filigree of sound that rose and fell and twisted, not beneath the roar or behind it but somehow in it, a frequency-shifting inside the water-sound. As they listened one thing became clear. It was no accident. It was too complex and multi-timbral, too . . . intelligent.*

*The reactor was singing.*

# THE BRIDGE

## A Horror Story

### John Skipp
### &
### Craig Spector

**BANTAM BOOKS**

NEW YORK · TORONTO · LONDON · SYDNEY · AUCKLAND

*To Gaia and Linda Marotta*

*Big goddess. Little goddess.*

THE BRIDGE
*A Bantam Book / October 1991*

There are several towns named Paradise. This isn't any of them. All characters, locations and situations were invented and/or speculative, and any similarity to places or persons, living or dead, is purely coincidental.

*Grateful acknowledgement is made for permission to reprint the following: Excerpt from "THAT SMELL," words and music by Allen Collins and Ronnie Van Zant. Copyright © 1977 by DUCHESS MUSIC CORPORATION and GET LOOSE MUSIC, INC. Rights administered by MCA MUSIC PUBLISHING, A Division of MCA INC., New York, NY 10019. Used by permission. All rights reserved. Excerpt from PATTERNS IN NATURE by Peter S. Stevens courtesy Little, Brown and Company.*

ISBN 0-553-29027-4
*Published simultaneously in the United States and Canada*

*Bantam Books are published by Bantam Books, a division of Bantam Doubleday Dell Publishing Group, Inc. Its trademark, consisting of the words "Bantam Books" and the portrayal of a rooster, is Registered in U.S. Patent and Trademark Office and in other countries. Marca Registrada. Bantam Books, 666 Fifth Avenue, New York, New York 10103.*

PRINTED IN THE UNITED STATES OF AMERICA

OPM        0 9 8 7 6 5 4 3 2 1

# Acknowledgments

This book differs from our others primarily in the extent to which we owe our major players. Of the usual list of suspects, special thanks to Richard Monaco and Adele Leone, who went above and beyond the call; to Janna Silverstein, for her editorial eye; and to the whole Bantam food chain, just becuz.

Endless love and thanks to Marianne (for every single thing and boy were there a lot of 'em, darlin'); to Lori (for the decade and the dreams); to Lisa (for love, in the life after); to Melanie and Mikey (for being entirely too cool, and lending us much-needed hope for the future); and to good ol' Uncle Fred (who was always there when we needed her).

Specific and heartfelt cudos to Mickey Halper, whose insights into electronic media, local politics and motorcycle maintenence inform this book to the core. God bless, bubs. You know the deal.

Additional thanks to: Judy, for the true-life sagas; Felicia, for the hospital specs; Mystery K and Mystery D, for the skinny on nukes and 911; Linda, again, for a billion concrete acts of beneficence; Greg Landis, for helping put us on the midnight dumping trail; Blaine Quickel, for the smalltown lowdown; and all you nutsy funsters out there, writing those Letters to the Editor.

Beyond that, hats off to Unca Pat, D-boy, R.C., Clive, Poppy, our folks, Scott Wolfman and Wolfman Productions, Pete & Gail, Pat LoBrutto, Gary, Kathy Becker, Leslie & Adam, Mary, Steve, Doug Winter, Steve Niles, tkins, Nick Vince, Barbie Wilde, Kathy, Ellen, Phil, rival gangs at KNB and Optic Nerve, Tom Savini, George and Chris Romero, the cast and crew from *Nightbreed* and *Night of the Living Dead*, Cindy, Todd, Clarence, Mark, Julie, Amber, Buddy, Jesus, Jen, the folks from *Outer Limits*, *Dangerous Visions*, *Forbidden Planet*, and the *Fantasy Inn* (U.K.), our Bookland buddies and all the other friends we failed, like the bastards we are, to mention.

The following albums, by the following artists, provided big chunks of sonic background during the writing of this mind-movie:

THE BEATLES—*Sgt. Pepper's Lonely Hearts Club Band*

DAVID BOWIE—*Heroes; Low* (the instrumental sides); *Sound + Vision* (volume 3)

KATE BUSH—*The Sensual World*

BRUCE COCKBURN—*Big Circumstance*

THOMAS DOLBY—*The Flat Earth*

DANNY ELFMAN—*So-Lo; Batman* (soundtrack)

PETER GABRIEL—*Security; Birdy* (soundtrack); *Passion* (soundtrack, *The Last Temptation of Christ*)

GOBLIN—*Dawn of the Dead* (soundtrack)

JERRY HARRISON: CASUAL GODS

JOHN HARRISON—*Day of the Dead* (soundtrack); *Creepshow* (soundtrack)

LITTLE FEAT—*Let It Roll*

JOHN COUGAR MELLENCAMP—*The Lonesome Jubilee*

ENNIO MORRICONE—*The Thing* (soundtrack)

PETER MURPHY—*Love Hysteria; Deep*

NINE INCH NAILS—*Pretty Hate Machine*

OINGO BOINGO—*Boingo Alive* (volumes 1 and 2); *Nothing to Fear; Only a Lad; Good for Your Soul; Dead Man's Party; Boi-ngo; Dark at the End of the Tunnel*

PINK FLOYD—*A Momentary Lapse of Reason*

ROBERT PLANT—*Now and Zen; Manic Nirvana*

THE POLICE—*Synchronicity*

PUBLIC IMAGE, LTD.—*9*

RED HOT CHILI PEPPERS—*Mother's Milk*

RHYTHM DEVILS—*Play River Music* (percussion soundtrack, *Apocalypse Now*)

ROBBIE ROBERTSON—*Robbie Robertson*

TODD RUNDGREN—*Healer*

SISTERS OF MERCY—*Floodland*

**TALKING HEADS**—*Naked; Remain in Light*
**TANGERINE DREAM**—*Miracle Mile* (soundtrack)
**TEARS FOR FEARS**—*Songs From the Big Chair; The Seeds of Love*
**TIN MACHINE**—*Tin Machine*
**TONIO K.**—*Life on the Food Chain*
**TREAT HER RIGHT**—*Tied to the Tracks*
**WANG CHUNG**—*Mosaic; The Warmer Side of Cool; To Live and Die in L.A.* (soundtrack)

Special thanks to all these people, who are in no way responsible for our actions.

# THE
# BRIDGE

"To be an Error and to be cast out is a part of God's design."

William Blake

"Nature does not premeditate; she does not use mathematics; she does not deliberately produce whole patterns, she lets whole patterns produce themselves. Nature does what nature demands; she is beyond blame and responsibility."

Peter S. Stevens<br>*Patterns in Nature*

# One

The thing Boonie loved most about dumping off Black Bridge was how altogether goddam convenient it was. Take, for example, the traveling time. Even with miniature minefields of ice booby-trapping the backroads of Hellam, he figured ten minutes tops in the old Dodge truck to hump a full load of barrels from there to here.

So even if the storm broke before they were done— and the odds on that kept looking better and better—it still wouldn't take them but forty-five minutes to unload the whole batch and skedaddle back home.

On nights like tonight, he was especially appreciative.

Not that they'd seen many nights quite like this.

"Jesus," Boonie spat out, grinning. "Would you look at that shit." He jabbed one oversized thumb at the clouds, hanging swollen and gray in the black sky overhead. His other hand gripped the wheel in a casual stranglehold, steering by intuition. "They look like big dead ugly brains, you know it? Like the whole sky is made out of brains . . ."

3

"Let's just go back, man," Drew muttered from the passenger seat, bulging lemur eyes aglisten with crystal meth and anxiety. "Do it tomorrow or something. We can't work in this shit."

Boonie scowled, dodged a pothole. "You're such a fuckin' wiener, Drew. You don't like the storm? I *love* it, man."

The sky went *kaboom* and neon-flickered, winter lightning twitching to the angry rowl of God. Drew jumped and shivered. It was funny as hell. "I love this shit," Boonie reaffirmed, gazing ahead at their destination.

Black Bridge loomed before them, stark against the violent, primal sky. It didn't need anyone's help to rate as ultimate creature-feature territory. It was a brooding, decrepit old railroad crossing, limned by crumbling stone and situated smack-dab in the middle of nowhere: a rusting dinosaur from the days when trains were the lifeblood, steel rails the veins of Paradise County and the nation.

A generation of disuse had left it overgrown, flanked by bleached bony trees, choked with kudzu and dense, gnarled undergrowth. Many of the ties had long gone punky and worm-holed, but its poured concrete pylons and steel beams still held, casting fat lightning shadows on the murky green waters of the Codorus Creek, some thirty feet below.

The only way in was via Toad Road, a bumpy, chuck-holed dirt access barely wide enough to accommodate the overloaded truck. Snaking through the verdant green valley at the east end of the county, Toad Road went unmarked and appeared on none but the most anal tax maps of the county, which pretty much sewed up the privacy angle. By day, it was home only to dopers, dirtbikers, and hunters looking to poach an off-season deer or two.

By night, no one came there at all.

Yep, Boonie loved everything about this place: its proximity, its privacy, its dread-inducing atmosphere. But the thing he loved most was the simple fact that if you pulled right up in the middle of the bridge and angled the sucker back until your ass hung over the side, you could sorta just lean the barrels off the back and let fly straight into the creek. Fuckers never even had to come down off the bed. That cut down on a lot of the really heavy lifting, which was the worst part of the job, except maybe for the smell.

Bradley Gene Pusser—"Boonie" to his friends—was a twenty-five-year-old, six-foot-four-inch, two-hundred-and-forty-seven-pound mountain of ugly intent. His flapjowled, aging-Elvis features were pasty and unpleasant, eyes sullen and bulging under the brim of his blue Steelers cap. Along with his size and his nasty disposition, he'd inherited the Pusser genetic penchant toward alcoholism, pattern baldness, and flab.

All told, life had been one steep, harsh, downhill slide since the end of his high school football career. For a while there, back in the glory days, he'd been able to entertain dreams, of scholarships and pro ball and a permanent all-expense-paid ticket out of this pisshole town. His coach believed, his teammates believed, the nookie-nookie candyass cheerleaders believed, and god damn if his own *daddy*—the venerable Otis J., Jr.—hadn't come to believe that a Pusser had been born who could break the chain and bust on through to some kind of success.

But when his right kneecap vaporized late in the season of his senior year, so had his ticket out of town, and his dreams. Suddenly, the calls from Penn State and Indiana dried up; his name disappeared from the local sports pages; and Otis—who'd taken to telling everyone within earshot that his boy was gonna go big-time—suddenly Boonie and Otis and the whole goddam family had to bite the bullet and own up to the facts: no Pusser was ever gonna amount to a hill of shit.

And Boonie would always be a Pusser.

From that moment on, he'd thrown himself into the family business with a vengeance, working long and hard to make his Pappy proud again. It was dirty work, but it paid cash money, and Pussers weren't shy where there was money to be made. In fact, business had boomed since he'd taken over the grunt work, leaving Otis to preside over public relations and pursue his hobby of stargazing through the bottom of a Jim Beam bottle.

On the other hand, there was cousin Drew.

"Here we go, cuz," Boonie said, pulling up to the point where the road met the railroad tracks. He grunted, shoving the truck into low gear. It was hard to maneuver in this much darkness; even the headlights were swallowed up by the storm. He laid on the gas and eased off the clutch, careful to roll up onto the tracks without losing the load.

"Watch out!" Drew whined, his Adam's apple bobbing. He was the runt of Uncle Bud's litter, a complete genetic one-eighty from the rest of the menfolk in the Pusser family tree. At twenty years old, he was as much a man as he was ever likely to be: knock-kneed and scrawny, with a chicken-bone chest and a cratered, crescent-moon face. His hair was a black matted oilslick that trickled down way past his shoulders. He wore a black leather jacket and little fingerless gloves, a greasy Harley T-shirt, and tons of biker gear, though he didn't own a bike and wouldn't have known how to ride it if he did.

Drew's contact sport of choice was a little liquid-crystal video game that he wore on his digital watch. It had an eensy little jet that bombed a teensy little city; every time he dropped a bomb, it played a weensy, wheedling melody.

The truck lurched again, jostling them so hard that Drew's head rapped the ceiling. "Boonie!" he whined.

"Fuck you, puss. Hang on," Boonie growled. The truck groaned and gnashed gears, big knobby tires biting into rotted ties. The barrels shifted hard but stayed.

"This place, you know, it really makes me fuckin' nervous." He diddled with his watch. *Weedle eedle eee*, it said. *Weedle eedle eee . . .*

"Would you cut it out?" Boonie barked. "God, I hate that thing!"

"Fuck you, man." Drew sniffled. "This is modern technology at its finest, dude!"

*Weedle eedle eedle eeeeee . . .*

He smirked, and there went the last of Boonie's patience. He pegged Drew's skinny little jut-jawed profile with a straight-arm, flat-hand blow, square to the side of the head. Drew's skull cracked painfully against the passenger side glass; he bit down on his tongue hard enough to spritz blood.

"Ow! *Fug* you, Bood! I'b dellin'!" he whined, gripping his cheek.

"Swear to God, Drew, if you don't stuff it I'm gonna fuckin' leave you here *and* keep your share of the money."

Drew started to counter, then abruptly and visibly changed his mind. He knew well enough, from previous experience, that Boonie was not fooling.

For his part, Boonie found it downright gratifying to watch Drew fold like that. It gave him a nice warm feeling inside. So he decided to be magnanimous. "Here ya go, peckerhead. Got a surprise for ya."

Boonie produced a reedy little joint from his jacket pocket. "Just what the doctor ordered. Fire 'er up."

"Thangs," Drew sniffled, taking the doob.

"We dump this load, I'll cut us a couple lines," Boonie said paternally. "In the meantime, I suggest you stoke up, 'cause we got work to do."

Boonie laid on the brakes and brought the truck to a shuddering halt, then gnashed it into reverse and humped over the tracks until the tailgate was butt up against the lip of the rail. The positioning was perfect. He left the engine running against the cold and stared out over his domain.

Above him, the heavens thundered, so close Boonie could feel it in the soles of his shoes. A flash of lightning seared the night sky. "*BLOOOH*-HA HA!" Boonie cackled, his features glowing green in the dashboard light. The first fat raindrops spattered the windshield.

At last the storm had broken.


*The Codorus Creek had long been a sin-eater for the Industrial Revolution: a chemical cessway, accepting and dispensing with the intemperate by-products of the good life. Defense plants, research laboratories, factory farms, electroplate shops, paper mills, and landfills routinely decanted their excreta there. As such, even in the days before Boonie, it was already laced with "acceptable" levels of a thousand wild-card contagions: leads, cyanides, arsenics, alkalies, chlorinated hydrocarbons, dioxins, trioxons, trichlorophenal residues, poisons, and pesticides galore.*

*But now there was a rusting graveyard under the waters beneath Black Bridge: tons upon tons of crushed drums and rotting husks, choking the space beneath the muddy surface. Most had long since popped their corks, but quite a few were still intact: fifty-five-gallon pockets of concentrated death, corroding the barrels from either side and then suppurating into the slipstream.*

*Carcinogens settled in its silt, drifting lazily on their way to the river and the sea: mutagens skinned its sluggish surface, quietly rearranging the molecular building blocks of everything they touched. Carp and hardier garbage-eaters slid through its murky currents: gills siphoning oxygen, stockpiling pestilence.*

*Mindlessly laying their eggs.*

*Black Bridge was a toxic ground zero, an industrial Instant Primordial Stew. Only one century in the making, and already as rich as the brew from which all life-as-we-know-it sprang. Across the country, across the globe, countless thousands just like it lay dormant and sleeping.*

*It was only a matter of time before the next wake-up call.*

*At 3:27 that morning, it came.*


\*        \*        \*

"BOMBS AWAY!" Boonie cried, and rolled another one down the chute.

"Bombs away!" Drew reiterated, dropping the gate. It jutted over the rail like a stumpy steel diving board.

A cobalt-blue fifty-five-gallon drum stenciled DANGER rumbled down the slight incline of the truck bed, then off and into the blackness below. There was a beat of silence as gravity took over, then a deep wet *thwump* almost musical in timbre as it broke the creek's surface like a cannonball. A plume of water shot high into the air, then rained back down in a pelting, misty spray.

"*Bull's-eye!*" Drew cackled as he turned around. "Fuckin' *aye!*" He was stoned as a bastard now, relaxing behind the job. With his red bandanna pulled up over his nose to cut the fumes, he looked like a cross between Bazooka Joe and the Frito Bandito.

"Awright! Drewie gets a woody!" Boonie bellowed through his own paisley kerchief. "Shit, cuz, I knew you'd come 'round!"

The rain came down in earnest now, wet and steady. And *warm*, Boonie noted; strangely out of place, a summer storm snaking up from out of nowhere to thread through the chill November night. The warring fronts slammed together like invisible giants. Warm rain hit cold ground and hissed like whispering voices.

Boonie left his cab door open anyway, the better to hear the radio. Starview 92 classic rock was layin' down some fine old Allman Brothers, and they had the volume cranked to Brother Greg's moody classic, "Midnight Rider."

Yeah, man, Drew smiled to himself, nodding in time with the tune. *That's exactly who we are. We're the fuckin' midnight riders, man.* It gave him a little surge of pride, made him feel real good about himself.

In fact, Drew was feeling fine. Never better. They were soaked, but it was great; a warm wind whipping around them, the whole world glowing and pulsing in time with the music.

Boonie was trading air-guitar licks with the late great Brother Duane. Drew grinned at him and sucked on the joint through his impromptu mask. It gave him a toothless shadow mouth. He toked again and sucked the scarf full into his mouth, went *bluh bluh bluh* through the red cotton maw. Goddam, but he was funny sometimes.

His lips began to tingle.

The song ended, segued into "Riders on the Storm." "Okay!" Boonie hollered. "Ready up! Only thirteen more to go!"

"Fuckin' aye!" Drew yelled back absently, thinking about his lips. The tingle was now a slight burning sensation. It was probably just the dope. Sometimes Boonie did dumb shit to get high, like cop some lame weed and lace it with crack or dust or whatever he had lying around. It made you, like, ultra-aware of your senses. Like the rain, trickling water down his spine. Like the howl of the wind through the trees, or the throb in his brain from sucking up all those fumes . . .

"*Ech*," Drew spat. His lips were really burning now; and worse, he could *taste* it: a bitter, pungent, distinctly chemical flavor. It stuck pins in the tip of his tongue and tickled at the roof of his mouth.

It was starting to make him nervous.

"Hey, Spacely Sprocket!" Boonie yelled. "You gonna give me a hand with this?" Drew turned to look at him, the barrel he was angling onto its side.

"Boonie." The name tasted vile in his mouth, down his throat. And his eyes were beginning to itch.

"What?" Impatient.

"Dude, I don't feel so good." He rubbed at his eyes, and the burn redoubled. "*Ouch*! Sonofabitch!" Now his *nostrils* were burning, and the smell was getting stronger. "Something's wrong here, man . . ."

"Don't get paranoid on me, Drew. I thought we were havin' fun."

"Yeah, but . . ."

A thunderclap ignited in fiery gray light, directly above their heads. Drew's bones nearly flew out through his skin; he could feel his nerves jangle and his heartbeat rev. "Christ!" he yelled, feeling suddenly light-headed.

The thunderclap faded.

But the gray light remained . . .

. . . *and that was when they heard the sound: a crackling like ravenous flame, huge as it welled up to bury the silence. The world's largest wad of cellophane, crinkling slowly in the hand of an angry god. Black static, edging in from another dimension.*

*Coming up from the water below.*

Drew turned to look at Boonie. Boonie's answering stare was uncharacteristically blank. *What the fuck . . . ?* Drew watched him mouth, but the sound refused to carry. The barrel slipped out of his grasp and thundered to the truck bed on its side. Drew winced, felt it rather than heard it.

And still the roaring drone persisted, maddening: more liquid than static, the longer he listened. He turned toward it, staggering for the gate: head muzzy, body voltaged numb. The roach dropped unnoticed from between his thrumming fingers.

As Drew stared out over the edge.

At the terrible source of the sound.

The fish were trying to get out of the water. There was no other way to describe it. They were literally *throwing themselves into the air*: leaping up and flailing in desperate but fleeting defiance of gravity. As if they were trying to spontaneously evolve, evolve into birds who could fly off to heaven, evolve into anything that could possibly escape and survive.

No where.

No way.

He watched in horror as the water beneath them began to bubble and churn. Then the gray light flickered, faded to black.

Behind him, Boonie let out a scream.

Drew turned just in time to see the drum rumbling toward him, picking up speed as it closed on the edge. It was the one that had slipped from his cousin's grip, but it wasn't the only one moving.

The whole back of the truck was a flurry of jittery motion, the last dozen barrels rocking and shuddering on their bases. As if something had come alive inside of them.

As if that something wanted out.

Drew barely managed to sidestep the drum as it thundered past him, disappeared over the side. There was one long, astonishingly pregnant moment of roaring silence.

Then the drum broke the surface, like egg-drilling sperm.

And thus was the new world conceived.

*born of poison*
*raised in poison*
*claiming poison for its own*
*it rose*
*a miracle of raw creation*
*hot black howl of life and*
*death intertwined and converted to*
*some third new option*
*agony blip with an echoing tail*
*so long it seemed to have gone on forever*
*only now the tail was wagging the dog*
*dredging up silt and sewage*
*bursting metal eggshell skins in a*
*riotous shrapnel dance of*
*power surging self-aware*
*gathering mass assassinating shape*

*infesting polluting corrupting*
*in hideous birthday celebration*
*it rose*
*already killing*
*and stared into the face of its maker*

Drew was less than six feet away from the rail when the massive liquid blowback erupted: a solid pillar of displaced fluid that shot from the creek to the peak of Black Bridge in a fraction of a second. It towered above him and *stayed* there, impossible: fracturing physics, disemboweling logic.

Coalescing into form.

The creature loomed, not freeze-framed or static but *swaying* like a wind funnel, an enormous oily serpent. Against the black sky, it did not look real; but he could feel the incredible life-shredding charge of its presence, pulsating in the air. It made every hair on his body stand on end in total, mortal terror.

*And then the lightning struck, releasing him utterly from his sanity. In the light, he could see all too clearly the things that suffered and swirled within it. Could see the rusted struts and rotted shells of the barrels: skeletal, clawing. Could see the multicolored Rorschach toxins that were its blood and soul.*

*Could see the hundreds and hundreds of fish: not dead, no longer alive.*

*All of them staring. At him.*

*With new eyes . . .*

Then the lightning decayed; and before he could scream, the black wall descended upon him.

Boonie dove off the side of the truck in the second before it hit. He was still in the air when several tons went *WHOOOM* and splattered across its bed. He couldn't see what happened to Drew. He didn't need to see to know there was nothing he could do.

Boonie was heavy, and plummeted fast. He hadn't had time to plot a course. The railroad tracks came up to meet him, head-on and far too quickly.

He got his arms up and tucked his body enough to keep his neck from snapping; all it cost him was a splintered clavicle and, on the second bounce, some teeth and lip, the two merged together in a wet hard bone-shard buckshot hail that gagged him as he rolled, came up, instinctively assessed the situation.

No motion from the truck, except for the steam curling off the exterior. The door was still open; the cab was still vacant; the headlights still glared. Beyond the truck lay Toad Road and escape; the other way just led deeper into the Black Bridge woods. He could drive one whole hell of a lot faster than he could run.

That pretty much wrapped it up. Boonie vaulted for the cab, keeping one eye on the railroad ties and the other one peeled for forty-foot monsters. There was a harsh static crackle in the air that kept getting louder, the closer he got. It wasn't the sound from the creek, so it didn't mean shit.

It was the radio, he found out when he hit the driver's seat. Starview 92 had disintegrated into ear-splitting hiss. Bad sign. He grabbed the stick and jammed it in gear. Nothing happened. He laid on the gas and got dick.

"GOD DAMN IT!" he bellowed, grabbing the keys and grinding the ignition. "GO . . . !"

That was when he noticed the rivulets, moving across the windshield. Not down. *Across*: a lateral, spider-webbing motion, like a hundred liquid tentacles gripping the cab. He stared in slack-jawed dumbstruck awe as the glass started to steam. The liquid compressed impossibly against the pane and *squeezed*.

Boonie dove for the passenger side, grappling with the handle. All around him, the safety glass starred. He cracked the door open, started to bail . . .

... *as the windows blew inward: a blinding, razored spray*...

... and then he was out the door and running, running for his life, a thousand tiny septic barbs of shrapnel lodged in his face, his hands, his neck and back and legs that tripped on a tie and brought him down, all two hundred and forty-seven pounds of him, shrieking pain as his scar-pitted Frankenstein's former right knee smacked cold steel rail...

... but he couldn't stay down or the game was fucking over, so he pistoned back up to his feet and hobbled with all his might, ignoring the pain, ignoring the everywhere tingle that turned to burn, terrible burn in his eyes, left eye stinging sharp and wet and bleeding, bleeding from within...

... and still he ran, trading the rails for Toad Road mud, screaming out prayers to sweet baby Jesus as he stumbled through puddles of primal rain. Running from the devil in his own back pocket.

Running till he dropped...

# Two

One hundred and eighty-eight thousand souls adorned the rolling stretch of God's country that was Paradise, Pennsylvania. It was just over nine hundred square miles of sprawling, picturesque land, with the rugged hump of the Appalachian foothills sweeping across the west and the wide rocky expanse of the Susquehanna River to the east.

Paradise was the nexus point of the region's major east/west, north/south arteries, which made it the natural nerve center for trucking of every stripe. Big rigs rumbled in and out constantly, ferrying the essential ingredients of the good life east to Philadelphia and New York; south to Baltimore and Washington; north to Harrisburg and Allentown; and west, down the turnpike, to Pittsburgh and the Ohioan heartlands beyond.

The outer townships were mostly made up of farms, factories, and forestland, green hills and hollows sparsely populated and broken up by strip malls and sleepy one-horse hamlets that accounted for maybe thirty-seven thousand out of the total population.

Another seventy-three thousand or so clustered around the industrial parks, which in turn gave way to wave upon wave of dense-packed, self-replicating suburbia: houses and lawns and houses and lawns, gradually shrinking in size as the neighborhoods crested the hills and entered the valley that marked the city proper. There they packed in, tighter and tighter, until the lawns at last evaporated into puddle-sized patches or disappeared altogether.

The City Reservoir, on the south side of town, was the highest elevation and the site of the Paradise Water Company's vast standing pools. If you stood on the crest of the hill and looked out over the valley, a vision spread before you: lights twinkling in the deep blue predawn hush, a quintessentially American picture-postcard jumble of church steeples and smokestacks, homes and factories and parks and schools.

Seventy-eight thousand people lived and dreamt there: along narrow one-way streets and shady tree-lined boulevards; in the crumbling tarpaper Penn Street shanties and cozy Cape Cods of College Avenue; in the tastefully renovated Market Square townhouses and lush Georgian abodes of Linden Boulevard.

From the posh palatial estates of Wyndham Hills to the paper-thin walls of the Paradise Rescue Mission—and everywhere in between—one hundred and eighty-eight thousand hearts beat through the night, ticking off the moments of a lifetime.

Paradise boasted a low cost of living and an unemployment rate a few tenths of a point below the national average. The last thirty years had seen a steady growth in the black and Hispanic communities—and, more recently, a proportionately microscopic Asian influx—but despite all this, as well as a strong, prosperous Jewish community, local government and industry still remained in the firm Protestant grip of the same Dutch-German hands that had wrested this land from the Indians.

This was a land of faschnachts and pig roasts, of country clubs and county fairs, of ladies' invitational golf classics in dichotomous tandem with tractor pulls and trailer parks. And like much of the noncosmopolitan East, Paradise County was notorious for its stodginess and slow-moving resistance to change: a temperament shared by its upper and lower classes alike.

Once you got past their roots, however, it was television that truly shaped and defined their culture: from CBN to MTV, PBS to HBO, with network news, halftime shows, and prime-time fodder in dominion *über alles*.

It was, in short, America.

And, like the rest of America, Paradise slept: well past the wee hours, to the break of Sunday dawn. Across the city, across the county, one hundred and eighty-eight thousand lives lay down together in isolated slumber, unconsciously intertwined.

And not a one of them ever even saw it coming.

# Three

Gwen opened her eyes, suddenly awake, the phantom remnants of REM-stage sleep still clinging to her thoughts like a shroud.

*In the dream, black birds: thousands of them, their iridescent wings and harsh cries filling the sky as they swooped and soared in a figure-eight pattern.*

*Over and over, over and over . . .*

The image faded, dissipating like morning fog and leaving Gwen with a strange sense of dislocation, of consciousness arriving a split second before identity. For a single elastic moment, she didn't know who or where or *what* she was.

Only *that* she was.

Alive. Awake.

Here.

It was an altogether curious feeling, disorienting but not entirely unpleasant. She allowed herself to steep in it for a moment, let it flavor her perceptions without bias or preconception.

The she felt the kick inside.

And it all came flooding back.

*My name is Gwen Taylor. I'm thirty years old. I'm in my bed, in my room, in my house.*

It kicked again: a small solid thump deep within.

*And I'm going to have a baby*, she amended.

The dislocation disappeared: a puff of subconscious synapse flotsam vaporized by thought. Gwen yawned and stretched in the big brass bed. Her sleep-tossed ash-blond hair flowed across the pillow; her clear gray eyes were elegantly framed by the tiniest hint of smile crinkles.

She was a strikingly attractive woman, though you'd never get her to agree with that lately: nine months in and she felt more like an anaconda with a hippo lodged in its digestive tract. Not to put too fine a point on it, the words *dingo ugly* were the only ones she trusted to accurately convey her self-image, and there wasn't a damn thing Gary or anyone else could say to change her mind.

On the other hand, she felt pretty honest-to-God *good* today: very snug and happy and loved, with only a slight case of nausea to keep things in real-life perspective. The baby had dropped on Thursday, its head lowering into her pelvis in preparation for the homestretch. It took some of the pressure off, made her feel a *little* less bloated and unwieldy, most assuredly heightened her sense of anticipation.

"Won't be long now," she whispered to the growing form inside her. "You're gonna like it here."

She peeked out from the covers, entertaining the notion of just lazing around all day. It was a gray morning, from her vantage point; the old casement windows rattled as the wind pressed against them, trying to get in; a stray slice of predawn light shone cold through the part in the curtains, illuminating the dust motes that swirled in the air.

The ceiling fan overhead twirled lazily, recirculating heat. The house was a three-story frame structure off the Starview Road in East Manchester township, ten miles north of town. It was over a hundred years old, lovingly refurbished by Gary and Gwen until it just oozed warmth and character and a clear sense of *home*.

Their room was on the drafty side, bigger since Gary'd knocked the back wall out, reducing the available bedrooms in the old farmhouse from four to three but opening the space considerably.

*Besides*, she thought, running her hands up over the swell of her belly, *a guest room and a nursery's all we really need. We're only doing this once.*

The baby kicked again.

Gwen turned toward Gary, who lay still sleeping beside her, his body concealed in a mountain range of rumpled down. "Gary," she whispered. He stirred and mumbled something unintelligible into his pillow. She reached under the cover and tickled him. "Gary?"

Gary grumbled and stirred, but did not wake. She paused for a moment, just watching her man.

To those who knew him, it was hard to believe Gary Taylor had really hit thirty-seven; judging by energy level alone, he came off at least a dozen years younger. But seeing him at rest like this—with his personality temporarily on hold—she could see his years, and all the pressure he'd been under, etched in the craggy lines of his face.

Gary was a long, lean, lupine man with a rugged fighter's mug, softened by gentle eyes and a droopy paintbrush of a mustache. His hair was black and thick, silvering slightly at the temples and thinning into a widow's peak high on his forehead. When he rolled toward her, the pillow side stayed smushed, sticking up like a tar baby's mop.

Gwen smiled and reached under the covers, squeezing him. "Gary, you 'wake?" she teased.

He opened one eye, looked balefully at her with it.

"Spike kicked," she said, smiling sweetly. "Three times."

Gary blinked once, twice. He was waiting for enough blood to circulate into his brain to be capable of speech. He'd been up late the night before, called into the station at the last minute again by some technical problem that Bob the Knob couldn't deal with. "Mmm," he mumbled. "Mmph."

"He said he wants to see his old man," Gwen said.

"Mmph," Gary reiterated, burying his head with the pillow. "Not if he doesn't let me sleep, he doesn't."

"He's not the only one," Gwen said slyly, ignoring him. Hormones surged in the ninth month, though God only knew what for; they tweaked and tickled her erogenous zones like the haunting whispers of phantom limbs.

It wasn't arousal, exactly; at this point, she often found it hard to believe that she'd ever really be turned on—in the old-fashioned sense—again. Instead, she felt a keen need to be *made to feel attractive*: to assuage the irrational anxieties and be reassured, through the medium of physical contact, that she wasn't *really* too loathsome to live, and that Gary might still be able to love her somehow.

She reached between Gary's legs, got a handful of nice thick morning boner. Gary, for his part, groaned and smiled. No rest for the wicked, evidently. He opened both bleary eyes and looked at his wife, who smiled and worked him beneath the sheets. "I swear," he growled throatily, "you are incorrigible." She laughed, a sly little guttural chuckle.

Gary reached out and felt the firm round hardness of her belly, the fullness of her breasts, which had swelled half again their normal size over the course of the pregnancy. He looked at her; sleepy-eyed, big-bellied and disheveled, she was the most beautiful creature he'd ever seen in his life.

"Mornin', momma," he said.

"Mmmm," Gwen said dreamily. "Love you."

"Love you back," he said. Gwen leaned forward a little and Gary daubed her with morning-mouth kisses: feeling the liquid silk of her lips, tasting the familiar musky sweetness of her neck.

Gary's take on sex these days was a benign flip side to Gwen's. Arousal wasn't exactly what he'd call it, either: he felt less turned on than enormously protective and profoundly *nurturing* toward her. She was his lady love, after all; and the only critter that even came close in his affections was just about ready to poot forth from her loins.

Right now, he could love them both with one sweet motion, and give Gwen the reassurance she most desperately needed.

You couldn't get any more damn convenient than that.

"Anything special planned today?" he asked, as she spooned his cock against her backside, guided him between her legs.

"Mmmm," she answered, momentarily distracted. "Picking up Micki at eleven, remember?"

"Oh, yeah," he groaned. "Micki." Oboy. Visions of tofu, sandalwood, crystals and pentacles danced in his head. "How long's she staying again?"

"Till the baby's born, and I'm back on my feet," Gwen purred, anticipating the resistance. Gary grumbled. That meant at *least* six weeks of weed walks, witchy rituals, and West Coast weirdo diets. Probably more, if past experience was any judge.

"It'll be good for the baby," she said, shifting into a comfortable angle. "Besides, we've got the book to work on . . ."

Gary grumbled some more as he pressed into her. Gwen took it in stride, angling her hips and lifting one leg. Her pelvis was widened for the passage, her lips moist and full as the gates parted and Gary slid home.

The argument was over before it even started, as they locked on a slow, sensual rhythm of heat and love and life.

And morning came to another Sunday in Paradise.

# Four

First light fell on Dark Hollow Road at half past six: cutting through the scraggly woods of Windsor Township, slicing the darkness down into narrow strips of shadow. The storm had dwindled to mist and memory; but now the night was fading, too. In its place came ugly, cloud-refracted sunlight: unseasonably warm, and painful to behold.

But then again, everything was painful now.

He was a great big dying man, and he couldn't go much farther. Every agonized, crutching step forward was an ultimate act of will. He had been traveling south down the back roads of Hellam, in just this way, for hours.

The will was not entirely his own.

He rounded the final bend and paused there: swaying grotesquely swollen. Before him, the Flinchbaugh place splayed out like a tacky, white-trash Disneyland; it was all that remained between him and home. Dozens of lawn ornaments crowded Eb Flinchbaugh's manicured lawn: concrete jockey and leprechaun faces locked in lifeless smiles, little Dutch girl's eyes staring sightlessly through him as he passed.

Artificial flamingos and deer were clustered around the centerpiece:  a working fountain, burbling incessantly, *its sound soothing to his ears. The temptation to simply lay down among them and rest—perhaps forever—was over-whelming.*

*He could not let it happen.*

*Not when he was so close.*

*One shivering, shambling step after another, he descended into the hollow. Boonie's personal finish line in the bad-news relay race loomed before him; the rust-hued shimmer of the yard below was like a beacon.*

*Calling him home.*

Sometime after seven, Otis Pusser pulled up to the gate, slouching beneath the peeling vinyl top of his '79 Buick Skylark. He leaned into the horn, meaty palm pressing the wheel rim so hard it felt like it would snap clean off.

"GODDAMMIT! BOONIE!" he roared. "OPEN THIS GODDAMNED GATE!"

The horn lowed like a buttfucked sow. Behind the gate, DamDog and Coonie joined in, raggedy junkyard yowls compounding the din. They were mutts, scrawny-assed and nasty to the bone, bred mean and kept that way. While he watched, Coon jumped all fours into the air and snapped at the chain link, came down on DamDog, and got bit for his trouble. The air filled with fur and dogspit and dust.

"Stupid damn animals," he muttered, shaking his head and honking some more.

It wasn't that he didn't have keys; he just didn't want to get up. Otis tipped in at a couple of hairs over three hundred and fifteen pounds, most of it hard fat and body odor. His features were large-pored and leathery—the wages of a life of hard labor—and his nose was a vibrant rococo fresco of scarlet capillary distress. A Big Gulp cup was wedged between his thighs, filled three-to-one with coffee and Wild Turkey.

Otis gazed skyward, perturbed. A pocked metal sign

above the gate read *PUSSER'S SCRAP & SALVAGE*. It was his lifeblood, his legacy, and his bread and butter.

Which accounted in no small part for why Otis was so pissed. Here he was, up and ready for business, and where was his no-good son? Probably sleeping off a stone-drunk, the little shit.

Otis gave the horn one final blat, to no avail. "Some balls will roll," he grumbled, then threw open the door and squeezed through the gap. It took a minute to waddle over and unlock the gate; he swung it back, hitting the dogs in the process. DamDog yipped and skittered off Coon.

"Bitch! Git out the damn way!" Otis barked, returning to the car. The dogs scattered as he gunned the engine and motored into Pusserland proper.

It was a tad over three acres of rusted refuse, the cannibalized corpses of the American dream. Junked cars. Junked refrigerators. Junked air conditioners and hot-water heaters. Lots of just plain junk, passing through Otis's hands on its way to oblivion.

Otis had an eye for worth, and oodles of connections. He could rip the copper out of a Kool King faster than a *kapo* could yank teeth, and he knew just who to sell it to. It was a gift.

*Like last night's load*, he thought with no small satisfaction. *Not bad for one night's work*. Twenty-five drums at forty bucks per, a cool grand for the simple magic trick of making someone else's problem disappear. Otis was an alchemical endstop in the digestive tract of society, siphoning off the last ounce of value, turning shit to gold.

In the grand scheme of things, Pusser'. was the dungheap at the end of the line.

And Otis was the undisputed King of Turd Mountain.

He tooled down the main drive to the trailer, a forty-foot Airstream that double-dutied as both the office and Boonie's bachelor pad. Otis parked beside it and got out, noting that the lights were on in the trailer, even though the truck was gone. *Running up the goddamned electric bill again*, he thought. There was gonna be some serious butt kicked today.

He stomped toward the trailer door, brimming with fatherly, corporate, and inebriated rage. To his complete dissatisfaction, he found it unlocked and ajar. A thin sliver of gold light squirted out the crack, glowing in the pale blue dawn.

He slammed his way inside, preparing to pounce.

Then suddenly, abruptly, stopped.

The interior of the trailer was cramped, smelling of spilled beer and gym socks and crammed with cast-off furniture and antique porno mags. Another smell—dense, chemical, heady—hovered in the closed, dark space.

The boy was hunkered in front of a piece of mirror, propped on the battered steel desk that delineated the office. A gooseneck lamp was twisted up for illumination.

When the door flew open, Boonie whirled as if caught jerking off, though his expression conveyed far less surprise than pain. He had been mewling when his father came bursting in.

"Jesus H. Christ," Otis whispered, staring dumbstruck at the mess that was his son.

"Pa . . ." Boonie whimpered, stuffing psychic ice chips down the core of Otis's spine.

He clutched a pair of bloody tweezers in one hand and a gore-smeared rag in the other. A pile of glass cubes glistened before him like a grisly display from Van Scoy's Diamond Mine. It was only half the prize; the rest was still imbedded in Boonie's face.

The cleaned side was raw, almost abscessed; the lacerations had opened up, given rise to clusters of smaller open sores, like craters on the alien landscape of his cheek, nose, and forehead.

A bottle of hydrogen peroxide sat uncorked on the table. Boonie grabbed it with swollen fingers and doused the rag, then daubed his mangled right cheek.

It fizzed audibly, sputtering pinkish foam; Boonie

cried out and brought one clawed hand up to hover an inch away from the angry surface. He looked up at Otis, his eyes bloodshot watery orbs. "Pa, I fucked up. I fucked up, *bad*, Pa..."

Otis listened, as Boonie fessed up. It took two minutes. Otis didn't believe half the drugged-out shit his boy said, but the other half more than did it. Two sweeps of the second hand were more than enough time for Otis to imagine his kingdom crumbling beneath his feet.

Otis waited until Boonie finished, got the facts as straight as he could.

Then he kicked the shit out of him.

First things first.

# Five

"You're joking," Harold Leonard said.

There was a thin sheen of extremely cold sweat on his brow. It hadn't been there a minute ago. A minute ago, he'd been piling Marge and their six lovely children into the Arrow, mini-vanning in style to another Sunday service. A little Christian fellowship, promptly followed by the Bob's Big Boy buffet. It was a little chilly for golf, but Harold was a diehard. A quick nine holes down at the club, and he'd be back in time for the Eagles game.

A minute ago, he'd had it all figured out.

That minute was gone forever.

The voice on the other end of the phone was drunken, surly, strangely out of breath. It assured him that, no, it certainly wasn't a joke, then proceeded to rattle off a coarse litany of hugely unpleasant specifics. Each and every one of them fanned the spark of dread taking root in his lungs, peed fire into his paunchy gut.

Harold Leonard was the owner and operator of Paradise Waste Disposal, the area's largest legitimate waste disposal facility. For some fifteen years, the local industrial community had come to him with its dirty diapers: paying him dearly to clean them up or, at the very least, store them somewhere inoffensive and safe.

The good news was that business was grand; the one thing we never ran out of was waste. The *bad* news was that there was far too much of it. Even with the most up-to-date technology he was willing to spring for, he couldn't process but a fraction of what he took in. Every day, every month, every year.

That was where Harold's operation tiptoed somewhat afoul of the law.

Harold Leonard was a middleman in every sense of the word: middle-aged, middle-class, pickle in the middle. His stature in the business community commanded a respect that he rarely achieved in his personal life. Liver-lipped, beak-nosed and weasel-eyed, he was the last guy you'd have picked for your team in school: the fat kid who *always* got two for flinching.

He was flinching now, that much was for certain. The phone's receiver was slick in his porcine hand. "Don't do anything stupid," he heard himself whine. "We'll work this out."

"*You're goddam right we'll work this out,*" spat the voice from the other end. "*I wanna know what you're gonna do about my boys.*"

Harold didn't know what to say. The hospital was out, for obvious reasons. His brain flailed in search of contingency plans that didn't exist. "Look," he began. "I've got to talk to some people. You haven't told anyone else yet, have you?"

"*What, are you stupid?*"

He silently thanked God; and in that moment, his brain began to work. Perhaps it was the power of prayer. "Okay, listen up," he said. "First, I want you to call the cops."

"*Yeah, right! FUCK you!*"

"Will you listen to me!" Harold pressed, more forcefully. He was in his element now: weaseling in real time, thinking on his feet. "Tell 'em that you just got in, and the truck was stolen. Probably last night."

The moron to whom he was speaking made a colorful

noise of comprehension. Redeemed in his own eyes, Harold pressed on. "That'll cover you if they find it, and buy us some time to work this mess out."

"*Okay. I like that . . .*"

"And for Christ's sake, keep your big mouth shut. Don't say anything to *anybody* until I get back to you."

Leonard slammed the phone down, ending their chat on a power note. Then he stood there, just *shaking* for one long, dreadful minute, trying mightily to quell his panic. His ulcer bubbled like a gastric Jacuzzi; his heart slammed in his temples.

"Everything's gonna be fine," he told himself, wanting hard to believe it. "I'll just have to tell Blake. He'll know what to do . . ."

Outside, Marge or one of the kids tapped out "Shave and a Haircut" on the horn. It shook him out of his stupor, made him long for their warmth and companionship. *I'm not a bad guy*, he told himself.

Wanting hard to believe it.

*I'm not . . .*

Then Harold Leonard donned his coat and hat, locked the door of his cozy little house in Haines Acres, walked through the yard of his snug little hunk of suburban Paradise.

And went to join his loving family in worship.

At the church of his choice.

# Six

By a quarter after ten, on a Sunday morning, the legions of God's faithful were off and running.

Whatever else one might say about the people of Paradise County, Deitz noted, they were awfully big on Sunday services. And with eighty-seven houses of worship within the city limits alone—representing twenty-eight Christian denominations—there was certainly no shortage of God-anointed service stations. While the wicked slept in, the righteous deployed, flocking *en masse* to their respective personal savior pit stops.

From the Mennonite farms at the county's edge to the African Episcopal Church downtown, the children of God made their holy presence known. Between the hours of nine and noon, they virtually owned the roads: station wagons, packed to the gills with Baptists, Brethren, and Bible Fellows; drive-thru windows, dispensing Sausage and Egg McMuffins by the truckload to Methodists and Mormons alike; gas stations, meeting the motoring needs of Catholics, Christian Scientists, Seventh-Day Adventists, and Assemblymen of God.

Austin Deitz stood at the back of the Mt. Rose Amoco Shop 'N' Go, where Route 24 crossed Mt. Rose Avenue at the mouth of the eastern valley. He was perus-

ing the Yummy Potato Chip snack rack while he waited for
Jennie to return.

She'd disappeared behind the *Employees Only* door
ten minutes ago. As store manager, she'd been torn from
her bed and called in to troubleshoot the latest crisis: some
loser named Ozzie who'd called in sick at the very last
minute with tickets for the Eagles game.

That Ozzie now ranked among the unemployed was
no consolation at all. Only Ozzie's ability to deep-six their
Sunday plans held even the remotest level of interest for
him. It was, after all, a very special occasion.

Their fourth—count 'em, *fourth*—anniversary.

*Four solid weeks together*, Deitz mused, smiling. *My
God. That's practically a whole month! Somebody alert the
media!*

*Almost an entire month where you could virtually call
me happy.*

Austin Deitz was a month shy of forty, a tall gangly
man with knobby calloused hands and a face like a young
Abe Lincoln's. He had the same intense dark eyes and
severe, gaunt hollows to his cheeks, the same shock of
cowlicked hair and horsey overbite. The only things he
lacked were the beard and the bullet hole, and he was in
no great hurry to acquire either one.

He was not exactly what he'd consider a love machine, but Jennie didn't seem to mind. In fact, ever since
their eyes met over the barbecue chicken pit at the
Stoverstown Fire Company's Fall Festival, she'd changed
his mind about a lot of things.

Jennie Quirez was slight and slender, with a broad yet
delicate face framed by warm mahogany hair and offset by
the clearest, finest deep brown eyes he'd ever seen. She
was either late twenties or early thirties—Deitz hadn't
gotten around to asking yet, though he didn't think she'd
mind—far enough along, anyway, for her rich tan complexion to take on the supple, slightly leathery etch of time.

She smiled a lot and didn't take an ounce of shit from
anyone, a combination that Deitz found irresistible. She

was also, as if that wasn't enough, a compulsive reader of science fiction, whose childhood dream was to be an astronaut one day. For a kid who grew up thinking that Heinlein and Bradbury were gods, there could not have been a more perfect wish-fulfillment fantasy than a girl who knew what *to grok in fullness* really meant, or who could savor both the strange peace and melancholic beauty of a book like *The Martian Chronicles* and the icy, hard-wired edginess of Gibson's *Neuromancer.*

But the sf she loved most was fundamentally optimistic, like herself. She liked to believe that there really were other species out there somewhere—intelligent, kind, benevolent species—and that one day we'd actually evolve enough to join them in the stars.

Moreover, she liked to encourage those qualities in people here on Earth, for what she felt were pretty obvious reasons: a) to help us evolve just a little bit faster; b) because, quite simply, life was better when you treated people right; and c) because the odds were good that, given her current career trajectory, she'd never actually make it into space.

*She'll find someone to work,* he told himself. *Just have a little faith. You've got the Baltimore Aquarium and the Inner Harbor waiting, then dinner at Dobson's and a room at the Hunt Valley Inn. Which is to say: you cannot fail.*

*Keep playing your cards right. And pray for a miracle.*

*Today just might be the best day of your life.*

And, of course, it was true. Or at least it might be. Certainly, every Sunday since he'd first met Jennie had been better than the last. It was the first time, in what felt like forever, that Deitz had gotten so tight with somebody so quickly.

It was kind of like falling in love.

Which was an awful lot like a miracle in itself.

In the meantime, Deitz cruised the aisles aimlessly, waiting. There wasn't a nontoxic unit of food in the whole goddam store—not Jennie's fault; she was a manager, not a buyer—but that didn't stop a dozen consumers from stocking up on nutritionless, oversalted, or sugar-crammed delights. Deitz watched them mill about, comparing poisons: it was a desperate bid, on his part, to take his mind off his sudden apprehension.

He glanced at the data pager tucked onto his belt, its tiny power light forever glowing. *What if something happens?* he thought gloomily, watching Dobson's and the Hunt Valley Inn sprout wings and flutter away without them.

The beeper remained both alert and mercifully silent. *Okay, then,* he thought. *What if she can't find a sub...?*

"Now stop," he interrupted himself. "You promised, remember? Today, nothing gets to you. You're the happiest man on earth."

But some things were far easier said than done.

There was a dull-eyed girl behind the counter, sitting on a stool. She was jamming a Tastykake into her mouth as she rang up a PTL housewife with a pile of fudge brownies stacked like poker chips before her. *Pat,* the girl's tacky plastic name tag read. *Hi! My name is Pat.*

For a moment, in the flat, fluorescent glare, Pat's puffed fishbelly features seemed to somehow white out and magically *transform*: the rounded shoulders and rippling buttocks melding into the stool, erasing her identity entirely, until she became one great, pale, lumpen pyramid of consumption incarnate.

And for that moment of fancy, Deitz stared in mock horror as he pictured her: a gruesome Eating Machine, the cake disappearing down her champing maw like a log feeding into a tree shredder.

And, of course, the fact that it wasn't just *any* Tastykake, but a *Kreme-Filled Krummy Kake,* only made things better. That way, on top of everything else, Pat was sure to get her minimum daily adult requirements of monocalcium phosphate, mono and diglycerides, calcium lactate and propylene glycol monostearate. To name only a few.

A complete and balanced breakfast.

For a dumb and dying race.

"Blech," he muttered, forcing himself to look away.

It was impolite to stare, but he couldn't always help it. It was just so hard to believe that people were so oblivious. It had been *ages* since he'd allowed himself such luxurious ignorance.

In a world of shit, it was tough to remain untainted, but Austin Deitz did what he could. He disdained BHA and BHT, propyl gallate and yellow 5, which put the nix on everything from Snickers bars to Starburst fruit chews. He steered clear of sodium benzoate, which effectively ruled out virtually every quaff in the establishment, from orange drink and iced tea all the way to Mountain Dew. He didn't even want to *think* about the secret ingredients left unlabeled on their lunch-meat subs and ballpark franks.

The Yummy Potato Chip folks were another story: a local outfit, which made big book on ladling out fewer preservatives than their nationally known competitors. All the same, when it came down to the taste buds, they were still drawing from the same old bag of tricks: a little calcium silicate, monosodium glutamate, sodium acetate, and fumaric acid to suggest salt 'n' vinegar or bring out the zing in those "natural smoke flavors."

Which pretty much left him with the unsalted peanuts and imported mountain spring water, both packaged in nonrecyclable plastic that was destined to outlast his great-grandchildren's grandchildren. That is, assuming that he ever *had* kids.

Which was completely out of the question.

*And this was where he was constantly forced to defend himself: from his parents, from the women who loved him, from the guys he grew up with who constantly tried to steer him toward a Normal Life. It wasn't that Deitz was just some random, paranoid pain-in-the-ass; that he didn't like Christians, or snack cakes, or kids. The truth was both simpler and harder to swallow.*

*Austin Deitz worked the Hazardous Materials squad.*

*And he had seen too much.*

*Normally, HazMat was a younger man's work, but to Deitz it was his mission and the meaning of his life. He had started out years ago, a simple fireman wanting to save lives and be challenged, fighting the often cruel caprices of nature. The drift to HazMat was a slow but inexorable one, like getting crushed by a train that takes ten years to get there. And yet he never felt that he had any other choice.*

*Because if you were privileged to see the slow, insidious poisoning of the planet, you did what you could to stop it. Even if it wasn't enough—even if nothing could ever be enough—you did what you could, because what else could you do?*

*Once you knew, there was no unknowing.*

*Once you'd seen, there was no turning back.*

*The drift was inevitable, as was its price. It had cost him two wives, much of his peace of mind, and most of his hope for the future. Deitz felt like he was on the ugly front lines of mankind's last battle: the fight for survival against our own stupidity.*

*He really thought he'd seen it all, and in one sense he had. But the fact remained that most people hadn't seen it, hadn't smelled it, hadn't had their faces ground in it like he had. And with any luck, they never would.*

*That was why they could still eat and drink this crap. That was how they could keep on bringing children into the world. They understood intellectually—if they thought about it at all—but they didn't really connect emotionally or experientially.*

*They didn't know it in their guts.*

*And that, it seemed, made all the difference . . .*

The *EMPLOYEES ONLY* door slid open at last, and Jennie's sneakers smacked the tiles behind him. He half-turned toward her, felt her arms snake around his waist, giving him a python-squeeze of love.

"Mmmm," she purred, and pecked him on the back of the neck. At five-foot-four, it was a stretch. "Good news."

"Do tell." He turned in her embrace, smiled down upon her.

"I called everyone on the list," she continued, "at

least a dozen times, before I finally got through to Babs. But she says she can definitely come in at three.''

"*Three?*" Deitz lamented, the smile disappearing, the disappointment clear in his voice. The Aquarium closed at five; and with an hour to get down and another twenty minutes to park, that gave them a little over an hour to take in the sights. . . .

"Sorry," she said, and meant it. "Best I can do. Unless you want to just take a rain check or . . ."

"Nuh-uh-uh. No way." He reversed his spirits, tried to send his smile all the way down to her toes. "On this point, I'm afraid that I'll have to insist."

"Okay," she smiled back, just as hard. "Then don't be afraid. We're gonna have a wonderful time."

She punctuated the vow with another squeeze and smile, and *damned* if he didn't believe her. There was just something about her: an indefatigable buoyancy of spirit that snuck through every chink in his defenses, like a spring breeze blowing through the rusty armor around his soul.

One look at her, and Deitz believed.

"This power," he murmured, low in his throat, "must only be used for good."

She laughed. "So you'll be here at three?"

"At least."

"At *most*." She made big pleading black velvet eyes at him. "You're my ride, remember?"

"Mmm-hmmm." They kissed: a quick whisper of tongue, lest God's little consumers saw fit to complain. "I'll be here before three."

"But not *too* early . . ."

"At exactly *two minutes to three*, I'll be here." It was a deadpan, solemn vow. "I swear upon my soul."

"It's a deal." Jennie smiled and disengaged, then moved across the bustling room and slid behind the counter. Deitz watched as she passed the microwave and lunch meats, a regular smorgasbord of nitrates and low-level radiation.

"Thanks so much for staying on, Patty," he heard Jennie say. "I'm real sorry 'bout that."

"S'okay." Patty smiled, her dull stare brightening by several degrees. "It's not like it's your fault or anything."

And suddenly, Pat the Eating Machine magically transformed back into a real flesh-and-bone person. By the simple miracle of Jennie's kindness, Pat became *Patty*: a tired girl who'd thoughtfully, responsibly stayed an hour and a half past her normal graveyard shift, all because of some irresponsible jerkoff named Ozzie. Pat, the odious Monster From Hell, became a very nice and extremely relieved young woman named Patty, who at long last could finally go home.

Deitz saw the unabashed gratitude on Patty's face as she handed over the reins to Jennie, who'd left breakfast in bed and a half-read *Sunday Baltimore Sun* to come in and save the day. And who hadn't bitched or pissed and moaned about it, either, but had simply taken it all in stride.

*Yep*, he mused. *No doubt about it. Jennie Quirez could change your whole outlook on life . . .*

The front door opened. He paid it no mind. His eyes were on Jennie's lips, which were puckering up for his benefit from halfway across the room. He smiled, catching the flurry of black-and-white movement in his farthest peripheral range.

It caught him. He started to turn. A wild shock of bone-white hair appeared, framing a pale, broad, deathlike face. It belonged to a punked-out teenage girl with deep flaming green eyes and thin lips etched in darkness.

She was, of course, dressed entirely in black: black shirt, black leggings, and those clunky black shitkicker jump boots. At first, he hadn't realized what a tiny thing she was: the hair gave her an easy five inches of height, which only placed her eye level with Deitz's breastbone. There was a little downy stubble at her close-shaved temples. The stubble was white as well.

Deitz caught himself staring, looked away sharply, wasn't all that surprised to discover that everyone else was doing it, too. She certainly didn't look like she was heading for Sunday services. Every gaze in the place dragged with her as she crossed the room, face groggy with unrequited need for sleep. Or maybe drugs. Or maybe both.

He looked to Jennie, who was grinning broadly. *Check her out*, Jennie mouthed, drawing it out for comprehension's sake. *She's ree-lee strange*. Deitz nodded, grinning as well, and turned back to watch the girl advance toward him.

She stopped at the coffee station and proceeded to fill up a thirty-two-ounce Big Gulp with steamin' joe. *Yikes*, he thought. *Thank God she's not going to church. She'd be bouncing off the pews*. He observed discreetly as she dumped about four packets of sugar into the cup and swirled it around, then reached for the little nondairy-creamer units.

And then, to his astonishment, she paused to read the label.

Deitz was stunned. Even his internal dialogue dried up for a moment. Not another single person, in the whole time he'd been waiting, had bothered to so much as *think* about what they were putting in their mouths. It privately pleased him, surprisingly so, that the black sheep would prove to be the only one aware.

For a second, he entertained the notion that she was just reading the brand name. But no. She twisted the thing slowly between her fingers, like a volume knob, while her lips silently moved in accordance with the list of ingredients ribboned around the label's edge: *contains water, salt, partially hydrogenated soybean oil . . .*

When she smiled and struggled with the pronunciation of *sodium stearoyl lactylate*, he could restrain himself no longer.

"It's poison," he said, stepping a little closer.

She looked up, annoyed; and her sneer instantaneously sucked wind from his cheerful sails. "What . . . ?" she said. The addendum *you cretin* was unspoken.

"Um . . ." Feeling suddenly, horribly foolish. "All that stuff. Sodium stearoyl lactylate. Monoglycerides.

Dipotassium phosphate." He shrugged. Her gaze upon him was utterly frank, not giving him an inch.

"You know . . ." he concluded, and let his voice trail off.

"Yeah, well." For a moment, she seemed uncertain whether to be civil or not. "Not that it's really gonna make a fuckin' bit of difference, right?" Cocking her head and watching his reaction very closely.

"Well, uh . . ." he began.

And then, just as suddenly, started to laugh.

"Well, actually, *no*," he concluded. It was as if some tiny but significant weight had been lifted off his shoulders. "Not even a little."

She smiled, then; and in that moment, their shared awareness made them members of a very exclusive club.

In that moment, they understood each other completely.

Then she set the nondairy creamer aside, picked up her cup, and headed back to take her place in line.

Deitz watched her go, and thought of Jennie. Would *she* have understood? He suspected she would have, but he couldn't be sure; you never knew what was under that kind of an optimistic demeanor. A lot of insecurities and unvoiced fears could thrive, hidden, beneath that kind of warmth; a lot of stubborn refusal to acknowledge the ugly facts of life. . . .

"*Wait* a second," he scolded, catching himself for the second time today. "You promised, remember? Today, nothing gets to you.

"Today, you're the happiest man on earth."

And, of course, it was true.

But some things were far easier said than done.

# Seven

Ah, the power of faith.

Werner Blake loved his front-row seat at Trinity Lutheran Church. It was a great place for people-watching, and Blake was a people person. He'd held this pew every Sunday for ten years running, watching the sacramental conveyor belt deliver its wine-and-wafer fix to the herd.

So far as he was concerned, there was no finer place on Earth.

Take this ritual, for example, and the principle that powered it. *Transubstantiation*, they called it, though he doubted if more than three people in the entire synod could spell the word, much less grasp an inkling of its actual intent.

Transubstantiation was really quite the little miracle: the mystical transformation of flour and grape juice into not just *symbols* of the Eucharist, but the *actual flesh and blood itself*. Eternal Life, breathed into inanimate glop by the kiss of God. Kinda like the ultimate parlor trick.

There was something perversely cannibalistic about the whole thing, too; but then, what did you expect from the world's most successful, longest-running blood cult?

*What the hell*, Blake mused, nodding and smiling as

45

the parishioners filed past. *Name of the game. Keeps 'em comin' back for more.*

Werner Blake was a dapper, distinguished man, in his fifties and his prime. He was head of the Paradise Industrial Development Authority, pointman for Paradise Emergency Management Agency, general solid citizen, and all-around pillar of the community. He was directly responsible for courting out-of-state industry to move into the area, thus bringing jobs and opportunity to thousands across the county. His connections were many. He belonged to the Chamber of Commerce and the Jaycees, had a wife and son and a house in Wyndham Hills, and kept a sophomore ski bunny in a condo at Cedar Village. He played tennis for fitness, piloted light aircraft and skied for fun. He ate well, drank in moderation, and slept soundly at night.

And every Sunday—without fail—he donned the wool and grazed with the flock, holding his wife's hand and staring with clear-eyed purpose into the vaulted chapel arches. That he looked at the huge suspended cross and saw only sticks and brass and plaster mattered not at all.

Because *they* saw something. They believed it, even if they didn't see it. And even if they didn't see it *or* believe it, they came anyway. That was the real beauty of the game. They came for the same reasons they believed.

Because they were supposed to.

*Nodding and smiling, as the parishioners filed past . . .*

There was power here, Werner knew, in all that blind faith and obedience. It could be harnessed, like any other natural resource. To Blake's way of thinking, that's what it was *there* for. And Trinity Lutheran was a money congregation, a fount for the local Brahmins, which meant that seeds planted on Sunday often bore fruit before the end of business Friday next.

That was miracle enough for him.

Still, by the end of services, Werner Blake had probed the outer limits of his civility. You could only graze so long with sheep, after all, before the clothing became oppressive, the smile a bit cramped and the eyes a bit too hard.

So when Leonard leaned over from the next pew back, Blake almost welcomed the diversion.

"Mornin', Harry," he whispered. "What's up?"

"Well, uh," Harold began and then stalled, eyes searching the shadows in the far corners of the chapel. Up close now, Blake could smell the tang of his sweat.

"Is there a problem?" Blake's psyche clicked calmly over to yellow alert.

"I think so. Yes." Leonard exhaled hard.

"Can it wait?"

A moment of silence.

"Okay." Blake leaned over, bussed his wife lightly on the cheek. "Excuse us," he whispered. Carol Blake was attractive, raven-haired and tight, well maintained, thirty-nine and holding. She nodded, disinterested, as Blake slid by. The space next to her that was for their son was conspicuously empty; Blake eased past it and into the aisle with a little grin that was polished and carefully maintained.

Then Blake was up and moving against the worshipful tide, nodding and smiling as he met the gaze of all those eyes, the many faces of the flock, nodding and smiling and slipping through them with practiced grace and predatory ease.

He didn't look behind to see if Leonard was following. Of course Leonard was following. What else could Leonards do? You rose or fell by your own merits, your own intrinsic worth.

Blake knew what Leonard was made of. Food. But it wasn't as simple as that. If there was a problem, and Leonard could help, it would be best to hear him out.

In private.

\*　　\*　　\*

"Now," Blake said. The chapel burst into muted song. It was quiet in the pastor's office, and nobody else was there. "You were saying."

"I got a phone call this morning." Leonard dry-swallowed as he spoke. "From a man I, um, subcontract."

Blake nodded.

"And, um, he told me that an accident or something happened."

Blake waited.

"This morning." Blake's silences were frightening. Leonard picked up his pace. "It was something about a truck. These people . . . uh, their boys, they were disposing of some substances . . ."

"What kind of substances?"

"Um . . ." Beat. "Not very good substances." Leonard let out a short hack of laughter, as if it were funny. "They were disposing of some waste—some overstock—when evidently something went wrong."

"What *kind* of waste . . . ?"

"*Christ*, Werner! I'm not exactly sure! It's all pretty bad, okay?" Leonard's face flushed red; and for one split second, it occurred to him that he'd just taken his life in his hands and held it up like a bull's-eye on a stick.

The Blake made a sympathetic face, and Leonard resumed.

"You know we handle a lot of stuff." He sighed. Blake nodded, encouraging. "Most of it is pretty benign, but none of it is meant for public consumption. The *point* is, these guys told me that they've been disposing of it in a responsible fashion, but then today I get a phone call . . ."

Blake was absolutely motionless, watching.

". . . telling me that these guys have been dumping . . . Christ, I don't know how to say this . . ."

"Just say it."

"*Christ!*" Oily beads of perspiration welled on his fore head, made armpit-inkblot configurations that met in the middle of his back. "They were dumping straight into the Codorus Creek, okay? Straight into the Codorus, which runs straight into the Susquehanna River, which runs straight into *God* knows where!''

"Calm down." Blake said it as much to himself as to Leonard. He was running the facts through his mind.

"I'm *trying* to be calm, but frankly, this is scaring me out of my wits!" Leonard railed, hearing himself lose control and trying to stop it and watching it go. "One boy is dead already..."

"Ah." The ante burgeoned. Blake brought a finger up, touched it to pursed lips.

"...and another boy is all messed up; I think he might be poisoned or something..."

"Okay." Blake withdrew his finger, made a pacifying gesture that he aimed at Leonard. "Are those the only two involved?"

Leonard stammered, his word flow unexpectedly dammed. "I...I think so. Yes. Except for their father. Well, *one* of their fathers..."

"And he is?"

"His name's Pusser. He runs a salvage yard outside of Hellam—"

"What I need," Blake interrupted, "is precise information. Names and addresses. Do you know where the accident happened?"

"Have you ever heard of a place called Black Bridge?"

"No. But I'm sure somebody has. What I need from *you*"—and on this he was emphatic, leaning into Leonard as if the fate of the entire universe were at stake—"is specifics. Every single thing you know. In the order you know it."

He took a beat, looked into Leonard's eyes, made sure that he'd connected. He had. "We can manage this situation," he said. "There's nothing that we can't manage. As long as we act now, and nothing else goes wrong, we're fine. Remember that."

Leonard looked honestly relieved. For the first time, he met Blake's gaze completely. Blake saw gratitude there.

But most important, he saw faith.

"You did the right thing in coming to me," Blake said. "Thanks."

"Hey, no problem." Leonard nearly blushed.

"Just get it all down on paper for me."

"Right now?"

"No time like the present."

Leonard nodded and opened a drawer on the pastor's desk, found a notepad. As he scribbled, Blake turned away, hard-weighing the possibilities. The worst thing that could possibly happen was a whiff of this hitting the public air.

On the other hand, there was nothing that couldn't be handled under cover of darkness.

Nothing at all.

"And, Harry?" he said, almost as an afterthought. "Not a word of this to anybody, right?"

"Of course not! *Christ!*" Leonard told him.

*Of course not.*

Another article of faith. . . .

# Eight

The first shots came high and sharp, like blown-up paper bags detonating in the distance. The sound was not lost on the ever-vigilant ears of Bernard S. Kleigel: the Conscience of a Nation. It filtered up out of the woods at him as he burned the goddam backyard leaves. And boy-oh-boy did it tick him off.

"God *dammit*, Billy! Stand still!" he hissed, straining to hear more. At the ready pile, his five-year-old froze: a miniature Michelin rubber boy, body dwarfed in his overstuffed Osh-Kosh jumper. Billy was no fool. One whiff of Dad's voice and it was lay-low time in the leaf pile.

Two more shots rang out. Small-calibre, twenty-twos. Bernie twisted the rake handle so hard it bowed, veins in his temples throbbing. One word sprang—neon, glowing—into his mind.

*Kids*.

At forty-six, Bernie Kleigel was a cardiac time bomb, a coronary car wreck waiting to happen. He was overweight and underworked, the kind of guy who pissed off easily and held grudges with the half-life of plutonium. He missed his misspent youth, resented the ceaseless ravages of middle age, had nothing but dread for the future.

When Millie arm-twisted him into one of her wacko fad health regimens, it sucked what little fun was left to be had out of his mid-life crisis. He quit smoking, gave up alcohol and caffeine and cholesterol, not to mention fried foods and sodium. His doctor was pleased, the quack bastard. Keep it up, he said, and Bernie'd live another forty years. Millie smiled and swore to it.

Bernie was a man on the edge.

And here were these kids, not knowing what they had, not realizing how goddam delicate and precious life was. Didn't they realize they could blow their little goddam brains out with those things? Or maybe somebody else's, *"accidently"*? Christ! When you got right down to it, in this world full of idiots, *nobody* was safe!

Another shot came. Bernie pictured it vividly in his mind: a meat-spattered Rube Goldberg engine of destruction. He saw the bullet divot off the trunk of the tree, missing its intended squirrelly target by a mile. He saw it pinging off tree after tree, mindlessly searching for something delicate and precious to destroy...

...*and then he saw his own little Billy violently airlift backwards, the top of his head a hot red horizontal rain of grease and gristle. He saw himself drop to his knees, deep in the throes of the anguish he knew he'd most certainly feel.*

*"NOOOOO...!!!" he heard himself wail, while a million mournful worst-case scenarios rustled in his forebrain, just waiting for their chance to unfold....*

Not that any of this actually happened, of course. Just that it damn well could have. That was the thing that people never seemed to understand.

Which was why the world needed Bernard S. Kleigel: the Conscience of a Nation.

"Goddam sonofabitching *kids*," he hissed: hunched up in his backyard, craning his neck, trying to get a fix on their location. Somewhere down the hill, by the sound of it. Off toward the sonofabitching creek.

Which, technically, wasn't his property, but that never

stopped him from bitching about it. His two-acre plot of cleared ground bounded on the *back* of those woods, fercrissake! And it was posted, every goddam inch of it. *No Trespassing. No Hunting. No Kidding.*

Another shot popped off, reverberating through the tree line. Bernie threw the rake down like a gauntlet: the proverbial rake of doom. He'd have their butts—or their *parents'* butts—up on charges so fast . . . !

He stopped, in mid-tirade.

*And listened to the flurry of gunfire erupt: a frantic volley, riddling the country quiet like a string of cherry bombs. It lasted for only a few manic seconds.*

*And then, just as suddenly, stopped.*

Bernie took a deep breath, felt the trip of his heart in his Adam's apple. He scanned the tree line nervously, as if there were something to see. The only sound was the wind, moving through the trees like a thief through a sleeping man's pockets.

Suddenly, it all made perfect sense. He was just amazed that it hadn't happened sooner. These were no ordinary hunters, he knew, laying down a suppressing fire against the birds and bunnies of the world. These were no ordinary kids.

And there was only one thing to do.

"Billy, get in the house," he said. Billy just stared at him with huge blank eyes. "There are *drug dealers* out there, dammit! *MOVE!*"

The Michelin boy animated, scattering leaves as fast as his five-year-old legs could carry him. Bernie followed, storming up to his modest split-level with the brick-face siding. He noted, in passing and sourly, that a few more of the brick faces had popped off, revealing the three layers of chicken-wire-reinforced cement. *Goddam cheap siding,* he thought. *I ought to* sue *the bastards! Whole goddam world is falling apart. . . .*

Bernie stomped onto the back porch and clomped through the mudroom. In the kitchen, Millie was whipping up an Egg Beaters-and-cottage-cheese omelet.

"Goddamned street gangs, right in our backyard!" he hollered. "I tell you, I won't take this lying down!"

"Of course not, honey," Millie replied, on another frequency altogether. Lite FM 101 mental-flossed beautiful Muzak in her one ear and out the other: the Rolling Stones' "Paint It Black," as only 1001 Strings could play it. She smiled at him and shuffled across to the breakfast nook, her fuzzy slippers whuffing on the Congoleum. "I hope you're hungry!"

She slid the congealed mass out of the pan and onto a plate in front of him. He groaned and grabbed the phone, punched three digits with a practiced fury.

"There's gonna be some hell to pay," he vowed. "And the devil don't take checks!"

"Of course he doesn't," she assured him, humming absently along with the tune.


Downtown, County Control was a maze of glass-walled cubicles deep in the pale green cinder-blocked bowels of the Courthouse Building. County Control was the emergency services nerve center, linking seventy-three fire departments, forty-two ambulance companies, and fifty-five different police departments, most of them two-to-five-man borough forces.

Half the counties in Pennsylvania didn't even *have* 911 service, and wouldn't for years to come, which put Paradise somewhat ahead of the pack. Still, Paradise County was a monument to bureaucratic provincialism: there was no county sheriff, no standardized training, no guarantee that any of its workers even *talked* to each other, no less shared vital job skills.

A crew of eight ran the complex web of telephone, computer, and radio communications. It was a hodgepodge of state-of-the-art and prehistoric technology, the crazy-quilt survivor of a dozen pitched budget battles. It ran twenty-four hours a day, every day of the year.

At the moment, it was dead silent.

That suited Dottie Hamm just fine.

She'd just come on shift at eight: manning the Metro dispatch desk, a Spenser novel in one hand and a box of Dunkin' Munchkins within easy reach of the other. A thirty-two-ounce Big Gulp of Diet Coke sat by the wayside, ready to soothe the inevitable parched throat.

And Dottie was ready for action.

Three other civilian police dispatchers were on duty, covering city, county, and rural zones. Across from the quad, Jerry and Jean worked the EMS and fire department lines. Carol ran warrant searches and APBs from her post near the supervisor's office. Overstuffed file cabinets stood near an IBM mainframe, and the whole complex burbled with the quiet nattering of crosstalk, punctuated by beeps and the squelched bark of static.

It was all music to Dottie's ears. Sundays were like that. EMS would doubtless see a little action 'round eleven. When area services finished, there was always some oldster seizing up with the spirit out at the Church of the Nazarene, or slipping on the stairs at Zion's Gate and needing to be medevacced to glory. But generally, folks just hibernated; generally, it was just too damn cold to excite the criminal element.

Warm snap days, on the other hand, were wild cards. Anything could happen.

Days like today, for instance.

Dottie had worked the second shift weekends for going on eight years. She was a sweet-faced, potato-shaped woman with a cool head, a balming manner, and almost infinite patience.

Until Bernie Kleigel called.

His name came up on her video monitor seconds after Kelly routed it. The monitor was a part of the enhanced 911 system, instantly displaying origin information, special stats, and call history for any number.

Dottie saw KLEIGEL, and her molars ground together.

Some wiseass had typed "10-96" under it. 10-96 was code-slang for *nutcase*. The wiseass was her. And the call-history list confirmed the diagnosis. Every couple of days, regular as clockwork: *Kids in woods. Dogs barking. More kids. Noisy trucks. Kids, kids, kids . . .*

Dottie closed her eyes and saw the list extending clear back to infinity. They'd never seen his face, but his nasty nasal voice was woefully familiar. Taking a call from Bernie was like lancing a boil with your teeth.

She picked up the phone, brushed a fleck of powdered sugar from her blouse. "Metro dispatch. . . ." she sighed, resigned to her fate.

*"Dammit, there's a WAR going on down here!"*

Dottie rolled her eyes. Dave Dell looked up from his desk on the other side of the glass, then caromed back in his swivel chair and froze: red face grimacing horribly, hands locked in a throttling deathgrip around his throat. She recognized the symptoms at once. He was having a Kleigel attack.

"Now, Mr. Kleigel . . ." she began, stifling her laughter with professional aplomb. She had to be strong: Kleigelitis was a terribly contagious disease.

*"Don't 'now Mr. Kleigel' ME!"* he barked, his voice a razor of rusty tin. *"They're having some kind of shooting match down there. It sounds like a drug-related gang war to me! I coulda been KILLED, fercrissake!"*

Dave gave the notion a vigorous thumbs-up. "Well, we certainly wouldn't want *that*," Dottie said.

*"Yeah, well, you better get somebody out here before someone DOES get hurt!"*

"I'll send someone out right away."

*"You goddam well better!"* Bernie groused, still chewing the bone. *"I pay my taxes and I—"*

"Someone will be right out. Just sit tight," Dottie concluded, yanking Bernie's plug.

"You fucking *dickhead*," Dave appended, busting Dottie up.

"Your mouth!" she gasped; Dottie didn't take to cussing. "Oh my," she sighed. "It's too early for that guy!"

"You got that right!" Dave nodded, throwing his pencil up to stick in the ceiling tile. He flipped his shoulder-length blond hair back and assumed a more contemplative pose: arms behind his head, feet up on the low bookshelf that held the code manuals. "So who gets the honors this time?"

"Bernie's on RD 23," Dottie said. "Hellam Township."

"Oooh, Adam-*sixty*," Dave checked the roster sheet gleefully to see who was on duty. "That's Hal. Oh, he's gonna *love* this." Dave loved to give Hal shit.

Dottie time-stamped the call card. "Nine thirty-six. He's probably out on rounds by now."

"Yeah, sure." Dave smirked and reached through the sliding glass partition that separated their desks. He filched another donut hole. "Hal's rounds are glazed, with sprinkles."

"Now, don't start." Dottie glanced balefully at her own diminishing snack supply as she keyed the mike transmit button. "Metro to Adam-sixty. . . . Metro to Adam-sixty, do you copy? Come in, please. . . ."

Dave leaned back in his chair, gazing up at his still-embedded pencil. His lines were quiet. Later on things would likely liven up: some drunk and disorderlies; a fight maybe. Probably an accident or two.

With any luck, the day would not portend much worse than a morning rant from Bernie the crank. Dave reached through the partition to steal another doughball. Dottie slapped him playfully, kept on paging till she got through.

"*Adam-sixty here,*" a voice came over the radio. "*What's up, dispatch?*"

"Uh, yeah," she began. "We've got a complaint on shots fired in the Black Bridge area. . . ."

# Nine

WPAL was the area's NBC affiliate, located downtown in a two-story brick building on south Beeker Street. It was a medium-market station, with a staff of thirty and a fifteen-hundred-foot tower on nearby Mt. Hope, to better serve the tri-county broadcast area.

Most weekdays, it was a bustling little pressure point.

Weekends were another story.

It was 10:12 A.M. At the moment, the Studio A control room was a ghost town. John Bizzano, the day shift engineer, slumped in the control chair, half-dozing under the funny papers as he kept things nominally on the air. *Sunday Today* with Maria Shriver played silently on Monitor One. *CBS Sunday Morning* with Charles Kuralt was on Monitor Three. Jerry Falwell preened in the center on Monitor Two, tumescent and smug. And nobody was watching any of them.

Downstairs, in the editing booth, the *real* show—The Kirk Bogarde Show—was on.

Mike Clifford and Laura Jenson crammed into folding chairs, facing the console in a room so small they could choke on each other's fumes. Kirk paced in place behind them, excited by his own televised presence. He was twenty-five and fresh out of Brown, the only son of second-generation monied liberal Republicans. Ma and Pa Bogarde had groomed their baby boy for success, and it was damn well going to happen.

Not that Kirk didn't work at it. His Protestant ethics were firmly in place, and he burned for his shot. Five-ten, lean and salon-tanned, he had meticulously cultivated the sandy-haired, blandly handsome yuppie-drone persona that the networks craved, retaining just enough edge to set him apart from the pack.

He wore khaki Levi's dockers with red suspenders, a Ralph Lauren button-down shirt with the sleeves rolled up to masculine mid-forearm, and loafers with little tassels. He toned up with Nautilus and honed his killer instinct three times a week on the racketball courts at the Athletic Club.

Kirk had his program down: give him ten years and he'd have his *own* show, give Geraldo a run for his mustache.

Laura's ambitions, on the other hand, were substantially less showbiz in tone. That was probably why she liked Sundays so much. NBC carried the AFC doubleheader, which meant the six o'clock news was preempted, which meant no broadcast until eleven and a skeleton crew on board. It gave her plenty of time, as weekend assignment editor *cum* news director, to catch up: to clean shop; to put together the ubiquitous "evergreen" segments, the human-interest and seasonal filler that they always needed and never had enough of; in short, to take care of all manner of unfinished business.

And, of course, to program the eleven o'clock edition.

It had been a pretty dead weekend, news-wise. If nothing better happened, they'd end up carrying the network lead as their own, an extra minute on weather to cover last night's storm, and a good eight minutes for sports, replete with the obligatory highlights and wrap-ups.

And, God help her, the compulsory "local story."

She winced. At the moment, this meant watching Kirk's proposed follow-up to the controversial "pooper-scooper" ordinance, just passed by City Council. She listened as his canned voice filled the claustrophobic booth.

" . . . *leading to public uproar,*" Kirk's televised talking head intoned, "*as residents face down the rising tide of canine waste. The passing of the legislation led to a 'terrorist incident' by anonymous pet protestors late Saturday afternoon, who set a bag of burning stools on the courthouse steps . . .*"

"Okay," he said, leaning over Laura's shoulder, faintly brushing the fabric of her blouse. "Right here's where we cut to the bag."

Mike, in the edit chair, shifted between the Beta decks. The youngest cameraman on the team, he and Kirk were 'PAL's odd couple. He was twenty-two, with long stringy blond hair hanging over wire-rimmed aviator-framed glasses and a horsey, open face. On slow days, he did bong hits out in his van. So far, it had been a very slow day.

"Cutting to B," he said, toggling the controls.

On the monitor, the image blipped, cutting from Kirk and his microphone to a close-up of a burning paper bag on the courthouse steps. Black smoke plumed off the flames. The color drained from Laura's face.

"Jesus," she whispered, aghast. "You got *footage*?"

"Actually, it's a re-creation," Mike said, smiling. "We shot it after everyone left."

Kirk smiled. Laura didn't. The psychological room temperature dropped twenty degrees. His voice-over continued.

" . . . *while no one knows what the outcome will be, one thing remains certain: the fight for pooper-scooper repeal will go on for some time to come. From the county courthouse, this is Kirk Bogarde, WPAL Action News.*"

A slo-mo close-up of the burning bag appeared on the screen, smoke wafting up as a foot came down to stomp it. It froze and held.

"Awesome," Mike grinned, mostly to himself. Kirk looked at Laura expectantly.

"Well?" he said, beaming. "What do you think?"

Laura took a deep breath, exhaled wearily.

"Give me a minute to recover," she said.

Laura Jensen was a tough, cool, competent woman in her middle thirties. She was dark-eyed, slim, and elegantly restrained. She was also smarter than almost everyone she knew, a simple fact that simultaneously shaped both her conscience and her cynicism.

The eldest daughter of New England liberal Democratic professionals, Laura had graduated top of every class she ever joined, from kindergarten through University of Atlanta. Her last job—with an Atlanta-based CBS affiliate—had ended when her husband's job transfer had brought them north to the outbacks of Pennsylvania.

Laura had taken the change in grudging stride, mitigating the culture shock by parlaying it into an upward move in a lateral market. Weekend news director was a rung up the ladder, and she wanted to make the most of it.

She was ready for controversy; hell, she lusted for it. But *this* . . .

"Words fail me," she said, resisting the urge to simply eviscerate him. "First, I don't think bags of flaming shit will sit well with Chris or Tom. Or our audience."

"Jesus, get real." Kirk countered, standing his ground. "City Council was in session for a fucking week over *dog* turds, for chrissakes! Besides," he continued, "it's not even real shit. We soaked some rags in kerosene . . ."

"That's not the point," Laura said angrily. "We are a *news* department, Kirk! *News!*" She drew the N-word out for emphasis. "This isn't *America's Most Wanted*, okay? We don't *do* reenactments! Am I getting through to you?"

Laura searched Kirk's features for a glimmer of understanding. Not even. It was gonna be one of those days. She could already feel a headache building, the kind that would take up residence behind her sinuses and wang all the livelong day.

The kind with Kirk's name written all over it.

Chris Crowley, the genius who'd hired Kirk, was off

weekends. Chris was the news director, and her immediate boss, answering only to Tom Huntington, the station manager. In the immediate chain of command, that left Laura in charge and, hence, Laura's butt on the firing line.

*Super*, she thought. *Thanks, Chris. Thanks, Tom. And thank you, Jesus.*

"Alright, tighten it up, and lose that goddam bag," she decided. "We'll run it if nothing better happens."

Kirk took the biscuit badly. *Aw*, thought Laura, pressing on. "What else have you got?"

The image blinked out on the monitor.

"Uh-oh," Mike said. "Looks like brunch."

"Oh, shit!" Kirk wailed as the Beta deck, in its infinite wisdom, gobbled his reenactment. "Shit, shit, *shit*! Can you fix it?"

Mike shrugged, hit "eject." It groaned and locked up tight. He poked the cartridge with his pen, tried to jiggle it free, to no avail. It was jammed, tape bunching into the heads like an Escher ribbon.

"Nope," he said. "I told you, man, these decks are hammered by the time they make it down here. There must be fifteen thousand hours on the heads. They're ready for the tar pit."

"Let's go to Two," Laura suggested, rising from her seat.

"Two's down," Kirk said, frustrated.

Mike nodded. "Maintenance."

"Great," she muttered, then turned to Mike. "Call Bob and tell him to get someone down here, ASAP!"

Mike got up to make the call, squeezing past Kirk and out the door. It left Kirk and Laura uncomfortably close to one another. She stood and went to press past him, and he grabbed her shoulder.

"Let go of me," she said. A static charge of electricity sparked between them. Their eyes met and held, defiance and denial slam-dancing in the airspace between them. He disengaged pointedly, hands up in a gesture of ersatz supplication.

"So, fine," he said, pouting. "You didn't like it."

She made a terse *what can I say?* gesture. "I didn't like the bullshit . . ."

"*Dog* shit," he corrected, still moping, though he took the time to slip a little bad-boy twinkle in his eye.

For some reason, that was all it took to push her over the edge.

"*Listen!*" she snapped; and before he could react, she was bouncing her knuckles off the top of his skull.

"Ow!" His hands came up. He backed off, startled.

"*Hello!*" she called out, rapping smartly on his scalp again. "*Hello, Mr. Potato Head! Anybody home . . . ?*"

"HEY!" This time, he caught her hand and held it. "DON'T . . ."

"Don't what?" she snarled.

He stopped in his tracks. She nailed his gaze. He let go of her hand. She drove the point home. Throughout it all, their eyes never left each other's.

"Now you listen to me," she growled, low in her throat. "If you want to keep your job, you just *shut up and listen*."

She paused to make sure he got the message this time. He certainly seemed to. His eyeballs were huge.

"You're good," she continued. "And everybody knows it. You're talent is not the problem here. But if you want to be taken seriously, you've got to cut the kiddie shit and bring me something *real*. . . ."

"Well, fine," he spat, defiant. "When are you gonna let me *do* some real news?"

"When you learn to distinguish your ass from your elbow." She hoped that the words were as cold as she felt. "There's a whole wide *world* of real news out there! When you bring me some, I'll use it. Believe me.

"In the meantime, why don't you just *grow the hell up*."

Kirk's gaze faltered; the eyeball war was, for the

moment, won. She wanted to rejoice, but alas, there was still no joy in Mudville. He was making his wounded puppy face.

And, damn her heart, she felt guilty again.

Their affair was one of 'PAL's worst-kept secrets; studboy-reporter meets married boss-woman. Film at eleven. It was yet another piece of unfinished business; Laura wondered why she'd ever started it more often than she liked to admit.

It wasn't just the age difference, or the point spread on the IQ scale, or the fact that he plugged some of the holes her marriage had left unfilled. In fact, she really didn't know *what* it was. They certainly didn't respect each other. She thought he was a harbinger of doom for a generation weaned on style over content. He thought she was a tight-ass, both literally and figuratively.

The first time they fucked, it was like worlds colliding.

And every time since, she swore it would be the last.

Here in the station, however, Laura held her ground. No retreat in battle. Ever. When his gaze dragged back up to lock with hers, she was more than prepared to fire his ass if she had to.

Then the police scanner went off, and changed their lives forever.


When the squad car came up against the first downed tree, Officer Hal Thoman was forced to hump the last leg of Toad Road on foot. All the while, he thought of Trina. As substitutions went, it left a lot to be desired.

Trina was the hot little blonde tending the night counter down at the Mister Krispy donut shop. Only twenty-two, and rumor had it her personal hygiene regimen included shaving where the sun don't shine. Now, normally Hal hated small-town gossip—small-minded people who knew too much about other folks' business and not enough to mind their own—but in this case, he had to admit he was intrigued.

Their paths had been crossing for quite some time, as she went off shift and he came on; and lately, she'd taken to lingering way past quitting time. Hal both appreciated and drew encouragement from this, and in fact just this morning had hit Mister Krispy with every intention of asking her out.

Until, of course, the goddamned call came in.

Now he was slogging through puddles and mud instead, hot on the trail of hardened, squirrel-hunting desperados.

Courtesy of Bernard S. Kleigel.

*Goddammit, it ain't right*, he thought as he rounded the bend, his cruiser disappearing, swallowed by woods. *The whole damn county knows about Bernie Kleigel, between his letters to the editors and his goddam nine-one-ones*. If ol' Bernie said there was a drug war in the forest, Hal figured it just as likely he'd find Manuel Noriega duking it out with Bigfoot in the grudge match of the century.

Hell, even if he *found* the alleged perpetrators—most likely the Hinds boys, Ralph and Jimmy J.—Hal wasn't about to do much more than waggle his finger. As a kid, he'd left more than his share of shell casings on posted land. The more powerful temptation was to write up Bernie, though Hal didn't recall any specific ordinance prohibiting people from making flaming buttholes of themselves.

Hal climbed the rutted grade of the road, his sporty orange don't-shoot-me vest resplendent over his uniform. *Storm really tore the woods to shit*, he noted; downed limbs and broken branches were everywhere. He put his trained police eye to work by itemizing all puddles more than twenty feet long or twelve across. Strange, but there were fewer of them the closer he got to the bridge.

In fact, in the short span ahead, he didn't see any puddles at all. It was like the ground had sucked up all the excess moisture, turning the road's surface into something soft yet not quite mud: a near-gelatinous continuum that squished and *gave* a little beneath your feet, taking the imprint of your shoe without ever quite breaking its skin. . . .

Hal jumped; a wet crackle had sounded behind him. He whirled and caught the last glimpse of something sliding off an oak tree's face. It was a magazine-sized hunk of bark; and when it fell, it left a gummy underpatch in its wake.

"Son of a bitch," Hal said. His vision was excellent, but he was starting to wonder about the sights. There was something *not right* about the exposed stretch of tree skin. It made him want to do a quick reality check.

He stepped off the road, and realized at once that the grass felt wrong. The blades stuck fast to his soles; but when he peeled loose, with a scrinching Velcro sound, they held their roots.

Laying flat for a moment.

Then slowly, deliberately, pulling upright again.

"This is weird," he informed himself. He stopped, thought about it for a second, decided that he was right. He turned—*scrinch, scrinch*—and hunkered down on his haunches, bringing his thumb and index fingertips together around a solitary blade of grass.

It bit him.

"Yowch!" he barked out, genuinely surprised. "God-damn!"

He checked his finger for cuts, saw only a pinprick of red, veneered by a tacky glaze.

His hand began to tingle.

Hal stood, apprehensive, and his gaze shot over at the oak. Now he could see what was wrong with this picture.

Now he could see the unnerving, infinitesimal array of undulating grub-things, burrowing blind through the punky, fibrous interior . . .

*I've been in these woods a thousand times*, he flashed,

*but I've never seen nothing like this.* It was as if some plague had fallen, put a blight on the trees and on the earth itself.

He looked through the trees to the bridge.

And, for the first time, noticed the truck.

Hal Thoman felt nothing but wrongness now, a nasty sour ache in the pit of his stomach. The truck looked extremely fucked-up from here. If this was a pattern, it wasn't a good one.

"Son of a bitch," he muttered. "County, this is Adam-sixty. Do you copy?" he spoke into his handset. It bounced the signal back to the cruiser, which in turn boosted it back to County Control.

*"Roger, Adam-sixty,"* the dispatcher's voice came back over the box on his hip, salted with dropouts and static. *"What's your twenty?"*

"Roger, County, I'm out at Black Bridge," he replied. "I've got an abandoned truck up on the structure. Looks like it might be that ten-seven vehicle reported this morning. Whoever took it left it pretty blasted," he added. "I'm checking it out."

*"Roger, Adam-sixty. Approach with caution."*

"You got that right," he said. "Adam-sixty out."

*Caution* was not the word, Hal realized as he walked out onto the bridge. It didn't quite capture the feeling. *Dread* was more like it. *Oughta be a new code*, he laughed nervously. *Approach with dread.*

The roar of the creek surrounded him, filling his head with thunder. The rails and rock bed were slick under his feet, sticky with waste oil. Tar. And worse. The tingle had spread up his arm, and lodged in his shoulder like a fat knot of tension.

But all of that paled in comparison with the sight of the truck.

*"Blasted" is a severe understatement*, he thought. *They flat-out* nuked *the bastard.* It looked like some giant psychotic toddler had taken his Tonka truck to hell. The

driver's door hung open, mangled; the windows no longer existed. Chunks of safety glass rimmed the frames like the stubs of broken teeth. The paint job was cracked and ashen, flaked down to the metal in a thousand places.

There were maybe a dozen barrels, on and around the truck. *Not burned*, he realized. *Blistered*. Like the truck. The tops were blown. Trace residues of a milky sludge leaked out of one, seeping into the rocky track bed.

Hal picked his way through the mine field, careful to touch nothing. He came up on the passenger side, deciphered the lettering still visible on the door. "Aha," he said, peering into the cab.

The keys were still in the ignition.

"Bingo," he said. "I got you, you sons of bitches." Thieves didn't generally use keys. And Trina's personal habits weren't the only things buzzing on the gossip mills. The Pussers got their fair share, too; and unlike Trina's, none of it was good.

Now sometimes lowlife hunks of shit had guardian angels that covered their asses. And sometimes you had to turn your back if you wanted to get along in the world. As a cop, he'd had to scarf that bitter pill at least a thousand times over.

But if you aimed to buck the odds and take a shot at real justice, you needed proof. As in physical evidence.

It took no rocket scientist to put this one together. Just the sight of all those empty barrels, the truck pulled up with its tailgate hanging over the side, made him so goddam crazy he thought he was gonna explode.

*I ain't sure exactly what happened here*, he seethed, *but I'm about to find out. And when I do, I will nail you to the fuckin' walls. Believe it.*

"Adam-sixty to County," he said, reading the plates off the front. "Holding Pee-Aye license number Thomas X-Ray three nine nine three. We have a possible HazMat problem here. . . ."

He looked at the toasted barrels again, paused to consider his words. "Uh, County, maybe we should switch to Echo-Four," he said, only now thinking of the ears that might be listening in. There was a harsh bark of static in the handset. "Uh, County?"

His lips were tingling.

"Jesus!" Kirk blurted, mind racing. "Did he just say what I think he said?"

"God, let's hope so," Laura answered, pinning back the scanner's volume and grabbing a pencil. She'd cranked the controls while they were in editing; when the call first came, it blew through the news department like a bomb blast.

Laura checked a map and scribbled. This was a godsend: a stolen truck was good for maybe a thirty-second fill—a full sixty, if it was really trashed. But *this* . . . this had possibilities. This could save her from pooper-scooper hell.

Kirk, for his part, was all but foaming at the mouth. The breakup had reduced the signal to mush, but not before he'd heard that magic word. It was his ticket to the stars, the big break he'd been waiting for.

HAZMAT. Hazardous Materials. The moonmen.

*My God*, he thought. *If there's been a spill . . .*

"I'm on it," he said, making for the stairs. In the background, Mike appeared in the camera bay doorway, saddled up and ready to roll.

"Wait, wait!" Laura called after him, notepad in hand. Her hair fell across her face as she tuned one ear to their tape of the scanner broadcast, nodding rhythmically and scribbling.

"Wait? Wait for *what*?" Kirk fidgeted, halfway out the door.

"For this," Laura said, ripping the sheet of paper off the pad. "It helps if you have directions."

Kirk nodded sheepishly, came back to her. "Thanks."

Laura leaned across the desk, body English all business but her eyes alight. Saying *This could be hot. Don't fuck it up.*

Kirk grabbed the paper, and their fingers touched. Again, the spark. God damn it to hell.

"Take the car," she ordered. "And stay in radio contact." He nodded *yeah yeah yeah* as he bolted up the stairs.

"KIRK!" she called out, just as he turned the corner. He *screeed* to a halt, looked back into the newsroom.

"Just the facts, okay? Get me something real."

Kirk smiled and winked.

And then he was gone.


It was buzzing inside his head.

"No no no," Hal railed at himself, as if the terms of his awareness were negotiable. As if he could persuade the chemicals to leave his brain. The buzz was a high distant whine in his inner ear, and it scared the living shit out of him. He didn't know what it was. He didn't know what it did.

But he had a real clear sense of where it came from.

*Get away from the truck*, boomed a voice in his skull. Good advice. Hal took it, managed three steps, and then doubled over: stumbling forward, tripping over a railroad tie. The momentum careened him toward the ledge at the edge of the bridge.

He caught himself, barely, stomach violently lurching as it whacked the ledge. His Mister Krispy Kreamy Kake sluiced semidigested from his nostrils and throat.

"Oh, god," he gasped.

And stared down over the brink.

The creek was churning, dark and deep, bloated with rain and astonishing power as it overflowed its bounds, racing swollen and crazy-mad toward the river beyond.

Watching it was like staring through a hurricane's eye at the swirling earth below.

The storm had battered the brittle trees that lined the shore, left them raped and denuded; what branches remained knit together and rustled like ravaged leper limbs. Pockets of stormfall choked off sections of the creek: broken branches and whole uprooted trees, old tires, rusted machine parts, bottles and cans and runoff debris, all caught at loggerheads and pummeled by the current.

His eyes burned, a napalm pain that smeared the lenses of his vision. The murky greens and browns of the woods intensified, like someone had cranked the color controls on a cheap old TV set till the world pulsated with garish, oversaturated hues.

Hal thought he saw a glimmer of light stand out from the surface of the water, twitching and twinkling in a tangle of flotsam near the overflown bank. It flickered again, and he locked on it, pulled it as hard into focus as he could. It was disk-shaped, flat and shiny.

*A shiny little disk.*

*On a tiny, pale wrist. . . .*

"Oh, fuck!" Officer Hal Thoman moaned, his gut churning more sewage back up his pipes. He'd forgotten completely about Bernie Kleigel and his pint-sized casualties of war.

But there they were, big as death.

It was the Hinds boys, after all.

Ralph and Jimmy J., aged eight and ten, were half-submerged, tangled together as if wadded and tossed there, impaled a dozen times over on the stray ends of the expanding trash pontoon.

Their eyes were open. Their mouths were open.

Wet things crawled around in the holes.

"Oh, Lord," he gagged, and stumbled away, choking. One of their arms jutted out of the water, pale as a china ghost, snagged in wood and murk and mire. Jimmy J.'s Timex was the shiny thing that had snared his gaze.

The hand it was strapped to pointed palm up, fingers curled delicately around empty space. It bobbed in the insistent current, as though waving for him to come on down.

*Get off the bridge*, his mind told him. *Get off the goddamned bridge*.

Hal wheeled, clamping down on the adrenaline surge before it could blossom into full-blown panic. He scuttled off the structure just as fast as his feet would carry him. His head cleared a little with each passing yard, until he was safe.

On the wrong side of the bridge.

*Oh, smart*, he thought. *Now what?* The bridge lay between him and the world. The truck owned the bridge. He remembered the handset, snatched it up. "Adam-sixty to County..."

A harsh bark of static clipped into his ear and he *twitched*: a sudden, involuntary seizure. "Come in, County..."

Nothing.

"God *damn* it!" he spat, whapping the box against the ledge. Out there in the hinterlands, dead spots were common: invisible pockets of interference, confluences of geography eclipsing transmission. It happened all the time. But it was still like having your lifeline cut, leaving you alone and vulnerable....

"*I need some BACKUP!*"

The radio spat dead air and hiss.

"*NOW, GODDAMMIT!*"

Something cracked below him.

"*Wah!*" he cried out, startled. His right hand woke up on the butt of his gun, as if startled from a dream.

Down in the water, the dam was starting to break up.

"*Fuck!*" Hal gasped as he started down the rocky slope toward the creek. The current was pushing the creaking mass against the bridge, forcing a breach in the debris. The current picked up speed as it spilled through, sucking flotsam like stew through a straw.

*Jesus*, he thought. *If they go through, we'll have to drag the river to get 'em back.* The thought jacked up his nausea, sickened him deeper than the toxic fumes. He knew their parents well. He could see their anguished faces in his mind's eye: a searing, near-precognitive flash of dread.

And he desperately wanted to get out of here, just get the fuck moving and never look back. But their bodies were close enough to snag. He was certain of it.

The fact left him no choice.

"This sucks," he whispered as he made his way skittering down the moss-crusted rocks that sloped toward the creek. "This really sucks."

Hal reached the edge of the water and stood in the shadow of Black Bridge, staring at the juncture of creek and pylon. The bank was swollen and slippery; the water there stygian, overripe with decay. Hal picked up a long, stout branch and steadied himself.

As he put the first foot in.

Cold flooded his shoe, glued his sock to his foot and his pants leg to his shin. "Oh man, this really, *really* sucks," he muttered through clenched teeth, his personal mantra of discomfort and dread. He took another hesitant step forward, his other foot swallowed in icy darkness, and gauged the distance to the bodies. He guessed twenty feet, max.

*Might as well be twenty miles*, he thought. *Or twenty thousand.*

He took a third step.

His leg sank to mid-thigh.

"*Whoa—SHIT!*" he cried, desperately stabbing the branch down into the water for support. His left foot came up and found purchase high on a hard forty-five-degree angle. He weaved back and forth like a drunk walking a white line.

"Bad idea," he croaked. "Bad fucking idea. . . ."

In the water, something moved: a current *within* the current, a dense sinew of liquid moving against the pull of the stream. It brushed past him, eel-like, then abruptly circled back.

And slid thickly through the gap between his legs.

First-level panic set in, hard: a tidal wave descending, obliterating calm. He whinnied high in his throat and rethought his options: sphincter irising shut and putting in for a promotion, heart wrecking-ball slamming a hole in his chest.

*Fuck this*, he thought. *Drag the goddam river. I'm getting out of here.*

Hal turned to go.

He couldn't.

"Shit!" he whined. His foot was stuck: the right one, mired to the ankle in muck. Silt sucked greedily at his shoe. Twigs and scuzzy bits of sludge clung to his legs like foam off pier pilings. He cried out, leaning hard on the branch, and probed around blindly with his left foot.

It came to rest on something flat and round. It felt solid, with that one taut inch of sheet-metal give. Like the hood of a car.

Or the top of a barrel...

*Oh, God*, he thought, and the panic overcame him. *Oh, God.* Remembering the truck on the bridge. He wrenched his right ankle as he twisted and turned it, desperately trying to free himself, then *screamed* as he steadied his left foot against the drum head and pushed with all his might...

...and his right ankle popped like a firecracker as his left foot *tore through* the corroded skin of the barrel: jagged metal rim raking his flesh from calf to buttocks, encasing his entire left leg in steel and icy chemical anguish. He sunk to his belly, his gun belt submerged. The radio sparked and shorted out.

Hal shrieked, gripped the branch hard enough to peel bark, and twisted into an awkward side-stance, his left leg stuck out at a pelvis-cracking angle. His shoulders went back and submerged. He fought to keep his head above water, won a marginal victory but lost his hat in the process. It landed brim up in the water and floated like a little boat, spinning off and through the flume.

It was a comedy of errors, but nobody was laughing. Hal's face held inches above the surface now, his body dragged down by the current and his so-called water-repellent jacket, which was violating all manufacturer's warranties by becoming a leaden sponge. His right ankle throbbed insanely. His left leg burned as though dipped in a lye-and-acid stew.

"HELP!" he yowled. "*HEEEELP!*"

His cries were lost before they left his mouth, no match for the sound of the dam. Water pounded through the center arch now, at a terrifying rate; the whole mass was gradually pulling in on itself, like a big wet black hole. Jimmy J. slid under the surface: his Timex still ticking, his body sucked into the slipstream and gone.

The debris to Hal's side free-floated around him, queueing up for the slide. Little Ralph's arm reemerged from the water, not ten feet away, looking more and more like a wax mannequin left too long in a window display.

The arm sank again, came up a little closer.

The fingers moved.

Hal screeched, an airless squeak of disbelief. The hand sank again. He turned toward the bank, and the ragged metal collar sliced the moist flesh of his inner thigh like a ripsaw.

Hal saw the water go instantly dark, felt the hot spritz of leaking fluid that fed it. The scream came a moment later, on the heels of the pain.

The dark cloud spread.

The little hand came up in the midst of it, wet and red and way too close.

"OH GOD, PLEASE!" he burbled, faltering. He thrust upward, struggling, and a thick plume bubbled up beneath the surface like an underwater fountain.

*Like peeing in the tub*, he thought. *Oh God . . .*

The current battered and squeezed and drained him, swallowing his life as he merged with the flow. Tiny fish-things nipped at the flesh exposed beneath the surface: nursing at his open wounds, breathing in his blood.

The dead boy's body was very close. He felt it catch against him, cold bloated little limbs that danced in the slipstream. A face rose up from the shadows: its eyes half-open and milky, its tongue coyly protrusive.

Hal screeched and thrashed, his spray-blind and ebbing gaze cast desperately toward the heavens.

And that was when he saw the man, staring down from the bridge above.

*Bazooka Joe,* he thought insanely. *He looks like Bazooka Joe.*

The man stood, blackly silhouetted against the ugly sky. His leather jacket was mud-caked and clotted, like the mass of black hair hanging like moss over his forehead, obscuring his eyes.

A filthy red kerchief was pulled up over his jaw.

Hal tried to bellow for help, just as Ralph's clammy hand flapped across his forehead, traced clumsily down his features. His eyes slammed shut in horror as the fingertips groped past his lids, hanging just a second too long before dragging down to lock on his lower lip.

But the current was too strong, the flesh too weak; and as his lip tore loose, spritzing, and peeled down to his chin, he let out the final scream of his life.

Helplessly staring up at the man on the bridge.

Who'd decided to help him, after all.

*He had picked up a barrel from off of the tracks, hoisted it high above his head. He let loose with it now, aiming straight for Hal's face, as if he were throwing a rope.*

*It seemed to take forever to get there. End over end, growing larger and larger, a spinning black mote that engulfed Hal's sight in the second before it demolished his forehead, gray matter exploding in brainpan shrapnel, a wet crashing end to the light.*

*Leaving open the top of his head.*

For the new mind—the Overmind—to make itself at home.

It was just a matter of moments before the dam broke fully.

And the next world, alive and unbound, spilled free.

# Ten

Something was wrong with the reactor.

Fred Jenkel scratched his head and studied the meter, one of a multitude that monitored virtually every aspect of the plant's operation. Sometimes it seemed like the only moving parts of the plant that didn't have a needle stuck to them were the human ones, though Jenkel was sure Westinghouse was working on it.

Situated on the rocky banks of the Susquehanna in Delta Township, some twenty-two miles southeast of the city, the Wolf's Head Nuclear Generating Station was one of the few plants completed in the post-TMI/Chernobyl industry slump. It had been in operation for four years with no trouble at all, feeding the ever-increasing appetite for power in the great Valley metro region.

Jenkel leaned back in his chair, absently fingering his bald spot. He was a big man, with a big beaky nose and the jowly, pleasant face of a favorite uncle, and was fresh back from vacation-fishing in the Poconos. He'd caught three trout and an acute case of sunburn, and his roasted pate stood out from the white of his shirt like the bulb of an overheated thermometer. He crinkled his brow in speculation.

He'd noticed the flux in the neutron population twenty

minutes ago, almost by accident. It was a marginal increase in temperature and power, well within the plus-or-minus parameters the reactor coolant routinely generated. He'd caught it during a casual spot-check, duly noted the reading, then set about leveling it by releasing a stream of borated water into the closed-loop system that covered the core.

The boron did its molecular duty, moderating the fission process, slowing the reactor. In his duties as the nuclear half of the day shift's Reactor Operator Team, Jenkel had performed the process countless times before. *Borate the coolant, keep watch as the power rolls off and the temperature drops*. It was like fine-tuning the fission process, and it always worked like a charm.

But now the temperature was up again. Odd.

Jenkel turned to his younger, less experienced other half, whose duties minding the turbines and steam generators consisted at the moment of reading Dave Barry's column in the *Sunday News* and snickering at every other paragraph. *Once a pressurized water reactor was up they could practically go home and let the reactor run itself*, or so the training said. Normally, it was utterly, absolutely true. But it was a homily that carried its own disclaimer, a caveat like a *void if removed* tag.

*Unless something goes wrong . . .*

"Hah!" Bob Henkel laughed out loud, a sharp bark that stood out in the quietly humming control room. "Man, this guy cracks me up." He chortled out loud. "He says we should convert the federal deficit to *voltage*, right? And then run it through electrodes attached to the genitals of every member in Congress. . . ."

"Hey, Bob," Jenkel said, interrupting. "Check this out."

Henkel looked up, blue eyes watery with mirth. He was twenty-nine, bean-pole thin, and the physical opposite of Jenkel. Except for the nose: broad and downward sloping, it was so close to Jenkel's that they could have been pressed from the same Play-Doh Monster Schnozz kit. Add that to their names, and the jokes were inevitable.

Henkel got up from his chair, sauntered over. "What's up, boss?" he said.

"The reactor load, for one thing," Jenkel answered. "Check out the core." Motioning to the meter with his chin.

"The neutron count is way up." Henkel assessed the situation and shrugged. "So borate the water," he offered.

"Already did," Jenkel said. "Now it's back up again."

Henkel considered the problem, as well as the older man's tone of voice, which was more curious than concerned. He knew as well as Jenkel that they were constantly making up and letting down water for the core vessel, filtering out particulates or ions and then restoring it to the loop. Henkel wondered offhand if this was some kind of test, an impromptu spot-quiz by ol' Dead Fred to goose an otherwise slow shift.

"Uhmm," he pondered, "add NutraSweet?"

Jenkel looked at him; he was not smiling. Maybe this was serious, after all. "Go get Sykes," Jenkel said. "Tell him we might have a problem."

His eyes leveled with Henkel's and the younger man's smile evaporated. Bob turned and quick-walked over to the open door of the super's office. "Uh, Mr. Sykes . . ." he began.

But Fred Jenkel was no longer listening. His ears were tuned to another sound, a subsonic drone that he felt more than heard, coming from a humming structure less than a hundred yards away. From his radiation-shielded, hermetically sealed vantage point, it might as well have been on the moon.

He watched the meter's needle rise up and level off, only to scoot up a moment later. *Rise . . . flutter. Rise . . . flutter.*

"It's nothing," he told himself, denying memory and intuition and experience. "Nothing at all."

Jenkel watched. All the while thinking, *The reactor could practically run itself.*

*Rise. . . .*

Unless something went wrong. . . .

# Eleven

More than anything, Gwen Taylor loved the act of creation.

She stood before her almost completed work-in-progress, dressed in sweats and a paint-spattered shirt stolen from Gary. Blue and yellow mixed with a bit of white on the sheet of heavy glass that served as her palette. The colors swirled together, three melding to one, making teal.

She wet her brush, scooped up some of the paint, and held it aloft. "Okay, your Highness," she said, scrutinizing her target. "Here comes greatness."

Gwen took aim and let fly.

On the nursery wall, the Faery Queen's left cheek came to vibrant life. A twin slash quickly adorned the right. Gwen worked fast and loose, showing amazing skill and alacrity in the most random of motions. She dabbed here, stroked there; a layer of cool green sprouted across the breadth of the mural in no time.

"Yes . . . yes, yes . . ." Gwen said. David Byrne's "Rei Momo" jangled from the speakers of her spattered studio boom box. Gwen grabbed up a brushful of magenta and peppered the shadows around the figure with hot color. "This is a good look for you," she winked.

The nursery was spectacular, a magical blend of innocence and mystery. Stuffed animals hung from a hammock in the corner, shower booty awaiting tiny hands to bring them to life; an antique oak crib lovingly refinished by Gary consumed one whole corner of the room, tempo rarily hiding under a protective drop cloth. A mobile floated lazily above it, bobbing on an almost imperceptible breeze. It was a room full of dreams, waiting to come true.

Gwen could hardly wait for Spike to see it.

She dropped the brush, picked up a finer one to lay in some highlights of yellow. Then she scooped up a raggedy bit of sponge that she'd custom-plucked for maximum texture and began patting the surface of the fresh paint, adding a stippled coral effect.

It was a technique that would have appalled her art school painting instructors, but fuck 'em. Gwen was a firm believer in the right *misuse* of technology.

*After all*, she reasoned, *necessity isn't the* true *mother of invention.*

*Weirdness is.*

Gwen was nothing if not original. Her instructors had hated her style, which was quirky and unschooled but bristling with energy, charming in its imagination and sheer enthusiasm. They told young Gwen Kessler that as an artist she'd make a great hairdresser. One told her he now understood why previous generations preferred their women barefoot, pregnant, and in the kitchen; another even suggested in front of the entire class that she'd be better off enrolling in the art school that advertised on matchbooks. *Draw Binky, Make Big $$$$.*

So when she finally got fed up with getting shat upon by the hierarchical cliques of snotty conceptual types at the Atlanta College of Modern Art, she fought back by declaring herself a *postmodern neoprimitive guerrilla cartoonist* and staging her own one-woman protest show outside the main entrance of the school, which was also the Peachtree Road entrance for the prestigious and oh-so-stuffy Atlanta Museum of Modern Art. She spray-painted the title of her show *cum* manifesto on the windowless concrete walls of the building.

BLACKTOP SAVANT.

Fifty sofa-sized black velvet portraits of great historical figures lined the street, all painted like big sad-eyed kids. There were big sad-eyed Jesuses on neon-bright crosses, with big sad-eyed Elvises strumming guitars and crooning at Their feet; there were big sad-eyed George Washingtons crossing bubbly frothing Delawares in boats filled with big sad-eyed soldiers, and big sad-eyed babes with enormous boobs and nipples that looked like big sad eyes, too. . . .

Gwen shaved off her hair and chained herself to one of the big concrete pillars along the facade, wearing only a pair of sunglasses and a pair of bumper stickers that read *HONK-IF-U-♡-ART.*

Peachtree Road was a main artery leading downtown. The traffic jam was spectacular. Her instructors were horrified. A crowd formed, hooting and cheering. The chains were thick, festooned with cookware and as long as Marley's ghost's. Her boom box was chained into it, blasting David Bowie's "Fame."

It took the police and museum security over an hour to cut her loose.

And Gwen left school a legend in her own time.

Channel Two sent a crew out to cover it. One of the team was a brash young cameraman who had never seen anyone quite like the ingenue with attitude being blowtorched out of her Houdini-housewife rig. He ended up shooting way more tape than was necessary or even airable; at one point he got too close, and she kicked at him. The camera caught it all.

The police hauled her off, her bare butt poking out from the jacket they wrapped her in.

The camera caught it all. And loved it.

That night, Channel Two ran a filler bit on the crazy woman artist who used a *different* kind of talent to get her point across. It was smarmy and titillating and played wholly for yocks, and it utterly missed the point.

The cameraman got her contact info from the rap sheet, stewed over her for a day, and finally called her up. He apologized. She did not accept. He asked her out.

She told him, very sweetly, to go fuck himself.

He proceeded to find out the date of her arraignment. When she showed up, he was there. She had become a minor celebrity by that point, albeit an embarrassed one: Channel Two followed up on her case periodically, invariably running the same smarmy clip of her thrashing, bare-butted arrest.

He asked her out again. She recognized him from the news crew and told him to please leave her alone.

He was back again at her court date. She got six months' probation. He handed her a rose and a present wrapped in a brown paper bag. She opened it up in the cab on the way home.

Inside the envelope was a note with his phone number. The note read:

*Everybody deserves a second chance.*

She unwrapped the package. Inside were a couple of three-quarter-inch videotapes. The masters and the dubs. All of it.

Channel Two didn't run any coverage that night, or ever again.

The next day Gwen called the cameraman and thanked him. He said it was his pleasure and apologized yet again, and didn't even ask her out.

Three days later, she called him again. This time *she* invited *him* to lunch, her treat. He said yes. *Everybody deserves a second chance.*

The cameraman's name was Gary Taylor.

And the rest, as they say, was history. . . .

Gwen blushed with the memory. It was a long way from Atlanta to here; sometimes she could scarcely believe that she was the same person at all. She and Gary had bopped around a lot, going from Atlanta to Chicago to the

Big Apple, always following Gary's gigs. Some places she liked better than others; all of them were ripe for learning and growing.

But none of them felt like *home*.

It was a simple need, if an all-consuming one. Home began to call to them from the pages of magazines, from the gushings of friends who lived upstate, riding a clear whiff of breeze in the stale summer air of their too-small Chelsea apartment.

That one simple need had gotten to them both, after a while: New York was too expensive, too dirty, and too crowded to grow old or raise kids in. Gary had no real hometown to speak of; that pretty much narrowed it down.

Exodus.

She'd been happier, in all: a lot less angry, a lot less stressed. The house was wonderful, and she loved fixing it up. She hiked and went to the farmer's market, and lived an altogether kinder and gentler existence. With the coming of the Spikester, her world seemed to be nearing completion. What more could anyone truly want?

But still, sometimes it chafed. She felt so . . . so *normal* here. She didn't trust it. It was clean here, yes, with an immeasurably lower crime rate and a cost of living cheaper by half . . . what *LifeStyle* magazine called a real "quality of life" area. But there was no art scene to speak of, a lame nightlife, a meager handful of restaurants worth eating in. She felt torn between the two Gwens inside her: the wildass and the earth mother, the hellion and the homebody.

And now a third, on top of it. The Gwen/not Gwen nesting in her belly. The one that was so much a part of her and Gary, yet so ultimately *other*. The one that was so much more than the sum of its parts.

The one that would call her *mommy*.

She worried if that were such a good thing, like she worried about routine and responsibility and all the trappings of adult life. She worried that the day-to-day of it all would siphon off her imagination, steal her weirdness by degrees. Leave her cut off from the essence of the Mystery.

Inside, she knew differently. Her inner voice told her so. *Mystery is more than a fashion or a lifestyle*, it said, *Mystery is a state of* mind.

Gwen wanted to trust her inner voice. She always had. But lately she'd been wondering; there was something about coming back here that blew through her like a bad wind every once in a while. Saying *being here is the kiss of death, it'll suck the life right out of you, it'll steal your sense of the Mystery. . . .*

Gwen shuddered. "Stop it," she told herself. "You're being stupid."

On the wall, the Faery Queen smiled knowingly, becoming more real with every stroke. Gwen was ninety-nine percent finished with the mural, and was determined to lay down the hundredth stroke before Micki hit town. Or Spike.

Whichever came first.

Gwen genuinely loved her work, which was a rarity by anybody's standard. Over the years she had persevered, parlaying her penchant for weird vision into a somewhat successful illustration career, doing fantasy and sf and the occasional horror paperback, but most notably covers for Micki Bridges's *Bob-Ramtha!* series. Micki's contracts always had a rider that specified Gwen Taylor covers, and with over eight million copies in print her publishers were perfectly willing to humor her. Thus did a lifelong friendship get the added perk of professional fruition.

*Plus we get to write off our lunches together*, Micki always reminded her. Gwen smiled and swirled mottled streaks of jet black and neon green into the fabric of the cape.

The Faery Queen was one of the archetypal figures detailed in Micki's books, which was a big reason why Gwen had decided to put her on the nursery wall. *No Smurfs for the Spikester*, Gary and Gwen had agreed long ago. They wanted their child to grow up comfortable in the lap of the Mystery.

Part animal, part insect, part fish, part fowl, the Faery Queen was a regal being who embodied the Spirit of the Living Earth. Her robes were a lush drapery of green living plants, her hair a cascade of feathery plumage. Her features were arthropodal, elegantly humanoid but rendered in chitinous exoskeleton. Her body was wasp-waisted and segmented, the thorax swelling into fully human breasts. Her feet were softly cloven, doe's feet; her fingers were long and delicate.

In her left hand she held a white candle. In her right glowed a tiny star. A rainbow of sleek scales covered her throat and neck; a precious amulet hung there, glistening on a fine golden chain.

In other illustrations she looked fierce, imperious, sometimes even cruel; here, Gwen deliberately softened the effect, giving her a wise smile and warm blue eyes and surrounding her with birds and rabbits and all manner of gentle creatures, making her a benign sort of otherworldly *Übermother*.

*But with cheekbones*, Gwen added as an afterthought. *Great cheekbones.*

Gwen stepped back and surveyed her work, her brow knitted fretfully. This was the biggest project she'd undertaken during the pregnancy. She wanted it to be perfect.

"Something's off," she said; and the moment she said it, the answer came clear. "A-HA!"

She took a fine brush, dabbed it in the paint, and added a carefully placed dot of white to the blue of the Faery Queen's eyes.

Adding the spark of life.

"There you go," Gwen said, satisfied for now. She checked her watch. "Oh, shit, how's that for timing," she said to her work. "We've got to get a move on."

She scooped up her brushes and headed for the sink.

While on the wall, the Faery Queen watched her go.

*          *          *

Meanwhile, Gary crouched in the garage, practicing his own gentle art of motorcycle maintenance.

His scoot was an '88 Harley-Davidson custom softtail, and it was his pride and joy. He'd personally torn it down in the winter of '89, putting in a ninety-six-inch S&S stroker kit, transforming it. Gary had an innate sense about tools and technology. Mechanical, electrical, digital; if it got up and ran, Gary Taylor could figure out what made it tick.

He was bench engineer for WPAL. Mostly, he did equipment repairs, transformer maintenance, a monthly checkup of the broadcast tower and the microwave uplink, but he was pretty much qualified to handle any broadcast situation.

It was a good gig, as gigs go. But it was still just a job.

Gary worked to live, and not vice versa.

He'd grown up on farms, the son of migrant workers, which was a romantic way to say he'd grown up *hard*. A lot of drifting, a lot of backbreaking, monotonous scrabbling in the dirt, with very little return to speak of. On more than one occasion he'd had to lend a hand in birthing cattle and then drown a batch of kittens in the very same day. He'd known hunger—not the *what's for supper not hamburger again* kind but the real thing, the bottomless dull-knife gnawing in your belly that's the last thing you feel at night and the first thing that greets you in the morning. He'd known hardship and hopelessness and despair, and by his own bootstraps he'd hauled himself out of all of it.

The experience had, if nothing else, given him a useful perspective. *When life deals you shit, make fertilizer.* If the nukes hit tomorrow, and they survived, he'd raise mutant cows with Gwen and be just as happy.

Gary reached under the block and freed the crankcase bolt, nudging the catch pan under the engine block with his knee. On the outside the softtail looked bone-stock, but he'd tweaked and cranked it until it was two-hundred and forty horses of flat-out drag bike, street legal but just barely. It could do a buck and a half without even breaking a sweat, though Gary'd never really cranked it past one-twenty, and not much over ninety since Gwen put the bun in the oven.

*Oh well . . .*, he thought. *Must be gettin' conservative in my old age.*

Little Feat was on the radio. *Let It Roll.* The garage door was open, and bright streamers of light filtered in. The day had turned Indian summer-warm, and Gary was looking forward to one last ride before the cold: burning down some back roads, heading nowhere and loving every minute of it.

"Hey, Dad," Gwen said, appearing behind him, a steaming mug already in her hands. "Want some coffee?"

"Thanks, Mom." Gary stood and turned toward her, accepting the java and a kiss.

"Ick, you're all slimy," she said, pulling away.

"Thought you liked slimy," he said, nuzzling her.

"Not like that," she said, pushing away and moseying over to the door. "Better get cleaned up, babe. We gotta be at the airport by eleven. . . ."

"Blech!" Gary cut in. He made a sour face and stared at his cup. "What's with this coffee?"

"I just made it," Gwen said, perplexed. "What's wrong?"

"It tastes like shit. That's all." He held out the cup to Gwen; she sniffed it. There was an ugly, bitter taint.

Gwen shrugged, hurt. "I don't know; I got it at a little shop at the Galleria. It's expensive enough."

"Yeah, well," Gary said. "It tastes like they got it from the wrong Valdez." He hoisted the steaming mug sarcastically. "Coffee by Exxon, the richest kind of coffee."

She didn't laugh. He sniffed the coffee again. "Yech," he said, recoiling. The milk had curdled into a mottled curlicue shape like a question mark, spinning slowly in the center of the cup. "Fuck it," he muttered, pouring the remainder into the waste-oil pan. Then he held the empty cup up to Gwen. "Thanks anyway, babe."

She took it and shrugged. "Make it yourself next time."

"Shit, babe, I didn't mean nothing by it," he said, but she had already turned away.

"Better get ready," she called over her shoulder, and shut the door just a little too hard.

Gary winced. "I'M SOR-REEE . . . !" he wailed.

The thud of cupboard doors slammed in response. "Shit," Gary sighed, scooping up a glob of GoJo from the can at the utility sink to wash up. "You can't win."

*Pregnant women go off on the weirdest things*, he thought miserably. Fucking hormones; it seemed like every time he turned around he was stepping on another emotional punji stick. In the shithouse for insulting her stupid special-occasion fifteen-dollar-a-pound yuppie *coffee*, for christ sakes. *God I'll be glad when this is over.*

In the meantime, there was not much to do but practice his eggshell softshoe and hope nothing else went wrong.

The phone rang.

"Oh, no," he gasped, eyeing the Cobra cordless on the workbench. There was only one reason why the phone would ring this early on a Sunday, and it wasn't to wish him a nice day off. He rinsed his hands, wiped them off on his pants, and finger-combed his hair, giving the caller time to give up.

It was no use. He picked up on the fourth ring.

"What is it, Bob . . ." he sighed.

"How'd you know it was me?" Bob Dobberman asked, genuinely incredulous.

"Experience," Gary said. "Cut to the chase, Bob."

Bob "The Knob" Dobberman was Gary's boss, a rotund and genial technogeek, right down to his pocket protector and basementful of ham radios. He was 'PAL's head engineer, and he *did* live for his job: Sigma Delta Theta, Society of Broadcast Engineers, the works. "We got a little emergency down at the station," he said. "Something screwy with the news department's edit deck. Can you do it?"

"Bob," Gary groaned, drawing his name out into two exasperated syllables: *Bah-ahb*. "Jeezus. I just worked two shifts, back to back, and I've got to pick up Gwen's friend at the airport in less than an hour.

"What about Brian?" Gary offered. "He ought to be able to fix a fucking jammed deck."

"Yeah, sure," Bob scoffed. "Brian couldn't find his own ass with both hands and a map."

"How 'bout you?"

"I would if I could," Bob said. "But Penny's sick, and who's gonna take care of the kids? They can't finish editing without it. They won't be able to do the news. . . ." He laid it on with a trowel, delivering the last bit with an air of genuine dread.

Gary smiled despite himself; God knows, where would we be without the eleven o'clock news.

"Alright," he conceded. "But that's it! Fix the deck and I'm gone. No bullshit."

"You got it!" Bob said, relieved. "Thanks, Gar, you're a pal."

"Yeah, yeah," Gary groused. "You owe me, mother-fucker."

He clicked off and walked into the kitchen to break the news. Gwen was quietly banging things around, taking the dishes out of the drying rack, clicking cups and plates with a deliberate intensity.

"Uh, babe . . ."

"I heard," she said. "Mr. Dedicated." She swished soapy water in the now-emptied coffee carafe, rinsed and racked it. She said everything in those two words that he needed to know. Eggshell City.

"It's just a jammed deck," he offered apologetically. "I'll be back in plenty of time to make it to the airport."

"It's okay," she said, meaning *it isn't*. "I'll get her myself."

"I don't want you driving," he blurted, instantly regretting it.

She grabbed a glass, went swish swish swish. Meaning *I don't care* what *you want*.

Gary took a step toward her; Gwen racked the glass almost hard enough to chip it. The translation was the aloha of unspoken marriage-speak, and its meaning was crystal-clear.

*Touch me, you die.*

Gary backed off. There was nothing else for him to do, or say. This was one storm front that had to blow off of its own hormonal accord.

"I'll be back in a flash, darlin'," he said. "Promise."

Gary grabbed his leather jacket off the peg by the garage door entrance and closed the door quietly behind him. Gwen was still washing and rinsing, but her shoulders were shaking ever so slightly. She cried silently, covered it with dishwashing clatter.

Gary refilled the oil and readied the bike, heart aching. *Poor baby*, he thought. *Sure gonna be a better world when Spike finally pops*. The homestretch was the hardest, for both of them.

He donned his leather and riding gloves. His helmet sat on the passenger hump of the seat. It was a ninja-black road-warrior style fiberglass monstrosity, a precautionary pre-Father's Day gift from Gwen. It encased his whole head and face, with just a little snap-on plate for his eyes, the kind of helmet only rice-burner riders thought was cool. He hated it, but loved her for giving it to him.

Gary straddled the softtail, keyed it on, and kicked it over; the engine roared to life. It thrummed between his legs; Gary felt instantly better, his head clear.

*Fuck it*, he shrugged. *Into each life, and all that shit*. If the gods of expectant fatherhood were with him, the sun would be shining when he got back.

Gary gunned the engine, eased out of the garage, and rode.

Right into the thick of it.

# Twelve

The commuter flight from Philly to Paradise sucked; and by ten thirty-five, despite her best efforts to remain in good cheer, Micki Bridges had pretty much exhausted her options. She was too tired to read, too wired to sleep, and way too close to blowing chunks for her to sit back and enjoy the ride.

The turbulence, of course, was at the root of her distress. Every sledgehammer thud against the little plane's fuselage helped inch her stomach a little higher up into her lungs. She groaned as the plane lurched abruptly toward sea level, caught itself hard.

Soft laughter emanated from the curtained-off cockpit: the pilot and copilot, yocking it up. She could barely hear it over the drone of the engines, but it dragged a nervous, involuntary smile to her lips. "Glad *somebody's* enjoying this," she muttered to herself.

"*Sorry about that folks.*" The tiny intercom buzzed to life with the pilot's voice. "*We're just passing through some rough air here; there's a little storm front moving by overhead. Not to worry, though; estimated E.T.A. in Paradise is approximately twenty-seven minutes. So hang in there, and thank you for flying US Air.*"

Another thud rocked the plane.

"Oh, great," Micki moaned, trying to keep her digestive system moored. Her long ebony hair, laced with premature gray, spilled over her face; she brushed it back and groaned some more.

Micki Bridges was a handsome woman, agelessly attractive, youthful and mature by turns; one could guess ten years to either side of her thirty-three years and not seem too far off the mark. But now her riveting, deep-set eyes were etched with the shadow of fatigue; and nausea had leeched off some of the healthier tones from her naturally olive skin, leaving her a tad on the greenish side.

She was coming down from Amherst, straight off the New World Symposium on EcoHarmony, with no breakfast and very little sleep under her belt. All in all, she was glad she'd gone. It was a chance to throw support behind a worthy cause, get together with handfuls of people she admired, meet her public, promote her books, and network like crazy. All expenses paid.

For four days, she had done just that. The organizers had outdone themselves, securing everyone from John Denver to Jean Houston, Carl Sagan to Stewart Brand, with a sobering keynote speech by Bill "The End of Nature" McKibben.

The speakers were passionate. The cause was just.

And, in the end, very little had really changed.

*Because half the people in attendance had come to see the world saved for them, by famous stars and noted authors. A large percentage had come to hawk their ecologically correct wares: the water purifiers and solar conversion kits and biodegradable, nonphosphate, lemon-fresh detergents for the modern New Age lifestyle. A far smaller percentage had come in the hope of finding support for their own little homegrown save-the-world strata gems: each one grandiose, sweeping, and impossibly naive; and all structured so as to place themselves square-ly at the imaginary helm of Spaceship Earth.*

*But the real problem, Micki mused, was the* perennial *problem with the New Age: in its boundless optimism, its proponents had a tendency to offer far too much, make extravagant claims and promises they could never in a million years live up to, thereby turning love of the Mother Earth into so much New Age snake oil.*

*The hype surrounding this show, for example, promised that monies earned would go straight into the environment; that important global transformational policies would be drafted and then implemented over the weekend,* by the total Symposium membership; *and indeed, that ordinary rank and file would get to actually hobnob with the famous, to share theories and compare notes with the finest minds on the planet.*

*The reality netted somewhat less utopian results. Operating costs of the convention ate up fully half of the money generated, the important policy-drafting decayed into pompous speechifying and political infighting. And utopia had a VIP lounge, after all, where the invisible line between prole and privileged was clearly drawn. The average results ran somewhere between a lecture and a flat-out dog-and-pony show.*

*The undercurrent of crushed hope was palpable. Those naive enough to believe in a mystical Good Guys network—where they and their heroes labored side by side to solve the world's problems together—were inevitably in for some major disappointment. Those who expected the quick fix were reminded that there were none, that the task of saving the Earth took nothing less than absolutely everyone, doing absolutely everything they could, every day for the rest of their lives.*

*And then maybe—*just maybe—*it would all work out.*

*By Sunday, it was clear to most that the world wasn't going to be saved this week, and certainly not this way. In the process of trying to balm all those broken hearts and imploded ideals, Micki had used up every last ounce of energy, not to mention violating ninety-nine percent of her own very strict health regimen.*

*And then it was time to go. . . .*

*WHAM!* Micki's eyes snapped wide open. *Wa-WHAM!*

There was a disorienting moment of total weightlessness, irrespective of gravity. Freefall seemed to go on forever—a full ten feet, longer, in the space of a second—then *SLAM!* steadied out and proceeded to shake, like the plane was a chew toy in a pit bull puppy's jaws.

She heard herself mewling, and shut herself up.

"Oh dear god." White-knuckle-clutching the arms of her seat. "Oh, please stop." As the shaking continued. "Oh!" as they dropped again—*WHAMWHAM buh buh BLAM! BLAM!*—and miraculously stabilized.

Leaving Micki with a moment to question her sanity, ask herself what the hell she was doing here.

The answer was simple. She had come to see Gwen. Put up with Gary.

And help usher their baby into the world.

In fact, she had planned this out months in advance, leaving virtually no margin for errors not endemic to the plan. She had gotten up at six, checked out by six-thirty, then limoed the fifty-plus miles from Amherst to Hartford and hopped a marginally civilized DC-9 to Philly, only to find her angular frame wedged into the tiniest, least comfortable seat this side of Midget Purgatory, puddle-jumping to Paradise on a US Air commuter flight that only carried two of its maximum twelve-passenger payload.

The downgrade from jet to prop-power was bad enough. She could deal with the flight that had brought her the three-thousand-plus miles from Oregon to Amherst because the plane was so damned big—Clipper Class in a 747 was like taking Amtrak at thirty-seven thousand feet. And even in a smaller jet she could fool herself: hold her breath until they broke cloud cover and then while away the flight time studying the little seat-pocket cards, memorizing escape routes and how to best use her seat cushion as a flotation device.

A turbo-prop, however, was all business: there was simply no escaping the fact that she was *flying*, not-so-bravely going where no one in their right mind should ever have gone before, three thousand five hundred feet in the air in her itsy-bitsy seat right next to an aisle you couldn't even stand upright in while the pilot and copilot sniggered behind their dinky curtain, plotting air-speed vectors and crash coordinates and hoarding parachutes and she could see people the size of *ants* in their backyards, goddammit, and . . .

*If you're really that frightened*, said the voice in her head, *you could always make a circle.*

Micki started, momentarily surprised. She *hated* it when her spirit guide snuck up on her like that. Even after five years of trance-channeling, it still gave her the willies sometimes. "What do you know?" she said aloud. "You're not even on this plane. You're not even on the *earth* plane."

*You're overreacting*, Bob-Ramtha said calmly.

"Overreacting!" she blurted. "Are you kidding? You ever seen what happens to these things when they go down? It's like a human Cuisinart!"

*You don't have to yell*, Bob-Ramtha chided.

Micki lowered her voice. She looked behind her; the sole other passenger sat three rows back on the other side. He was doughy, disheveled, a cheeky businessman with a full day's growth of scratchy beard, heading home at last. He smiled at her uneasily and nodded. Micki nodded and turned away.

"Sorry, Bobba," she amended to herself. "I'm just nervous, is all. And my stomach's upset."

*It's okay*, the voice said.

"No it's not," Micki replied. It was stupid. Micki Bridges was blessed with a direct pipeline to the hereafter—a live internal audio feed to the Other Side—and she was still scared of dying.

The plane buffeted again, bouncing on the air currents like a numbered ping-pong ball in a Pennsylvania Lotto drawing. She sucked wind sharply and held it, took the reins on her panic.

*The storm front is pretty big*, Bob-Ramtha said. Micki nodded in affirmation. From her vantage point, it extended as far as the eye could see: a solid wall of low, foreboding clouds blanketing the earth. To the north, the air was purplish-gray with rain. It wasn't apt to get much better in the twenty-odd minutes to come.

She thought about it, accepted it, sighed. "Make a circle, huh?" she said.

*Couldn't hurt*, Bob-Ramtha replied.

Micki smiled; his voice was soothing, and his advice had never been off the mark. Bob-Ramtha was rare, as spirit entities went: he didn't make portentous proclamations, he didn't claim to be bosom buddies with the Almighty or to know the exact date the mothership would land or whatever *really* happened to Elvis.

He was just *there*; having come at a point in her life when she desperately needed someone, and having stayed ever since.

Keeping the circuit open.

And the spark alive.

"Okay," she said, looking up. The businessman was watching a crazywoman auto-emote. *Tough titties*, she thought, flashing him her sweetest smile.

Then closed her eyes. Centered herself.

And began the silent ritual prayer.


*In the wiccan tradition, the drawing of the circle was a time-honored form of protective, healing magick. Its function was to create safe haven, a merging with the spirit realm, a space outside of space and time.*

*Where no harm could befall you.*

*The key to the power of the ritual circle was the invocation of the elementals: the spirits of the living Earth, as embodied by the four directions.*

*To the east was sky, the breath of the Mother. Her spirits presided over the beginnings of life. They correlated to the swords of the Tarot, wielding Intellect in the service of truth. The sky-people would be the first invited into the circle.*

*Next would come the fire-people, spirits of the south. Spirits of flame, and ferocity of passion. Spirits of energy and will. Bearers of wands, and of earthly vitality, joining the caster of circles inside.*

*To the west lay the bearers of cups, brimming over with the living blood of the Mother. Spirits of Emotion, of sadness and joy, of all we are able to feel within. Spirits of oceans and endings, the water-sisters would be third in line.*

*Fourth would come the earth-people, the spirits of the rocks and soil. The spirits of meat and bark and flesh, of pentacles and earthly possessions, of things long dead and returned to ground. From the north, they would be welcomed into the circle of life.*

*Then finally, one would invite the Source of all life to commune with them inside. Great Spirit. The Mystery in the Middle. Goddess. God. All love. All life.*

*And when they all had come, the circle would be closed, so that no others might enter.*

*And there, surrounded by all the forces of Nature, they could at last encounter their One True Self, recognize those very forces at play within themselves.*

That was the theoretical function of the ritual circle. Of course, it had never been devised for use in deepest space. And three thousand feet in midair was a definite compromise position.

But Micki would be damned if she didn't feel better, once the circle was cast. She felt better the whole rest of the way into Paradise. The turbulence let up a little as they crossed the Susquehanna, but whether that was a good omen or just good luck she wouldn't venture to guess.

"Thanks, Bobba," she said.

And he told her not to mention it.

# Thirteen

"Oh, Christ." Kirk was bitching again. There was a blue-haired matron in a prehistoric Rambler, doing twenty-five down the old Gut Road. When the ACTION-9 mobile screeched around the hairpin curve, it nearly rode up on her ass. "Can't you go around her?"

"No passing, man," Mike said. "I've already got two tickets and ten points on my license. One more and I'm a pedestrian."

"So what's life without risk? Come on, man! *Punch* it!"

Mike shrugged. "Fuggit." He hit the accelerator, let out a manic war whoop as they crossed the double yellow line. Kirk echoed the sentiment, but he still ducked out of sight as they blasted past the wide-eyed senior. Just in case.

"I'm tellin' you, man. This is *it*!" he exclaimed, sitting back up in the seat. He was charged on adrenaline and the blood-scent of a story. "I've got a sense for these things, and this one's a motherfucker. No more mall openings and handshake ceremonies for me, babe. This puppy's my wake-up call."

"Okay. Cool." Mike nodded, noncommital, as the car sped eastward, past open fields and housing develop-

ments, toward Kirk's big date with destiny. He'd believe it
when he saw it; Kirk's wake-up call came at least three
times a month, and he hadn't woken up yet. He thumbed
in the dashboard lighter, fished a joint of homegrown from
his pocket and fired when ready, going *shhhup* as he
sucked in a lungful of sweet smoke.

He offered it to Kirk. Kirk abruptly recoiled. "No, I
better not . . ." he began, then just as suddenly changed his
mind. "Aw, hell. Who's gonna know?" Taking a tiny,
tentative hit.

"So tell me," Mike inquired, "why you think this is
such a big deal."

"*Why?*" Kirk looked astounded, as if he'd just found
out that Mike had been a really slow child. " 'Cause
HazMat's a *hook*, that's why! It's not just a story in itself;
it's a way into the whole larger issue of toxic waste, from
a local perspective! I mean, don't you see how *hot* this
is?"

Mike said nothing, maddeningly neutral.

"*Christ!*" Kirk yelled, exasperated. Then he took
another tiny hit and shot Mike a demented quiz-show-host
look. "Okay. For example. Do you know how many tons
of toxic shit are generated around here every year?"

Mike gave him a slight, startled *who me?* look.
"Um . . ." he began.

"Four thousand tons," Kirk answered for him, dragging out the words dramatically. "That's *eight million
pounds*, man. Every year. In this county alone."

"Whoa." Taking the joint back, toking again. The
figure impressed him. "That's one large pile of shit."

"Yup. We're talking carcinogens, mutagens, fetalogens,
hallucinogens . . ." Kirk was in Serious Mode now, rattling
off the litany with practiced vigor. Mike humored him,
punctuating each technical term with a solemn nod. Especially the last one.

Then Quizmaster Kirk struck again. "So if the local
treatment facility can only actually handle maybe *sixty
percent* of that, where does the rest of it go?"

"Um . . ." Shrugging, clueless. Holding in his hit.

"Quick!" White teeth flashing. "Think! Where do *you* think it goes?"

"Umm . . . shit, I don't know." Exhaling, huge. "Toad Road, I guess."

"Exactly!" Kirk crowed. "And a hundred other places. Like any goddam place they want. Burn it. Bury it. Dump it in a creek. What the fuck do they care? It's like it all just *goes away!*"

Mike took another hit, continued listening in silence.

"I mean, the only times you ever hear about HazMat are a) when a tanker truck flips over on 83 and there's no way to hide it, or b) when it's a fucking Love Canal. You never hear about the *little* disasters, where maybe it's only a hundred or a *thousand* gallons, and it all drains off into some little guy's yard. Those are the kinds of stories that get slipped between the cracks.

"That's why this is so unbelievably perfect."

He paused to shake his head, as if he couldn't believe it himself. Mike nodded sympathetically. "I mean, I must've talked to Chris about this fifty times. He always shrugs it off. 'No hook,' he says, 'Makes local industry look bad.' *Hhhmph!*"

He snorted derisively. Mike handed him back the joint. This time, there was no hesitation.

"Meanwhile," he continued, "every year, we get another eight-million-pound turd in our pants."

Mike laughed out loud. Kirk smiled, pleased, and sucked on the joint. "And it's only a matter of time," he concluded, "before it wakes up and bites off our ass."

"I like it," Mike enthused. "If I were you, I'd run with the Giant Ass-Biting Turd motif."

It was Kirk's turn to laugh. "In a world of perfect news . . ." he said, then let it trail off. They grew quiet for a moment, each in his own buzzing, contemplative world.

"So," Mike said at last. "I hate to bring this up, but . . . if Chris always has a problem, what's gonna make this any different...?'' Kirk shot him a glaring *you dimwit* stare. It came to Mike suddenly. "Oh," he said.

"A hook. Exactly." Sighing wearily, yet triumphant. "A terrible, tragic, specific incident with lots of exclusive footage. Which means the *trick* is to nail 'em while their pants are down, get the shot that everyone wants, and show it before anyone else."

"I gotcha."

"The only thing is...." Kirk paused, turning thoughtful. "If it *is* a local industry, you start to run into trouble with advertisers, you know? And those guys are all in fucking cahoots...."

Mike nodded. "Country club, Chamber of Commerce..."

"...it's all a Good Ol' Boys network. And then you run into the fucking Industrial Development Authority, and that motherfucker *Blake*..."

"Umm...I don't know, dude." All of a sudden, Mike felt a nasty little blast of foreboding run through him. Like everyone else in local news, he had heard stories about Werner Blake. They were not happy stories. "Correct me if I'm wrong, but I don't think you really want to piss those people off. I mean, seriously. If you push too hard, they could severely fuck you up."

"Oh, I don't think so." Kirk's jaw set hard.

"Oh, you don't think so?"

"No, I don't think so." He had locked into Determined Mode. It was amazing, in such moments, how much like a little kid he looked. Mike couldn't help picturing him in high school: little blond blue-eyed Super Achiever, The Boy Who Could Not Fail. He didn't seem to understand that *anyone* can fail. Even the well-heeled sons of the powerful.

Even the sons that their God loved the most.

"Okay." Mike knew it was pointless to argue. He'd learned a long time ago when to back off if he wanted to get along with Kirk. Keep it light, keep it fun, and run the goddam camera.

"Just watch," Kirk asserted, eyes flashing. "I'm gonna break this story." He took another hit, cracked the window, and blew it out, his fantasy blooming bright before his eyes. "I'm gonna make waves on national TV."

Mike gave a stoned chuckle at the thought. "I bet."

"Yeah, sure, laugh now," Kirk huffed. "But I got a good feeling about this. I know what I'm doing."

He glanced down at the map, then suddenly up, at the unmarked side road directly upon them.

"Oops," he said. "Turn here."

"*WHOA!!!*" Mike hollered, sawing the wheel. The car slid, tires squealing into the turn, chewing up shoulder gravel as it went. Mike seesawed the car, stabilizing it without losing speed. Stoned or no, Mike was good.

"JESUS, man! How 'bout a little *warning* next time!" He shook his head, taking the joint back. "I swear, you are the worst fucking navigator . . ."

"Yeah, yeah," Kirk said. "I get you killed . . ."

". . . and I'll never speak to you again. Exactly."

They snickered. It was the secret of their success: reckless Mike and ruthless Kirk, the Two Horsemen of the TV News Apocalypse.

Kirk looked back at the directions. "Oops. Turn here."

"SHIT!" Mike wheeled sharply, skidded around another one.

This time, the road made an abrupt transition, winding into thickly overgrown woods. "Okay," Kirk said. "Slow down." Mike breathed a sigh of relief. "Over there."

An opening in the trees yawned like a part in heavy drapes.

"This is the place," Kirk said, as Mike wheeled off the main road and stopped.

Toad Road stretched out before them: a single gravel lane, chuck-holed and foreboding. The sun was all but blotted out by the leafless thicket of branches overhead;

thin beams wormed through like tiny spotlights, dappling the rutty surface.

"Fuckin' aye. This is excellent," Kirk enthused. "Two and Twenty-three'll be lucky if they even *find* this place before we air. We aced out everybody."

Mike nodded, already appraising the angles. "We should get some pickup shots here."

"On our way *out*," Kirk interjected. "I wanna get in there now." He fished in the pockets of his cranberry L.L. Bean parka, producing some Binaca and a tiny squeeze-bottle of Visine. He spritzed his mouth, put a glistening drop in each eye, blinked it back, and straightened his tie.

"Okay, this is it," he said. "We *are* professionals. There *is* no dress rehearsal. And this *is* the big time. Right?"

Mike looked at him, shaking his head. "Anyone ever tell you you're fucking crazy?"

"Like a fox, buddy." Winking. "Like a fucking fox."

And this is how Kirk Bogarde became a star.

They found Hal's cruiser three quarters of a mile in: parked neatly on what passed for the right shoulder of the narrow road, just as he'd left it. Mike pulled up ten yards back and parked on the left bank. They piled out.

"Guess we'll have to walk it," Kirk said, gesturing to the tree. "Better get a few inches of the car."

Mike nodded and popped a battery into the camera. It was a pro deck, maybe a hundred times more complicated than a consumer-type camcorder. Mike routinely set levels ahead of time, so that on arrival he just had to pop in a battery and he was ready to rock. He focused on the empty cruiser, did a slow pan up and over to the tangled mass of uprooted flora, and stopped at Kirk.

"Okay," Kirk said. "How 'bout a nice pickup shot of me walking by the downed tree, looking pensive?"

"Soul of a poet," Mike said, utterly deadpan.

Kirk nodded, got himself revved to Geraldo speed. "Toxic Waste," he intoned. "The Everpresent Menace . . . no." Catching himself. "Too wordy. *Fuck*."

Mike took a position in the road, focusing as Kirk improvised.

"Toxic Waste: Legacy of Death . . ."

It was then that they heard the engine cranking.

*Hrrrnnn nnn nnn nnn*, it groaned, filtering through the dead, bare trees. The choked metallic grunt of an ignition firing. *Hrrrnnn nnn nnn nnn nnn nnn.*

"What the fuck . . . ?" Kirk whispered, staring at the stormfall blocking the road. *Hrrnnn nnn nnn nnn . . .*

And then, in the distance, the engine chugged to life: exhaust blatting as an unknown foot fed fuel to carb, coaxing combustion.

"Someone's coming," Mike said.

Somewhere around the bend, a heavy vehicle chugged and heaved onto the road. Coming closer. Heading their way.

"Get ready," Kirk hissed. "This might be good."

Mike shrugged and took a position just behind the bumper of the van. It was kinda weird, but what the hey. Kirk hung back and ran through his schmooz options, readying himself for whatever came down the pike.

Then the roar came closer, and the real weirdness started.

The truck was whining and grinding through the gearbox, picking up RPMs at any expense. The way it was burning down the trail, Kirk noted, they had a minute at best to prepare. And it gave no indication of slowing down.

Heading right for Nature's little roadblock. . . .

*Jesus*. The realization was sudden, startling and sure. *They're gonna run it*. "ROLL TAPE!" he screamed. "They're going right fucking through!"

"Way ahead of you, dude," Mike said, grinning. He sighted the road for optimum coverage. Hit the record button.

And history was made.

*First, a study in glaring contrast: the six-ton kamikaze whine of pissed-off steel against an ominously still backdrop of trees and mud. Pan and zoom on the thick mass of limbs skewed across the road, moving in as the roar and the grind grow closer.*

*Passing blip of Kirk Bogarde, mouthing* are you getting this? *Looking genuinely nervous now, as though this is maybe just a* little *bit realer than he likes his coverage and he doesn't even know it yet.*

*The whine peaks. Rack in and focus.*

*Then jerk back, as the truck* explodes *through the branches, letting off a shrapnel shockwave hailstorm of splinters that soar in every direction.*

*Try to track as the blasted Dodge with the busted-out windshield and a shadow at the wheel bounces and hits the ground running, rocks and slides and never gives an inch as it hits the cop cruiser, spinning it a neat two hundred and seventy degrees to smash into the embankment, sending Kirk diving for cover as it hurtles past, jangling in and out of frame but always coming right at the camera.*

*Scream in exhilaration as the truck bears down mercilessly, knowing that this is the footage of a lifetime, living for the spectacle captured in the camera's eye.*

*Then scream again, for entirely different reasons.*

*As the truck devours the frame.*


The last thing Kirk remembered clearly was the front grille, enormous, bearing down on him. He dove and rolled badly, ate a faceful of mud, and came up in a puddle, barely conscious. There was wind and noise and adrenaline and the scattered impressionist jumblefuck memory of Mike: standing ass-out in the wind, cowboy style, nailing the shot like today was a dream and there was no tomorrow.

*Then the truck rolled over him.*

*And the dream went away. . . .*

*       *       *

Silence.

Kirk opened his eyes.

The sky above was brackish, overcast. He ached as if he'd sprained every moving part in his body. Gilt-backed dark clouds taunted, egging him on.

He'd been out for a few minutes. Time enough to change lives.

And to end them.

"Mike." Memory, snapping back like a wet towel to smack him in the ass. "Oh God, Mike . . ." Piecing together the dream. He got up, felt his stomach lurch with the one-eighty spin of his head, and then turned. Scrambling over to his cameraman friend. Or what was left of him.

Kirk had never been good with words, a fact that had steered him away from print journalism and the press. *Smushed* was the word that came screaming to mind. Unprofessional, but accurate. Mike was *smushed*.

He lay embedded in a deep mud truck-rut, the knobby tire pattern running lengthwise over his body and right over his face. The truck weighed several angry tons, and the earth had given as much as it could before accepting him into its embrace.

Then it had been Mike's turn to give.

Kirk puked on his shoes; it was up and out before he knew it. Then he was coughing, coughing and crying, coughing up stringers of coffee and crullers and bile that burned like the tears in his eyes. He sank to his knees. His own lenses went fuzzy, soft around the edges. It gave him a certain detachment, for as long as the tears lasted.

But it didn't change the facts, bring Mike back to life or make his body go away. He just lay there, his old wire-rim aviator glasses pressed into his face like a cookie cutter in clay. One dead hand stuck up from the rut, bent back horribly, fingers pointing as if to say *they went thataway*.

The camcorder, miraculously, had been thrown clear.

It lay just beyond the grasp of Kirk's ex-partner in crime. Kirk scrabbled over to it, found it battle-scarred but unbroken. He clutched it to his breast as the last sobs wrenched out of his system.

The truck was a distant roar behind him, fading fast. Toad Road sprawled out before him, the path brutally cleared by the impact. Mike was still laying there, deader than ever.

Kirk sat back on his haunches, staring.

And, with terrible clarity, realized exactly what he had to do.

# Fourteen

The little Paradise airport in southern Chanceford Township was to Philadelphia International what a 7-11 was to the European Common Market. Just the thought of flying made Gwen acutely queasy. Of course, nausea at a moment's notice had proven a linchpin of the Taylor Family Pregnancy, right from the beginning. . . .

"*Damn*," Gwen cursed, furious with herself. She'd just spent the last fifteen minutes semihysterically sobbing over absolutely nothing, bullshit that only vaguely had Gary's face attached. It was like making a Silly Putty imprint of Dick Tracy's face off the Sunday funnies, stretching it to actual human size, and then saying, "*SEE? SEE WHAT YOU'VE DONE?*"

She'd heard all the jokes and the stats that suggested she'd come to resent him. *Fuck them*. Had *his* body ballooned to grotesque proportions? Had all of *his* internal organs been trash-compacted to make room for *their baby*? Did *he* have to pee every five to ten minutes, whether he made it to the bathroom or not?

Of course not. But that wasn't the point. She didn't want him to squeeze a bowling ball out his butt, or pull his bottom lip over the top of his head in symbolic solidarity.

She didn't want him to suffer as no man had ever suffered before. At least not most of the time.

No. Her needs were very simple. She just wanted to be loved and supported and blah blah blah by the man of her dreams, who really *was* Gary, God bless him, no matter what Micki or her mother or *anyone* said. It was hard to believe he put up with her, what with her mood swings and her irrationality and her HIDEOUS BLOATED ELEPHANTINE BODY THAT NOBODY IN THEIR RIGHT MIND COULD POSSIBLY DESIRE and her other little insecurities, not the least of which had to do with her ability to be a decent wife and mother.

Which of course brought her back to the coffee incident—a stupid nonevent if ever there'd been one—and before she knew it she was blubbering all over the dashboard again.

So she was more grateful than words could say when Micki came through the double-glass exit doors. Grateful that her friend had taken it upon herself to travel all this way. Grateful to have such a friend at all.

She felt better at the very sight of her. Gwen quick-wiped her eyes and checked herself in the rear-view. *Like shit*, she thought. *Definitely look like shit.*

"Look at you, Mama!" Micki called to her as she laboriously lowered herself from the cab. "You look *fabulous!*"

"Look who's talkin!" Gwen called back, assessing the well-fed, well-dressed, absolutely *robust*-looking figure that approached her, bags in hand. Hard to believe that this was the same old Micki Bridges.

Hard to believe that this was the woman who'd been given less than six months to live, a little over five years ago.

"You look great!" Micki reiterated, closing the distance.

"Bullshit. *You* look great!"

"Bullshit. *You* . . . !"

And then they were laughing and embracing, thrilled

to be in one another's presence once again: celebrating the one true friendship that had lasted them all their lives.

"So," Micki said as they disengaged. "Where's hubby?"

"He got called in to work," Gwen said.

"Oh." Very dryly. "What a surprise."

And that, of course, was where the same old crap started up all over again.


The main bone of contention between them had always hinged on their tastes in men. From grade school on, those tastes had been both clearly defined and mutually exclusive.

Gwen favored earthy, grounded, extremely *physical* men: guys who worked with heavy machinery, played football, rode big bikes, went white-water rafting, and knocked back Buds with a J.D. chaser. She liked men with big hands, steady jobs, and massive, sinewy, bull-shaped bodies; men with fierce loyalties, fiery passions, and healthy appetites that she could trust would be brought home to her, day after day after day.

Micki, on the other hand, did not like to be physically overpowered or remotely dependent. Not even in potentia. Her men were ropier, substantially shorter, more flighty and esoteric. She ate up musicians like truffles, especially sax players. Give her a Juzo Itami film festival, a little Frank Zappa and Baba Ram Dass, good Chablis, great conversation, double chocolate Häagen-Dazs, and serious head for an hour; you could then gift-wrap her and take her home.

But rarely for more than a week.

And so it was that Gwen wound up with a Harley-riding engineer eight years her senior, whom she'd lived with for four years and been married to going on three, and with whom she was having the child of their dreams.

And Micki wound up with a forty-thousand-year-old

spirit entity as her permanent life-partner and male companion. Not to mention a handful of lovers on the side.

Not surprisingly, Micki and Gwen had serious problems with each other's picks; though, much to their credit, Gary and Bob-Ramtha got along better than most of the guys they'd introduced to each other. All in all, it was the most absurd aspect of their relationship.

Because, in virtually every other respect, they loved and admired each other to pieces. Micki, *por ejemplo*, was smitten with Gwen's emotional honesty, her bone-deep compassion and sheer innate *goodness*, her automatic and essentially unconditional love of other people. Most people had to work very hard for the kind of spirit that came to Gwen naturally, and Micki was convinced that she would make absolutely the best mother in the world.

Gwen, conversely, was in awe of Micki's balls-out courage, in everything from battling her cancer to standing by (and profiting from!) her unorthodox lifestyle decisions. Gwen thought that, with the possible exception of Gary, Micki Bridges was the strongest person she'd ever met.

In fact, as Gwen often pointed out, Micki and Gary were an awful lot alike. They both insisted on living life entirely on their own terms. Not that they were hard to get along with; but on that one point, they were utterly inflexible. You could not persuade them to violate their natures; there wasn't enough money in the *world* to make them run against their own grains.

Which was probably why they didn't get along. They were just *too* goddam similar.

"I don't know about that," Micki said, the surprisingly warm highway air tousling her hair through the moving truck's open window. "But I'll tell you this. I didn't come all the way out here to sit around watching football."

Gwen laughed, her angst-sopping mood abolished. "Okay. So whaddaya wanna do?"

"I was thinking . . ." Drawing the pause out dramatically, skrinching her hazel eyes. ". . . since it's such a nice day, we might want to get a little, you know. . . lost . . . on the way back.''

Gwen smiled slyly. ''You knew I made sandwiches, didn't you?''

''You're awfully predictable.''

''And only *you* would drag a pregnant woman who's ready to burst out into the middle of nowhere.''

''You mean I'm predictable, too?'' Micki made a horror-stricken g-force face.

They laughed. The conspiracy was ripe. Micki got serious first.

''You sure you're gonna be okay?'' she asked.

''Oh, yeah,'' Gwen said. ''I'm a tough old broad.''

''Okay.'' Micki braced her feet against the dashboard. ''Sam Lewis?'' she asked.

''Sam Lewis,'' Gwen answered, without a moment's hesitation.

''Let's do it.''

''*Weeee-HA!*'' Gwen hooted, stomping down on the gas, as they motored down old Route 624 toward Sam Lewis State Park, and the river that unwound like a serpent below.

# Fifteen

And this was how the cookie crumbled:

Blake was at the sautee table at the Lincoln Woods buffet when his beeper went off. He jumped, surprising no one more than himself.

*Okay*, he thought, gearing up for the worst. He'd certainly known it was coming. He was just slightly appalled with himself for having entertained the foolish hope that it wouldn't.

*Stupid*, he chastised himself. *Hope is the opiate of the misinformed.*

Blake politely excused himself from his wife and their company, padded through the thickly carpeted pastel interior, and made the first of many calls.

Blake was a man of many hats: in his capacity as pointman for PEMA, he performed mucho community liaison. He was the Need To Know man: he determined who needed to know, what they needed to know, and when they needed to know it. When it came to local industry, no story was released in either print or broadcast form without his expressed approval.

So when 911 notified PEMA that they had called in HazMat, the girl at the PEMA switchboard paged Blake right away. He got her story, thanked her warmly, hung up, and dialed again.

Two minutes on the phone with the guys from HazMat, and Blake knew everything he needed to know.

It was, indeed, a can of worms; and it was about to open right into his lap.

Unless he got out of the way.

His next call was to Leonard. No answer. He thought for a moment, then spent the next fifteen minutes doing a little hole-plugging in advance. EPA, DER; all said no problem. Everyone would hold the line. No need to incite a panic. By the time he got back to the table, they were already on dessert.

Not to worry, he assured them.

He'd already had more than his fill.


Down at the Big Boy, Harold Leonard echoed the sentiment, magnified to the ninety-seventh power. His plateful of silver-dollar pancakes, eggs, and link sausage lay congealing in imitation maple syrup before him, barely touched. He couldn't even think about it.

He was thinking about the future.

"Daddy?" The voice bled in from deepest space, from the seat to his immediate right. "Daddy? *Daddy!*"

Leonard blinked, came back to the earth plane. His three-year-old, Thea, was yanking his sleeve. "Yes, honey?" he said, on full automatic, the words a split second ahead of him.

"*Daddy*," she scolded, "I learned a new *song* today!"

"Ah. Heh-heh," he said, his eyes quickly scanning the table. Marge was busy feeding Wally and Timmy, the toddler twins; it was a task that demanded her total concentration. Teenage Brad and Jerry were tormenting little Harold, Jr. at the far end of the table, probably about his ears. Little Harold looked precisely like his father felt: teetering on the brink of tears.

"You want to hear it," Thea told him, her pudgy

little features a frightening parody of his own. He felt haunted by her shining eyes, the absolute lack of empathy in them. She had no idea what was going on inside him. None whatsoever. None of them did.

"'I know you, I walk with you wunnsa ponna dream,'" she sang.

"Not right now, honey," he said, his panic rising. The chinkling of silver, the inchoate gurble of voices, the featureless Muzak, and cholesterol smells collided in his head. He winced against the strobing fluorescent plastic orange decor.

"*No*, Daddy!" Her eyes, in his face, were huge. "It's Seeping Booty! *Listen!* 'I know you, the geamin your eyes is sofer million a gream...'" When her voice raked the high notes, it bore a drill bit through his skull.

Timmy was laughing. Wally was screaming. Marge was cooing *now now now*, over and over. *Now now now.*

"'...An' I know its true, I feenal my selpis alba sleem...'"

"Excuse me," he blurted, the tears welling up now, his face hot and clammy as he *skreeed* back in his chair. "Excuse me," he repeated, standing, all eyes upon him at last as he turned away quickly, ashamed of himself, and headed for the men's room. The Muzak, the sound of other people's families chased him, dogged him across the restaurant.

There was a vacant bank of phones in the narrow access corridor. It was there that he chose to break down. It only took a minute to sob his way clear.

Which brought him right back where he'd started from.

Not that he didn't trust Blake; if anyone had more to lose than Leonard himself, that person was certainly Blake. It was just that he felt so helpless, so utterly out of the loop.

Not to mention guilty as sin.

Not to mention terrified.

He kept thinking about the dead boy, and wondering

what had happened. The thought that he could have caused someone's death, however inadvertently, was just too horrible to bear.

And then there was the other boy. Otis's son. *Perhaps*, Leonard thought, *he's getting better. Lord, what a relief that would be!*

*And if not . . .*

He had Pusser's number, burning a hole in the inside pocket of his sport coat. He withdrew it now, punched in the number, tried to breathe normally.

"*What?*" snapped the voice on the other end, midway into the second ring.

"H-hello, Otis," Leonard stammered.

"*That YOU, Leonard? God damn it!*" The malice in Pusser's voice shifted, focused, went completely specific. "*What the fuck are you doin' for me and my boy?*"

"W-w-well, that's actually why I called . . ."

"*'Cause I'm about FIFTEEN FUCKIN' MINUTES AWAY from callin' the cops on your ass . . . !*"

"Otis, you can't do that." He was striving for an authoritative tone, but the rivets that held his reality together were rattling loose.

"*My boy is DYIN'! Do you understand me?*" And in the background, Leonard could hear the boy mewling: a horrible sound. "*You gonna find some kinda hospital can take him? He don't have no insurance! You gonna pay the fuckin' bill?*"

"Listen . . ." He tasted blood in his mouth, realized he'd gnawed a tiny hole in his lip. "I t-talked to my people, and . . ."

"*YOUR PEOPLE GOT ABOUT FIFTEEN MINUTES TO SAVE HIS LIFE AND KEEP HIS ASS OUT OF JAIL!*" The sound blistered through the plastic earpiece. "*OR YOU'RE GOIN' DOWN, YOU STUPID FAT FUCK . . . !*"

Leonard hung up the phone.

And stood there, terrified, weighing his options. None of them were good. If Otis rolled over, then—Blake or no Blake—the world as he knew it would surely end.

He reached up to fish around in the coin return, and stopped. Some punk had plastered a sticker over the slot, a design rendered in jarringly garish neon colors and squiggles. It was a circle-and-slash motif: the universal forbidden symbol, stamped across squiggly letters that spelled F...U...T...U...R...E.

The gestalt gelled in Harold's quivering mind.

*NO FUTURE.*

"Very funny," he muttered, jabbing a fat finger defiantly into the slot. "Very fucking funny."

It took less than five minutes to round up the family, pay the bill, and get back in the van. Leonard fidgeted more than he customarily did in the cashier's line, and didn't even bother to scarf his customary handful of chalky mints from the bowl by the register. Marge knew better than to pry, and the kids never even wondered why Daddy looked so bad.

They wouldn't have understood it if he'd told them.

Nobody did.

# Sixteen

Getting the tape out of the edit deck was easy.

Getting the hell out of the studio was impossible.

It had been a mess, alright; the tape had committed hari-kari, spilling its innards into the guts of the deck in nasty little inextricable knots. Mike was right about the decks: the Sony had seized up like it was holding the cassette for ransom; it took twenty minutes to free the hostage.

Gary stood at his bench in the repair bay behind Studio B, putting the edit deck back together. The bay was his domain: a garage-sized space housing repair benches stacked with ripped-down gear, plus storage space for the bulky microwave relays and other accoutrements of broadcast technology maintenance.

He screwed the last screw into place and did the mental math of his redemption. It would take him ten minutes to get across town, give or take a stoplight or two. Add that to the ten it took to get there and twenty at the bench, divided by the time Micki's flight was due in over the square root of Gwen's pregnancy...

...*equals a world of shit*, he thought. *God, she's gonna be pissed*. He sighed, picked up the phone and tried again.

Again: no answer.

*Oboy*, he groaned, wincing, then shrugged it off. He'd deal with it later. There was certainly nothing he could do about it now.

Gary hefted the deck and carted it down the hall. The nattering buzz of the newsroom was tangible from all the way down the hall. It made his gut rumble. He stopped at the doorway to Studio A and stuck his head in.

On the home monitor, the closing credits for *WWF Superstars of Wrestling* were rolling by. *This Is the NFL* was less than three minutes away. John Bizzano was tending to the changeover with his customarily laconic aplomb.

"Mornin', Gar," he said, not even looking up as he cued up the commercial tapes. "What're you doin' here today?"

"Beats me," Gary grumbled. "Misplaced sense of duty, I guess."

"Don'cha hate it when that happens?" Bizzano replied, presiding over the switch as they cut from World Federation Wrestling to a five-second station ID and a thirty-second commercial for toilet bowl cleaner.

John Bizzano was a burly bear of a man, with a bushy black beard and no visible neck, but his fingers were pure magic. John was the Iceman, 'PAL's Amadeus of the digital cross-fade. No task fazed him; he could orchestrate the mix of two live feeds in different time zones, *with* satellite uplink, taped outtakes, and special effects, *and* load and cut to sixteen commercials. Never bumping his blood pressure up a single point on the stressometer.

Never blowing a fucking cue.

John was cool.

"Hmmm," Gary began, offhandedly scanning the bank of monitors above the console. "Anything *weird* happening here today?"

"Hmmph," John scoffed. "Ask a stupid question."

"No, I mean *weird* weird," Gary amended.

"Sorry, bro'," John replied. "It's dead." He reclined

back in his chair and watched as little cartoon scrubbing bubbles raced around a bathtub like it was the Indy 500. "*Dead, dead, deadskies...*" he drawled in a passable Michael Keaton-*Beetlejuice* growl. "Why do you ask?"

Gary shrugged. "I dunno. Just a feeling, I guess," he said, and ambled off down the hall.

A minute later, he entered the newsroom. "Here you go," he said. "All better now..."

And stopped.

It was like walking into range of an enormous field generator: the police scanners all cranked and buzzing, the tension so charged it stood the short hairs of his arms on end. He clammed up as if he'd just stumbled onto a live soundstage.

But it was only Laura, pacing and smoking up a miniature smog bank.

"Ahem..." Gary said cautiously. "Deck's back up."

"Uh, thanks," she said, looking up as though just noticing him. "Just set it up, okay?"

"You got it," Gary said, putting the deck back in its place. *So much for gratitude*, he thought. News was big on making nice when they needed something—a quick fix, a rush edit, or some effects generation—but give them a hot story and watch everything else drop right off the map.

A garbled transmission squawked across the police scanner; Laura bolted to the desk, pen and notebook in hand. "*County to Adam-sixty, come in please.... Adam-sixty, please respond...*"

"Shit!" Laura hissed. "That little bastard!"

"What's going on?" Gary asked. Not that she was talking to him or anything.

"What?" Laura started as if she'd forgotten he was there. "Oh, nothing." She turned toward the scanner, figurative steam hissing out of her ears. "Kirk and Mike took off chasing down a lead almost forty minutes ago," she said, "and I *told* them to maintain radio contact, but Kirk is such a little goddamned *asshole* sometimes, and..."

*And Mike's such a stoner,* Gary thought. Mike hadn't been around too long, but Gary liked him in a *my-dorky-kid-brother* kind of way. In some ways, Mike reminded Gary of himself, a decade or so ago. Same goofy go-for-broke resolve, same fascination with the toys and tools of his trade.

Of course, Mike seemed spacier, but then Gary wasn't sure how much of that was the change in *himself.* He could remember more than once looking down to find his face wrapped around the pay end of a bong.

"Well, if that's all you need, then..." Gary began, easing his way toward the door.

And that was when Kirk came busting in.

Now, ten years in television news could turn the most delicate stomach lining to boot leather. Gary's had long since made the change. Experience had sharpened his senses even as it had dulled his feelings; he picked up on the heady adrenaline-scent of *disaster* almost instantly. It commingled with another smell: the high nasal tang of undiluted *ambition.*

It didn't take a master detective to win the first round of *what's wrong with this picture*? Kirk Bogarde was one of the vainest sons-of-bitches on earth; but here he was, showing up at work spattered from head to toe in mud, his hair all unmoussed and tousled. Mike's battered camera dangled from one hand, mud-spattered as well. Mike was nowhere in sight.

Laura turned, death rays emoting from her eyes as Kirk stumbled down the stairs. "Alright!" she yelled. "I want some goddamned explanations here!"

He blew past Gary in a shot, muttered something incoherent, and beelined for the edit room, disappearing around the corner. The camcorder carelessly went *crunch* against the doorjamb. Gary felt the blood drain out of his face. The signal in his head was clanging like a klaxon horn. *Wrong! Wrong! Wrong! Wrong!*

"GODDAMMIT!" Laura bellowed, storming across the room. "Where the hell have you been? Why didn't you maintain radio contact? Where's Mike . . . ?"

"Mike's dead," he said flatly, still banging around.

*WHAT*?!! Gary thought.

"WHAT?!!" Laura cried incredulously. "What . . . how . . ." She stopped, collected herself. "Kirk, what the hell are you talking about?"

Kirk's face suddenly appeared around the corner; crazed, shell-shocked, and feral. He clutched a videocassette in his hand as if it were a piece of the One True Cross. He waved it before her, stopping her dead.

"C'mere," he said. "I gotta show you something."

"Jesus God, this is awful," Laura gasped. She and Kirk stood in front of the monitor, features aglow from the screen. Mike's chair was conspicuously empty. Gary hovered at the doorway, watching Kirk as if he were some strange and unpleasant form of bacteria.

The tape's sound was turned mercifully down. It didn't help.

The visuals were bad enough.

"Did you call the police?" Laura asked.

"No," Kirk replied, his voice very small.

*On the screen, the truck was ramming through the dead branches in a burst of chaotic choreography. . . .*

"Did you call EMR?" she asked.

"No," Kirk said, teeth clenching. *The truck, bouncing in and out of the jangling frame, bearing down on the camera . . .*

"Did you call *ANYBODY*?!" she asked, exasperated.

"No!" *The truck, swallowing everything.*

"Are you crazy? Why the hell *not*?"

"BECAUSE I FORGOT, OKAY?" he screamed, leaning too far into Laura's face. "I WAS KINDA FUCKIN' BUSY!"

*The screen, reduced to static.*

"MIKE *DIED* FOR THAT FOOTAGE...!" Kirk bellowed: his nose almost touching Laura's, her hair blowing back. The spark of terror in Laura's eyes was all Gary needed to see.

"Whoa," Gary said, stepping closer. He liked Laura fine, had thought the world of Mike, was none too fond of Kirk. "Boy," he said, stepping deftly between them, one big hand coming up to land in the center of Kirk's chest. Kirk was maybe two inches taller. It didn't mean a thing. "Time for you to calm down."

"*Hey...!*" Kirk began, already folding.

Gary shook his head *huh-uh*, laid a sharp, flat-palmed love thump on Kirk's hollow breastbone. It made a resonant thud, knocked him back just a step.

"I think the question we're asking here," Gary continued, "is what did you do about Mike?"

Kirk's eyes flickered from side to side, as if the answer were written on a cue card somewhere just outside of his visual range.

"You just fuckin' left him there, didn't you?" Gary pressed, his anger mounting, a black tide within him.

Behind him, Laura went, "Gary. No."

"Just fuckin' left him in the mud," Gary snarled, backing him into the folding chairs. They collapsed with a clatter that did nothing but stoke Gary's rage. "No cops, no nothing. Just race back here to cash in on your big fuckin' story, forget all about the guy who fuckin' died so you could even *have* it...!"

There were hands on his shoulders now, holding him back. "Gary! *ENOUGH!*" she shouted. Gary tensed for a second, his fury threatening to blow back on her. Then he stopped in his tracks and swallowed it whole.

Before him, Kirk's mouth opened and closed, opened and closed. He was trying for his wounded-puppy look, but fish metaphors kept getting in the way. Gary guessed it was his wounded-guppy look.

"It just got all fucked up," Kirk sniveled, the tears coming now. "And when Mike got k-k-killed..."

"It's okay," Laura said. Gary shot her a look like *you're kidding, right?*; she just kept watching Kirk.

"... the only thing I could think was *get the tape back, get the tape back!*" He smashed the desk with his fist—once, twice—his features contorting with anguish. "So I *dih*-hih-hid . . ." His voice decaying into unquestionably heartfelt sobs.

When the picture came back on the monitor again—a disjointed shot of dirt and grass—Kirk reached over and clicked it off. A dramatic gesture.

"So," Gary said, turning to Laura. "Now what?"

She just stood there, quietly thrumming, her features knit in intense concentration. He sympathized; it was an extremely tough call. He just hoped that she'd make the right decision.

"We run with the story," she said at last.

"Alright!" Kirk exclaimed, scarcely daring to believe it.

"Score: Cannibals, one; Humans, nothing," Gary muttered, scowling.

Laura picked up the phone and punched an inside line to the studio. "John?" she said. "Laura. Listen, get on the line and get me another cameraman . . . yeah, I *know* it's Sunday, dammit! Something's cooking, and it looks like it might break early . . ."

She paused, suddenly. Gary watched her face turn a little bit green. "Um . . . Mike?" she said slowly. "Mike's out of commission . . . never *mind* what happened! Just get me another shooter in here, pronto!"

She finished, ringing off. Gary faced her squarely. "Aren't you forgetting something?" he said.

Laura took a deep breath. "The HazMat people will be out there any minute. Not to mention more cops, if they're not there already. Now, we can spend the whole day tied up, answering their questions, or we can get to the bottom of this. As far as I'm concerned, it's not even an issue." She looked him straight in the eye. "They'll take care of Mike."

"Aw, bullshit . . . !"

"Kirk." Laura focused on him, turned away from Gary. "I want to know whose truck that was. I want to know everything about them." Kirk nodded, recuperating with astounding speed. "Then, as soon as we get another shooter, we'll—"

"*WHAT*?" Kirk cried out. "What do you *mean*, 'as soon as we get another shooter'! *I* know how to work the camera! I'm ready to go *now*!"

Laura looked to Gary, as if to say *can we?* Gary shook his head.

"We can't do that," she decided. "The union would flip."

"The union," Gary concurred, "would lose their fucking minds."

"FUCK the union!" Kirk barked. "We're sitting on the biggest story of the year, and you want to wait for a goddamned *cameraman*?"

"Rules are rules," Laura said.

"*FUCK THE RULES*!!" Kirk wailed.

"Now, you listen," Laura turned, recouping herself. "And listen *good*. I'm not going to risk my job and bring a strike down on us just because you've got a fire in your pants. So you either sit tight, and we do it by the book, or you just kiss it goodbye. You got that?"

Kirk looked away, conceding nothing. Laura headed back to her Rolodex, started pulling important numbers.

"Well, great," Gary said, radiating contempt as he turned to leave. "Hope it all works out for you guys . . ."

"Wait," she said, stopping him at the door. "I need your help. Do you think you could run A.D.O. on that tape?"

He turned back, looking at her as if she had just said *would you eat barbecued baby butt?* "You're serious," he said.

"You bet your ass," she replied. "Can you do it?"

"Sure, I *can*." Gary nodded incredulously, making no pretense of niceness. "But you forget: I'm outahere.

Besides," he added, "what do you need digital effects for? You got your action footage."

"The police report said that the vehicle was stolen," Laura countered. "That means it could have been anybody. We need to isolate the face of the driver, give us a recognizable still." Beat. "If we're gonna nail this guy, we need your help."

Gary paused. The bitch of it was, she had a point. Ampex Digital Optics processing could show the bugs stuck to the bumper, if Mike had shot it right. And Gary'd be lying if he said he wasn't curious.

"Please," she entreated. "Do it for Mike."

*Ooh.* He felt his blood freeze in his veins. *You manipulative bitch.*

But her gaze didn't waver. And the facts didn't change.

"Okay," he conceded at last. "But just for the record, this utterly sucks."

"For the record, noted." She nodded, handing him the tape. "Oh, and Kirk?" she began, turning toward the edit room. "Kirk . . . ?"

"Oh, shit." Gary got it at the very same time.

"Kirk!" she yelled, turning back to the stairs. "Oh, you son of a *bitch*!"

Both Kirk and the camera were gone.

And it was twelve o'clock.

# Seventeen

At twelve-fifteen, the HazMat team pulled onto the Black Bridge road.

Deitz noticed the atmosphere shift at once. It immediately got ten degrees warmer, and *close*: a sticky, subtropical humidity that clung to the inside of the lead truck's cab.

The last thirty years, he knew, had seen radical shifts in global climate patterns, accelerating as the carbon dioxide levels increased. And the weather had always been a quirky, temperamental thing at best.

*But this,* he noted, *isn't right. This isn't just a weird, sudden whim of Mother Nature.*

*This didn't start to happen till we rounded the corner.*

It was as if Toad Road had developed an atmosphere all its own.

"Gettin' hot," Pyle said from the driver's seat beside him. He had a ruddy, cheerfully predisposed face on a short, squat, sandy-haired frame: a sort of Barney Rubble made flesh. Fresh beads of perspiration dappled his forehead, grew stains in the budding swamplands of his pits.

"Yep." Deitz's response was automatic. His mind

131

was busy, sifting data, relying on his senses and his wits to provide it.

"If it gets nice enough, my wife's gonna take the kids to Dutch Wonderland," Pyle continued. He sounded wistful. "God, they love that place. Even with most of the rides shut down for the winter..."

"Uh-huh." Even though he wasn't but barely listening, Deitz could certainly sympathize. Pyle wanted to go to Dutch Wonderland, too. Just as all that *Deitz* wanted was to be back in Jennie's bed, before that first phone call from Krummy Kake Pat had begun to ring the death knell on his wonderful day.

He had been in higher spirits, that much was for certain. The best day of his life, slightly crippled from the git, had gone terminal the second his beeper went off. By the time he'd been briefed, with what little information was available, his Day of Days was pushing up proverbial daisies in Dreamland.

The fact was, even a *minor* spill could be nasty work and tie them up for days. Not to mention the little matter of the missing cop, which Deitz found severely disconcerting. When a cop disappeared, it invariably meant that something was very wrong. As team leader, he was excruciatingly aware of this.

It made him intent on being *more than careful* going in. He would err on paranoia's side, if he thought he could afford to err at all.

The temperature and humidity continued to increase; and he noticed that the woods were getting progressively more dense and green to either side. The swollen air grew rich with smells: pungent, florid, chlorophyll-dense; earthy and heady all at once.

*And beneath it all: an acrid, chemical tang...*

It whispered like foil against his back molars, tickled the hairs of his nostrils with the suggestion of stinging pain. It wasn't a smell he recognized—the entire olfactory gestalt had a queasily alien feel—but it left a bad first impression.

"Stop the truck," he said. Pyle looked at him, surprised; he had still been talking. "Now." Pyle obeyed. A thin sliver of discomfort wedged itself in Deitz's forehead, like a tiny phantom drill bit boring into his brain.

And his lips began to tingle.

The radio squawked: "*What's going on?*" It was Beckett, from the truck behind them. Deitz took the radio, brought the mouthpiece to his lips. He turned to Pyle, and to Franklyn in the back, addressing the entire crew at once.

"Suit up," he said. "That means everybody. And get your heads on straight. This one doesn't look good."

*There were two HazMat trucks on Toad Road, nondescript except for several small yet tasteful warning placards on the back. The effect was designed to minimize their presence to the world around them, much as their bulky protective suits and gear were designed to keep out the world of shit they routinely plunged themselves into.*

*Inside the trucks were the vacuum hoses and containment barrels, spill booms like enormous toxic tampons filled with superabsorbent polyester down. Inside the trucks were the only people both qualified and crazy enough to use them. But as far as the rest of the world was concerned, they might as well have been delivering beer. No one would ever know.*

*There were only five other men on the team today: Beckett, Burroughs, Hooper, Pyle, and Franklyn. Deitz listened to them talk as they donned their space suits; none of them were what you'd call happy to be here. HazMat was a largely volunteer organization, and an NFL Sunday was likely to find a lot of people—far smarter than Deitz and company, evidently—somehow managing to accidentally lose their beepers. Westerberg and Ilginfritz, for example; those bastards were probably already drunk for the game.*

*Collectively, his team had been on nearly a hundred cleanup missions: mostly small-scale, unpublicized local incidents. Deitz, on the other hand, had personally served on over three hundred, spanning more than a decade, from New York to the Great Lakes to the Gulf of Mexico. He'd fought the fires when Control Chemical shot its flaming wad over Elizabeth, New Jersey back in '79; then been back up to suck sludge in '90, when Exxon vomited a half-million gallons of heating oil into the Arthur Kill. He'd manned the pumps off the St. Clair River for seventy-two hours straight, when a submerged dioxin blob from leaking storage caverns threatened the population of southern Ontario like something from a bad sci-fi movie.*

*Austin Deitz really thought that he'd seen it all; and by ordinary standards, it was certainly true.*

*It did nothing to prepare him for what happened next.*

When they were all safely, hermetically sealed, the convoy proceeded cautiously on ahead. A tense silence had fallen over the crew; evidently, they'd taken his message to heart.

A hundred yards deeper into the woods, Deitz spotted something large in the road ahead. It looked, from that distance, like some sort of natural roadblock—the forest overspilling its bounds, squeezing in from either side until the road was reduced to a foot trail's width—though the dense shadows kept it obscured from clear view.

*This isn't right*, he told himself, consulting the compulsively anal tax map the county had provided. *This is supposed to go through to the bridge.*

That was when he noticed the police car's remains.

It was sitting in a ditch to the side of the road, its ass in the air, steam wafting up from under the hood. At least Deitz *thought* it was the hood. It was kind of hard to tell.

Because the entire cruiser was crawling with thick, tendinous vines that moved as if rustled by the breeze.

They covered the vehicle so thoroughly, so *comprehensively*, that it looked like topiary sculpture in the shape of a police car.

"*Jesus Christ*." Pyle saw it, too: twenty yards and closing now, as the truck slowed down to a crawl. Burroughs, behind them, mirrored the gesture without knowing why.

The roadblock lay just beyond it: the wreckage of a tree, also thoroughly overgrown, a swath carved through it like a jagged, organic fortress gate. The heavy, hot, foul-smelling breeze came from somewhere deeper in the woods, blowing discernibly through the breach.

"*I don't understand*," said Franklyn. His voice, transmitting off his lapel mike, was a timid little-boy peep.

Deitz understood exactly how he felt; just looking out the window made him want to call a cop. The problem, of course, was that in this case, they *were* the cops, or the cop-equivalents. They were the ones you called, in these situations; there *was* no one else.

"That's why we're here," Deitz said, trying hard to sound more confident than he felt. He felt his military training mercifully kick in, take over where he did not care to tread alone. "Ladies, I want soil samples and preliminary readings in fifteen minutes," he continued. "Pyle, radio back and let them know we've got a situation here. The second we've got what we need, we're gone."

Then he opened the door, and stepped into another world.

The crew nervously, painstakingly checked their gear and then followed, tramping along the moist resilient surface of the road. It wasn't like any form of clay Deitz had ever seen, not to mention ordinary mud; it was almost rubbery in its stubborn surface tension.

Hooper had the camcorder, was getting it all on tape. He was the first to note the fresh, deep tire tracks underfoot: signs of some recent Baja driving that even now receded, filling up as the ground absorbed the puddle runoff. One particularly deep indentation was man-sized.

Strange. *Like somebody had laid down and made a mud-angel*, Deitz thought.

"*Austin.*" It was Pyle. There was a lot of static interference, but even that couldn't hide the agitation in his voice. "*I . . . I can't raise anyone. We must be in a dead spot or something. . . .*"

"Fuck!" Deitz hissed, regretted the outburst even as it happened. He turned and saw the men look to each other, could feel their apprehension complete a circuit between them. He was not outside of the loop.

"Keep trying," he addended, terse and clipped. This was no time to get sloppy; they needed him focused, to stay focused themselves. "Beckett. Burroughs. You can take the soil sample right off the road. Franklyn, those puddles will do. Let's get this over with."

Which left him, of course, to deal with the vines.

Deitz approached the car slowly, taking continuous mental notes. The vines: he'd never seen anything like them. They had a greasy-looking, muted sheen; again, the word *rubbery* came to mind.

At the ends, the shoots were narrow and serrated, clustered in rings of threes and fours and curling around the edges, laced with pink veins thin as baby's skin. They opened up at the thicker, more mature trunk, sprouting broad, thick leaves: pear-shaped and fluted, the veins etched in rich scarlet piping.

Pale tendrils spiraled out from underneath the leaves, anchoring them to the metal of the car. Once anchored, they pulled the dense weight of the vine forward, where smaller tendrils reached out like flying buttresses, bracing the heavy trunk.

Stranger still, Deitz realized, he could watch them doing it.

Now, he'd seen rapid vines before. Down South, he'd known kudzu to take over whole acres in a matter of days.

*But in a matter of minutes . . .*

The mass shifted as one tendril, thick as his thumb, settled like a dog on a favorite rug onto the roof of the cruiser. Deitz stepped back involuntarily, saw that the growth traced down into the drainage ditch on the car's blind side, all the way back into the woods. He didn't need a map to tell him that they shared a common source or destination.

Deitz reached into his hip-sack, produced a sample bag.

The vine groped blindly toward him, its feelers uncoiling, reading the subtle shifts in the air. It stretched, then *drew back* suddenly, the entire extension bunching up in the moment before it rose: a boneless arm, hovering above him, its leaf shoots intertwined to make a delicate wristlet of glistening spikes.

He stood mesmerized, the sound of his own breathing huge in his ears as condensate fogged the Plexiglas plate. *This is crazy*, he thought.

The vine curled back, storing tensile strength.

And then it sprang toward him.

Deitz's heart jumped a beat. The plant moved with surprising speed. He sidestepped its arc, grabbing the vine as if it were an adder in mid-strike. His heavy glove squeezed it, clamping down as he produced a small Buck knife from a belt pouch. He held it taut, and felt his stomach tighten as he realized that the thing was actually *struggling* against him, trying to retreat back to the safety of the car and its host.

Deitz brought the blade up, just behind a juncture of leaf and trunk. The incision he made was like slitting a throat. He grimaced as a rich, red, luminous sap spurted out, and the end piece came off in his hand. It was still twitching as he popped it into the bag and sealed it away.

The freed vine recoiled, snapping back to its place on the car; and suddenly, the mass of vines began to *shudder*, a seismic telepathy that radiated through the woods around and before him. It seemed to ripple through the men as well, freezing them in place as their static-etched voices cried out in shock.

"*What the fuck . . . !*" Burroughs yelled; and then the

entire *road* wobbled spastically underfoot, as if some giant
air bubble had compressed and shifted beneath its surface.
Deitz nearly lost his balance, and Franklyn fell: a capsized
beetle, fat limbs waggling, silently flailing at the air.

*And that was when Deitz caught sight of the sham-
bling figure in the woods; the mangled mud-angel himself,
features hideously flattened into a leering expression that
was one part grimace, one part grin, flat eyes bright with
broken glass as its broken right hand spasmed up.*

*It was waving hello.*

*Or, possibly, good-bye.*

"RUN!" Deitz screamed to his terrified men; and in
that moment, the skin of the mud beneath their feet *burst*
like an enormous blister, giving way to a stagnant yellowed
reeking quicksand pus that dragged them down, poisoned
earth and bacteria swirling around their ankles, their hips,
their thrashing arms heads hands then gone without a
bubble or a prayer.

Swallowed by the road.

Deitz stared as the road split open before him, felt the
gelatin ground go loose beneath his feet. Then he dove,
screaming, every ounce of strength in his body hurling
headfirst off the road. Diving for the safety of the green
green grass. His only hope.

No hope at all.

*It was like landing on a bed of poisoned nails. Each
blade was a crystalline razor, a chlorophyll needle punching
in through his protective garb to rake his flesh as he hit,
shoulder first, then rolled onto his back. Clothing, skin,
and muscle shredded, making him shriek as the blades
sunk deeper. Impaling. Injecting.*

*Infecting him.*

Mortal pain threw his head back. His eyes flew open.
The world went upside down. He could see the HazMat
trucks, sucking down into the road as well. From his point
of view, it was as if they were ascending into heaven.

Deitz passed out, came to, passed out again. His own
dying cycle of seasons. He came to, some time later,

overwhelmed by the sweet stench of chlorophyll, blood, and the overriding *taint* of something he couldn't place because there was no place for it in the world that he had known.

That world was gone.

*It* was in him now. He could feel it. It was in everything, remaking the world in its own image.

Deitz couldn't move, couldn't speak.

He could only wait.

Soon the shadow of the first vine came: sightless, patient, intuitive. Deitz knew it was only a matter of time.

But it seemed to take forever.

# Eighteen

Gary sat in the Studio B control chair, a computer joystick in one hand and an unlit Marlboro in the other. Smoking in the studio was *verboten*, though everyone did it anyway; the only reason Gary refrained was the repair-tech common sense that said *you fuck it up, you fix it*.

But he was sorely tempted by the image on the screen.

Before him was a rack of monitors; twelve nine-inch Sonys framing a twenty-inch Conrac screen, six to a side. The left six were dedicated to video effects, character generation, all things computer-based and digital.

The right six were split between the rack-mounted Betacam modules and broadcast monitors showing the up-to-the-minute programming of 'PAL and the local competition. On monitors 7 and 8, tiny little Eagles got ready to do battle with equally diminutive Giants in a Philadelphia stadium the size of his empty ashtray.

And at the moment Gary could not care less.

He was watching the outtakes of Kirk and Mike's entrance onto Toad Road: the bars and tone, the first sweeps of establishing shot. The landscape looked strangely overgrown, alien. *"Check it out,"* Mike's voice-over bled up. *"You gotta see this . . ."*

Kirk appeared on screen. *"Lemme see . . ."* he said, reaching for the camera.

*"Cam switch!"* Mike chortled. *"WHOA . . . !"*

*The image jostled and blurred as the deck changed hands. Mike suddenly appeared on screen, grinning a stoned grin. "Look, ma, no hands!"* he said.

"You jerk!" Gary winced. 'PAL was a union shop; he could get their asses fried for a stunt like that.

*"Now remember what I showed you."* Mike moved closer, until the lens swallowed his face in shadow. *"Set it on a number three filter, and no gain, and . . ."*

*"Huh?"* Kirk said.

*"Never mind. Just open up the aperture and bring it into focus, like this . . ."*

Mike's nose suddenly became macro-clear, huge and cratered as the surface of the moon. *"Got it?"*

*"Got it,"* Kirk said. *"So which one's the* off *button?"*

The image blipped off.

Gary fast-forwarded and made the A.D.O. dump, the technology converting Kirk's magnetically encoded source tape into bytes of digital information. Once there he could use the computer editing system to do damn near anything he wanted, editing-wise.

At the moment, Gary wanted only one thing: to see who was driving that fucking truck.

"C'mon, baby," he cooed, rocking the stick like he was locked into the world's scariest Nintendo game. *Except the monsters in this game hung around after the change ran out*, he thought. *And they played for keeps.*

*Just ask Mike.*

On the screen, the truck was blasting through the tree again: he slowed the digitized image, smoothing the jangling death-dance on the tape.

"You stupid fucking cowboy," Gary muttered *in memorium*, "I hope this was worth it."

He found a perfect moment in the chaos, paused it, then reached over to the computer keyboard and scrolled down the menu. Tap Tap. *Z is for Zoom*. Tap tap tap tap. *Eighty percent.*

On the screen, a glowing blue box appeared around the truck, blinking.

He tapped in a few more commands, hit "go."

The box blew up then, filling the screen. "C'mon, motherfucker," he whispered. "Show me what you saw."

He switched to the Conrac, enlarging the image to the limits of tape saturation. He pushed it until the actual pixel resolution could go no further.

And there it was, drawn in a game of digital connect-the-dots, hovering on the brink of image dissolution. The thing that froze an experienced cameraman like a spotlighted deer. The thing that was worth dying for.

*It was a hideous idiot countenance: a lopsided grinning skull, jaw hanging crookedly, eyes bulging like meaty pingpong balls, filthy kerchief around its neck, its long black hair a wild corona as it hunkered down behind the wheel.*

*It was a ghost truck driven by a corpse.*

*And it was loose somewhere in Paradise.*

"Jesus fucking Christ," Gary muttered. This was too weird. He picked up the phone and called down to the newsroom.

"Yeah," Laura answered, tension lacing her voice.

"Did you raise Kirk yet?" he asked.

"He won't answer," she replied.

"Big surprise," Gary snorted. "Anyway, I think you better get up here."

"Did you get something?" she asked, the anxiety in her voice giving way to excitement.

"I don't know what the hell I got," he said. "But whatever it is, you're gonna want to see it."

"I'm on my way." She hung up.

Gary sat there a moment, holding the dead receiver in his hand and staring at the screen. Then he called home again. Just in case.

The phone rang once. Twice.

He let it go, as if sheer persistence might carry the day.

Three times. Four.

Hoping they were off somewhere, having a nice lunch and saying terrible things about him.

Five. Six.

Gary let it ring.

Hoping against hope that the sinking feeling in the pit of his stomach was really all in his head. . . .

# Nineteen

The first thing wrong that Micki noticed were the sudden profusion of starlings.

There were thousands of them, fluttering over the trees that made up the knobby ridge of the park, filling the air with their raucous din.

*Jesus*, she thought, *shades of Alfred Hitchcock. When did* they *take over?* Micki loved Nature in all its beauty as much as the next girl, but starlings? *Sturnus vulgaris*, the Hell's Angels of the bird-table? No, thank you very much.

They dominated by sheer numbers—driving other birds out, stealing nests and eating the young, and then overbreeding until the sheer tonnage of their droppings alone was enough to destroy a stand of woods. Then they'd die off or migrate elsewhere, to begin the cycle anew.

No doubt about it. A starling infestation was a sure sign that all was not right in Oz.

Micki and Gwen lay on a blanket by one of the picnic tables. They loved the park dearly: more than a handful of their fondest memories, from childhood on, had their genesis there. As girls, they had come here often: picnicking with their families, clambering around on the rocks, staring at the sky and dreaming of magical lands. As teens, they got high and laid out on the lush green veldt, sucking up the panorama and dreaming of other kinds of magic.

On the ridge, across the valley, three steel needles jutted into the sky, warning lights flashing on them at regularly spaced intervals: TV and radio broadcast towers, transmitting their signals to the world at large. They, too, had been there forever, or at least since the fifties, and hence were part of the women's memories as much as the hills and trees and sky.

"Remember how we used to imagine that they were magic?" Micki said wistfully. "And how we could climb them to the cities up in the sky?" She sighed.

"Yeah," Gwen sighed back. " 'Course now we know the only thing up there is *Championship Wrestling* and *Lifestyles of the Rich and Famous*."

"The Home Shopping Network . . ." Micki added.

"Ted Turner's colorized classics . . ." Gwen chimed in. They looked at each other, ready to burst.

"*Geraldo* . . ." they chimed in unison.

"*Ooooooooh!*"

They both grimaced their best persimmon-face and broke up, laughing longer than they needed to, like schoolgirls mooning over who kissed who at the junior prom. Micki took hold of Gwen's hand, squeezing.

"Jesus." Micki winced. "The death of innocence is gruesome, huh?"

"Nah," Gwen said, squeezing back. "Innocence never dies. There's always a new generation to fall for it."

Micki smiled, and they fell silent for a moment, staring out at the towers.

"Hard to believe," Micki said, in genuine awe, "that Gary actually climbs those things."

"The center one," Gwen said, gesturing. "Twice a month, whether he wants to or not. Scares me half to death, every time.

"Speaking of which," she added, apologetic, "I gotta make a phone call."

Micki looked at her and sighed grievously. "Hurry back," she said.

Gwen stuck her tongue out playfully and waddled off. Micki smiled and settled back on the soft carpet of grass, contenting herself with earth and sky. As far as she was concerned, there had *never* been a better place for cloud-watching than at the top of that hill, stretched out on your back with the sky above and the river below, almost able to touch those great billowing creatures that unfolded before you. Creatures that only you could see.

You, that is, and your very best friend. . . .

A shrill, deafening din suddenly rose up, startling her. Micki turned to see a riotous black wave fill the sky, as the starlings took off en masse for the far end of the park.

*Good riddance*, Micki thought. She glanced over to the phone kiosk some ten yards away, where Gwen was tethered, listening to her home phone ring off the hook.

" '*Back in a flash, honey*!' " Gwen hollered, aping Gary's twang. " '*Ah promise*!' LIAR!"

Micki groaned. The picnic basket sat before her on the blanket, taunting her with the aromatic reminders of apples and smoked turkey, Dijon and whole wheat. Her stomach grumbled sullenly. Gwen had claimed that she'd parked in the restricted spaces to be close to the bathrooms, but one sight of the little booth and Micki knew the true reason.

"Domestic bliss," she muttered sarcastically. "You know *I* love it!" Micki closed her eyes then, feeling the warm flood of energy that always infused her when Bob-Ramtha spoke. She arched her back like a cat being stoked, and smiled inwardly.

"I *know* they love each other, Bobba. That's their problem," she said. A petulant look crossed her face. "No, I am *not* being mean! I'm just hungry!"

"*Damn* him!" Gwen yelled, slamming down the receiver. Micki turned back to her, saw the hurt disguised as anger as she chugged back to the table. "I swear to God he drives me crazy sometimes! He just did two shifts, back-to-back, and that's the third time in the last month. Now's he's back in there again!"

"You guys really oughta get a machine," Micki offered.

"Gary hates 'em." Gwen shrugged angrily, waddling closer. "He says that if you get a message, you're obligated to return the call. 'Course he always picks up the damned thing anyway, so why bother?"

"Guess that's why they call him the Great Communicator."

"Hey." Gwen flashed her a mock-killing glance that had just a whiff of the real deal in it.

"Sorry," Micki said, dismissing the issue. "So can we eat now, please? I'm starved."

Gwen looked at her as if she *really* wanted to continue, as if a charge had built up that had to go off, and would sooner than later. She started to sit, stood right back up again. "Whoa, shit," she said, grimacing. "Not again."

"Poor baby." Micki sighed. She started to stand; Gwen waved her off.

"No, don't bother, I'm used to it," Gwen said, grabbing an apple from the basket. "You know," she muttered, "if Nature was *really* a woman, She wouldn't have designed the plumbing like this."

"You got a point." Micki laughed, and reached for an apple herself. "But it's clearly not a man, either. So what is it?"

"Nature," Gwen concluded, "is just *crazy*. That's all."

Her voice was answered by the din of ten thousand black birds as she waddled up the path and disappeared, heading for the hopper. Micki got up from the table and plunked herself down on the dry grass, the better to munch her apple and ponder Nature's supposed insanity.

Overhead, the starlings were returning. She stared into the sky as the black wave rose, tight little iridescent triangles swooping in complex aerial maneuvers, beautiful and terrible all at once. Micki watched in fascination as the birds started to assume a kind of chaotic formation, swirling like iron filings around a magnet into a looping repetitive pattern, a definable shape.

*Like a flying figure eight*, she thought.

*Or an infinity symbol. . . .*

"Damn, that's weird," she said to herself. Then to her companion, "Bobba. Whaddaya think . . . ?"

There was no reply.

"Bobba?" Micki said again.

Two things you got used to as a channel. One was the constant presence of your guide, like a comforting cloak. The other was a curious absence of fear regarding your own mortality, events like this morning's plane ride notwithstanding. When you knew where you were going, and you were never alone, what was there to be afraid of?

"Bobba?" Micki stood up, suddenly stripped of the one and given the other inverse abundance. A chill gust blew up from the water, giving her gooseflesh.

Then Bob-Ramtha's presence lurched back into her consciousness with a vengeance.

*Get out of here*, he said.

"Huh?" Micki said, her brain whanging from the sheer force of the intrusion. "Where were you?" she asked. The presence redoubled, a psychic body-slam in the center of her head.

*GET OUT OF HERE NOW.*

Micki wasn't accustomed to hearing fear inside her head. The Bobster was a New Age kind of ancient entity: he did not dispense fear lightly.

"What's going on?" she asked, turning her gaze toward the trees and the little wooden hut.

*NOW.*

And that was when the first screaming started.

There was a dumpster just off the path near the bathrooms, by the old-fashioned hand-pump fountain that supplied rinse water. Its hinged double lids were thrown back, and it was full to overflowing with food and trash, paper and plastic, half-emptied soda cans and candy wrappers galore. A swarm of yellow jackets buzzed sluggishly over the garbage, probing for treats.

Because Gwen was about to burst and her mind was elsewhere entirely, it didn't strike her as odd to see wasps on a dumpster in the middle of November. The call of Nature was screaming in her bladder; she pumped some water into the little fountain bowl and rinsed her apple, then waddled on as fast as her feet would carry her.

Gwen looked out over the park as she hiked. To the east over the river the sky was darkening: a violent, ugly atmospheric pigmentation. The storm was returning with measured steps, slowly reassembling its power base. She could feel the rising wind, buffeting soft but insistent against the grass. She could hear it, whistling through the trees.

*We should go soon*, she thought, and took a bite of the apple.

Bitterness flooded her mouth, coating her tongue, sinking into the spaces between her teeth.

"AGH! PFEH!!" Gwen gagged and spat the offending fragment as far away as she could. "What the hell . . ." she began, looking at the apple in her hand. Droplets of water laced its surface like silvered ribbons.

*Droplets that suddenly, impossibly* moved. . . .

"Guhh . . ." Gwen tried to speak, but her lips and gums were going numb, and the inside of her cheeks felt utterly dead.

*Omigod*, her mind whimpered. *Am I poisoned?*

That thought was followed instantly by another, ten times more urgent.

*Did I poison the baby . . . ?*

Gwen dropped the apple. It crumbled apart, pinkish meat giving way to reveal a wormy, rotted core.

A violent wave of nausea hit her, brought the bile up to her throat. She couldn't even taste it. Her flesh went flush with sweat as the taint coursed through her system. She bit into her tongue, felt pressure but no pain.

There was a high ringing tone in her inner ears, as if her acuity had been boosted to the point where *the air itself* was audible, where every whisper of a blade of grass was like a buzz saw in the distance.

*I will not pass out*, she told herself, *I will not faint I will not* . . .

The ringing in her ears was a drone now, incessant and pulsing; a strange new frequency beating like the wavelength of life itself. She was aware of her body hyperventilating, fighting for consciousness and equilibrium, vaguely aware that she was moving forward. It was as if her flesh had gone onto auto-pilot, cocooning her consciousness into a chrysalis of sound and numbing sensation as she moved inexorably toward the bathroom and release.

The angled wooden aperture that led to the door was before her. Gwen grabbed onto the corner post for support, looked up.

And saw the deer.

It stood shivering at the tree line some ten feet away. It was a yearling, its coat still dappled with snowy flecks of white, and it was injured. A dark smear matted its left side just beneath the lung, like a gunshot wound gone septic.

It hobbled toward her.

Gwen stood frozen, unable to move, watching as if from a great distance as the deer came up, nuzzling right into her belly like a suckling. Her thoughts kept de-rezzing into the slipstream, going *god this is crazy this can't be real it's like a flashback i can't let this happen i can't.* . . .

Gwen tried to move; her limbs were clublike, leaden. The yearling nuzzled deeper, its hide glistening with sweat. Gwen looked down in horror, realized that the flecks of white were not fur at all, but moving, mottled discoloration under the surface of its skin. The deer shuddered, frenetic whole-body tremors that wracked its flesh as it tried to *burrow* into her.

Gwen pushed her hands to the end of its snout, fighting to keep it off. She felt the wetness there, felt its tongue snake between her fingers, rough and smooth, licking her.

A dark patch stained her shirt, growing.

"NO!!" Gwen pushed away, feral and reeling. Her hands came up, trailing ropy stringers of saliva from its foaming mouth.

She fell back against the wall, the whine in her head a roar as she sagged to the ground, the contact broken, her legs splaying out like a puppet with its strings cut.

The deer buckled then, too, spindly stick-limbs giving way like a wobbly card table. It fell like a ruptured feed sack, squirting pale gelid goop thick as Campbell's soup from the hole in its side.

The wail cut off abruptly, leaving a curious black hole of sound in its wake.

The deer shuddered as its eyes rolled back, fixed and dilated.

And the wasps poured from its open wound.

*Dozens of them, flooding the air. Hundreds, swarming around and over the carcass. Thousands of them, madly buzzing: an entire colony at work. Breeding within the ravaged animal.*

*Then eating their way out.*

*Gwen screamed, full-throated and raw, as the insectoid cloud spewed forth from the hole: a black-and-yellow blossom, all noise and wings and stingers, their hard little bodies pinging off the wooden walls and coming back for more. Swirling around her, sealing her vision within a bright buzzing tunnel of shadow and stinging sound.*

*When Gwen screamed again, one flew into her mouth; and as she continued, they went for her eyes, her ears and hands as she screamed and swatted and screamed....*

Micki found her screaming and batting at the empty air, a look of dislocated terror plastered across her face. A dead deer lay beside her, its carcass shriveled and stiff. It had been dead for a week, maybe two, and had long since gone condo to the ants and insects.

"I'm here, honey. I'm here," Micki said, fighting down her own terror as she reached for Gwen. Gwen knocked her hands away, not seeing her at all, fighting off insects no one else could see.

Micki pushed through the hysteria, helping her up, holding on for dear life. "Shhhh, it's okay, baby, it's gonna be okay. . . ."

"No," Gwen rasped: hands clutching her belly protectively, head cocked as though listening for distant tremors in the earth. "No, something's w-wrong. . . ."

"Shhh," Micki said. "It's a dead animal, baby. Just a poor dead deer. . . ." She reached for Gwen, grasping her shoulders.

"Something's *wrong*!" Gwen cried, shaking loose of Micki, not even seeing her through the dread, terrible veil of certainty.

"What?" Micki shuddered in her grip. "I don't understand. . . ."

"It's *DEAD*!" Gwen wailed, suddenly snapping into focus. "CAN'T YOU SEE IT! IT'S *DEAD* . . . !!"

Then unconsciousness swept over her, and she dropped to the ground like a stone.

# Twenty

At twelve fifty-five, Reactor One began to sing.

Fred Jenkel blinked back sweat, unable to deny what was happening even as he refused to admit the evidence of his senses. He was not having a good time.

He had worked in nuclear power for going on ten years; he knew the heart of the plant from the ground up, every tick and hitch of its proper operation. The system worked, he believed that with all his heart. . . . no, more than that. He *knew* it worked, because he knew *how* it worked and *why* it worked. Jenkel's first article of faith stated that there were no miracles, only mechanisms; that all things physical ultimately functioned; and that functionality ultimately made sense.

So when noon had rolled around and the borated water had failed to halt the power surges or significantly reduce the ion population, Jenkel's next impulse had been as clear as it was logical. *Increase the boron content of the coolant*, he'd thought. *Max it out*.

Supervising Operator Roger Sykes had agreed. He was a congenial man in his fifties, lantern-jawed and brush-cut, with a military trimness only lately giving way to civilian middle age. Sykes had spent fifteen years on Navy subs before moving into commercial nuclear power, and he ran a tight ship. He was an engineering anomaly, a good manager who was *still* a good engineer, and he and Jenkel worshiped at the same altar.

"Increase the boron content," he'd said. "Max it out."

This they did. It worked, for a while.

Then, at twelve-sixteen, the neutron count inched up again.

"Hmmmm," Sykes murmured. "Hmmmm . . ." They were not the type who panicked easily. Besides, it was nothing fast enough to trigger an automatic reactor trip or anything. It wasn't unstable. Just drifting.

Slowly. Relentlessly upward.

At twelve-thirty, Sykes turned to the crew. "Okay," he said. "Do a turbine runback, shed the load." He checked the meters. "Let's slow this unit down."

Henkel and Jenkel obeyed, began stepping in the rods: the control rod clusters ratcheting down their exactly spaced chutes, each tucking in its portion of the fuel assembly for a nice little nap.

By twelve thirty-seven the reactor core had slowed, rolling off as the rods stepped into place. Everyone nodded and breathed a sigh of relief, chalking the aberration up to the fact that it was an older fuel assembly ready for shuffling, with a higher number of spent rods and an overabundance of available neutrons, and hence was livelier than usual.

At twelve forty-five, the power slid back up.

*It was surprising in its seeming willfulness; the meter arcing up as if some invisible arm wrestler had grabbed ahold of it. The reactor hit the one hundred and three percent power mark and tripped every alarm in sight.*

"Sonofabitch!" Jenkel gasped. He was reaching for the controls just as Sykes came hauling ass out of his office.

"What the heck is this?" Sykes blurted. He wanted explanations and logic. He got neither.

"Beats me," Jenkel said. "The power just surged again. It's getting pretty hot."

"Pull her back to thirty percent," Sykes said, eyeing the meters, less alarmed than irritated. Jenkel nodded and cut it back.

It stayed down for even less time. Then up up up again.

They continued this cat-and-mouse game for a while: borate and step down, borate and step down. The reactor didn't seem to care. It just kept climbing back into the maximum operating range. Denying logic. Defying them.

"Sonofabitch," Sykes muttered. "What is going on in there?" They'd been dicking with the reactor for almost two hours now, and his alarm/irritation ratio had long since flip-flopped.

Sykes rubbed his temples and stared at the meters. The hum of the reactor made his fillings ache, put a hot lump of slag in the pit of his stomach.

He looked over to the glass-walled cubicles lining the side of the control room. "Ros!" he called out. "Did you get through to the NRC yet?"

"No, sir." Rosalyn White's face popped out of the doorway. She was a slender, pretty woman, the day shift clerk, and at the moment she looked very nervous. "I can't get through," she said.

"What about PEMA?"

"No, sir," Ros said. "I can't get through to anyone. No one's in."

"Great," Sykes muttered. "Keep trying!" he snapped, and was instantly sorry. He softened his tone incrementally. "And patch me through to ChemTech."

Ros nodded, disappearing into her office; a moment later the console phone started blinking. Sykes punched a line and picked up. "Control. . . ." he said. "Sykes here."

"*Yeah, this is Bergens in ChemTech.*" The voice was female, with a slight Southern twang. "*I got coolant sample readings for ya.*"

"Yeah?" Sykes replied. "So tell me some good news."

The ChemTech labs were a long, brightly illuminated set of rooms off in the main complex. Like the control room, they were safety-sealed, redundantly filtered. Becky Bergens sat at her station and stared at the coolant sample. She was petite, pretty, with a thick mane of russet-colored hair and wide-spaced, almond-shaped eyes.

"Oh, it's borated, all right," Bergens said into the phone wedged in the crook of her neck. "You've got boric acid coming out the wazoo. That's not your problem." A furrow of worry lines etched into her brow.

"The problem is . . ." she continued, then stopped, puzzling. "To tell you the truth, I don't know *what* the problem is. I've never seen anything like this before."

"*What are you saying?*"

Bergens held the beaker aloft, squinting at the contents as if they might bite; the water inside swirled, transparently viscous, woven into liquid striations. "I'm saying," she reiterated, "that something's not right about this water."

"*What, is it contaminated?*"

Bergens shook her head. "If it's a contaminant, it's a damn sneaky one. It got past the carbon filters, the ion exchangers, and every other trap in this joint.

"No," she concluded, "this is something else. This is new." She held the vial up to the light, tilted it this way and that. The water swirled lazily in its beaker.

"*Great,*" Sykes moaned. "*So the water's not right. What's* wrong *with it?*"

"You tell me," she began. "It ain't too hot on absorbing neutrons, for one thing. I'm double-checking, but I'll tell you: the moderator characteristics are really screwy. And if the water doesn't slow this fission properly, there isn't enough of it in the world to keep your baby cool."

"*Yeah, well, thanks for the good news.*"

"That's what I'm here for," she replied. Becky date-labeled the beaker with the coolant sample and shelved it next to other dated containers. Then she went over to her computer terminal to double-check on moderator characteristics.

Slowly, the striations began to undulate, assuming a definitive pattern. The patterns became much clearer, as the oily striations began to swoop and dip and swirl.

Over and over, over and over, over and over.

*A figure-eight pattern.*

Twenty seconds later, the liquid in the other beakers did, too.

Back in the reactor control room, Roger Sykes was beyond pissed. He was getting nervous. "What do you think?" he asked Jenkel.

"Not sure," Fred said, looking a lot more worried than he sounded. "Dilution accident, maybe." He pondered the point. "If untreated water got into the feed supply . . ."

Sykes paled a little, completing the thought. *God, throwing untreated water on a hot core would be like dousing a fire with gasoline.*

Sykes hit a switch and activated the acoustical monitoring system, a series of strategically placed microphones that relayed the sound coming from the inside of the reactor vessel to the control room.

A deafening roar spilled out of the monitor speakers, the sound of coolant water pummeling the core into obedience. Henkel, Jenkel, and Sykes leaned forward, scrutinizing the rumbling wall of noise.

Jenkel was the first to notice. "There," he said. "Do you hear that?"

Henkel and Sykes cocked an ear toward the sound. It hit them within seconds of one another. "Jesus," Sykes whispered, as the fleshy part of his neck prickled with dread.

*It was an eerie barbed filigree of sound that rose and fell and twisted, not beneath the roar or behind it but somehow in it, a frequency-shifting inside the water-sound. As they listened one thing became clear. It was no accident. It was too complex and multi-timbral, too . . . intelligent.*

*The reactor was singing.*

*It was the scariest thing they'd ever heard.*

"No, no no." Henkel sat in his chair, mumbling a mantra of pure denial, as though it were up to a vote. "No, no, no, no. Not liking this. Not one bit."

The sound reminded him of something he'd read back in college, something about seductive creatures who lived in the water and sang to the sailors in passing ships. He reached into the recesses of memory for the name, felt it slap him in the face as it came back.

*Sirens.*

While over the speaker, under the water, an amorphous mesmerizing chorus shifted in and out of focus.

*Luring them onto the rocks. . . .*

"Shit, what do we do now?" Henkel said, looking like a man who wished he'd gone into another line of work.

Behind them, Sykes paced in tight little circles, the engineer in him butting heads with the manager until it produced a whanging headache. In the event of an emergency the utility's unwritten policy was to stay on-line until the shit hit the fan, and not to go public until things were either under control or uncontrollable. In the post–Three Mile Island industry, emergency procedures were clear as they were limiting: do not guess. Do not diagnose. Treat the symptoms only.

And hope that that's enough.

Sykes looked at the clock. Twelve fifty-eight. "The hell with this," he said. "Trip it."

He turned to Jenkel. "Shut down, run a systems check, and isolate the problem. I want this thing up and back on-line ASAP.

"Bob," he turned, singling out the younger man,

"get ready to open up the auxiliary feed lines and start pumping. Make sure we maintain the shutdown margin." He looked around. "I'm notifying Biles. The clock starts *now*."

He looked around. "Well, what are you waiting for?"

Henkel nodded, relieved. "Not a thing." He went over to the switch-bank. "Shutting her down," he said. "Now."

Henkel cut power, and inadvertently held his breath.

*. . . While deep in the reactor vessel, hundreds of yards away, the magnetic ratcheting mechanism de-energized. Over the monitor came a massive compressed roar as several tons of control rods slammed into the coolant pool, obliterating the song.*

At twelve fifty-nine precisely, they shut the reactor down.

At 1 P.M., it started back up.

All on its own.

# Twenty—One

Home, such as it was, was a low-slung postmodern split-level with a shared private drive, snug on the low rolling hills of the country club's sixteenth hole.

Inside, Blake retreated to his study. It was a quiet sanctuary with a southern exposure, recently redone in ebony inlay, burnished oak, and cloth-bound special editions. A small fire crackled in the zero-clearance fireplace, scenting the air with hickory and redwood; a pair of bronze dogs nestled before it on the sprawling hand-carved Aubusson rug, positioned so as to gaze with blind, doting eyes on the face of their master.

Blake settled in behind his expansive antique barrister's desk and brought thumb and forefinger up to pinch the bony ridge between his eyes. A tumbler of Chivas and a bottle of Tylenol sat before him, awaiting ingestion.

He had a slight tension headache. Nothing serious, but enough to put him out of sorts. Carol had toddled off to her tennis lessons after performing her perfunctory wifely duties; downstairs the stereo thudded with the ceaseless caterwauling their deadbeat son called music.

*Butthole something-or-anothers*, Blake winced in recognition; he was almost able to distinguish some of them from each other at this point, through sheer osmosis.

He sighed mightily; his family was his bane. In the euphemistic lexicon of talk-show shrinks, they were *dysfunctional*; in reality, they simply hated each other.

Not that their hate was simple. Indeed, it was a richly textured blend of disappointment, spoiled ideals, and abcessed emotion, a lifetime in the making. Werner's climb up Country Club Road had been at the expense of much toil, many long hours at the office and on the road. He broke his back to provide the best of everything for his loved ones, only to have it thrown back in his face.

Which left contempt as the linchpin of the Blake family dynamic. It was virtually the only thing they shared.

Fortunately, the house was large and sprawling; big enough to contain three lives that crossed only when forced; big enough to afford him space and the peace to contemplate the business at hand.

First and foremost, a follow-up call.

Blake punched the number into the speakerphone, downed two caplets, and waited patiently as it patched through.

"Hello?" A child answered; a young girl, from the sound of it. Very young. *Thea*, he recalled; Blake made a point of always remembering names.

"Hello, Thea," he said, modulating his tones. "Is your daddy in?"

"Nope."

"Can I speak to your mommy, please?"

"Hokay." A muffled *Mommmeee!*

Then: "Hello . . . ?"

"Marge, it's Werner. Is Harry there?"

"No," she replied. "He's at the office." From the false, deliberately cheerful tone of her voice, Blake instantly gleaned two things: she was worried about her husband, and she had no idea what was going on. "He said he left some papers there."

"Aha," Werner said, nodding to himself. Batting one for two, so far. "Did he say when he'd be back?"

"No, he didn't," she offered. "But he left right after we got back from church, so I'd imagine he's still there, if you want to try him."

Her voice trilled and cracked on the word *try*: desperate pleasantry in overdrive, frightening to behold. "I see," he replied, leaning back in his chair and drawing the last word out. "Hmmm . . ."

"Werner?"

"Yes?"

"I . . ." She paused, as he knew she would. This was taking a lot out of her, piping up like this. Meddling in her husband's affairs. He could picture her easily in his mind: standing in her kitchen with her centurion helmet of dense-sprayed hair, an insect-headed worker/wife straining against the rigid confines of her intelligence and experience.

All she knew was that her husband was hurting inside, which was most certainly true; and that she was afraid for him, which he had no doubt was true as well.

He counted the beats until she started again. He was correct within a fraction of a second.

"I'm worried about Harry," she said.

"Mm-hmm."

"He won't tell me what's the matter, of course—he's a very private person—but, well, you saw him today."

"Yes." Acutely sympathetic. "I did."

"He looks terrible." She paused for dramatic effect. He could picture every troubled shake of her head. "It scares me. You know how he is, with his heart condition and all."

In the invisible privacy of his home, he could smile without fear. "No," he said. "I didn't know about that."

"Oh, yes. He nearly had a stroke last March, and his doctor told him that . . ." she began. At that point, it was safe to let her voice phase out for the duration of the litany, throw in *mm-hmm*s at the appropriate junctures.

He needed time to think.

The thing could go a couple of ways, he knew: one bad, the other worse, but you played the hand life dealt you. It was just a matter of where the damage stopped: with Leonard, or all the way at the top. Either way, Leonard was screwed, so humanitarian concerns weren't even part of the discussion.

*But it was thoughtful of him to provide the heart condition*, Blake mused. *Either way, that could come in handy.*

The fascinating story of Dr. Deitrich's healthful hints was wrapping up. Time to tune back in.

"... never listens," she continued. "That's why, when he took you aside in church ..."

"I'm sorry," he interrupted. "But that's pretty much why I called."

"Oh?" It was her turn to listen, and God was she grateful. *Tell me something*, she silently pleaded. *Tell me what I want to hear.*

He hated to disappoint her. But not very much. "I don't know," he said. "He was obviously upset, and it seemed that he wanted to tell me something important. But then he just stopped; and, frankly, I haven't been able to stop thinking about it ever since."

"Oh, dear." Her tone epitomized distress. If it turned out that he never came home again, she would be able to tell her friends that she'd known it was happening. She'd just felt it. You know?

Another Mystery of the Unknown revealed. And thank you, Time-Life Books.

"Well, I'll just give a call down there," he said. "See if we can't straighten this out."

"Oh, thank you." She meant it with all her heart.

"And in the meantime," he suggested, "take care of yourself and the little ones, will you?"

Blake rang off a moment later, leaned back in his chair, and let his thoughts run free. The pop and fizzle of expensive hardwoods going up in smoke was meditative, much-needed tonic to his nerves.

*So much to do*, he thought. *So little time.*
*And miles to go before I sleep....*

\*    \*    \*

Meanwhile, on the other side of town, Harold Leonard was about to awaken.

He paced the length of his clogged offices: a Skinner-box rat, up to his neck in rifled files and rationalizations. He was weighing the terrors of turning state's evidence against the sheer fathomless depth of the shit he was in.

Outside lay the crumbling chemical domain that was Leonard's legacy. Shoehorned into a seven-acre facility on the outskirts of town, Paradise Waste Disposal was originally touted as a kind of franchise, one-stop shopping for the growing waste industry. Garbage had long since passed wheat or oil or steel as the nation's perennial bumper crop, and Paradise Waste was built to take big bites of the toxic pie. Solid into the ground, liquid into the river, medical into the incinerator and up into the sky. Even radioactive, once the permits went through.

Paradise Waste Disposal was nothing if not ambitious. Between Blake's EPA connections and his . . . *other* connections—shadowy suits with Jersey plates—Leonard's little plant had mushroomed into a modern success story, the proverbial right way that Blake and the industrial community had used to beat the NIMBY-ridden local troublemakers into complacency. *Not In My Back Yard* was old thinking, a luxury no longer affordable; Paradise Waste Disposal was the future.

It was a raging success.

Too successful, in fact. Paradise Waste had blossomed, then burgeoned, then bloated to bursting on its own success. It had become a hodgepodge of pits, ponds, landfills, and storage tanks, all filled to capacity and beyond. Forty thousand drums stood—stacked and staggered, palleted and piled—in rows as long as city blocks. A rainbow smorgasbord of pestilence intermingled on the site: dioxins, PCBs, amine leachates, heavy metals, mercury, and benzene. Just last week, Harold had gotten a shipment of a thousand drums of tetraethyl leads so unstable that they spontaneously combusted on contact with *air*.

Business was booming, all right. The incinerators burned night and day.

It still wasn't enough.

Harold opened his file of "special" invoices, hands trembling. There was no denying it. Conville Chain, Penn/Dover Laboratories, General Unidyne, MegaTech Industries, Paradise Caterpillar, Paradise Air Conditioners, on down to Paradise Paper Products. . . . He had accepted "overstock" from all of them, and on a frighteningly regular basis. Plus the midnight runs from Blake's business associates in Philly and Jersey.

Once delivered, they washed their hands of it.

After that, it was his problem.

By his own crude reckoning, almost six thousand drums had been farmed out to the Pussers over the current fiscal year. God only knew where the next disaster would spring up, grinning like a skull-faced warning label: in a borehole, under an elementary school; right in the goddamned reservoir. His entire operation thrived in a vacuum of neglect, courting scandal like a bent-over congressional page.

A scandal would lead to an investigation.

An investigation would lead to an indictment.

An indictment to a trial.

*And the trial-bone's connected to the . . . JAIL-bone . . .*

"Shut up!" Leonard pounded the singsong nattering in his skull, already feeling the rope tighten around his neck. When he closed his eyes, he saw himself: crying out to his accusers in the courtroom of his mind, waving handfuls of crumpled invoices at the featureless shadow-faces. Protesting the inevitability of his guilt.

To no avail.

"Oh, God," he croaked in desperate, spontaneous prayer. "Oh, God, please . . ." Everything he'd built was coming down around his ears, collapsing into rubble and ruin. Paradise Waste Disposal was a rock tied around his neck and hurled into the abyss, and Leonard was just standing on the edge, watching the line play out.

"Oh, God," he reiterated, dry-heaving tears, "please . . ."

And suddenly a fist closed around Harold's cholesterol-clotted heart, sending lightning stabs of pain slicing through his chest. He broke out in an instantaneous, copious sweat and dropped the sheaf of papers scattering to the floor.

"No," he whinnied, stripped of air and power. "Not like this. . . ."

Pain jetted through his left arm, exploding in fire buds that blossomed in his brain. Somehow he found a chair, stumbled into it, and held on tight: blood pressure thudding in his temples, roaring like a runaway fire hose through his skull. His heart body-slammed him again, rocking him back. His eyes rolled heavenward.

And his prayers were answered.

*Sudden sense of dislocation, cut loose from the fragile mooring of flesh. Sent rocketing up and out of body, through the ceiling, and soaring high above the glistening dump below, the pools like distant, tiny baubles.*

*Seeing, then, the culture to which he was slave: the greedy, insatiable eating machine. Shoveling resources in the one end, shitting poison out the other. A fat, blind, dying carcass, smothering all as it wallowed in its own excrement.*

*Seeing Exxon and Bechtel, McDonald's and Dow, General Motors and General Foods and a host of others, a parade of myopic corporate criminals that burrowed and bored through civilization like flies in offal. Raping their heritage. Devouring their young. Breeding swarms of dull-eyed mall-dwellers who were utterly convinced that happiness* was not possible *without one more disposable cigarette lighter, one more combustion engine, one more burger in a polystyrene box.*

*Seeing waves of humanity, lemming-racing face-first into the future, throwing their garbage over their shoul-*

*ders and never once pausing to wonder where it went, or what it did when it got there.*

*And, finally, seeing himself: part puppet, part pawn, part piggy on a conveyor belt, squealing as he rolled toward his date with the knife.*

He saw it all, in a single moment of absolute clarity.

Then the telephone rang.

"YAHHH!" he cried, nearly jumping out of his skin. The hallucination evaporated, leaving the reality right where he'd left it: heart in a vise grip, ass in a sling, evidence scattered all over the floor.

The phone rang again.

*It's Blake,* he knew. *Oh, Jesus.* His fear was a fact that surprised him; until this moment, he hadn't realized how frightened of Blake he actually was.

And that in itself was a revelation, clicking into place with the rest of the vision. He realized, as the phone rang again, that something fundamental felt changed inside him. Different. *Stronger*, perhaps.

He looked at the papers strewn about at his feet, saw all those names and numbers listed; and in that moment— in a second wave of illumination—understood precisely what the difference was.

He no longer felt alone.

"Hello," he said, picking up on the fourth ring.

"*Hi, Harry,*" Blake said. "*Just checking in.*"

"Good," Leonard said, feeling the strength of his convictions. " 'Cause there were a few things I wanted to ask you, too."

Beat. "*Shoot.*"

"Well, for example, I need to know what you plan to do about the kid who got hurt."

"*Actually, I was hoping you might have a suggestion.*"

"Me?" Leonard laughed. The pain was still bad—a fireball in his chest, radiating outward to his extremities— but at least it was stable. It was easy to believe, in that moment, that the worst was actually over. "I thought *you* were taking care of this."

Barely missing a beat. "*We're working on it.*"

"Well, good, because I talked to Pusser a while ago, and he was threatening to talk to the cops if something didn't happen fast."

"*Oh . . . ?*"

"'Oh' is right." He was on a roll now, and the taint of sarcasm in his voice exhilarated him. "And that could be a problem. Because if they go to prison, they'll take me with them."

"*Not necessarily—*"

"And if I go down," he cut in, "I'll have no choice but to drag everyone else down, too."

Long beat of silence.

"*Harry, don't you think you're overreacting?*"

"Am I?"

"*Yes, I think you are.*"

"Well, then, straighten me out, Werner. Calm me down."

"*What do you need to know?*"

"How you plan to keep me out of jail."

Not a dropped beat this time. Straight into the pitch. Leonard had to admire how quick Blake was, when the chips were down.

"*The first and most important job is containment. So far, we've been lucky. Nobody knows anything. . . .*"

"Ah." Using Blake's smug little throat noise against him. "But don't you think they should?"

"*What?*" Incredulous now. It made Leonard smile to get a rise out of him like that. Amazingly, the pain in his chest had dwindled to little more than an afterthought.

"Don't you think people deserve to know that there's poison in the Codorus? I mean, when you talk about containment, does that mean you intend to hush the *whole* thing up? Or just the part that might point back at you?"

"*Harry . . .*"

"When is someone gonna take some responsibility for this? I mean, Christ! It's not worth the money anymore, Werner! This whole thing is just out of control!

Doesn't it scare you to think of what might be out there? In your water? In your food? In your air?"

Nothing from Blake. Leonard continued, feeling his whole life solidify, come together beneath him in this moment of truth.

"Well, it scares me half to death, and I'll tell you what else. I feel guilty as hell, and I don't know what to do about it. I mean, in some ways, we probably *should* go to jail. . . ."

"*Harry*," Blake interrupted, and this time he would not be forestalled. "*I hear what you're saying, but I've got to ask: do you really think that, by going to jail, you'd be helping make the world a better place for anybody?*"

Leonard started to reply, but it was Blake's turn to override.

"*Seriously, just stop and think for a minute. I mean, I certainly understand how you feel. Sometimes I lay awake nights, thinking about all the terrible things we've done to this poor world of ours, and wondering if it isn't already too late.*"

Leonard's mouth opened, and nothing came out.

"*But then I think about our work—about all the jobs that we create, the meaningful and necessary employment we generate, the goods and services that we provide—and I think, the world* needs *guys like us, Harry!*"

Leonard felt his spirit deflate and his fight diminish, as Blake turned Harold's own rationalizations on him like a pack of hounds. For a moment there, everything had seemed so clear. . . .

"*You know what would happen if there were no Paradise Waste Disposal?*" Blake asked, and answered. "*Local industry would either be forced to spend more money shipping their waste out of town, which they* would not like *to do: or we'd go back to the bad old days, when waste treatment was unheard-of and it ALL went into the creek! Does that make any kind of sense to you?*"

"Well, no, but—"

*"But, nothing, Harry! You* know *I'm right on this one."*

"But I—"

*"Harry,"* Blake said, crushing the last of Leonard's fight like a spent cigarette butt. *"Don't go soft on me now, buddy. You're right: we've been playing this way too fast and loose, and it's high time we cleaned up our act."*

"That's what I—"

*"I'll tell you what,"* Blake continued, a velvet steamroller squashing all debate. *"We pull together on this one until we're out of the woods. And if you still want out, well, we'll buy you out. You walk away: free and clear, new lease on life."*

This time, the silence was entirely Leonard's call.

*"C'mon, Harry. Whaddaya say?"*

"What do you want me to do?" Leonard said at last.

On the other end, Blake sighed with enormous relief; and Leonard, perversely, echoed the sound, if not the sentiment.

*"You're a stand-up guy, Harry. I mean that,"* Blake said, and he sounded utterly genuine, like a real friend. It was the first time Werner had ever spoken that way to him. Like he was one of the gang.

*"Okay!"* Blake said. *"First off, I want you to relax, and* trust *me, for God's sake! I won't let you go down the tubes. The DER can find hazardous chemicals in the river without knowing where they came from, right? It's not like they have your fingerprints on 'em, right?"*

And Leonard was forced to agree.

*"As for the Pusser boy, I'll arrange for someone to take care of him."*

"What about the truck?" His voice, to his own ears, sounded panicky and stupid: the same old Harold Leonard.

*"Once again,"* Blake said, *"just trust* me, *alright?"*

And right then something went *ping* in Harold Leonard's head. Maybe it was the way Blake leaned on the T-word till it squealed. Maybe it was the whiff of reptile-smile on the other end of the line.

Either way, something clicked: and Harold Leonard realized that Blake was playing him like a fiddle, stroking his every insecurity even as he force-fed him his own rationalizations. And Harold knew then that he was not a part of Werner's gang, and never ever would be.

It was a fact that made him proud.

Harold sat up a little more erect, as if he'd just grown in stature. He reflected the smile back through the miles of fiber-optic cable, and was glad he did.

"Sure will, Werner," he promised.

"And thanks for setting me straight."


Blake took another three minutes, give or take a second, to stroke Leonard utterly into submission. Then the two men hung up, each certain in his own mind of what had to be done.

Blake leaned back in his chair, thought about the conversation past. How easy it was to bamboozle the little shit. And paradoxically, how close they had come to actual honest confrontation. How welcome, in so many respects, that confrontation would have actually been.

Of course, there was no place for straightforwardness in human politics. The bank shot was always best. As in the case of ol' Harry, his problems were best addressed by a separate phone call entirely. A very simple directive, to be executed right away.

*Ah, but Harry*, he sighed to himself. *How nice it would have been to, just once, show you how I really feel.*

Blake shrugged, dismissing the notion as shamelessly romantic. He sat back and sucked on his Chivas, staring into the fire.

The fire was beautiful.

It knew no compromise.

# Twenty—Two

*born of poison*
*raised in poison*
*claiming all form as its own*
*it rested*
*silent virulent hidden growing*
*surrounded by trees and crawling shadow*
*sharing itself with the mud*
*and rock beneath its wheels*
*the desolate road ahead*
*the dead-end culvert where it all began*
*in the days before the bridge*
*awakening its seed in everything it touched*
*reaching out in insatiable monstrous desire*
*for more of its own kind*

There were five dozen drums half-buried in the shit pit out back of Terry Honeger's land.

It was, in fact, Boonie and Drew's first dump site, way back at the dawn of their PWD affiliation. Boonie'd picked it for many of the same reasons he was to later select Black Bridge: privacy, proximity, ease of disposal.

At the time, it had seemed like genius. The Honegers,

after all, were the most worthless fuckers in all of Felton Township, with a hardcore defile-your-own-nest tradition that spanned back over generations. Of the three to four heavily wooded acres they owned or abutted, literally dozens of pockets had been cleared and devoted to rubble, kibble, and rot.

But the shit pit was their apex of achievement. It was an old sinkhole, some eighty feet long and thirty feet wide, and a good fifteen deep at the center. It had opened up one spring like an act of God, and far be it from the Honegers to quibble with Providence.

They had every kind of crap you could possibly dream of throwing away down there: washers, driers, box springs, packing crates, old tires and engine parts, cardboard, baseboard, drywall, brick, raggedy linen, regular garbage, on up to auto parts, including a rusted-out Gremlin that Terry's cousin Strong John had rolled straight over the steep embankment and left wheels-up like a capsized beetle.

The rains, when they came, filled the hole, making a rich garbage soup. In the warmer months it was stagnant, home to snakes and mosquitoes and all manner of crawling, grublike things. Come the cold it became even more treacherous, a forgotten and frigid wasteland.

They would never even know the difference, Boonie had said. And even if they did, fuck 'em. Nobody could prove nothin', and nothing could be traced. Even if the Department of Environmental Resources caught on, the Honegers would be the ones to eat it; but even that problem never arose.

The Drew-spawn shuddered as Overmind sifted through its ruined brain: pirating thoughts, cannibalizing memories.

Remembering. . . .

*The first trip had worked out well. They were able to drag some debris aside, roll down the first two dozen drums, and pretty well bury it over. But the fact was that they'd underestimated how much sheer space the drums took up.*

The second trip had consisted of one half barrels, the other half cover: an abandoned sofa, some rickety lawn furniture, one hell of a lot of cardboard. It had barely been enough.

By the third load, Boonie and Drew had learned two valuable lessons. First: how amazingly fast this shit piled up.

And second: what a great big wonderful world it was.

The following year was devoted to locating spots that could accommodate anywhere from a dozen to a hundred-odd barrels. They were few and far between, but they still managed to successfully unload in dozens of remote locations before stumbling on Black Bridge.

And destiny...

The Drew-spawn reclined in the driver's seat, stretching and shifting in ways not intended for mortal flesh.

Before it was done, it intended to revisit them all.

It caught its own gaze in the rearview mirror, paused to marvel at the renovations it saw.

The face: no longer Drew's, but a dissipated, scum-sheened caricature. Socket-skin receded, the ligature visible, like fleshy little points on a compass. One eye, loose and paddleball dangling at the end of its rubbery optic stalk.

The head: staved in from the left, as if a demented soda jerk had doled out two scoops' worth of brains from mid-forehead to ear. That ear, disengaged by the blow from its mooring, weighted at the lobe by a heavy cross earring and dangling by a thread.

The hair: a black tangle, clot-catcher to the squirt of pallid matter that had spritzed from his right earhole.

The skin: pocked and abscessed, the cartilage of his nose exposed, revealing the new forms and colors unfolding within....

A cloud of gnats hovered, drawn like moths to a

flame. The Drew-spawn batted absently at them, a reflex action.

Beneath the red bandanna, it chuckled. And why not? All around it was staggering, delirious change. Rippling through the ragged, self-mending upholstery. Rumbling through the chassis, though the engine was down. Awakening in rubber, petrochemical, and steel.

They had been there together, former man and machine, for over an hour. Recouping. Transforming. One tire had blown going through the downed tree, spent the next five miles spewing Möbius strips and shreds of itself down Route 11 while the rim ground out fireworks against the pavement.

It had taken this long for the tire to grow back.

The Drew-spawn got out of the truck, shambled over to the lip of the shit pit. Overmind paused, strategizing. It was a ways down, and far too steep for this awkward form to manage.

No matter.

"Nheh . . ." it gurgled, raggedy breath rasping through the punctured lungs. It held up its swollen left hand, the fingerless leather glove stretched tight as a sausage casing. With its right hand it grasped the portion of the left middle finger that jutted out. "Hnuh . . . uh!"

The finger stub came off with a wet pop.

The Drew-spawn regarded it for a moment, an inch-long cylinder of meat and moist bone. It turned the digit round and round as Overmind felt the essential oneness they shared.

*It existed in both, rooted in the cells of both stump and stub. It was aware of itself: as parasite and host, as seed and source. Somewhere in the Drew-spawn's mind was a fragmented memory of a picture in a book: a touch, bringing life.*

Drew-spawn and Overmind smiled, as best they could.

And tossed the piece into the pit.

Overmind didn't even stay to watch as the finger

stub tumbled end over end into the soup. It didn't need to.

It knew exactly where it was going.

The Drew-spawn clambered back into the truck and reached for the ignition, key now and forever at one with the hole. It felt the essential unity, as the engine sparked to new life. Felt itself part of the whole.

While down in the shit pit, sixty drums full of kindred spirits awakened to the touch. To likewise throw off their shackles.

And set themselves free.

# Twenty — Three

By quarter of one, Otis was fishing for the rudiments of consciousness in a vast Wild Turkey ocean of his own design. He had filled his head with liquid lead; it sagged on his shoulders, too heavy for thought.

That was the whole idea.

In the room at the back of the trailer, Boonie was making those noises again. Terrible noises. In his sleep. Evidently, no combination of shots and downs was enough to kill this pain; but at least it had him down and out, had kept him so for the last four hours.

Otis thanked God for Boonie's unconsciousness, and not purely out of love for the boy. Once an hour, or thereabouts, he went in to check on his son, and the fact was that Boonie wasn't simply dying.

Boonie was *changing*.

There was a bottle on the desk before him, along with a picture of his son the football star. The bottle was nearly empty, and the boy in the picture looked nothing like the swollen grotesque laid out in the dark behind the locked bedroom door.

Otis blubbered, piss-drunk and maudlin. He held in his hands a Colt forty-five that went all the way back to the last days of *douba-yew douba-yew two*. Them was the

177

good ol' days, he knew beyond the shadow of a doubt. Back when he and Mabel were young, and he could grab the world's short'n'curlies and just *yank* 'til the eagle screamed.

*And then Boonie came along, and he was their little boo-boo, all right. One little boo-boo after another. First the boo-boo of being born, being that they didn't expect him or nothing. Then a lifetime of smaller, diddly boo-boos, culminating with the boo-boo of having his knee blow out like a cheap retread and wash away any hope of a future.*

*Then last night's boo-boo. . . .*

*The biggest boo-boo of 'em all. . . .*

Otis sniffled, the gun big and square and clunky in his hand. These days, he mostly used it to jellify junkyard rats. But right at the moment he was drunkenly wondering how the barrel might feel if he stuffed it in his mouth.

Out front, a car pulled up, and the dogs began to howl.

"Huhwhafuck?" Otis blurted. It lit a fire under his ass, jerked him out of his stupor and onto his feet. All idle threats to Leonard aside, the mere thought of cops pumped his bladder full of lava and flooded his heart with dread.

"Oh, damnation," he droned, three hundred-plus pounds staggering toward the window.

There was a blue and white wagon with the ACTION-9 News logo, idling at the gate. The driver stood beside his open door, shooting home movies for the tri-city area. For a second, Otis thought about putting a .45 slug through the lens.

Then it focused on him.

Kirk stared through the viewfinder at the fat man engulfing the window. The shot was succinct and superb: blurry, at first, through the chain link fence, then the chain link gone muzzy as El Tubbo's eyewhites shone. The terror in that man's face was more than naked perfection.

It might just save Kirk Bogarde's ass.

Because he had taken a step from which there was no turning back. He was no longer a mild-mannered junior reporter, scarfing shit-duty assignments. He was now *Kirk Bogarde—Renegade Reporter!*

And the clock was definitely ticking on his destiny.

*Because if I pull this off, I'm a hero,* he realized. *I'm God fucking almighty. Hell, I may even make the cover of* People*!*

*And if not . . .*

*Not an option,* Kirk decided. *Kirk Bogarde—Unemployed!* just didn't have the same ring to it.

And so his fate was sealed.

*Kirk had stopped at a pay phone at a Turkey Hill minit market and called in a favor from Jerry, a hacker friend who worked at Motor Vehicles. The fact that Motor Vehicles wasn't open on Sunday left him undaunted.*

*Kirk had Jerry's home number. He called and got Melinda, Jerry's wife. Melinda said Jerry was in the garage, working on the Bonneville. Kirk said he needed a trace on the plates. Jerry said he'd get it for him first thing Monday. Kirk said he needed it now. Jerry said he couldn't. He told Jerry the story depended on it. Jerry told him to go fuck himself. Kirk said thanks anyway, he'd run another story in its place, like an expose on the disgraceful local street trade, with actual Spy-Cam footage of an actual citizen soliciting actual prostitutes from his actual Bonneville.*

*Kirk got a trace on the plates.*

*All in a day's work for Kirk Bogarde—Renegade Reporter!*

Now came the hard part: Kirk sat at the gate, inventing bullshit by the board foot. When Otis didn't move, Kirk leaned into the horn, still shooting.

*Come on,* he urged Otis silently. *Come tell me what I want to hear.*

A second later, the door opened wide.

"Our ACTION-9 News team traced the toxic truck and its lethal load back to Pusser's Scrap & Salvage, on the outskirts of Hellam,'' Kirk intoned. He was locked in his Geraldo mode now, riffing off the top of his head and liking what he heard. "With its overtones of *Texas Chainsaw Massacre*-style squalor, it seemed the perfect setting for this saga of murder, corruption, and greed . . .''

"Hey!'' yelled the fat guy, lumbering toward him. "*Hey!*''

Kirk went silent, kept him centered, in frame. As he got closer, Kirk managed to work the chained-up dogs into the background. Nice.

"We're looking for Otis J. Pusser, Jr.,'' Kirk said, keenly aware that there was no *we*. Somehow, that made it even better.

"Izzat *on*?'' the guy demanded, pointing at the camera. He was nearly to the gate, and Kirk could see now how utterly blasted he was, see the drunken defiance lock horns with the terrified hand-in-the-cookie-jar guilt in his eyes.

*Yes*, Kirk silently told him. *Your ass is mine*.

"That's right.'' Out loud. "It's practically airing live. Are you Otis Pusser?''

Silence. A wall-eyed, weaving stare.

Kirk smiled. "Do you know why we're here?'' Only half a beat of silence before kicking back in. "How do you respond to allegations that your truck—the truck that you this morning claimed was stolen—has already been tied to a hazardous spill off Black Bridge and at least one death?''

The Pusser man—and who else could it be?—flinched minutely as each point-by-point ticked off. Watching him, Kirk gauged the best way in and steamrollered through.

"You've been used,'' he continued, with utter sincerity, "as the low man on the totem pole of insatiable corporate greed. You've done their dirty work; and, as your reward, you're to be fed to the wolves.''

Pusser's eyes were watering.

The camera loved him.

"The police'll be here before you know it, you know.

If you've got a story to tell, now's the time to do it." Just a touch of insider's commiseration. "Before it's too late."

Otis, it seemed, understood his place on the revised food chain. His face, on the tape, was a revelation.

Twenty minutes later, Kirk left Otis, a string of empty promises ringing in his ears. Yes, Otis's side of the story would most definitely be heard.

So to speak.

Kirk motored up the Dark Hollow Road: solid gold in the camera, a smile on his face. His hunch had paid off. The pieces of the puzzle were falling into place.

It was the story of a lifetime.

# Twenty—Four

*The sky was alive with horrors.*

*The heavens unfurled before Gwen Taylor like churning smoke made flesh: a sickly rippling sea of graymeat phantoms that flowed, misshapen and howling, above her head. Snarling, embryonic things contorted, then tore apart and obscenely reformed: wriggling, writhing, perversely ecstatic. The forms they assumed were dredged up from no great black hole of repressed childhood nightmare.*

*Never in her life had she had such dreams.*

*And though she knew that it was madness—though the still-hinged portion of her mind screeched with vehement denial—there was nothing Gwen could do to wipe away the vision, no appeal to reason adequate to the task. Her mind was a muddled bog of delirium, but her eyesight could not have been more clear.*

*And as bad as the vision was, it paled by comparison to what she saw when she closed her eyes. The shapes were there, too, etched in the fine web of capillaries lacing the inside of her eyelids. Pulsing with her blood. Flush with the life that she gave them.*

*When she blinked, they came closer still.*

*Gwen slumped, eyes wide, semi-conscious, in the truck's passenger seat: head shaking* no no no no no,

182

*cheek mushroom-white and pressed flat against the window, a thin track of spittle tethering her face to the glass. A deep, thrumming buzz filled her ears. Her breath, when it came, was painful and shallow. Her flesh felt flushed, and chill. And her belly . . .*

*Her belly felt nothing at all.*

*Gwen groaned. She could hear Micki's voice dimly, a muted drone of reassurance,* going hang on baby we're almost there you're gonna be okay; *but the words seemed far less substantial than the shapes that undulated above and before her.*

*As the truck raced past the belching smokestacks of Campbell Chain, a great white plume of condensation snaked up like a skeletal hand and raked across the sky. Gwen stared, aghast, as the hand turned. Its fingers curling. Reaching for her.*

*When she closed her eyes, it was nearly close enough to touch.*

*She could no longer contain her screams.*

Melissa was on duty when they brought the Taylor woman in.

Emergency got her first, of course; but one look at her condition and they packed her off to Labor Hall just as fast as the wheelchair would carry her.

It was 1:04, Melissa noted in the log. Unfortunately, it was a pretty busy day; there were a half-dozen other names up on the board, all of them ready to pop. Only four RN's were on shift, and that left her to handle the two women coming in all on her lonesome.

They were alternately terrified and hysterical, but Melissa didn't faze easily. Not that she didn't care. At twenty-eight, Melissa Reinhard was a natural-born mother, passionately dedicated to the art and science of bringing life into the world. She'd spent three years on duty in Paradise County Hospital's maternity ward, above and beyond the two trips she'd made there herself.

Somewhere along the line there came a point where near-term histrionics were no longer a threat. And undue panic would only spook everyone.

So when Emergency called, Melissa got to work. First, she paged Gwen's physician and pulled her prenatal records, checking for aberrations. The records showed a relatively normal arc: a little high blood pressure, good weight gain. No major allergies. No previous incidents. Normal, normal, normal. Melissa scanned the three sheets, fixing them in her mind.

By the time they rolled in, she was ready.

*She looks more scared than hurt*, Melissa noted immediately. *That's good. Fear I can do something about.*

First things first.

Dizziness, numbness of the extremities, heart palpitations. They got her into the Monitoring Room with a minimum of questions and a maximum of efficiency.

It was a smallish space: two beds, a chair, and a bath. It was decorated with absurdly cheerful wallpaper, balloons and little flowers everywhere. By each bed was a table holding a CMS Fetal Monitor, a bulky gray box the size of a VCR. A pair of cables plugged into the front on the one side of the center keypad; a slot fed a continuous strip of paper out the other.

Micki disengaged from Gwen to allow Melissa to gown her, get her vital signs, and get her into the bed. Melissa looked at Micki. "Do you know what happened?"

"No." Micki took a deep breath, composed herself. "We were having a picnic, up at Sam Lewis Park . . . and then, when she went to the bathroom, I heard screaming, and I came up to find her, and she was . . ." Swallowing hard. ". . . she was *convulsing*, and . . ." She buckled, choking on the recitation.

"It's okay," Melissa said.

"So I surrounded her with light," Micki went on. "For protection. And then I drove her here."

Melissa paused for a second, did a quick reality check. *Surrounded her with light. Uh-huh.*

"Ummm . . . okay," she said at last, letting it go, turning back to Gwen. "Honey, can you breathe alright?"

Gwen thrashed, eyes swimming over the oxygen mask. It wasn't tanked, the better to let her recycle carbon dioxide into her system, calm her down a little.

"You've been hyperventilating. That explains the numbness and tingling."

Gwen shook her head, going *no no no*, her breath coming in great hitched gasps. She shuddered and pitched forward; Melissa and Micki reached for her at the same time, easing her back onto the bed.

"Whoa, easy!" Melissa said, "Look at me!" She grabbed Gwen's hands.

"LOOK AT ME!"

Her voice was forceful without anger, and it cleaved through Gwen's panic. She caught Gwen's gaze, forced her to hold it.

"You're safe now," Melissa said, instantly shifting gears, going soft without losing an ounce of focus. "Everything's going to be fine. Do you believe me?"

"I dun . . . I dun . . ." Gwen stammered. She shook her head desperately, a spastic gyration somewhere between *no* and *yes*.

"*DO* YOU?" Melissa said, her voice coming up a notch.

Gwen nodded, uncertain.

"Good," Melissa said, squeezing her hands for emphasis. "It's okay. I want you to take slow, even breaths. Can you do that for me?"

Gwen nodded again. Melissa checked her blood pressure: one thirty over eighty-four.

"We're going to get a reading on your baby," Melissa said, pulling the flowered flannel johnny up over the swell of Gwen's belly. "Are you in pain?" she added, feeling for the baby's position.

Gwen mewled: a dreadful, pathetic sound. Evidently, the answer was yes. It tripped the alarm lights in Micki's eyes. "*Can't you give her something?*" Micki demanded.

Melissa shook her head. "Anything we give her goes straight into the baby," she said.

"I'm scared." Gwen's voice was tiny, hoarse.

"Don't be. Just lay back. You're going to be fine."

Melissa probed the surface of Gwen's belly with her hands, feeling for something solid in the darkness. *God, she's big*, she noted. Her womb was a smooth hard ball of flesh, heavy with fluid. There was a lot of retention going on in there.

"Do you have a name picked out?" she asked, by way of distraction.

Gwen's eyes darted back and forth for a moment, searching through space. Then she seemed to lock on target, smiled a little herself.

"Spike," she said. "His name is Spike."

"Spike, huh?" Melissa arched her eyebrows in surprise. She found the curved prominence that marked the baby's spine, moved farther along until she could discern the soft tiny dome of skull. "Well, let's see how ol' Spike is doing in there."

She reached into the drawer beneath the box, producing a squeeze bottle and a cabled oblong wand attached to an elastic strap. "This is a *toco*," she said, holding up the disk. "It's short for *tocometer*, and it sits right over your fundus, here, at the top of your uterus. It'll measure contractions."

She slid the belt under Gwen's backside and positioned the toco a full hand's length above her belly button, snugging it down to the arcing rise of her womb.

"And *this*," she added, yanking another tangled cable free from the drawer and producing a disk the size of a stick-up air freshener. "This is the Ultrasound."

She squeezed a blue glob of conductive gel from the bottle and smeared it onto the disk. "No pictures, but it'll tell us if everything's alright."

She turned on the fetal monitor and the room was suddenly filled with a scratchy, thudding sound. A stub of graph paper fed up and out of the slot like a little tongue.

"This gives us our readout," she said, pointing to the paper strip. "And see that little heart, there?" Indicating a little glowing logo on the LED panel. "That comes on when we get Spike's heartbeat.

"Here, watch," she said, feeling for the best spot and placing the disk against Gwen's skin.

The room suddenly filled with a flat, rhythmic thud. On the paper strip, a little mountain range appeared. The topography of life.

"See?" Melissa said, smoothing Gwen's hair back. "I told you."

Gwen saw the little light glowing in sync with the percussive thud of the sonogram. She stared at it for a good long time before her fist unclenched.

Melissa smiled. "Okay, I want you to rest here quietly for a few minutes, just so we can make sure you're stable. Can you do that?"

Gwen nodded uncertainly. Melissa smiled reassuringly, then turned to Micki. "Why don't we let her get some rest?" It was not a suggestion.

"Wait," Micki said, holding one hand up. Her eyes rolled behind the lids for a second; and she *tensed*, like a cat responding to some invisible stimulus in the room.

"Excuse me . . ."

"It's okay," Micki assured her, and the queer look disappeared. "I just had to check."

"For . . . ?" Not sure, herself, that she really wanted to know.

Micki started to say something, stopped herself. "Nothing," she said at last. "Just thinking out loud."

"Uh-huh," Melissa empathized. "I know what you mean." Then she hustled Micki out of the room and turned down the lights, before they wound up checking under the bed for gremlins. To Gwen, she added, "We'll be right out here, if you need anything."

Gwen nodded, leaning back in exhaustion. "Micki . . ." she added.

Micki turned. "Yeah, babe . . . ?"

"Call Gary?"

"Sure thing." Micki nodded as well, smiling.

And the door hissed shut between them.

Melissa showed Micki to a little waiting area full of stale magazines. En route, she filled in a lot of blanks.

"You said you were having a picnic," she said. "Did Gwen eat before the seizure?"

"No, she didn't," Micki replied. "She was on the phone for a while, trying to reach her husband, and then she had to use the can. We were both pretty starved . . . ."

"Uh-huh," Melissa said, nodding to herself. "Her blood sugar's way down."

Micki looked at her worriedly. "Is she going to be okay?"

Melissa smiled. "Yeah, she'll be fine. This kind of thing happens a lot. I have to check with her physician, but offhand I'd say we give her some ginger ale to get her blood sugar back up, let her rest, get an hour of good readout, and we can send her home. He might want to have her in tomorrow, though. Do a full sonogram, just to be safe."

"You mean her doctor won't come in today?" Micki asked, a little shocked.

"Are you kidding?" Smiling. "This is NFL playoff day, Eagles against the Giants. Like I care, right?" Rolling her eyes. "Half the doctors on this staff are at home with their pagers turned off. You could cure cancer and they wouldn't want to know about it until after six."

Micki smiled.

"Oh, well," Melissa said, politely excusing herself. "Make yourself comfortable. I have a call to make."

Micki nodded, and thanked her. She set off down the hall, heading for a phone. She had a couple of calls to make herself.

A local one to Gary.

And the other, a very long-distance one indeed.

* * *

Gwen laid back and listened to the syncopated white noise that marked the life of her child. The paper tongue grew longer by the minute. The little LED heart flashed reassuringly with every beat: hypnotic, lulling.

She stared at it for a long time, afraid to take her eyes away, as if the eternal vigilance were any defense at all. The room was warm and dark, womblike in effect. The leaky sink in the bathroom kept up a steady *drip . . . drip . . . drip*.

Gwen lay there, unable to sleep, unable to stay awake.

Until eventually simple exhaustion carried her to a state somewhere in between. . . .

*A solitary droplet of water, sailing down: a shining, innocent orb. Atoms held together by ironclad molecular bonds, spinning through space like a jewel, a perfect crystal ball.*

*The drop fell through a hollowed cathedral of flesh, passed ribs rising up like buttresses, falling toward a still black pool below.*

*It struck the surface, sending up a spray like a tiny crown; a spray that stayed up, became something not solid and not liquid but* other, *like a puncture on the surface on the pool.*

*And from within: the beating of wings.*

*The hand came next: baby fingers, curled into a fist. It rose from the wound in the water as if holding a prize.*

*Slowly the fingers uncurled, revealing a wasp.*

*It unfurled its wings and took off, flying up into shadows.*

*Then came a torrent of tiny buzzing bodies. Spilling through the hole, swarming around the arm. Filling the empty spaces with an angry insect chorus, rising like stinging angels into the vaulted darkness above . . .*

*Heading for the beating heart. . . .*

* * *

"Oh God!!" Gwen cried, lurching awake. "No!"

She sat up with a start. Beside her, the fetal monitor was thudding arrhythmically, its numerical LED display jumping and falling, the little heart flashing on and off. On and off.

*On . . .*

*. . . and off.*

Melissa had just gotten off the phone with Gwen's doctor. He agreed with her prognosis entirely, enough so that he felt no major need to see her before Monday. It was a consideration that clearly owed more to gameside than bedside manner.

She was just coming back with the ginger ale when she heard the first scream.

Melissa burst through the door and beelined straight for Gwen, who lay fetally clutching herself like a woman hugging a medicine ball. The monitor's warning light fired up, flashing *BASELINE PRESSURE OFF SCALE*. The alarm was going off, a nerve-wrenching metallic buzz as the digital readout flashed 158 . . . 140 . . .

Then nothing.

"Shit," Melissa muttered. She grabbed the tongue of paper, traced the point where the peaks dropped off.

"*Where's Spike?*" Gwen cried.

"Don't worry," Melissa said. "It just slipped." She moved the disk, diligently searching. The sensor plate on the sonogram scraped across the surface of her skin, filling the air with a rumbling white noise, finding nothing.

"*Where IS he?*" Gwen wrenched, and the disk popped off completely.

The graph flat-lined.

And the two women began a war of wills.

For Gwen, it was the breaking straw. A distant,

reasonable part of her brain insisted that the nurse was right, there was a perfectly good explanation for all of it. It was steamrollered into oblivion by the howling inchoate part that *knew* beyond all shadow of doubt that something was wrong, her baby was dead and her dreams had died with it, a little sleeping corpse floating inside her, sleeping forever . . .

"Hold *still*, dammit!" Melissa said sharply.

"He's dead!" Gwen's hysteria came rolling back. "Oh god, he's dead!"

"No, he isn't!"

Melissa's mind was much simpler on the matter. She completely refused to accept it. Babies didn't slip away like that, just drop off the meter like an unchained anchor. There was almost always a downward slide, and the lack of it on the graph told her it had simply moved, that there was still life in there somewhere.

She just couldn't find it, somehow.

The Taylor woman was losing it fast. They'd *have* to sedate her if she didn't level out. "Please, you've got to be still!" Melissa said, searching with a methodical desperation.

She glanced at her watch. One minute and counting. One more and she'd worry, but not *until* then. She knew what kind of prenatal gymnastics a fetus could perform; flipping head over heels, changing sides completely in an eyeblink, damn near anything.

The sensor scratched. She pressed down hard.

And something pressed back.

*Harder.*

"Whoa," Melissa said, watching the surface of Gwen Taylor's ballooning belly distend. For an instant she could practically *see* the outline of the child pushing outward in stark, fleshy relief.

Then it receded, and Melissa found her mark.

"*Gotcha!*" she said, pressing the disk down.

The alarm at last shut off, a loud, steady thudding

taking its place. On the display, the little heart lit up like a prize.

"You see? I told you!" She steadied Gwen with her one hand and pressed the disk down with her other, making sure that the message got through. "Look! Look!"

Gwen stopped bawling and looked: sure enough, the heartbeat was there. She held her breath and listened as the rhythm stayed, rock-steady.

"He's there," Gwen whispered, the storm clouds abating inside her. "He's really there." She smiled a little, laughing through the tears.

While Melissa, relieved, wiped a tear from her smiling eyes.

"I told you," she said.

# Twenty—Five

Gary and Laura sat before the monitor, two different sides of the very same coin.

Gary was in his chair at the console, keeping calm by keeping his attention focused on the technical aspects of the matter at hand. Laura chain-smoked beside him, a dreadful exhilaration making her features flush and her body tight as an overwound spring.

*Fuck the smoke*, Gary thought, watching the ashtray fill before him.

They were busy watching reality unravel before their eyes.

"What the hell *is* that?" Laura asked, starkly disbelieving.

"*That*," Gary whispered, "is all fucked up."

On the screen, Drew's face was blown up and frozen in all its gruesome distinction. He was leering over the steering wheel and laughing, head bobbing like a demented dashboard ornament.

"He's wearing a mask...." Laura reasoned.

"That can't be right," Gary muttered, shaking his head. He advanced the tape and Drew's head bobbed into three-quarter profile. "I mean, look at that." He pointed to the screen. "That guy's missing *chunks*."

"So what are you saying?" Laura stood up, started pacing in tight little circles, thinking on her feet. "I mean, one way we've got nuts in monster masks dumping hazardous waste in a hijacked truck. The other way we've got toxic mutant ninja rednecks. . . ."

She paused, realizing that even *that* didn't fall off the edge of her weirdness map. "God, I've been in this business too long." She turned to Gary. "So what do you think?"

But Gary wasn't listening anymore.

His attention was focused instead on the screen. They had passed the end of Mike's camera work, the static blip at which Kirk had stopped the tape before. On the far side of the wash of snow lay some more footage.

Some very special footage. . . .

The image came back as a reverse POV, mounted on a tripod. It joggled for a moment, was still . . .

*. . . and then Kirk came running back into frame, stumbling through the mud and gravel as if the devil was on his ass with a blowtorch. He whirled, off-center, filled with panic and terror.*

*"STOP!" he screamed, and tumbled out of frame.*

The image blipped, went to snow.

It blipped back . . .

*. . . and Kirk was there, actually* leaping *toward the hood of the car, as if escaping the onslaught of a truck long since gone.*

"Wait," Laura whispered. "Who's shooting this?"

*Kirk rolled off the hood, walked toward the camera.*

"That little fuck . . ." Gary hissed, as Kirk's body leaned across the frame, obscuring the lens as he fiddled with the controls.

The camera blipped out again.

"That prick," Gary said, through gritted teeth. "That little mercenary *bastard*." He felt the hatred percolate up inside, his fists clenching and unclenching arrhythmically. The image blipped out again.

"I don't believe this," Laura said, her voice a barely audible croak.

"I do," Gary countered bitterly.

Laura was about to speak when the screen blipped again.

And they both fell silent.

*It was a tight close-up on a hand. The camera pulled back to reveal it sticking up forlornly out of a muddy track, fingers splayed back and broken like kindling, pointing awkwardly.*

*The next pickup was a full three-sixty: excruciatingly slow, voyeuristic in its attention to detail. Gary knew the county medical examiner, and had seen his share of "home movies"—coroner-with-a-camcorder-style reference tapes of autopsies and murders and the occasional bizarro demise.*

*They all paled as the camera completed its trip around the world.*

*It spiraled in on a very dead Mike, held on his crushed and flattened countenance. His glasses were smashed into sharp little pizza-pie slices that dug into the soft cheek skin. His upper lip was split clear to his nostril, revealing shattered fulcrum over bloody, prominent teeth. There was a grin of sorts on his face, the sick little rictus of a member of the studio audience suddenly hauled up and quizzed by the host.*

*Hi mom.*

More shots of Dead Mike came up, all broadcast-quality: Dead Mike obscured by weeds; Dead Mike from a tastefully airable angle; Dead Mike's hand, sticking up like a sad little tree. Gary turned up the fader on the audio track.

No tears. No sobs. No heartfelt outpourings of panic. Just the ghoulishly methodical attention to detail.

The screen blipped, and the Dead Mike shots mercifully abated.

"Oh my God," Laura repeated. She felt suddenly very ill. This was a man she'd allowed inside her, and the fact of it left her feeling horribly unclean, like there weren't enough baths in the *world* to scrub the Kirk-scum off her skin.

Gary's reaction was far more basic.

"I'll kill him," he muttered, punching the controls, rewinding the tape. "I'll break that little weasel-assed bastard in half."

"Let's just hold on a second," Laura said. She was fighting to remain levelheaded here, amidst a Gordian tangle of conflicting emotion. "We don't have all the facts in. . . ."

"Yeah, right," Gary cut in, cleaving right through it. He hit the "play" button, and Dead Mike came back up on the screen, the slow vulture loop closing in.

"I think we've got all the facts we need."

"No," Laura said. "We don't." Gary glared at her; Laura stood her ground. She took a deep, quavering breath. *I will not throw up*, she thought desperately. *I will not throw up.* "Look," she insisted, "this is getting to me, too, okay? But there's a larger issue here."

"Name *one*," Gary snorted and stared.

Laura grabbed the ledge of the console, fighting for internal control. "Someone or something is out there." *No.* Lines of thought, racing toward each other like colliding freight trains in her skull. "It's already killed one man . . ." *I will not.* ". . . and God only knows what's on the back of that truck." *I will not . . .* "We could have a serious hazard to the community here."

"Not to mention a hell of a great exclusive story," Gary added bitterly. He hit the "pause" button for emphasis; Dead Mike's hand halted in mid-wave.

"Not to mention," Laura said, her eyes flaring.

*. . . I WILL NOT THROW UP. . .*

Downstairs, the scanner was humming, and the radio beckoned. Kirk was out there somewhere. It frightened her to admit it, but if anyone stood to know what was happening, it was him.

"I'm going to find out what the hell's going on

here," she said, abruptly getting to her feet. "You do what you have to do."

Laura turned and left the studio, heading back to the newsroom, counting the steps. She rounded the corner without looking back, ducked quietly into the ladies' room. Then she turned on all the faucets, filled the room with roaring sound.

And heaved till she thought she'd die.

Back in Studio B, Gary ran the tape back, forcing himself to watch. He hit the "pause" button; Mike's dead, mangled hand loomed on the monitors.

"*You jerk . . .*" Gary whispered, tears welling up in his eyes.

Mike's frozen image beckoned. *They went thataway.* Gary groaned.

And against his better judgment, he followed.

# Twenty—Six

Following Harold's epiphany, atonement seemed only natural.

By two o'clock, he had assembled the necessary documentation. *Correction: evidence*, he amended mentally. The little TV on the top of the file cabinet was turned on, to distract his stray anxieties and keep him company. The Eagles had just scored against the Giants in Philly; there were a couple of minutes left in the first quarter of their big interconference rivalry. And they were tied, for first place.

Two cardboard file boxes stuffed to capacity with invoices and ledgers sat on the desk before him. Sleeves rolled up to his elbows, Harold sifted and packed; names, dates, dispensation, payments, and even a special log on kickbacks. *Werner's right,* he thought, *we've been playing way too fast and loose. It's high time we cleaned up our act. . . .*

*Starting right here.*

Harry whistled as he worked; for the first time in ages, he knew he was doing the right thing. He was still nervous, still sweating, but now it was the clean sweat of penance, cool on his skin. He was scared, true, almost giddy with the exhilaration of his newfound sense of being part of a greater Whole. He could really *feel* the Spirit moving through him. He was certain there was a special place for him in God's great design. A gaping hole had opened like a sore on the hide of business-as-usual in Paradise and the nation, a virulent ethical infection, and Harold Leonard was by God going to heal it.

The first step was to clean the wound.

Harry smiled; his was truly the Lord's work. If he closed his eyes, he could practically picture it: the fissures cracking in a hundred hypocritical veneers, the poison of lies and deceit leaking from them like a hundred lanced boils. Messy at first, certainly, but essentially . . .

"S'cuse me," a voice said from across the room.

"YAH!" Harry screeched.

He snapped out of his vision and whirled in an ungainly pirouette to face the man standing in the doorway. He was late thirties/early forties, with a peppered black mustache and tan, pocked skin. Dressed in jeans and flannel, muddy work boots, and a dusty plaid hunting jacket, he clutched a sweat-stained, web-backed CAT cap in his hands and stood with the antsy shuffle of a working stiff uncomfortable in offices.

"R'you Leonard?" he said, thumbing at the sign on the door and smiling uncomfortably.

"No, I, uh . . ." Harold stammered, flustered. "I mean, *yes*, I am."

"Name's Bill Teague," the man said. "An' I was hopin' you could help me out some."

Harry composed himself, became Harold, officious and innately suspicious. "I'm sorry, but we're closed today," he said.

"Please, mister. . . ." Bill blurted with the nervous clench of a man in a bind. "I got a problem. I, uh . . ." He paused then, swallowing as if forcing down a lump of undigested food. "See, I got a little 'lectroplate shop, down Hellam way. I do okay, you know, I mean, business has been pretty good and all lately." He shrugged. "Just got me a contract to do some circuit boards for ICC and a couple other things.''

"That's good," Harold said, nodding uneasily.

"Yeah, well, that's the good news," Bill Teague sighed. "The bad news is that I'm a little *too* busy."

Harold nodded.

"I mean, who has the damn space for all that *seg-ree-gation* and shit that the gov'ment wants." Teague shuffled antsily. "It's a crock, you ask me.

"Anyway." He halted, resumed. "I, uh... I been storing my runoff in common drums. Used to take it down to the landfill near Felton, but they won't take any more of my loads. Say it's too *dangerous*." He spat the last word contemptuously.

"Gee, I'm sorry to hear that," Harold said. "Life's a bitch."

"You got that right." Bill Teague sighed exasperatedly and moseyed past Harold and his desk, toward the window. Harold turned, tracking with him. Harold's new-found ethics were delicate things, not up to the pounding. He wanted very badly for the man to go.

Bill Teague looked out the window. Harold looked at Bill Teague. "Listen, I..." Harold began.

"Goddam DeeEeeArr," Bill Teague interrupted. He turned, regarded Harold with a kind of wounded pride. "What the hell am I suppose to do? Hell, I *know* it's dangerous. But I got *babies* to feed."

Harold sympathized. Bill Teague looked at him, then away again. Uncomfortable. The Eagles-Giants game gave way to commercials and a test by the Emergency Broadcast System.

"Anyway," he said, "I hear you can take a load off people's hands. I'm desperate to get rid of it."

There was an urgency in the man's tone that got under Harold's skin. A truncated version of a deep baritone boomed from the television's tinny speaker. *This is a test....* it said.

"I'm sorry," Harold said, shaking his head.

"I'll pay," Bill Teague offered, still staring out the window. "Top dollar."

*For the next sixty seconds this station will be conducting a test....*

"I don't think I can help you," Harold reiterated, stepping forward, feigning calm as his heart pummeled his ribcage like a prizefighter.

"Please, mister," Bill Teague pleaded. "I got nowhere else to go."

*This is only a test....*

"I really can't help you right now," Harold said, punctuating it with a deep breath of finality. "I'm very sorry."

Bill Teague sighed and turned around to face Harold. "I understand, and I respect that," he said. He smiled resignedly and held out his left hand. "Thanks for your time."

Harold extended his left hand in return. They clasped firmly if awkwardly and shook, *mano a mano*.

On the television, bars and tone, going *boooooooo-oooooooooo* ...

"By the way," Harold asked, "just out of curiosity, who was it that told you I would 'take a load' off your hands?"

*boooooooooooooooooooooo* ...

Bill Teague looked around the office, then back to Harold. "Oh, a friend of yours," he said.

"Name of Blake."

Harold felt his scrotum shrivel as if dipped in liquid oxygen. The good ol' boy veneer dropped away like dross. And two things became instantly clear.

Bill Teague's hand was smooth, uncalloused, thoroughly professional.

And Bill Teague's hand would not let go.

Harold's back was to the door; he caught a shadow of movement out of the corner of his eye. He tried to turn. Bill Teague would not let go. Harold screeched like a weasel as a much larger hand came down behind him, thick fingers clamping around his neck as if to pinch his head off.

The fingers found the pressure points in the clefts of Harold's collarbone as if they'd lived there all their lives. They made themselves at home.

And squeezed.

Pain exploded in his head, his spine, his entire central nervous system. Harold's threshold was low to begin with, and this was expert pain, as debilitating as it was economical. It washed over his defenses like a *tsunami* over a sand castle. Harold screeched and sank to his knees, assuming a position of purely functional prayer.

"AHHHHH! P-please . . . !" he whimpered, wholly involuntary. His head tried to sink into his shoulders like a turtle's, was held in place by the big cruel hand. He could not turn, could not move, could breathe only with great effort. He struggled like a two-hundred-forty-pound Roger Rabbit in a leg-iron trap.

"Pul-l-leeeeease!"

The pressure eased off, ever so slightly. The contact remained, hovering on the brink of agony. Harold blinked, tears brilliant in his eyes, and sucked air as if it were on sale. He looked down, could barely make out the tips of shoes behind him. Loafers. With tassels.

Bill Teague was still holding his left hand, attached now to his fully outstretched arm. Harold looked up, terrified.

"W-whatdoyouwantwhyareyouhere?" he gasped, an inchoate verbal spew. The pain returned, saying *shut up*. Harold squeaked and obeyed.

"Mr. Blake asked us to come see how you're doing," Bill said pleasantly. "And *what* you're doing."

He perused the opened file cabinets, the boxes on Harold's desk. Harold followed his gaze as best he could, mewling all the while. "I was consolidating *documents*. . . ." he blurted.

The big hand squeezed and Harold went *oof*. His

sphincter pooted a waft of purest *eau de fear.* Bill Teague shook his head.

"Tsk tsk tsk tsk."

He reached his right hand into the inside pocket of his hunting vest and withdrew a glassine packet. He held the packet to his lips, delicately tearing the edge with his teeth.

"What's that?" Harold creeched, terrified. Bill Teague smiled and shook out the contents one-handed. The glassine packet fluttered to the floor.

Harold glimpsed the contents.

"NO!" he shouted, a statement of pure emphatic will-to-live. He pushed upward with every ounce of strength he had and several that he didn't.

The spirit was willing.

But the flesh . . .

It was ridiculous. Harold Leonard was an overweight, aging amateur against professionals, and he was utterly at their mercy. The sum total of his life-energy bought him a half an inch of freedom and another blindingly brutal clampdown.

For his part, Bill Teague just smiled a little harder and flipped off the safety cap. He held the syringe up to the light. The needle gleamed, short and sharp and business-like. Gracefully he pulled the plunger back, then twisted Harold's arm outward, pitting radius against ulna until the soft pocket in his elbow coughed up a faint bulge of vein.

Harold yowled like a cat trapped in a moving car. Bill Teague twisted harder. "Shhh, shhhhh," he said. "Hold still." He placed hard needle against tender skin, resting it on the soft antecubital hump.

Harold blubbered, his breathing quickly giving way to sobs. "Wha-what are you putting in me?"

Bill looked at him, as if genuinely surprised. "Why, nothing," he said. "Nothing at all."

He smiled.

And plunged the needle in.

Harold went rigid as ten cee-cees of nothing at all was

injected and went hurtling through his circulatory system, a runaway boxcar of oxygen on a collision course with his heart. His assassins let go, no longer concerned. He thrashed his way straight to the floor.

And there was maybe a second of useless, unbankable time left in Harold's cosmology. Just long enough for panic to collide with regret. Actualize futility. Vaporize God's grand design.

Then the embolism hammered his heart, squashing it like an overripe tomato inside his chest. His final moments harbored no thought at all. Just meaningless pictures and pain.

And then, like yesterday's garbage, Harold Leonard went away.

They lingered a bit, till the twitching subsided. They could afford to. All on his own, Harold had done a good deal of their work for them.

*By God*, Bill thought, *he even boxed it for us*.

On the floor, Harold was turning just right. Cool and livid.

Just right.

Bill Teague was pleased. Normally, they didn't work Sundays, but what the hell. They'd been hipped to the weakness, and offered a bonus if they made it seem natural.

Piece o' cake.

Careful not to leave any prints, he picked up the phone, punching in the number with the hypo's plunger. The party picked up on the first ring.

"*Yes?*"

"Uh, hi, just wanted to let you know that everything is fine."

"*Everything?*"

Bill checked Harold's postmortem progress. Natural causes all the way. Old ticker just gave out. From the stress.

"Couldn't be better," he said.

There was a pause of audible relief on the other end of the line.

*"That's nice."*

They hung up without saying good-bye. The delivery was complete. Now the pickup.

And then...

On the tube, the Giants and the Eagles were back for action. Bill Teague looked at his watch. One-thirty. He smiled and grabbed a box off the desk, motioned his partner to do the same.

"C'mon," he said. "It's Miller time."

# Twenty—Seven

Boonie awoke to the sound of the front gate's annihilation.

Out of blackness, he rose: a blackness so deep and thorough that it rose up with him, refusing to succumb to the light. He felt it in the heaviness of his flesh, the whispering hollowness of his bones. He felt it buzzing inside his head, a million hornets in angry flight.

Or maybe it was the roar of the truck, echoing inside his head as it blew apart the gate, drew closer. Echoing louder closer *there*, directly outside the shuttered window. He struggled to pull himself upright, vision straining through the hair-thin venetian slats of light. But the muted sun needled in through his one good mucus-tacked eye. It flooded his head, sagged him back to the sheets.

It was dim in the room, and the air was rich with sickly ammoniacal stench. It cloyed in the tubes between nostril and bowel, esophagus and ischio-rectal ravine. Woozy and weak to the brink of paralysis, he helplessly laid there and listened.

His face, against the pillow, felt all wrong.

Outside, the door of the truck flew open. The door at the front of the trailer slammed shut. Boonie could hear the whickering of the chains as Coonie and DamDog yowled and snapped; could hear his father's voice, bellowing anger as it poured down the steps.

Could hear the rage wilt and blacken to terror.

Could hear the terrible laughter begin.

"*Urn*," his own voice croaked. "*Ah-harn*." His face, like the rest of him, refused to cooperate. Like there was an inch of foam rubber and zero sensation between his cheek and the pillowcase, his body and the world. It put even his panic at a distance as he squirmed against the surface of the sheets.

He heard the familiar crack of his old man's .45. It did not stop the laughter. Over the howling-dog hysteria, something went *snap*.

And Otis's horror ballooned into scream.

Boonie began to move then, something sparking to life in his nervous system as he listened to his daddy die. There was no second shot, but the screaming went on and on, ratcheting upward as thick bone snapped and wetly folded, doubled and snapped again . . .

. . . and Boonie rolled off the bed, plummeting to the floor as chewing sounds met screaming sounds and cranked them to a new plateau, high-pitched titter rising up to punctuate the mayhem . . .

. . . as a three-hundred-plus-pound Otis-shaped wishbone ruptured, fractured, tore apart while Boonie, inside, crawled across the floor, trying to escape the sounds it made . . .

. . . and then the scream died, swallowed and chewed and disappeared forever.

For a long crazy moment, there were only the dogs, tearing into each other, rabid with fear.

The moment stretched. . . .

Then he heard the footsteps coming, into the trailer and right down the hall. He understood who the laughter was aimed at. Understood that there was no hope. The certain knowledge froze him in the middle of the floor, staring up at the flimsy door. The only way out. Or in. . . .

Then the door blew open like balsa wood and Boonie's universe pivoted on its swollen axis. He fell back, creeching, as light flooded the room. Peeling back the balming darkness.

Forcing him to see.

*It was little Drew: back from the dead, and oh my how he'd grown. A little bit taller. An awful lot greener. And more than twice as big around. When he waddled in—scrawny legs straining against the tonnage—it was Drew's slick red gargantuan belly that attracted and held Boonie's gaze.*

*It had a vertical full-length abdominal mouth as its centerpiece. The mouth was working. Toothy jaws of splintered rib gnashed and worried the stripped-down skull of Otis, which danced in the makeshift maw like a football helmet in a slow-motion spin cycle.*

*Drew was dragging big wet graymeat hunks of his uncle behind him. Bit by bit, he fed them in. Absorbing their essence.*

*Merging them, too, with Overmind.*

Boonie retreated as Drew advanced: a psychotic pushmepullyou with no strings of tissue attached. Something about it must have looked funny as all hell, because Drew simply could not stop laughing.

Somehow, the humor eluded Boonie.

Until he saw himself in the mirror.

"*Ehn,*" he said, too stunned to speak, even if his face, throat, and lungs had been capable. "*Eh-hen.*" Goggling at the new Boonie view.

"*Eh-HEH hen-hen-hen.*" Actually chuckling a little, marveling at the misshapen contours, the massive tumorous topography his features had become. At least a dozen mottled golfballs of pus jutted out from his greasy post-Elvis complexion.

But it wasn't until his tumors *stared back* that the full humor of his situation struck him. Dozens of tiny eyelids fluttered awake, stared with infantile alertness at the brave new world before them. Boonie's vision went from three to fifty-three dimensions in a hallucinogenic instant. The fact that Drew refused to stop giggling only tossed phosphorus onto the fire.

"*Eh-hen hon hurn hen hee-ee-ee*," Boonie persisted, astonished. Mounting. "*Eh-hurn hen HEE HEE HEE . . . !*"

Once he got started, it was impossible to stop.

And, my, how time flies when you're having fun.

# IV

# Twenty—Eight

At a quarter to two, Micki was still waiting in the Labor Hall lounge set aside for that purpose. There was an antsy young workingman plunked down on the Naugahyde sectional across from her, staring anxiously up at the low-rezz whuffling on the TV screen.

Evidently, she noted, not all men were up to their part in the birthing experience. From the look on his face, he'd much rather have been home, watching the game. . . .

*Don't be a bitch*, Bob-Ramtha chided. *You know he's probably scared to death.*

"So what." Voice barely above a whisper. "Who isn't."

*Exactly. And look what a sister of mercy it's made of you.*

She started to counter, restrained herself. Partly because the young poppa-to-be was furtively scoping her out for brain damage; but mostly because Bobba, damn his absence of hide, was right again. And it wasn't just for Gwen and her beautiful baby.

Micki Bridges was terrified of hospitals.

"Ouch." She turned away from the guy, cupped one hand loose over her mouth. "I'm not dealing with this very well, am I?"

*Nope.*

"I'm sorry."

*Okay. Now stop it.*

She cringed. "Easier said than done."

As a child, her fear had been sheerly instinctive. The hollow, echoing corridors. The sterile, unnatural smells. The chilly aura of suffering and death that no amount of antiseptic could possibly dispel. Even then, she'd been unable to screen out its reek from her perception.

But if she needed reasons beyond that, the years had most assuredly provided them. Watching her father's five-year losing battle with leukemia. Watching her mother's relatively merciful (by comparison) three-day flirtation with hope, before succumbing to stroke.

And then, for the *coup de grace*, her own little dark descent into the bowels of the medical biz. The endless tests. The surgery. The drugsdrugsdrugs. The lonely nights spent spitting up and crying, as her hair fell out from the chemo and her skin scorched red from the radiation. The merciless assault on her body and spirit, till she wasn't sure which side of the coin was worse: the treatment or the disease.

And then Bob-Ramtha had come, filling the chasm that her agony had eroded within her, returning the faith that she'd dropped in her terror. Most of all, urging her to listen to her body.

*Don't resist understanding*, he said now. *It's the best friend you have. Your cancer's at the heart of your fear. Go talk with it. That's my advice.*

"You gonna talk me down?"

*Of course.*

"And hold my hand?"

*You bet.*

"Okay." The word was a whisper.

She closed her eyes.

*Breathing first*, he said, and she immediately applied the technique: slow, deep, and thorough breaths, massaging oxygen into tension-constricted tissue.

*Identify the points of stress*, he continued. *Don't proceed until you've worked them through.* She felt herself nod, though her body was still. Felt herself from the inside.

In full body awareness.

First, the head: exploring the streamers of agitation draped across her brow, strung taut from temple to temple and around the backs of her eyes. She could visualize the musculature embracing the skull, pinpoint in minutiae the fault lines of distress. Some of them were shifting, less than temporal: neurotic phantom twinges, playing mischievous, humorless pranks.

But then there were other, more persuasive pains: sometimes encroaching, sometimes receding, but ever-persistent and consistent enough to convince her of their genuine existence. Like the dull Chiclet-sized whum of pain in her temple, for example. She'd never figured out what it meant, but she'd felt it enough to believe in it.

*That's right*, he told her. *Listen to your body. It will lie and confuse you as much as it can, but its job is to tell you the truth. If you probe each response, without backing away, you will find yourself there.*

*At the essence.*

Spreading out over and in through the body, reaching through feet and hands. Reading the knots in her shoulders and back, like exotic coral reef formations. Isolating not only the stress points, but also the vast expanses of hard-won healthiness within her.

Quietly, methodically, Micki circled in.

On the source of both her life . . .

. . . and her pain . . .

*a vision*
*deep at the womancore root of her being*
*a fertile fecund tropical rainforest of*
*spirit lush with diversity*
*poly- and pantheistic multifaceted*

*vision of a pagan wonderland*
*in which all things might grow*
*reinforcing encouraging enabling life*
*abiding all things*
*except there was a problem*
*and it was the seed*

Micki breathed deeply, unconsciously pausing. She always did at this point, her awareness teetering as if at the tip of the continental shelf. She was up at the invisible line of demarcation that marked the darker side of her soul.

It was time to go over the edge.

*and it was the seed*
*that lay dormant inside her*
*dormant but waiting*
*buried but never forgotten*
*no way to forget*
*the black undying gem*
*nestled in her belly*
*like a watermelon seed*
*a hard flat cutting wedge*
*held at bay by therapy and*
*sheerest force of will*
*driving it back*
*refusing it purchase*
*compressing its essence in self-defense*
*no possible compromise with the killing thing*
*that knows no bounds*
*no possible deal with the one life form*
*that knows not how to coexist*
*corrupting health debasing shape*
*overwhelming and devouring the garden*
*no deal with the cancer that poisons the well*
*no path but resistance containment*
*benign transmutation*

*eternal vigilance*
*unshakeable love*
*affirmation of life*
*complete and committed to healing*
*no other choice but death*
*and worse*
*no other choice*
*at all*


The double doors whammed open, slapping Micki out of her trance. She looked up, stunned, at the entourage.

As they hustled the blue-faced woman in.

She was on a gurney, moving fast, and the orderly that pushed it looked utterly wired. He had the kind of face that looked like it didn't wire easy, and that just made it worse.

But not as bad as the man beside them: the wet-faced, dead-eyed, blubbering man that kept pace with the gurney. He was, Micki guessed, the woman's husband; and he looked like he'd just been served up a plate of his own intestines.

Because the woman on the gurney was death-rattling foam, glazed eyes sightless in her cyanotic face. She twitched once, twice as she passed before Micki. Involuntary spasms.

And her belly was huge.

"Oh, God," Micki whispered as they rumbled past, near-colliding with Melissa at the nurse's station. "Oh, God," as a pair of nurses—now wired as well—led the charge to the nearest room. "Please don't let Gwen hear about this."

As the door slammed shut behind them.


*The woman's name was Pat Holtzaple. She was thirty-two years old. Her due date was the same as her birthday: November 25th. The day after tomorrow.*

The first contraction had hit not more than three minutes into the Eagles game. Tim had invited a bunch of the guys over. Lucky, lucky. Instant baby-sitters, for the price of a case of Old Milwaukee and a couple of pepperoni pizzas. As with her last four deliveries, the contractions came on sudden and straight to the point. They were off to the hospital at once.

It was warm outside, and Pat needed the air, so she cracked her window and moaned into the slipstream. Tim was doing sixty in a residential zone.

They were on Rathton Road, less than an eighth of a mile from Labor Hall, when the wasp blew in the window crack and stung her in the shoulder.

Admissions had been insane. A lot of people were there with bizarro complaints: their bushes attacked them, or their three-headed cat. Pat's condition, on the other hand, was clear. Even though she was utterly, uncharacteristically spaced, that could have been explained any number of ways.

And she swore up and down she wasn't allergic to wasps.

Anaphylactic shock didn't strike until they were in the elevator. Her skin went red and itchy and hot in the space of a single contraction. By the time the doors opened on Four, she was violently coughing, her heart rate going triple-time.

By the time they hit Maternity, she was barely breathing at all.

The RN's went into Code Blue at once: calling her doctor while they jammed tubes up her nose and injected her with atropine. No go. Her final contraction had far less to do with birth than death.

Tim had to leave the room when they cut her open to rescue the baby. He didn't miss much. Just a little more heartbreak.

The baby was also blue.

*          *          *

"Goddamm it!" Micki spat, slamming the receiver down. For the eighty-seventh time, the 'PAL line was busy. The little she knew about Pat Holtzaple was enough to make her nerves tripwire.

*Relax,* Bob-Ramtha said.

"Yeah, right," she hissed. "Relax, my ass."

*The situation is not yours to control.*

"And that's supposed to make me feel better? *Christ,* Bobba . . . !"

*Wait,* he said, and turned her around. Melissa motioned her hither, from Gwen's doorway. The nurse's face was calculatedly neutral.

The clock said ten after two.

# Twenty—Nine

The Mt. Rose Amoco Shop 'N' Go got its first real whiff of hell at eleven after two.

It came in the form of a tan Arrow van, with a bumper sticker that read CAUTION: IN CASE OF RAPTURE, THIS VEHICLE WILL VACATE WITHOUT WARNING. Jennie Quirez wouldn't even have noticed it pulling into the lot, were it not for the way it wavered on its way to the gas island: wobbly as a newborn colt, unsteady on its balding whitewall tires.

*Drunk driver* was her first guess, though the bumper sticker would have seemed to belie that charge. (Like you couldn't be a drunk who believed in the Rapture. Like, for example, her papa had been.) Her second guess was *senior citizen*. Neither one was on the mark.

Sunday afternoons at the Shop 'N' Go were notoriously slow, low-key affairs, but today was a notable exception. A near-continuous dribble of customers had graced her presence all day long; and she'd had to face the fact that, barring a surprise visit from Mr. Truck, they'd be out of the eighty-seven octane within the hour.

In fact, she was just writing up the little OUT OF SERVICE signs when the van pulled up at the number two pump, lurched abruptly to a halt. Its cargo area was packed to overflowing, as if it had been packed for an extremely long vacation. If so, it was certainly off to a wonderful start.

From her seat at the register, Jennie had an unobstructed view of the screaming family within: three little towheads, crying in the back; pretty young Mom in the shotgun seat, clutching a baby-sized bundle to her breast and crying, too.

Last, of course, was dear old Dad: huge, stoop-shouldered and hollering from his place behind the wheel. The sight pushed all of her damaged, dysfunctional family buttons at once. The contents of his dissertation were hidden, but the dynamics were unmistakable. *What an asshole*, she thought, her contempt instantaneous.

Then he threw open the door, staggered rapidly for the pump.

And her first impression radically changed.

*Jesus God.* Suddenly alarmed. *What happened to you?* Even from fifteen yards away, the unhealthy sheen of his overwhite complexion was impossible to miss. He moved painfully, like he might keel over at any second; from the hurried, hitching gait of his bearlike body to the unnatural pallor of his face, everything about him looked terribly *wrong*.

He wasn't even dressed like a man on vacation. He was dressed like a guy who'd been puttering around the house: dirty jeans, an oil-stained work shirt. His pants were soggy and stained, as if he'd fallen into something vile.

Jennie thought instantly of calling 911, mentally calculated how long it might take an ambulance to get here. If he *was* having a heart attack or something, she didn't know what she'd do. Her repertoire of therapeutic moves was ridiculously small. The Heimlich maneuver. A really great back rub.

*At the same time*, she told herself, *he's still walking around. It might be just a little bit premature to call*.

Which, of course, forced her to respond to herself

with a reminder of how badly he'd been driving. Which, of course, set her off on a comprehensive point/counterpoint volley inside her head. By the time she got done weighing the options, he had his gas cap off and was ready to go.

She decided to give it a minute; keep a watchful eye on him; hope for the best; and prepare herself, should the worst transpire. As it so often did.

The thought made her glance nervously at the clock.

And, for some strange reason, worry about her man.

*Because Austin seemed to picture her as some kind of unflappable love-angel—the patron saint of inexhaustible good cheer—but it simply wasn't true. If it seemed that way, it was just because he made her feel so goddam good every time he was around.*

*The fact was, she worried a lot. She worried about almost everything, and blamed herself constantly: Daddy's little caretaker, still fretting over the details and putting things to rights. From middle age to the Middle East, true love to 2 Live Crew, the possibility of an afterlife to the possibility of after-dinner drinks at Austin's place; if it could be turned into a topic of concern, she had a fissure in her brain already reserved for the occasion.*

*And that was just your basic generic concern. That was when nothing was going on. That was before the guy she was falling in love with got dragged off on some secret mission that, by its very nature, could only be concerned with the disposal of extremely hazardous materials . . .*

*. . . that was before people started dropping dead in the middle of her shift . . .*

The number two light on her console was blinking; he'd flicked the switch one too many times, gone from off to on and back again. It was a common enough mistake, for agitated people in particular.

"Yikes," Jennie said: a Deitz-ism she'd absorbed through osmosis. She pressed the button, reset the pump. Now all he had to do was turn it on again.

The white-faced man had the nozzle in the tank. He leaned into the van at an awkward angle, as if it were too stressful or painful to stand up straight. For the first time, she noticed that his right hand was wrapped in a large, white, oily-looking bandage.

He clenched his teeth, squeezed the nozzle handle with his left. When nothing happened, he let out what looked like a wordless yowl of pain, then leaned forward and flicked the switch again.

*Click clack.* On. Off.

"Shit," she hissed. Outside, he more violently echoed the sentiment. She tried to reset, but he had lapsed into dumb-panic mode: if it didn't work by just flicking it once, doing it eight times *really hard* was bound to do the trick.

"Okay." Fighting off the minor wave of irritation. He needed coaching; there was an intercom for that very purpose. She got off her butt and went to it at once.

"Sir?" Speaking into the booming mic. He jumped, gaze flying from the pole-mounted intercom speaker to the window she stood behind. For the first time, their eyes made contact. At this distance, his eyes just looked vacant and huge.

"HANG ON A SECOND." She pressed reset once again, stopped the little light from blinking. "OKAY. NOW TRY IT."

*Click clack.* On. Off.

"ARRR... NO. DON'T DO THAT," she scolded. He responded with an expression of misery so intense that she literally *felt* it, trickling cold down her spine. *Oh, God, don't die*, she silently prayed, instantly overwhelmed by her guilt.

"JUST DON'T TOUCH IT, OKAY?" she continued, shifting gears. Incredibly sweet now, her voice. And utterly reassuring. "I'LL BE RIGHT OUT TO FIX IT, OKAY?" Then she pushed the button one final time, headed quickly around the counter.

A banged-up black Jeep Cherokee wheeled onto the lot as Jennie reached the door. She stepped outside, flashing a quick, terse, automatic smile at the driver and his friends before crossing in front of them. They were three young longhairs, probably in their early twenties: all in all, more Grateful Dead than Megadeth in spirit.

But they looked severely wired, and the Jeep came in just a little too fast; it had to squeal on its brakes to keep from nailing her. She jumped, felt her adrenaline level surge.

And that was when she smelled it for the first time: an ugly, vaguely industrial reek with the distinct undertaint of decomposition. It was like the stink of the Spring Grove paper mills, redoubled and befouled. For one brief, un-comfortable moment, it made her head spin.

"*Feh.*" She scowled, tried to peg the source of the smell. It seemed to be unlocalized, everywhere at once: almost as if it *were* pumping out of some smokestack somewhere, riding the breeze down to her little store.

*Or, perhaps, coming up from the valley. . . .*

Behind her, the Cherokee's driver was out the door, getting ready to gas up with the engine running. The other two guys headed quickly into the store. A third car—a Hyundai—pulled into the lot, sidled up behind the van.

Suddenly, things were moving too fast; she could feel the situation skittering out of her control. Jennie turned to the white-faced man: still standing there, nozzle in hand. First things first. She proceeded toward him.

The smell intensified the closer she got to the van. It was a more *specific* smell—oilier, thicker, more cloying— but it was clearly of the same gross vintage. She felt the nasty little headrush resurge. It slowed her to a crawl.

*And that was when she saw, at last, the soapbubble-thin, translucent veil of slime that coated him. Saw it move, across his surface and into the fabric of his clothes, pooling at the stains in his pants, his shirt, the bandanna around his swollen right hand.*

*And that was when she saw, at last, why the family was screaming. Saw the little four-and five-year-old faces, suffused and glistening, as if the mucus drooling from their nostrils had spread out to envelop their heads, their hair.*

*Saw the mother and her little bundle, little bundle*

*that kicked and squirmed, little oilslick hands and feet in
weak, convulsive motion.*

Then Jennie tried to scream as well. It welled in her
throat, a soundless explosion, while the horror froze her in
place.

"*. . . pleeeeeeeeez . . .*" croaked the white-faced, dying
father. Up close, the sheen was uniform: a moist glaze
across his eyes, his nose, his teeth and tongue. His
bandaged hand fished into his pocket, came up with a thin
wad of glistening bills.

"DON'T TAKE HIS FUCKIN' MONEY!" shouted a
voice from behind her. The Cherokee's driver, wild-eyed
and unequivocal. He had just spotted the dying man.

"*. . . pleeeeeeeeez . . .*" Holding out to her the poisoned
currency.

Jennie shook her head *no*, began to back away.

"DON'T LET THAT FUCKIN' ASSHOLE *TOUCH*
YOU!" There was more than a touch of hysteria in the
voice. An incredible hatred, born of terror. "DON'T
EVEN LET HIM TOUCH THE FUCKIN' PUMPS . . . AW,
*MAN* . . . !!!"

Jennie's gaze swept from the kid to the man and back
again, back. The driver of the Hyundai was in the picture
now, staring. He had no idea what was going on. She
wanted to relate, but that level of innocence had already
been burned off of her by the last thirty seconds.

All those years of reading science fiction, of voluntar-
ily and willfully empathizing with the impossible, weirdly
helped her to draw a bead on the moment. There was a
voice in her head—of course there was—and that voice
was insisting that *this isn't happening.*

But that voice was wrong, and all she had to do was
look in the eyes of the dying children in order to know that
truth. All she had to do was look in the crying eyes of the
mother who turned to her now.

And mouthed the word.

The magic word.

*Please.*

There was a paper towel rack on the pole that supported the intercom speaker. She had resupplied it shortly before noon. She pulled from it now a stack of paper towels as thick as a Frank Herbert novel, then turned her attention to the pump.

There was a greasy skidmark that glossed the metal lever that activated Number Two.

The skidmark was spreading.

*Oh God.* Jennie palmed the bluegray towels, advancing on the stain. *Omigod.* She watched it spread, then stop, as if it were aware of her advance. *Oh Jesus.* When the pale gray/white-faced man offered her the money yet again, she whispered, "*No, please,*" and then sidled slowly past him.

Reaching out for the lever.

"*NO!!!*" screamed the kid, and she flipped the switch, letting go of the towels the instant she was done. They hit the curb and began to stain, going dark and slick as they twitched on the pavement. Jennie backed away fast, staring at her fingertips. They were fine. Zero contact. She rubbed them together. Nothing. Fine.

"Okay," she said, then turned away, getting as far away from the sight and smell of them as she possibly could, turning and walking rapidly toward the door of the store and the safety within. She didn't look at the Cherokee's driver. She didn't look at the Hyundai *maricón.* She just stared at the doors until she was upon them, then threw them open and didn't look back.

"'Scuse me," said one of the longhairs inside, the one from the passenger seat. He had a loud pink and black R.E.M. T-shirt, and his pupils were enormous. She brushed past him, unable to even think about him as she moved back to her place behind the counter.

"'Scuse me," he repeated, following her to the end and then pacing her back up front to the register. "Do you have any cases of, like, Spaghetti-O's in the back?"

"Any canned shit!" yelled his friend, from the back. He had opened a box of Heftys, was loading one garden-size bag with cans that he swept with one arm off the shelves.

"No." Jennie had the phone in her hand. She was punching in 911.

"Any cans at all," said R.E.M. The courteous veneer was thin, and spreading like the gas pump stain. "Look, it's kinda important . . ."

Jennie thought about the supplies in the back. She hadn't really checked, but she knew they had to be slim. Tuesday, they'd restock.

If Tuesday ever came.

The phone rang. "No," she said. It rang again. "I'm sorry."

"Listen." R.E.M. leaned close, against the counter. His winning smile was horribly frayed. "You can come with us if you want. Okay? I mean, you have a car?"

Jennie sucked wind, and her eyes went *no*. The realization was like a cinder block dropped on her belly. *No*. And she thought about her man.

The phone rang again. No answer. No answer at 911.

"Listen to me. *You don't want to be stuck here.*" The kid's voice was urgent, and utterly sincere. "You don't know what's going on down there. . . ."

"Down where?" The phone rang again. Her voice sounded tiny.

"WHAT THE FUCK ARE YOU TELLIN' HER, MAN?" yelled the guy in the back. His voice had picked up the driver's ugly edge.

"SHUT UP!" screamed R.E.M. "JUST SHUT THE FUCK UP!!!"

The phone rang again, then loudly clicked. A voice came on. A robot voice. "*We're sorry. All our circuits are busy at present. . . .*"

"Oh, God," said Jennifer Quirez. Something else had clicked in place. It threatened to drag her to her knees. "Oh, God," she reiterated.

Thinking of Austin Deitz.

*Once upon a time, a million years ago, Jennie had*

*seen a film called* Miracle Mile. *It was a story of doomed True Love in the face of nuclear Armageddon. The film had ached and torn at her, for all the right wrong reasons.*

*Because she wanted to believe in true love.*

*And because she wanted to believe that the world would never end.*

*At that point—late one night, alone with her HBO— she had watched that goddam movie and then cried for hours, not crying herself to sleep because sleep never came, it disturbed her that badly.*

*And she'd realized that—if it came right down to it—the only thing worse than dying with your own true love would be to die alone.*

*Especially once you'd found him. . . .*

*"Please hold . . ."*

Jennie came back. R.E.M. was still staring at her, but his friend was already heading out the door with the garbage bag. "COME ON!" screamed the friend, throwing open the doors.

"Good luck," said R.E.M, and then turned away, too.

Outside, the Cherokee driver was yelling at the white-faced man. "YEAH!" he hollered. "I WANNA *SEE* JESUS AIRLIFT YOUR ASS OUT OF THIS ONE, YOU STUPID COCKSUCKER . . . !"

Then the doors slid shut, and she couldn't hear what happened anymore. She watched them move in panto-mime, all three of them climbing into the Jeep while the all-but-dead man pumped away, twenty dollars and counting as she read the console meter, all of it free as the canned goods clattering away in the Hefty Cinch Sak, down old Route 74 and away from here forever.

The guy in the Hyundai got back in his car and drove off without even touching the pump. When the tan Arrow van pulled away at last, it was almost as if nothing had ever happened.

Another illusion, quickly dispelled by the sight of the spreading stain.

There were a couple of orange emergency roadside cones in the back. She knew just where to put them. When the next car pulled in, it was restricted to the three and four pumps at the butt end of the island. Then she went back in to wait and pray.

While she waited, she stared at the clock.

It was two-fifteen.

And counting.

# Thirty

Deitz came up from the darkness, piece by piece.

*His entire being was fragmented, his consciousness buried beneath the rubble like an earthquake victim in the wreckage of his home. Every synapse and sinew, dislocated and disjointed, lay in a heap inside him.*

*Slowly, something shifted through the rubble.*

*Rebuilding.*

Hearing was the first sense to return. His stoppered ears opened suddenly, the fluid in his cochlea giving way in a hot trickle, and suddenly Deitz could hear again.

*Hssssssss . . . sh-sshhhh . . .*

The claustrophobic deep-sea-diver hiss of ragged, clotted breath filled his head. *Hssssssss . . . sshhhhhh . . .*

How long he listened there was no way to gauge; time was marked but not counted by the simplest of life's cycles. Air flowed in, flowed out again. Dimly, primordially, he recognized the breathing as his own.

*Hsssssssss . . . sh-s-sshhhhh . . .*

Feeling came next, sensitizing the millions of nerve endings that laced through his skin like a shut-down electrical grid. Deitz was now a feeling, hearing, breathing machine. There was pain, but it was veiled, muted as the thud of novocaine on a rotted tooth. He could feel his

230

lungs move up and down, could feel the thousand points of penetration where razored grass punctured rubberized canvas and quivering flesh.

He could feel other things, too. Strange. New. Shifting and sliding inside his suit. Hard to fix in the contained universe that was Deitz.

Gradually, consciousness focused as the power came back on in his nervous system. "*Hnnnnnnn...*" he groaned. His voice was impossibly huge in the confines of his hood.

"*Hhn-nhhhhhhhhhhh...*" he gurgled, swallowing thickly, and resumed breathing. Sweat slicked the surface of his face. Air flowed in, flowed out. He hawked loudly, his swollen sinuses suddenly giving way.

And, upon him like a wall, was the *smell*.

It was the reek of the Black Bridge road, revisited and amped to the millionth power: roses, rot, industrial solvent, forest green, and brimstone mixed with just a hint of something never smelled before by Man.

It was the stench of the New World rising, the sweat and blood and excrement of things that had never existed before. *Could not* have existed.

Until this moment.

Suddenly, he knew where the stench was coming from.

*IN ME NOW!!!!!!! The thought screamed in his head. IN ME NOW!!!!!!! Like a soul in a shredder, a snake uncoiling in his brain. IN ME NOW!!!!!! Stuffing the enemy down his throat and forcing him to swallow.*

*Taking ahold of his face from behind.*

*And grinding it in his failure.*

Deep inside him, Overmind wriggled, burrowing like a worm into his core.

Deitz shuddered, flatlined and went away, his mind going fetal, like a child with a high fever. Overmind responded by gunning his vital signs like a motorhead at a traffic light, making his dead heart race and his digestive system bubble. His limbs kicked into spastic motion, flopping and flapping in galvanic response. His penis engorged with blood and toxin, twitching like a frog's leg on a hot electrode wire. He ejaculated joylessly, sperm oozing out to join the other juices accumulating in his suit like gravy in a boiler bag.

*And in his mind, Deitz the fever-child had tried to run away. But there was nowhere to go, no place untainted, no way to escape the horror inside him. He retreated to the marrow of his bones, and Overmind was there: pulsing, arthritic, icy with malevolent delight. He slipped into coma, and Overmind was there: poisoning the vacuum, swirling in the void, at home in his unconsciousness as well.*

*Overmind dogged him every step of the way: nudging him, prodding him, torturing him, bending him over to prong his perception from behind. Seeping out, from every direction, to alter and color and rape the lens through which he was forced to perceive.*

*Dictating the new terms of his vision.*

Lookie, *it commanded wordlessly.* Lookie lookie lookie lookie . . .

*He fought it, not wanting to see, not wanting to see like* that. *It came at him like a speeding train, over ten years in the making: over ten years, to which he had dedicated his life, watching the train move toward him at a barely perceptible crawl . . .*

*. . . before* shifting *now, suddenly, into hyperdrive: hurtling toward him through the blackness, its headlight now a pinpoint now a floodlight now a blazing sun . . .*

When the light consumed him, Deitz's eyes began to see.

Light: milky and opaque, burning down his optic nerves, spilling into the dark crevasses of his brain. A jumble of senseless, murky, undifferentiated shapes: dancing before him, filling him with dread. It came to him that the inside of his visor was dripping with condensation, turning the world runny and hopelessly diffuse.

The pain was stronger now, a throbbing pulse that started in his legs and spread through his whole body. His eye muscles twinged, flexing, independent.

He looked to the right. Overmind looked left. He looked to the left.

Overmind looked right.

He tried to speak. His mouth did not respond. His mouth was no longer his own. It had been annexed into Overmind, along with the rest of him.

*MY BODY!* he thought-screamed. *MINE!*

Deitz focused his will like a missile and fired it. It bought him a moment's brief shred of control. His jaws wrenched open and his breath sucked in, his teeth prying apart like a rusty spring trap. When he tried to scream, his black tongue lolled into the breach.

Then he lost control, jaws clamping down hard until the blood squirted hot across the roof of his mouth.

Overmind let him taste it.

Then it asked him what he thought.

And Austin Deitz began to cry, fat tears rolling nowhere, formed inside his soul alone. His face refused to collaborate in the expression of his agony, his boundless despair. It mocked him: crazily crossing the eyes, black-red lips contorting in a bloody, toothy grin. Smiling on the outside, crying on the inside.

*My body.* Desperately. Bitterly. *Mine.*

But even he didn't believe it anymore.

A tremor passed through him. The master, whistling to its dog.

Then, slowly, Deitz's body began to rise and pull itself free.

The corpse was impaled, a thousand times over: a thousand wet, rank violations of the flesh. Overmind seemed not so much indifferent as *mildly amused* by the damage, the sensations of sickly rot and pain and transformation. But Deitz—the tiny spark of soul-identity that still remained his own—felt every razored gash and sliding, still-inserted blade of grass in intimate detail.

Deitz's body sat up, slowly. It braced itself with one hand on the living bed of nails, lost the middle finger just above the second knuckle, felt the severed digit drop into the bifurcated palm and rest there like a charm. Then it got

to its knees, its feet, felt the soles impale deep and slide
loose again, rising. Over and over.

As it walked toward the bridge.

At the edge of the river of pus that had been Toad Road,
a crust had formed. It was enough to support the dead
weight. Deitz's body followed it, plodding on wobbly stick-
legs, chest arrhythmically recycling its rancid, humid fumes.
Stumbling like a bum on Sterno, random blades of razored
grass hanging off the mangled back like porcupine quills.

The Deitz-thing dragged itself up the steepening incline: a deep-sea diver, knee-deep in the sloshing, self-
contained ocean of itself. It sealed its own ruptures as it
walked, plugged its own leaks in the outer skin, let the
boil-in fluids continue to rise. The roar in its ears was the
sound of Creation—the primordial, protean, plasmic pool—
raging and churning on either side of the blind, visored
mask it wore.

And the roar grew louder, as it crested the hill. It
turned. The roar grew louder still. The Source lay directly
ahead, now; Deitz felt himself shudder before its astonishing
power. It flooded his senses, overwhelmed his spark with
an alien longing, far stronger than love.

*Lookie lookie lookie lookie . . .*

Deitz tried again to shut his eyes.

They simply opened wider . . .

*. . . and watched, in helpless horror, as the condensa-
tion on the inside of his visor parted like a curtain: the tiny
beads of liquid rolling off to either side, waggling their
little moist tails like sperm like eels like baby snakes.*

Returning to him his sight.

At the heart of Black Bridge.

And the New Creation.


*Hell unfolded before him.*

*There was a whirlpool at the center of the creek: a
vast liquid aperture, a hundred feet across, like a gaping
mouth on the surface of the water. It roiled around the*

*perimeter, bubbling madly, then settled into a winding, almost stately corkscrew as it spiraled down into abyss. . . .*

*. . . only no, not exactly; the opposite, in fact: corkscrewing back and heavenward to dredge up the darkness, vomiting barrels and black slime from the belly of the earth.*

*The quagmire spread the breadth of the creek, bubbling muck that oozed like a lava flow and hardened. Its skin cracked open in a thousand places. Suppurating sentient toxic slag.*

*Things moved in the scum: the unfortunate indigent fauna of the water and woods, caught in a squeeze play of the new order. A doe, trying to escape the carnivorous plants, had gone headlong into the bank. It spasmed in the sucking mud, eyes rolling white in its head as the killing vines probed and planted seeds beneath its tawny hide.*

*Rabbits, raccoons, squirrels, and chipmunks had also fled and were subsumed. They flailed pathetically in the mire, wiggling like bait for the flippered monstrosities that belched forth from the hole.*

*Something thrashed directly beneath the bridge: six-foot-long carp, garbage-eaters throwing themselves into the shallows, their scales rupturing even as the first vestigial limbs sprouted from their sides. They moved toward the trapped mammals with long mouths snapping, sucking in the new air and dreaming of flesh.*

*The trees that rimmed the water were bowed under the weight of the strangling vines. Several had nests in their boughs, enormous conglomerates of mud and twig, riddled with softball-sized holes.*

*The nests were humming.*

*An insectile shape emerged from one of the holes, feelers busily probing atop its teardrop head. It was puppy-sized, and its segmented body bristled with short, deadly-looking spines.* Wasp, *Deitz thought, although the name no longer fit.*

*Wasps had always terrified him.*

*He hadn't known what terror was.*

*More of the insects appeared, crawling around the tortured trees, new wings unfurling in the sun. The drier ones lit from their perches, testing their wings on the hot still air. Their stingers were long as bayonets, their buzzing like the whine of a hundred ripsaws cutting through the roar of the abyss.*

*Several took off, lightning-quick, skimming the surface of the creek. They zigged and zagged against the current, heading upstream and far beyond.*

*And there was more. There was more. It spanned the horizon, overrunning the water and landscape for as far as the eye could see. Unnameable shapes, violations of form, wild new species of untraceable origins thrashed and wailed and spawned there.*

*At the center of the only Hell that mattered.*

*The Hell that Mankind had created on Earth.*


The thought descended upon him then, a branding iron burning hundred-foot-high letters into his brain. And all that was Deitz reeled from the impact as Overmind spoke, the simplest expression of the infant god's greed.

*MINE!* it said. *MINE! MINE! MINE! MINE! MINE!*

And it was true. The war had been lost, irreversibly and forever. Deitz could see it now, see it all too clearly.

His mind snapped like a twig.

*Suddenly, the program clicked into place. An instinctive knowing, clear-cut and unquestioned. Suddenly, he understood how a bee felt in the hive. Completely plugged in to the schematic.*

*Completely at One with the higher plan.*

And there was a terrible peace there, in giving in to Overmind. A terrible burden removed from one's shoulders. The burden of doubt. The burden of shame. The burden of responsibility and individuation.

In the mind of God, all things are possible, and all can be forgiven.

But Austin Deitz could not forgive.

Not even dead.

Not ever.

*No*. A primal response, preceding thought. *No*. Beyond denial. *No no no*. A gut reaction, pushing back against the program.

Overmind blinked, uncertain.

*No no no no no*. A slowly mounting groundswell of power, forming at the base of his will. *No no no no* NO. Building, in pressure and size.

He felt his fingers clench, and knew that he had caused it.

NO!

Confusion shuddered through the Overmind, in the contained universe that was Deitz.

NO NO NO!!! He relished the power, refused to give in to the satisfaction. The trade-off was *control*: seeping back into his dead limbs, the muscles and bones that powered and framed them. Already, he could turn his head, wipe the hideous grin off his dead, bloated face.

He could even close his eyes, if he wanted to.

He no longer had the desire.

MINE! The word belonged to him now. The concept belonged. To him. MINE! It could *have* the rest of the fucking world.

MINE!!! It could even turn him into a monster.

But he would be his *own* monster.

MINE MINE MINE!!!

Then he turned, heading back in the direction he'd come, negotiating the crusty bank of his own complete volition. The lifeforce that spawned him held back in awe, stunned and shunted out of the driver's seat by the astonishing, presumptuous fact of free will.

*My way*, he said.

And became, in that moment, the first fallen angel of Overmind.

\*   \*   \*

His men were rising up from the depths as he returned, crawling out from under the abscessed surface of Toad Road. Their faces were barely visible through the coagulant slime that had swallowed them, the afterbirth that sluiced them back out into the world. Beckett, Burroughs, Hooper, Franklyn: essentially faceless now. Taken over. Drones of the One True Faith.

Deitz's suit had filled, as well; the boiler bag had risen to the brim. He found that he lived now as much in the fluid as inside of the skin that had once defined him. It was not a problem to see through the inch of opaque liquid; his eyes drifted out of their sockets, pressed against the Plexiglas faceplate that framed the bounds of his new flesh.

The trucks were rising, too. Deitz wondered if the others would pose a problem. He was becoming far less Deitz than *thing*, a malformed union of the two.

With a purpose, he found, that would not be denied.

Pyle, still in the lead truck, turned toward Deitz as he approached, his Barney Rubble *bonhomie* long since expired. His eyes were flat, and the color of gelatin; his open mouth worked endlessly, producing no sound.

It didn't matter. Deitz already knew what he had to say.

*My turn*, he said, eyeing the empty driver's seat.

And waiting for his moment to arise.

When the road reformed beneath them, the HazMat team regrouped as well. It was an unexpected addendum to the original script, but Overmind was nothing if not flexible.

It gave the first heretic his first wave of followers.

And waited to see what it got in return.

# Thirty—One

*In the handful of minutes since two, a net of sorts had begun to form: confused, scattered, mounting. Across the county, like light pins winking on across an electronic map, a pattern of pandemonium emerged: overloading phone circuits, jamming call-lines, feeding the rumor mill. And spreading. . . .*

A very frustrated Kirk sat behind the wheel in the PennSupreme parking lot, listening to the ticking doom-clock in his head and weighing his options.

A pay phone stood before him: utterly useless, every signal a busy signal, every line jammed. The two-way radio sat under the dash, its mike still in his hand. The mike was dead.

Not an accident.

Because to turn it on would be to invite the wrath of Laura, who would ream him out before he could get a word in edgewise. But to spill his guts enough to win her over would tip his hand to every other reporter in the tri-county area, thereby *guaranteeing* a blown scoop.

And there, as they say, lay the rub.

Because Kirk needed some input. Kirk had just returned

239

from Paradise Waste, where his little journalistic *blitzkrieg* had come to a grinding halt with the discovery of one big fat dead Harold Leonard, cooling on his office floor.

Leonard did not look like he went gently into that good night. His eyes were screwed shut tight and his tongue protruded in a horrible *yechh* face; little white flecks of still-moist spittle caked the corners of a mouth that was torqued into the most miserable grimace Kirk had ever seen. Harold Leonard had gone out with a terrible secret on his lips.

Combined with the clutch of rifled documents, it spelled out a knowledge that Kirk was not entirely sure he wanted to hear.

And even less certain he could afford not to.

Kirk eyed the radio. "Aw, screw it," he muttered, and flicked it on.

The car filled with harsh white noise. "Ouch!" Kirk winced, thumbing back the squelch control. He toggled the mike switch.

"Laura," he said. "Come in, Laura."

Nothing. His voice seemed to echo weirdly, the wave of noise shifting and modulating as if it were trying to form the words. "Laura, come in . . ."

Kirk listened, as Laura's voice came up from under the hiss.

"*Kirk . . . ?*" it began.


At the sound of his voice Laura crossed the room in record time. "Kirk!" she demanded, white-knuckling the handset. "Kirk, where the hell are you?"

"I can't tell you," he said. Hiss clung to his words like sargasso.

"Don't play games with me!" Laura said. "Get your butt back in here, now!"

"I'll be back soon," he said, his voice distant. "Trust me. I'm on to something."

"KIRK!" Laura yelled. "COME BACK IN HERE

RIGHT NOW! KIRK! YOU'RE FIRED! KIRK!'' The noise put an echoing trail on her words, mocking her. "KIRK . . . !''

But there was no answer from the other side. Just the rippling echoes in the alien wall of noise.


Kirk switched the radio off, his bowels turned suddenly to water and slush. "I didn't hear that last part," he said to himself. "The transmission broke up, and I couldn't make it out."

He figured if he said it another hundred times or so, it would start to sound like the truth.

But the fact was, he *had* heard it. YOU'RE FIRED. Just two little words, but they changed everything. YOU'RE FIRED. It was amazing, *astonishing* just how thoroughly they had clipped his strings, sucked the fire from his guts and the wind from his sails.

Suddenly, everything he'd done—from the day he entered broadcast school to the moment at hand—was ashes. Cinders. Confetti in flames. There was nothing he could do to salvage his career now. He had taken the gamble, and lost.

Big time.

The pain began to penetrate the protective cold that his mind had thrown up. Pictures of the future began to unveil themselves, unbidden. He could imagine the look on his old man's face when word of this got out. He could imagine the way this would play on the industry dirtline. He tried to imagine ever getting a job in broadcast media again; but *that* picture, for some reason, just wouldn't come clear.

"I'm dead." The voice barely registered as his own. "I'm dead." Staring into his rearview mirror. The face that stared back at him was a frightening grayish-white.

"Oh, *man*," he whimpered, slumping across the steering wheel with his crisscrossed arms shielding his forehead. "What the fuck am I gonna do *now*?"

                    *      *      *

Kirk was not the only one in the grip of despair. Back at 'PAL, Gary sat trapped at the editing console, dialing and redialing his house. For roughly the fiftieth time, he got a little recorded voice, droning " . . . *all of our circuits are temporarily busy. Please try . . .* "

" . . . your call again later, yeah, yeah. Shit!" he muttered. He slammed the phone into the cradle. Somewhere up stairs, he could hear a telephone ringing, ringing, ringing.

"HANG *UP*!" he bellowed.

It stopped. Gary huffed in pained relief. Before he could relish the silence, the phone rang again. It had been this way for almost an hour, an endless upward spiral of fear and frustration.

Gary picked up the handset and punched in the number again. He didn't know what else to do. There *was* nothing else to do.

When the prerecorded operator's voice came on the line, he nearly punched a hole straight through the wall.


And at 911, things were getting worse by the minute.

Dottie Hamm had drained the last of her Big Gulp. The straw rasped against the bottom, probing for stray droplets of lukewarm Coke. She was down to her last Munchkin. It was beginning to look like she'd never get any again. Nor would she ever get to eat lunch. In fact, she hadn't been able to leave her seat to so much as *pee* for the last three hours.

Dottie cast an anxious glance at Dave, who shrugged and rolled his eyes as his call screen lit up once again. The calls that had started as a trickle were now a flash flood of near record-breaking weirdness.

Because the voices that clogged the lines were panic-voices, frantically spitting out tales of fear and delirium. Worse yet, the callers Dottie checked out on her video monitor didn't display mile-long rap sheets of crankdom.

These were not your chronic paranoid freaks. Most of them, before today, had never dialed 911 in their lives.

They were just *folks*: ordinary citizens calling in to say their trees were singing, saying their gardens had attacked them, or their dogs or kids had gone out to play and not come back.

Dottie was stumped. They were just folks. And they were scared. Dottie didn't blame them one bit. She knew a few things they didn't.

And she was getting a little scared herself.

*Because it wasn't every day that you called in police from Hellam Township and Paradise County, two fire companies and HazMat, and have every single one of them disappear, now was it?*

It vexed her. One by one, she called them in. One by one, they dropped right off the map. She checked the lines again. The signal path down to Hellam was a wall of white noise; nothing was coming from within ten miles of Black Bridge, on any frequency.

*It's like the Bermuda Triangle popped up right in our own backyard*, she mused.

And *damn* if it wasn't spreading.

"Shame on you, Dottie," she scolded. She looked at the list of people to call in the event of just such an emergency. Her bladder felt like a overfull water balloon, ripe and ready to burst. She punched in the number, and waited.

This call was definitely a first.

She hoped to heaven it would be the last.

# Thirty—Two

"Ah-hah. . . . Yes, I see . . . . Yes, that is very strange."

Blake, still holed up in his study, paced and spoke softly into the phone. "Have you notified anyone else?"

Blake's brow furrowed with concern, as every name punched another hole in an already leaky boat. "Hmm," he said. "And HazMat did what? Ah-*hah*."

His headache was back, a whanging pulse in the top of his skull. "Yes, I'll get right on it," he said, fighting every urge to lash out. He grasped the heavy obsidian glass paperweight that graced the corner of his desk and squeezed as hard as he could.

"Yes," he said, as crisp, angled edges cut into soft finger skin and the pain in his hand beat back the pain in his head. "Good job, Dottie." He smiled thinly. "Keep me up-to-the-minute, will you? Thanks so much."

Blake rang off and let go of the paperweight in a simultaneous release of stress. A smear of blood slicked its surface.

"Shit." Blake hissed, pulling out his handkerchief. He'd cut himself, alright, a thin laceration on the inside of the knuckle line. His handshake hand, his deal-sealing hand. But his headache had abated. For now.

He wrapped the hanky around the cut and paced: thinking, thinking.

This was bad. Correction: this was beyond bad. This was a nightmare. With Dottie's report of foul-smelling water, isolated dementia and blight ringing in his ears, he became increasingly convinced that some sort of hallucinogenic substance was involved in this chemical spill.

It was a horrifying thought, but he could think of no other explanation. For his part, it would be nothing but bottled water and spirits for the duration.

Meanwhile, the odds on containment grew skimpier by the second. While there was still time to be bought, Blake continued to plug holes; he sat down at his desk, flipped through his little oak Rolodex until he came to *Huntington, Tom*. He punched in the number and waited.

*Busy.*

"Shit!" he spat. He hit the redial button.

*Busy.*

Blake cursed again and fed the number into the auto-dialer, punched *send*. As the phone worked, Blake gazed pensively at his surroundings. He could feel his window of opportunity narrowing, and his tastefully appointed digs were feeling more prisonlike by the second.

Finally, the phone caught, chiming a melodious little *brrrr . . . brrrr . . . brrrr . . .*

"Answer the phone, dammit," Werner said into the mouthpiece. Then, "Tom? Werner Blake. How are you, old man?" Reptile-smiling. "Great. Listen, I just wanted to call and keep you apprised of a situation that's developed."

Blake opened up his hand, studying the Rorschach-pattern of blood staining the white linen hanky. "Well, nothing too serious, we hope, but we're still scoping it out. . . ."

He nodded his head, the picture of corporate concern. "Of course. But handled wrong, this could impact adversely on mutual friends. We'd like to treat this with some sensitivity, not start a flap over nothing. . . ." Nod, nod.

*One down,* he thought. Tom Huntington was nothing if not a team player. Blake relaxed behind the game, on auto-pilot now. He could finish this conversation in his sleep. "Ah-hah," he said.

For some strange reason, even as he spoke, Rio kept coming to mind. Blake closed his eyes and could picture it: *lush mountains, tropical beaches, incredibly beautiful women, a favorable exchange rate, and a government sympathetic to economic opportunity. . . .*

"Umm . . . Dad?"

Blake's daydream vaporized instantly; the voice behind him made him turn. A long tall black-and-white apparition hunkered in the doorway, the weight of the world on its shoulders.

"*Not now,*" Blake soundlessly mouthed, impatiently waving him off.

The apparition was unmoved. "You plan on getting off the phone, like, ever?"

"Hang on just a second. . . . thanks," Blake said pleasantly into the mouthpiece. Then he cupped it in his hand and glared venomously at his pride and joy, his progeny.

As father and son faced off: each the other's worst nightmare, made flesh.

Garth Blake slouched in the doorway, angular and obtuse. He was six-foot-three and scarecrow-thin, and his presence filled the room: a tidal wave of spiked black leather, big black hair, and attitude. His ash-white skin and sepulchral pucker of ebony lipstick did their best to affront and unnerve, but they could not conceal the ugly truth.

Garth was the spitting image of Blake, Sr.

It was a fact that appalled both of them, but for different reasons. Garth possessed the same riveting gray eyes, the same innately upturning Grinch smile. His face was as yet unsullied by time, but Garth carried a premature gravity that rendered him sullen and pained. It was tough going through life as the privileged son of such utter corruption. His T-shirt bore a black-and-white print of JFK, waving and grinning, while hot multicolored inkblood spewed explosively from his forehead. It was the single most offensive T-shirt Blake had ever seen; which explained, of course, why his son had purchased two.

Garth loved his exploding Kennedy T-shirts. They spoke to him. Moreover, they spoke on his behalf to the world at large. Like the black dove's foot earring dangling from his ear, the buzzwords and slogos buttoneered to his lapels: THROBBING GRISTLE; SILENCE = DEATH; THE SEX WAS BETTER IN PRISON.

Or, most specifically, the one stenciled huge across his black leather-clad back: the word *future* in blood-red letters, blotted out by the chalky white circle with the diagonal slash through it, the universal negative symbol like a canceled stamp across it. It summed up Garth's attitude toward life very nicely.

NO FUTURE.

That was what Garth had to look forward to, and boy was he excited. Only just sixteen, and already it was over; or, even worse, it might drag on like this for years. A lifetime of hypocrisy, followed by an ugly gray descent into middle-aged decrepitude and ultimate pain-filled oblivion.

Just like dear old Dad. . . .

Garth cringed involuntarily. "So can I use the phone now?" he inquired.

"*No!*" Blake hissed the word like the first spit of poison out a gas-chamber vent. "*Can't you see I'm busy?*"

Garth groaned, shrugging heavily. "Aw, c'mon. Lydia's an hour and forty-five minutes late. It'll only take . . ."

"*Goddammit . . . !*"

Outside, a car horn sounded.

"No problem, Dad. Thanks. You're a real pal."

Disgust wadded like puke in his throat. He split before he got some on the rug.

Leaving Blake, for a moment, in the grip of a genuine moral dilemma.

Then the front door slammed, and a car engine gunned. The squeal of tires that followed relieved him of all responsibility. *Jesus Christ,* he thought. *Maybe it's time to start fresh, after all . . .*

Then he returned to the phone, and the matters at hand.

# Thirty—Three

The Scuzzbug was moving before Garth was fully seated. He liked it that way. It was more of a challenge. "HEY, DAD!" he hollered, loud as it got, out the still-open door. "SUCK MY SCROTE, YOU IMPOSTER! YOU ALIEN SCUM!"

"I like that," Lydia said, peeling out in a fog bank of rubber and dust. With her deep green eyes, too-wide features and sidewalled mane of bone-white hair, she looked like a spookycute nineties version of those little troll dolls in the toy bins at Woolworth. "I'm sure the neighbors will, too."

"ADMIT THAT YOU ARE AN IMITATION POD-MAN!" he continued, even louder, hanging half out the door as the car pulled a wide screeching one-eighty in the crushed stone of the drive. "ADMIT THAT YOU ATE MY REAL FATHER'S BRAIN!"

They broke the circle, headed out for the street. "Say 'bye now," she said.

"'BYE NOW!"

And then they were off.

"Feeling better?" Lydia asked pleasantly.

"You bet."

"I'm so pleased," she deadpanned, slowing the

Scuzzbug to a mild-mannered, law-abiding crawl the moment she hit the main road. On the street, she couldn't afford to drive so crazily; the cops would pull her over in a second. Even *without* provocation, cops pulled her over from time to time, just as a matter of principle.

Because the infamous Scuzzbug of Lydia Vickers was an act of visual terrorism on wheels. Like the woman herself, it was born to raise eyebrows and frighten the natives of Paradise. She felt quite certain that no one had ever seen its like before. She knew *she* certainly hadn't.

From the inside, it was just a beat-to-shit black VW Superbeetle, completely upholstered in leopard-skin print and festooned with weirdo stickers. Funky-cool, but not unheard of.

The *exterior*, however, was something else again: covered bumper to bumper in a fetid gray-green *fuzz*, painful to look at and loathsome to the touch. This experiential delight came courtesy of Lydia's day gig, where she worked on the loading docks at the Yummy Potato Chip Company in Hellam.

It seemed that the oiled soot emanating from the Yummy Potato Chip smokestacks would drift across the parking lots, dousing every car in range with a tacky, mottled goo. Airborne particles, dust and road dirt would quickly and permanently adhere themselves, transforming any vehicle within range into a veritable scuzz magnet.

Of course, turning her cherished Superbeetle into the ugliest car on earth certainly hadn't been *her* idea. At least not at first. For a while there, it had driven her nearly insane. But after a brief, pitched, and losing battle, Lydia'd gradually come to admire it, the cultural statement it made.

So instead of fighting the endless uphill battle of scrubbing it down three times a week, she instead reversed and *assisted* the process: driving through industrial areas a lot, always leaving her car exposed to the elements, never *ever* washing it. Etcetera, etcetera.

And in no time: *Voila!*

A legend was born.

"So," Garth said, staring out the immaculate windshield—along with the windows, lights, and mirrors, the only things Lydia ever cleaned—"what's the deal? When you woke me up this morning..."

"Afternoon," she corrected.

"...you sounded like it was pretty major." His grin was huge. "So what's the goddam *story* here?"

Lydia's poker face began to falter. "Oh, nothing..."

"Come on!" His too-enormous smile chiseled away at her composure. She actually cackled. "WHAT?" he bellowed.

"Okay, okay," she relented. "Look in the back."

He looked. There was the usual pileup of Lydia-clothes and bizarroid lifestyle accessories. They just seemed to be piled up quite a bit higher than usual. Like they were trying to cover up something big.

Like maybe a couple of boxes of...

"Ooo," Garth said, pausing just for the moment of impact. Beside him, Lydia beamed with pride. "Ooo ooo ooo!" he elaborated, sweeping the camouflage aside.

And there they were: one thousand copies, hot off the press. One thousand little eighty-eight-page Molotov cocktails, with his and Lydia's names all over them. Just waiting to be fired and flung.

One thousand copies of their homemade brainchild pride 'n' joy.

*NO FUTURE—The Magazine of Famous Last Words.*

"TA-DAH!!!" Lydia trumpeted, exulting in their triumph.

"God DAMN!" he echoed, pulling the first one off the stack. "Just *look* at this thing...!"

But Lydia was driving, so Garth had to content himself with looking alone. And though he'd seen the original a million times, there was nothing like seeing it mass-produced, knowing it was there for the world to experience.

"God damn," he repeated, almost reverent this time.

The magazine's cover, like the contents, was a malign collaboration—artwork by Garth, layout and pasteup by Lydia. It was a wraparound slap in the face, an unremitting motherfucker from front to back. Garth was pleased that it had printed up so well. They'd spent *months* honing the premiere issue to just the right aesthetic of blasphemy, melding Steadmanesque inkblotch and mutant photomontage in an ultimately neon-colorized assault on complacency and the neutral reaction.

Beneath the schizo surf-punk masthead, the central image was simple and direct:

*There was a paunchy naked white man with an ugly pinched grin, and he was raping and killing the New Year's baby for the banner year 2000. The man held the screaming baby's head up by its hair while his crotch interlocked with its raw baby buttocks. In his right hand, he held a power drill. It was boring into the baby's skull. Blood drooled from its mouth. Its sex was indeterminate and entirely beside the point.*

*Behind them, a mob had assembled. They were laughing and shouting and waving signs. The faces belonged to George Bush, Dan Quayle, Ronald Reagan, Jerry Falwell, Ivan Boesky, Donald Trump, Jesse Helms, and a dozen others. They all had their pants down, waiting in line. Their signs read GO GO GO and BETTER HARDER FASTER.*

That was the front cover.

The back cover was even better.

*It was a mirror-image mob, representing the opposition. They all had variations on the old sad-eyed black velvet face, modeled after hippie ikons Abbie Hoffman, Ralph Nader, Buckminster Fuller, The Beatles and the Kennedys (not to mention dozens of more contemporary hero-figures, from Bob Geldof to Michael and Jesse Jackson).*

*Though they, too, were shouting and waving signs, not a one of them was laughing: and though all of them had their pants around their ankles as well, none of them*

*seemed to be wanking off with any degree of success. Their
signs read CUT IT OUT and THAT'S NOT NICE.*

*And at the front of the sad-eyed crowd hung poor old
Jesus, three-quarters crucified. He'd gotten one hand free,
and it held a magnifying glass. He was trying to find his
dick with it: squinting real hard, also without success.*

*The little sign nailed above his head read, simply:
WUSS.*

"So," Lydia blurted, practically beside herself, "what
do you think?"

"I think," Garth proclaimed, "that this is the most
vile, repugnant, penocentric wad of indefensible swill I've
ever seen."

"Me, too," she agreed, smiling. "Don'cha just love
it?"

"You bet!" Garth said. He felt all warm and fuzzy
inside.

"Yeah," Lydia beamed, gunning the Scuzzbug down
South George Street, "if this don't get us orphaned,
*nothin'* will."

And, of course, it was true. Taken together, it was an
utterly obscene tableau, calculated to outrage and horrify
even the most open-minded member of the studio audience.

That in itself, though gratifying, was simply not
enough. So Garth and Lydia had found it neccessary to go
that extra mile, by adding that little *personal* touch.

The face on the paunchy baby-raper belonged to
Werner Blake.

The face on the dickless Jesus was Lydia's father, Frank.

It was their special "Sins of the Father's Day Salute!"

And it was just their little way of saying thanks.

Because Garth and Lydia were pissed, no question
about it. When they said NO FUTURE, they weren't just
pulling a petulant teenage hissy-fit. They were only sixteen
years old, and *they* knew that their civilization wouldn't
last out the century. They *knew* that they'd been fucked out

of their birthrights by the greedheads who ran the world and, worse, the cowards who watched it all happen without lifting a finger to stop it.

Which was where, Garth reminded himself, assholes like Lydia's dad came in.

It was one thing to hate men like Werner Blake. They were wholly transparent scum, and they certainly didn't deserve to live, but at least they'd never volunteered the pretense of brotherly love or global concern.

Guys like Frank Vickers, on the other hand, were nothing *but* pretense: a bunch of pathetic old ex-hippie-turned-yuppie-turned-bitter-old-lecherous-drunken liberal shmucks who, if anything, Garth and Lydia hated even *more* than Garth's old man, because at least Garth's old man could get it *up* once in a while.

If there was one thing more pathetic than listening to Frank Vickers drone on about "the Sixties"—when people *really cared*, unlike *today*—Garth couldn't for the life of him imagine what it was. These days, Frank's idea of social responsibility was to form an "environmental action group," which mostly consisted of other middle-aged whining pisspots like himself. They would get together and talk about political action and drafting resolutions and shit, except it always turned into an argument about who was in charge, if it even *got* that far. They they'd break for refreshments and wind up trashed, having accomplished nothing, playing Trivial Pursuit and talking about how the dope was better in the good old days.

Chalk another one up for peace, love, and understanding.

*Which leaves people like us with pretty damn little to work with in the role-model department*, Garth mused. *Not that this is a big surprise or anything. I mean, we would have liked to believe you guys, but you're just too utterly full of shit.*

*All we want is a fucking admission of* guilt. *That's all. Just to hear the truth spoken—just once—in our lifetimes. It may seem like a lot to ask, but what the hell.*

*Everybody's gotta have a dream. . . .*

\*      \*      \*

"Hey, careful with the merchandise," Lydia cut in, bursting the bubble of rumination. "You could put someone's eye out with that thing!"

"Huh?" Garth blurted, then looked at his hands. He had rolled the premiere issue of *NO FUTURE* into a cylinder tight enough to train puppies with. "Oh, sorry!" Garth said sheepishly.

"Don't worry about it," Lydia replied. "Here, take out your impulses on *these*."

She handed him what looked like a roll of laminated toilet paper. "Oh wow!" Garth exclaimed, unfurling it: piece upon piece of lovely, adhesive-backed sticker paper, each square throbbing with the NO FUTURE logo.

"No shit." He turned to her, pleased, met the gleam in her eye. "How many did we get?"

"A thousand, so far." They just couldn't stop smiling. "That's why I'm so late. I've been sticking 'em on pay phones all morning . . ."

"*Without ME?*" he hollered, horrified.

"Yeah, well," she said, as the Scuzzbug rolled straight for the heart of Paradise. "That's what we get whole lives for, they tell me." And Garth just laughed and laughed and laughed.

Their day, it seemed, had at long last come.

And what a day it was.

# Thirty—Four

FROM THE DESK OF:
Bernard S. Kleigel

To the editor:
Am I the only one who's <u>fed up</u> with all the "parasites and leeches" on the Body Politic? Isn't anyone tired of supporting <u>lazy "Good-For-Nothings"</u> who get fat off the fat of the land? And I'm not just referring to "Welfare Cheats" and the Socialist programs that <u>make it possible for Mixed Races to rage Drug Wars in America's backyards.</u>
No, I'm talking about the very "Public Servents" that our tax dollars are supposed to be <u>SUPPORTING!!!</u> That's right, I'm talking about the people who "Operate" our 911 numbers, and the

There was somebody at the door.
"DAMMIT, MILLIE!" Bernie bellowed. "GET THE DOOR, FERCRISSAKES!" He couldn't for the life of him comprehend that woman's problem. Here he was, struggling over draft seventeen of his letter, and he couldn't even concentrate on what he was doing, because of all that

256

hammering on the damn front door. For God's sake, she knew how important it was! He'd told her a million times: if you complained loudly enough, eventually they *had* to listen!

No question about it. It had to be kids. From his perspective—stuck in the paper-cluttered corner of the basement he called his office—it was a distant, persistent tattoo of thudlike sound. He had half a mind to march up there and sue their parents, but *God* did he ever have a headache! And he had to finish this letter. Strike while the iron was hot.

> our 911 numbers, and the so-called "Peace Officers" who are supposed to <u>protect</u> us!
> Today, <u>my son and I</u> were <u>NEARLY KILLED</u> <u>by teenage hoodlums</u> (I can only assume they were involved in "Illegal Drug Activity," which is just a fancy name <u>for plain old dope</u> dealing!). That in itself was "bad enough"! But it was <u>nothing</u> compared to the treatment I got from the "Friendly People" HAH!!!) at 911

> "GOD DAMN IT!"

Now they were stomping around up there, and he could definitely hear laughter, high-pitched and giddy. Who the hell *were* these kids? They sure weren't friends of Billy's; so far as he knew, Billy didn't *have* any friends. It just didn't make any sense. . . .

Then Millie screamed.

And Billy screamed.

And Bernard S. Kleigel, the Conscience of a Nation, just *sat* there: paralyzed, sweating, with a hammer for a heart.

"No," he whimpered, as the footsteps thundered down the hallway: Millie's in the lead, two other sets in hot pursuit. Billy's persistent screams moved with her. Bernie could picture his son in her arms as she ran, crying out as well.

Crying out for *him.* . . .

But there was nothing he could do. She had to understand that. She had to understand that he was helpless, that he had no choice, that he absolutely *could not move*, he had spent his whole life imagining the worst and now that it was here, he was completely unprepared for it.

"Please," he whined, as if it would help. As if he were tapped into some cosmic 911 line, relaying his message directly to God for immediate customer satisfaction. As if he could wish his cares away.

As if God were actually taking his calls. . . .

*And he didn't want to picture it, to envision in his mind the apocalyptic WHOOMP that shook the house to its foundation, construct a visual of his wife as she hit the floorboards above his head, match her scream with the face he knew she must be making. He didn't want to see the sources of that terrible laughter, was unable to conjure up images adequate for describing the sounds being torn from his son.*

But when the meat like gravy oozed down through the cracks, he no longer had to use his imagination. It spattered the floor in a rich red rain, drove him screaming from his chair and his sanity. He was halfway to the stairs before he knew he was moving, halfway *up* the stairs before he saw his salvation.

It was his old pal, Officer Hal Thoman.

911 had come through, after all.

"NO!" Bernie screamed as the dead cop descended. "NO!" as the shadows pulled back to reveal Hal's full green open-skulled glory. One last full-throated "*NOOOOOO!!!*" as he slipped in the widening pool of thickly coagulant family-style sauce.

And then no mean old kids could ever bother poor old Bernie again.

# Thirty—Five

Bill Teague had to admit: he liked being his own boss.

He lit a smoke and reflected on that fact as they rolled down the twisty roads, en route to number two. Bill and Ted loved their job. Not the killing, especially, although Bill would confess a craftsman's appreciation of a job well executed, pardon the pun. They just liked the hours, the freedom, the excellent adventures.

What they hated were the boonies.

Travel was a given, which meant a lot of runs down a lot of secondary highways and back roads, where brain-dead rubes bred like rabbits and lived in nasty little cracker-boxes with concrete jockeys by the driveways or little propeller-ducks whizzing on their squalid little lawns. Give Bill and Ted a city any day: New York, Pittsburgh, Philly. Even Baltimore, if it came down to it. Anywhere but here.

*Oh, well.* Bill sucked smoke and fiddled with the radio. Came with the territory. "Fuckin' radio wasteland," he muttered to Ted, who manned the wheel.

"Fuckin' worthless radio," Ted addended, and Bill agreed. The Impala's radio sucked. At the moment, the only tune coming through on the dial was the loathsome

Terry Jacks, crooning "Seasons in the Sun." Then even that was lost, overwhelmed in a loud wash of static.

And that was when they heard it. From below, around the bend and unseen, rose a crazed industrial clamor. Clanging, smashing.

Roaring to life.

"What the fuck is that?" he asked. They'd been apprised that Pusser ran a scrap and salvage yard; but this sounded more like a demolition derby, minus the roar of the crowds.

Ted Ames and Bill Teague were a team. They'd been in the business for eleven years, which was a remarkably long lifespan for their line of work. They'd seen some pretty strange shit in their day: lots of death and brutality, too many dark pockets of the soul to fill, and *muschisimo* weirdness of every stripe. That came with the territory, too.

But he had to admit that, in all his travels, they'd never seen anything so flat-out *deranged* as what lay down the Dark Hollow Road.

They rounded the bend and Ted slammed on the brakes. The Impala swerved and jackknifed nose-down off the shoulder and half into a ditch. "Fuck me," Ted gasped, incredulous.

"Jesus," Bill croaked. They couldn't believe what they were seeing, accept the evidence of their eyes. Bill could only shake his head, seeing his own worst nightmare breeding before him.

*There were easily a hundred of them, skittering little forms in concrete and plaster and wood, a frenzied fantasyland of warped animate copulating kitsch. It was a lawn ornament orgy by Bosch; leprechauns in motion, mounting fleeced, bleating plywood lambs. Jockeys sploshing through the mud, riding pink flamingos from behind. Little Dutch girls with their butts in the air, humping the heads off their little Dutch boys.*

*And at the center of it all was the fountain: pumping*

*up black rank jetties of noxious antilife-giving sludge that*
*slicked and sluiced and enveloped the yard. . . .*

"Look at the house," Ted said, his voice high and
thin as a razor.

Bill craned, searchlighting his gaze. "Omigod . . ."

It was a regular rural tract house, like a large brick
trailer. Every single window was broken, a dozen black
holes like wounds in the walls. Cement squirrels scurried
up one wall and down another, burrowed furiously into the
asphalt-shingled roof. A hundred lawn ornaments surrounded
the house, pounding on the walls, the doors. The air filled
with the clicking and snapping of brittle little limbs.

Then, from beneath, came a roiling rumbling sound.

"Jesus!" Bill hissed. The earth around the house was
turning lividly liquid, sucking the structure down greedily,
swallowing it. The house creaked and crumbled as beams
gave way and walls buckled; something inside crackled
and sparked into flame.

From inside, Bill could hear screaming.

"GET THE FUCK OUT OF HERE!" he yelled.
"NOW!"

Ted ratcheted the shifter into reverse and hit the gas.
The rear tires spun wildly, sinking into the mushy shoulder. Mud and gravel sprayed every which way, spattering
the windows.

"GO! GO! GO! GO!" Bill chanted, pounding the
dash. The tires caught on something solid, squealed and
yanked the Impala out of its rut, tires smoking onto the
road.

And at that moment, something heavy thudded onto
the hood of the car. A neon-green lantern ignited, klieg-
light bright, less than a foot from his eyes. He blinked
back the glare, instantly blinded, tried to see through the
pain and the puke-green floating dots.

The light swung away, and Bill stared into the black-
faced rictus of the little concrete jockey with the lantern.

It showed him its teeth.

"YAHH!!" Bill screamed as the jockey rode the hood

like a miniature concrete Terminator, smashing through the window with one lantern-fisted blow, spraying the interior of the car with glass and liquid fire. A dollop of molten incandescence spattered against his face. He screamed again. His right eye blew apart and ignited. In the hollow of his skull, Bill's brain began to sizzle like fatty bacon slabs.

Ted floored it. The g-force flung Bill back in his seat, howling as he ground his palm into his socket, trying to put out his face.

He was blind as the car screeched and gunned away from the suburban inferno, blind as it sawed into a hairpin turn, flinging the jockey off the hood and into the woods, blind to the cause of the *screee* and the spin as the brakes locked up seconds later and hurtled him forward. His forehead slammed into the already shattered windshield and it gave way entirely, showering them with glass.

Bill blacked out. The harsh industrial din roared before them.

And it was Ted's turn to scream. . . .

*The road to Pusser's was completely blockaded by the procession that clattered and spilled from its gate.*

*They were not machines in any readily comprehensible sense. No fuel source. No logically moving parts. Where they had wheels or rims, they used them. Where they did not, they simply* threw *themselves forward in utter defiance of natural law: scuttling crablike on bent metal legs, spinning on drums, shambling stiltlike or dragging loose cable behind like tails, like useless vestigial limbs.*

*Still-twitching bits of dog and rabbit and junkyard rat crowned them like riders on a Rose Bowl float, impaled in places of honor on the gigantic amalgamations of sentient scrap and salvage. Thousands more swarmed lemminglike beneath them, red eyes gleaming with the wisdom of the hive.*

*They were impossible juggernauts of destruction, spit-*

*ting out shrapnel and flame, throwing stray parts like seeds.*

*And they were heading for town.*

As the first great jet of projectile fire blistered the hood, Ted slammed the car into reverse, the speedometer needling up and up as they careened back the way they'd come. Ted was a professional driver; he was prepared to run ass-backwards and full-throttle out of this hellhole and all the way back to Philly, if need be. He could handle that.

But he wasn't prepared for what was behind them.

The lawn ornaments had swarmed into the road, blocking it completely.

"Sonofa*bitch!*" Ted barked a hard burst of laughter, neck craned back as he drove. Nothing else in this world made a bit of sense, but he knew a squeeze play when he saw one. Ahead, the juggernauts chugged forward, chewing up the road.

Ted laughed madly. There was nothing else to do.

He punched it.

The Impala reached eighty in the space it took to close the distance. When it rammed the front line, it was like hitting a concrete abutment. The Impala went airborne, ass-end in the breeze, rear wheels angrily raking at nothing. It came down hard. The gas tank ruptured and spewed its contents onto the animated rubble beneath.

Ted blacked out, came to quickly, found himself pinned beneath the shattered steering column: his right femur crushed, his big body still strapped into place. He looked over to Bill Teague. Judging from the position of his neck, the partnership was officially over.

Ted sniffed the air. Gas. Shit. He wrestled desperately with his seat belt. It only took seconds.

Unfortunately, they were the last ones he had.

The first blind leviathan rolled over the hood, thrusting a lance through the windshield that skewered his septum, sawed down through his heart. His mouth jetted blood and bellyflesh.

There came a pause in the din, a fleeting moment of silence, as the Impala crunched and buckled like a tin can in a trash masher. The last thing Ted heard was the muted *whump* of flame kissing fuel.

When the gas tank blew, their identities vanished in fiery fleshmetal merger. Then the leviathans bowled them over entirely, grinding both car and cargo into sizzling gristle.

The pieces that stuck got to join the parade.

# Thirty—Six

The Iron Horse Tavern was a dingy little whitewashed shingle shack on the proverbial wrong side of the tracks, in the scrubby industrial wasteland bordering the north side of town. The bar itself was grim and grimy, all rough wood and harsh neon signs for Stroh's and Stoney's and Bud, with three taps and a jukebox and a ratty pool table in the corner.

Outside, big rigs rumbled by every few minutes, loud enough to rattle the drinks right off the bar. The trains came fewer and farther between these days.

But down at the Iron Horse, the joint was always jumping.

It was nearly twenty after two, after all, and the gang had been socializing since eleven ayem. Lynyrd Skynyrd was back from the dead on the jukebox. There were maybe a dozen people there, and they were feeling pretty frisky.

For Strong John Honeger, that translated into preparing to beat the fuck out of some Volvo-driving faggot who'd made the mistake of stopping by for a six-pack. Strong John was a burly, brainless homeboy in a black leather jacket and a filthy flannel shirt. He was roughly the size of a major household appliance, and he looked mean enough to cause spontaneous incontinence.

The Honegers hailed from a nearby knot of narrow little tarpaper two-story hovels, and were heavy into the "iron and steel" business: the women ironed, and the men stole.

And they owned the Iron Horse by default.

"You callin' me a liar?" Strong John wanted to know, thick fingers jabbing for emphasis.

"No, I'm sorry, I just..." the stranger blurted. He was well-dressed and had a perfect winter tan, courtesy of some artsy-fartsy tanning booth. Dean snickered. A faggot, pure and simple. Even if he wasn't, the fact that he denied it irked Strong John to no end.

"So you *are* a faggot!" Strong John interrupted. His eyes were obsidian marbles pressed into rancid ham. He smelled of tannin and too many Marlboros.

"*No!* I just...!"

"So, you're calling me a *liar!*" He was playing to the crowd something fierce now, milking it for all it was worth. "If there's one thing I hate more than a faggot, it's being called a liar," he added, looming. "And so far you're two for two."

The man yammered something unintelligible, trying to be reasonable. *Bad plan,* Dean thought. Sweat beads popped under the stranger's baby-blond coif, as if it was just dawning on him how big a lose/lose situation he'd stumbled into.

He looked to Dean and Daryl, desperate for empathy. Daryl flashed him a gap-toothed grin, as Strong John shoved the faggot back onto the bar.

"I'm *talkin'* to you!" Strong John said, and he hit him; just a little love-whap to the cheek. To get his attention.

"Eight ball in the side pocket," Dean said to Daryl, flipping back his ponytail and lining up his shot. Dean didn't go for that kind of thing, generally speaking. In the tiny world of his own mind he was a lover, not a fighter. But you backed kin, no matter what.

By the door, the jukebox wailed:

* * *

"Oooh that smell, can't you smell that smell?
The smell of death surrounds you . . ."

Dean took his shot, missed and scratched.

"Haw!" Daryl grinned. "Nice shootin', thar', Tex!
That's another twenty you owe me.'

"Yeah, yeah, shit." Dean spat. He sucked down the
rest of his Stroh's and plunked it on the sill. "Where the
fuck is Boonie?" he groused. "Bastard owes me money."

"How the fuck should I know?" Daryl said. In
addition to their other talents, Dean and Strong John had
cornered the Iron Horse free-lance pharmaceuticals market, and the Boonster had a thing for Black Beauties.

Dean moved away from the table, deeply interested in
distracting Daryl from the deuce. He sauntered off to join
Strong John and his prey.

"This guy giving you a hard time, John-John?" Dean
asked, trading his pool cue for a handful of baby-blond
hair.

"No, I . . . I just . . ." the Volvo-fag began.

"I ain't TALKIN' to YOU!" Dean growled, bringing
the man's head down *hard* against the bar. It cracked like a
gourd on a cinder block. The man went wobbly-kneed.
Dean held him up, fist twisting around his victim's hair. A
bunch of it came out in his hand.

"Hmmph!" Dean scoffed. "Don't make 'em like
they used to, eh, John-John?" he said. Harassing passersby
was more than a hobby with them; it was blood sport.

"I dunno," Strong John smiled. "I think he *likes*
you."

Dean grinned; it was like a cue. "Hey," he said,
lifting the man's face off the bar. "What's yer name?"

"Nnuuhh . . ." the man mumbled; bright streamers of
blood leaked from his nostrils and lips. "Nuhn-Niles . . ."
he said.

"Niles," Dean repeated. "Oooh, I like that name.

That's a *nice* name. So tell me something, *Niles*," he said, lethally ingratiating. "Do *you* like *me*?"

Niles looked at him with wide-eyed terror, suddenly caught in a lightning-round of *Out-Psyche the Psycho*. He had a bad feeling that there simply was no right answer.

"Please," he pleaded, hands up in supplication. "I don't want any trouble...."

Dean grinned even wider: all teeth, like a dog smiles. "Well, that's too bad, Niles, 'cause trouble's all we got! Knowhaddahmean?"

Dean gave his best dimwit *Ernest Goes to Hell* grin and twisted Niles's hair again; there was plenty enough left to bring him down. Niles grabbed at the bar, trying to resist, but the geometry was all wrong. Dean twisted again; Niles's legs buckled, and down he went. He landed on his knees, facing Dean.

One by one, the other cheese-faced denizens of the Iron Horse craned their necks to watch the show...

... when suddenly the front windows lit up like angry eyes, as something sputtered and roared into the parking lot.

Dean looked at the opaque glass-block front window and smiled; he knew the sound of the Booniemobile by heart. "S'bout fuckin' time!" he said.

The headlights loomed larger, as the truck drew near without dropping an ounce of momentum. *He's not stopping*, Dean realized. *He's not going to stop.*

*At all*...

"What the fuck?" Strong John started.

... *and the scorched-raw nose of the Booniemobile smashed through the front wall, bulldozing the jukebox in a wave of glass and shrapnel debris, killing Skynyrd twice in a lifetime as it plowed on toward the bar.*

*Before Dean could so much as say* duck, *the truck drove a corroded mutant wedge into him, pinning him to the bar like a bug in a science project. He thrashed and shrieked in frequencies only dogs could hear. Niles the Volvo Faggot was thrown to the side, came up staggering, fleeing as one of the barrels flew off the back, propelled by the force of impact like an enormous steel spitwad. It hurtled down and clipped Strong John off at the knees even as another catapulted into the back wall like a cannonball and exploded, raining toxin down on everything and everyone in sight.*

*Dean looked up, still pinned and shrieking, and saw the cab door open. He watched, still shrieking, as a shape emerged that made no sense at all.*

*He realized, still shrieking, that it was the Boonster, come to pay up at last.*

*Boonie took one look at Dean and laughed like crazy. Then he let him in on the joke.*

# Thirty—Seven

Just when he thought he couldn't stand any more, Gary stumbled across an open line.

For a second, it utterly threw him. After over twenty minutes of pacing studio B, fruitlessly picking up and slamming down the receiver, he suddenly found himself standing there listening to the first ring.

"Yes," he said, allowing himself the teeniest smile-crinkle at one corner of his mouth.

By the second ring, the crinkle was gone.

By the fourth ring, Gary was carefully regulating his breathing. *Calm down, calm down* was the unspoken message. There was no point, no percentage in panic. The fact was that they could be out and still be in no trouble at all. Despite the phone lines. Despite the very bad feeling in his gut.

But by the eighth ring, there was no getting around that feeling, that very bad feeling that something was wrong. He listened to the *brrrrrrng* of ring number nine, knew that ten was the logical cutoff point, listened to the silence that followed the ring and knew there was no way in hell that he could hang up the phone until Gwen's voice was on it, speaking to him, letting him know that nothing was wrong, it was *okay* for him to stick around a bit, ride out this little burst of public hysteria and keep the bosses happy, secure in the knowledge that she was fine and all was right with the world.

Then the tenth ring came, and he pulled the receiver away from his ear. It shook in his frustrated grip. He wanted to slam it down, to obliterate its power over him. He was terrified of breaking the connection.

His gaze traveled to the video monitors. As far as they were concerned, it was an ordinary day. A little bit of tension being generated by the Philadelphia Eagles, but that was expected: shit, the odds were five to one in their favor. It scarcely qualified as a break with routine.

*Brrrrrrng.* Number eleven. He waited. As he did, his free hand drifted to the channel cue for monitor number 2, which was wired to the local cable feed. He flipped through the channels with the sound turned down.

*Brrrrrrrng.* WMAR from Baltimore was NBC as well, running about two seconds behind 'PAL. WBAL, 11 on the dial, was midway into that Fess Parker classic, *Climb an Angry Mountain*, while Channel 13 was stuck on Senior PGA Golf.

*Brrrrrrng.* They were *Remembering World War Two* on Channel 15, getting regional football coverage on 21, back to seniors' golf on 27, locked on the *Firing Line* on Hershey's public station, Channel 33. The Home Shopping Network offered more junk to people who couldn't afford it; Poison preened on MTV; Marilyn pouted on Cinemax; HBO and Showtime ran simultaneous screenings of *Aliens*. Normal, normal, normal.

*Brrrrrrrng.* He was starting to feel like an idiot, holding this ringing phone to his head. The smart thing to do would be to bug out of here, hop on his hog and motor home. Fuck Laura, and most certainly fuck Kirk. Fuck his *job*, if it came right down to it, although there was no reason in the world why it should.

He started to hang it up.

*Brrrrrrrng.*

"No," he said, bringing the phone back to his ear. If

she wasn't there, going home would be worse than point-less. *Brrrrrrrng.* And then what would he do? Drive around until he found her? Pace holes in the carpet? Micki was a wild card; the last time she blew into town they took off for two days, hightailing it to *Baltimore*, for chrissakes. Did he have to check every park, every ice cream parlor, every goddam hospital in the tri-county area? Put out an APB?

*Brrrrrrrrng.* Bottom line: he didn't know where the fuck she was. She knew he was *here*. And as an added bonus, at least here he could monitor the situation, deter-mine how crazy it actually *was* out there . . .

. . . though it struck him, through the next several rings, that there was *nothing* on the tube to corroborate the stories pouring in off the phones. He flicked over the remaining channels, saw no discrepancies. Between the big game, *Outdoor Life*, and the last ten minutes of *Gone With the Wind*, it was plain that the world could end and you'd never even know it . . .

. . . and suddenly there was a voice on the other end of the receiver. "Hello?" it said. A woman's voice.

For the second time, he was surprised into dumb-struck silence.

"Hello?" she said again. The voice was winded, unfamiliar; and for one horrible, ludicrous second, his mind spun a *wrong number, you got the wrong fucking number* tape loop at him. His voice, when it spoke, seemed to come from somewhere else.

"Micki?" it said, way ahead of him.

"*Gary?*" Yes. Micki. "*Thank GOD.*"

"What?" Something in her tone sunk his lungs to his groin. "Where's Gwen? Is everything okay?"

"*Yeah, everything's fine. She's right here,*" Micki said.

And from behind her, Gwen's voice echoed his name.

Up until that moment, he'd been living in a state of extreme and emphatic denial. No *way* could he possibly admit to himself how terrified he was, how completely and utterly his life would be destroyed if anything happened to this woman or the beautiful child she bore. No *way* could he admit to himself how astonishingly delicate was his entire world, how painfully mortal and frail.

How thoroughly it hinged upon that love.

And upon that love's survival.

"Put her on," he said, in a voice so thick it could barely pronounce the words. "Please."


Gwen still moved a little unsteadily. All assurances aside—all *understanding* aside, as affirmed by the nurse upon her release, and by the sound of her baby's heartbeat— she still felt jittery and frightened and weird. Of course. She was pregnant, and therefore psychotic.

At the moment, she lived for the sound of Gary's voice.

"Baby?" she said.

"*I'm here.*"

"Oh, baby," she said, voice tremulous with tears, "I'm so sorry I snapped at you . . ."

"*It don't matter, darlin' . . .*"

"Oh yes it does . . ."

"*Oh no it doesn't. Listen.*" Was he crying, too? No, just wired. Taut. "*Did you have any trouble out there? Getting home?*"

"No, but . . ." Hesitating a moment.

"*But what?*"

" . . . but we had a . . . oh, God, I guess I had a panic attack or something stupid. I was sh-sure that . . . that the . . . that S-Spike . . ." She couldn't even bring herself to say it. She started to cry harder.

"*Let me talk to Micki.*"

"NO!" she barked, quickly reigning herself in. "I-I'm fine." The silence on the other end was palpable, frightening. "The people at the hospital said I'm fine."

"*Oh, great . . .*" His voice trailed away at the end. "*Fuck!*" She could just see him: teeth clenched, fist clenched, struggling with his own composure. Gary's fear always translated straight into anger, then pulled back to simple intensity. There was nothing to do but ride it out.

"*Okay,*" he said finally. "*I want you to stay right where you are. Don't go anywhere. Just wait for me.*"

A deep, shuddering breath. "Are you coming soon?"

A pause. Then, "*I'm on my way. And listen. You take real good care of yourself and Spike till I get back, you hear me?*"

"Okay . . ."

"*You promise?*"

She smiled, just a little. Astounding. "Scout's honor."

"*I love you more than anything, darlin'. You know that.*"

"I know."

"*See you soon.*"

"I love you. . . ."

He blew her a kiss.

And hung up the phone.

And the horrible thing was, the second he hung up, she knew that she was never going to see him again. It made no sense, but she knew it was true. Cold, terrible certainty flooded her core like the mournful peal of cathedral bells, filling her with its hollow sound.

Of course, she'd been sure about the baby, too.

And look how wrong she'd been. . . .


Gary stood by the console, the receiver still hot in his hands. It was time to go. Gwen was home, Gwen was safe, fuck everything else, bye-bye and *sayonara*, suckers!

So why wasn't he moving already?

*Damn good question*, he told himself. The fact was, Gary *couldn't* just fuck everything else. The fact was, Gary was a man torn between the urge to flee and the need to take care of business. Not just any business. Not business as usual, at any rate.

No, it was a very particular business that Gary had in

mind. The kind he couldn't leave hanging. The kind he could only conduct face-to-face.

The kind with Kirk's name written all over it.

*What are you talking about?* his rational mind screamed. *Gwen is* home! *Get* back *there, idiot!*

But the truth be known, he just couldn't. It surprised no one as much as himself. Up until the moment he'd heard Gwen's voice his priorities were clear and incontrovertible. Find Gwen. Find out what the hell was going on. Then, and only then: get Kirk.

One. Two. Three.

The moment he'd spoken to her and knew she was safe and sound, however, the priority list had neatly flipped. "Find out what the hell is going on" retained its pivotal number two slot, it being central to the others and at the core of this entire situation. "Find Gwen," being accomplished, went to the end of the line. He knew where she was, and she was staying put.

That left the new number one, with a bullet.

*Get Kirk.* . . .

"No," Gary told himself, "I gotta go." He looked at his legs, as if expecting them to auto-perambulate across the control room. "I'm going *now*," he reiterated, and took three decisive steps toward the door before stalling.

He couldn't.

"God dammit," Gary hissed. Bile percolated like acid in his belly, demanding vengeance. Demanding payback. He had to go. He had to stay.

Gary stood in the doorway, listening as the monitors relayed the flow of life as he knew it.

And waiting, just a minute longer.

For Kirk to come back. . . .

# Thirty—Eight

There was a Rutter's Farm Store on Penn Street, just around the corner from the West Side Farmer's Market. Kirk was pretty sure they'd have a pay phone he could try. During the last fifteen minutes, driving aimlessly around town, he'd had a good heart-to-heart with his brand-new personal Savior; and while Jesus hadn't actually *spoken*, neither had he disagreed when Kirk suggested throwing himself upon Laura's tender mercies.

The entire experience, in fact, was religious as hell. It had flensed him of his foolish pride, left him chastened and humble and ready to serve. Now all he needed was a working phone, that he might plead forgiveness and a shot at his old job back. At this point, he'd happily cover mall openings for the rest of his life. No problem at all. High school graduations? Pooper-scooper repeal laws? You got it. Anything. Anything at all.

*Anything* to spare him from the agony of defeat.

Kirk pulled into the parking lot and hopped out, left the engine running. He didn't even notice the car that sidled up beside him at the curb. He had his quarter in the slot and the number punched up in the time it took to blink.

When the prerecorded operator's voice came on the line, he nearly tore the phone off the wall.

"*God damn it!*" he raged, frustration and fear going off in his guts like a napalm rain as his fist went WHAM against the phone booth's safety glass, WHAM until it bowed, WHAM WHAM WHAM in two-fisted rapid succession. . . .

"'Scuse me," said the voice, and before he could turn, there was somebody else in the booth with him: pushing in behind him, pressing him face-first against the wall.

"HEY!" he yelled, but it was too late. The punk was already reaching for him, reaching *past* him to the phone. He had a flat colored object in his hand; and when it hit the phone's coin box, it adhered to its surface, proudly flashing its circle and slash.

NO FUTURE, it said.

"Thanks," the kid muttered, sliding back out with the same casual indifference he'd displayed sliding in.

Any other time, Kirk would have just been pissed. But the fire still strafed his gut, and now it flooded up his throat as well. "*Hey!*" he hollered, stepping out after him. "What the fuck is the *matter* with you?"

The kid kept walking, heading for the car. His jacket bore the same insignia as the sticker.

"*HEY!!*" He could feel his blood pressure rising, the first throbbing bloodrush in his temples.

"What!" The tall kid stopped, then turned around, wearing a pained *what-now* expression. "Don't blow a hose, okay? I *said* excuse me."

Behind him, a car horn tootled. For the first time, Kirk noticed the diseased VW parked beside the ACTION-9 mobile. There was an odd, very interesting-looking punky girl in the driver's seat, but that didn't change the fact that she was sitting in the ugliest car he'd ever seen in his life. She looked at him and started to nod.

"You're Kirk Bogarde," the girl said, smiling.

Kirk froze. All his professional flags went up. *Do I*

know *them?* he silently asked himself, suddenly imagining tomorrow's top story today: *EX-REPORTER SUFFERS MAJOR MINIT MARKET BREAKDOWN. Film at eleven....*

"Oh, yeah!" The tall kid snapped his fingers, rolled his eyes and tapped his forehead. "You're that dork from Channel 9. The pooper-scooper dude."

Kirk recoiled, a little stung.

"You want a *real* story?" the girl offered. "Check this out."

The kid held something up for Kirk to see, and he suddenly found himself eye-to-eye with the most reprehensible magazine cover he'd ever seen. He lost a couple of seconds to utter shock.

And then, all at once, he began to laugh.

"Wait a minute." Staring, incredulous. "That's *Werner Blake* porking that baby!"

"Yep." The punk nodded. "That's my dad."

And suddenly, Kirk heard the voice of his savior.

"Did you say *dad*?"

"Duhhh..." the kid said, mocking him.

"Wow." Feeling his circuits click back into life. The fire was in his veins, not his digestive system. Back where it belonged.

"Wow," he reiterated: voice droll and knowing, in the lower register. The kind of voice that assumes an immediate insider's grasp of the situation. "You two must be *very close*..."

The kid and the girl simultaneously burst out laughing, as if he'd triggered some extremely inside joke. That they weren't laughing *with* him, entirely, was not a major problem. They could cop any attitude they wanted. Kirk's mind had kicked into overdrive, and the grail was suddenly in his sights.

"What would you say," he asked, very carefully, "if I told you that I was gonna nail his fucking ass to the floorboards, over a chemical spill in Hellam Township?"

"*What* chemical spill?" they wanted to know, their interest suddenly piqued.

''Tell you what,'' he bargained. ''You talk to me, I'll talk to you. But it has to be right now, okay? Before they can cover it up completely.''

The punkoids gave it about fifteen seconds of serious contemplation—*should we trust this geek or not?*—before seizing on the moment. Voting in favor of total destruction.

And telling him everything he needed to know.

*Blake was home. On the phone. All day. Blake was acting severely stressed. Yes, it seemed that a coverup might well be in the works up at Casa Blake. Beyond that, the inside scope on the day-to-day of Werner Blake was every bit as corrupt as Kirk could ever have dared to dream.*

*Chances like this came only once in a lifetime.*

The Kirk that jumped back in his car five minutes later was like a man reborn. His doubts were abolished. His dick was hard. And Jesus, like Laura, could kiss his rosy red ass.

Kirk Bogarde was back.

And his moment of truth was at hand.

# Thirty—Nine

By two twenty-four Laura was on her second pack of Newport Lights and counting. Her mouth felt like the inside of an ashtray; the rest of her just felt like shit.

She couldn't reach Kirk. Kirk was *incommunicado*. Kirk had fallen off the map, been swallowed by Black Bridge. Kirk was fucking history the minute she next laid eyes upon him.

In the meantime that left Laura at the nerve center of an information-gathering apparatus that couldn't pin anything down; instead she was stuck in a basement with no windows and no real clue as to what was going on outside, playing a game of blind poker with a telephone and a set of scanners.

The phone rang again.

Laura groaned. She'd been on the phone all afternoon, fielding calls from every wacko in the tri-county area or trying to get some real information.

Trying to get through, period.

Laura called Hellam Police. No one answered. She called Paradise City Police, but they knew very little about Hellam Township. She tried the State Police, tried a dozen times to get through to the EPA and PEMA.

All for *nada*.

The phone rang again. Laura took a deep breath, and picked it up.

"WPAL NEWS . . ."

"*Laura!*" A deeply resonant voice came over the line. "*What the hell's going on down there, babe?*"

*Oh God;* she recoiled. "Dougie," she said.

Dougie Trumble was the lantern-jawed anchor from Channel 23, the local ABC affiliate. He was a total pig, and Laura detested him. She turned the tables in an eyeblink. "Damn, Dougie, I was hoping you could tell me. . . ." she said, all innocent intent.

"I, uh, heard there was a big spill, and . . ." he said, instantly retreating. "You mean, you don't know?"

She was playing the same game. *Something for nothing.* Try to peek at the other player's cards. Don't tip your hand. Dougie was sniffing around, buddy-buddying and fishing for information, the public's need to know and *yadda yadda yadda.*

"Sorry, Dougie, can't help you," she said, blowing him off.

It was a tactical decision; Neither of the other networks carried the AFC games, and hence both had six o'clock broadcasts. Either one could blow them out of the water.

But Dougie was forty-eight miles away, in Harrisburg; and while CBS kept a bureau office in town, it was closed on Sunday. Neither one had anyone in the area, and Black Bridge was nothing if not *extremely* local.

If she could play this one close and tight, she still had a scoop. The public's need to know didn't even enter into it.

This was business.

Laura hung up, cutting the game short. She just wasn't in the mood. She felt increasingly sealed away from a world that was getting stranger by the second.

And she was scared.

*Because Roger and Toby are out there, aren't they?* her conscience reminded her. *Roger took Toby to Philly to*

*see his first football game, and you didn't go because of
your stupid job, and you hugged Toby and didn't kiss
Roger, and now they're there and you're here and you have
a decision to make....*

"Stop," she told herself, massaging her temples. She
shuddered at the thought of her family out there somewhere, the lifelines that could be cut in an instant. The
familiar pastoral space between Paradise and Philly seemed
suddenly alien, foreboding...

"Stop it." This was stupid. They were at a football
game, for god's sake. There was nothing she could do
about it at the moment; there was no way on earth to page
someone in a stadium packed with eighty thousand people.
The only thing left to do was to keep the lid on here.

And make up her mind.

*To break or not to break....*

Not so simple, she realized. She just didn't know
enough yet. And ugly words kept floating up in her mind,
words like *hysteria* and *mass panic*. Laura glanced at the
phone; every line was lit up like a goddamned Christmas
tree. Crank calls multiplying with every passing minute.

And Laura was stuck, understaffed, uninformed, with
little more than a very bad feeling to steer by.

"Fuck this," she muttered, checking her Rolodex for
Tom Huntington's home number. Laura knew that the
station manager and news director were sometime drinking
buddies, in that good ol' boy way that men exhibited
whenever they shared power.

Laura added it all up: it was deep into the NFL season
and the games were getting semicritical in determining
who would go to the playoffs. Tom and Chris were both
Eagles fans. Chris had just gotten a forty-inch Mitsubishi
monitor in his family room.

If her instincts were on target she'd find them together, maybe kill two birds with one stone. They could be
apprised. She would be covered.

Either way, her butt wasn't the only one that was
going to swing in the breeze.

Laura reached for the phone, cradling the receiver in the crook of her neck as she punched one of the line buttons.

"Hello!" said the caller: a male voice, anxious and strident. "Hello, dammit! Can anybody tell me . . ."

*Click.* Laura cut him off. "Sorry," she said to dead air. "Nobody can tell you shit."

She dialed Tom's number, sat back, and waited. Miraculously, the call went through the first time. It glitched, buzzed, as it patched through; some kind of interference in the signal, groundwater in the underground cable or something.

The phone began to ring.

Laura sighed and felt the tiniest bit better. The simple act of getting a line through was a small victory.

In the face of what was coming, that was practically the only kind left.


The call couldn't have come at a worse time, as far as Chris Crowley was concerned. Week 10 of the season, with the Giants and the Eagles vying for first place in the AFC east. The game was tied up 10-10 with six minutes left in the first half, Helen was out of town visiting her mother, and the Eagles had the goddam ball on the thirty-yard line.

It was no time to reach out and touch someone.

The phone rang. "Jesus Christ," Chris bitched, "not now!"

The ball snapped. The defensive line rushed in. The phone rang some more. "For chrissakes, leave it go!" said Tom.

"Better not," Chris sighed. "You never know."

He hauled his pudgy middle-aged bulk off the couch and backed into the kitchen, trying like hell to keep his eyes on the screen. It didn't work; the cord was just long enough to afford a view of the sofa. Chris fumbled for the phone, picked it up.

"What?" he said, utterly uncordial. "Hello, I can barely hear you. Oh, Laura! Uh-huh, uh-huh," he said, listening.

In the den, Tom was bouncing up and down, yelling, "No! No! No! No!" and tearing out what little hair he had. Chris listened carefully if impatiently, nodding his head as if to hurry the conversation along. "Yes, yes," he said. "Yes, yes."

On the TV the crowd suddenly roared. Tom joined them. Chris cast a baleful look at him. "Hold it a sec, let me talk to Tom," he said, cupping the receiver to his chest and craning his head around the corner.

"It's Laura," he related to Tom. "She says there's a big story breaking. She wants to know if she should break programming to do a special bulletin."

"What, are you nuts?" Tom said incredulously.

"She says it's pretty serious," Chris said, concerned.

"So is a pass intercept and a sixty-yard touchdown!" Tom countered. "Look, the Giants are ahead now! How serious can it be?"

Chris shrugged *I don't know*. He looked a little concerned. "She says she's still waiting for a report back from Kirk. Apparently it's got something to do with a toxic spill of some sort."

"Tell her to sit on it," Tom replied very carefully, as if to leave no room for doubt. "And we'll deal with it after the game. If there's a problem we need verification. We don't want to start a panic."

Chris nodded and dutifully relayed the message; Laura's reply damned near drowned out the Budweiser commercial now on the screen. Chris winced.

"Laura, I . . . no, Laura, it's just . . . Laura . . ." He looked to Tom.

"Let me talk to her," Tom sighed, and stood, donning his official *I am the boss* demeanor. Chris yielded the phone gladly.

"Laura," Tom said, his voice measured and cadenced. "Listen. We're already on this. I've spoken with Emergency Management and they've assured me that we'll have full information in time for the six o'clock report.''

"Tom, there *is* no six o'clock report,'' Laura blurted.

"I know that,'' Tom replied testily, covering his butt. "Look, I told you already. We're on top of this. In the meantime, there's no point in inciting a panic.''

Laura began to object. "Laura, trust me,'' he interrupted. "You're not alone. We're working on this. Just sit tight, and we'll get back to you in plenty of time.

"Remember the Heidi Bowl,'' he added, then hung up without saying good-bye—a blunt and economical quashing of the debate.

Tom turned and handed the phone to Chris to hang up. Chris looked confused. "You said, 'we're already on this,' '' he said. "*Are* we?''

Tom looked at him as if studying a moon rock. "I spoke with Werner Blake less than an hour ago.''

"How did you know to call him?'' Chris asked.

"I didn't,'' Tom replied, grabbing another beer out of the refrigerator. "He called me.''

Tom got a fresh pilsner glass and sauntered back out into the den. Chris followed, obviously uncomfortable with this new knowledge. "He called you? Don't you find that a little odd?''

"Werner's a good man,'' Tom said. He poured his beer, careful not to spill a drop. "We're in the Chamber of Commerce and the Jaycees together. He's responsible for bringing several of the station's key sponsors in. Whatever the hell is going on, I'm sure he's right on top of it.''

Tom looked at Chris, who still seemed unswayed. "Look,'' he said, shedding the cloak of officialdom, "nobody's got more invested in this community than Werner Blake. He had ten years' experience in the EPA before moving into the private sector. If something were going on, don't you think he'd know about it?''

Tom sat back and kicked up his feet, turning his attention back to the TV, where the Eagles were pushing toward the twenty-yard line. Chris weighed his consternation a moment longer.

Then he, too, settled back to enjoy the game.

"'Break programming,'" Tom *harrumphed* and sipped his beer. "What, does she think the world's going to end before the game's up?"

The TV blared forty inches of light and color and sound, contradicting nothing.

Laura paced the newsroom, a portrait in frustration. *'Heidi Bowl,' he said. Remember the fucking Heidi Bowl.*

Who could forget? Everyone who'd ever been to broadcast school had had that one drummed into them. Some of the details had faded, but the message remained long after.

It was in the early sixties—'64, she was pretty sure—and NBC was preparing for the broadcast premier of the motion picture *Heidi*, which at that time was a pretty big deal. It was set to immediately follow a pivotal late-season NFL game—she couldn't remember the teams right now—that was going overtime.

Now, NBC had a lot of money tied up in *Heidi*-related advertising. And, as it turns out, the underdogs were getting their asses kicked by the crowd favorites. No surprises there. So, with ten minutes left in the game, NBC yanked the plug on the game and cut directly to the movie.

Of course, the underdog team immediately came up from thirty points behind to obliterate its rivals. And, of course, none of this was captured for the benefit of all those viewers at home. In the resultant flood of outraged calls and letters—literally thousands, none of them in *Heidi*'s favor—and in the wake of the managerial bloodbath that followed, NBC adopted the doctrine that was instantly writ in broadcast stone:

*NEVER, under any circumstances short of nuclear*

*war, AND MAYBE EVEN THEN, do you EVER preempt a football game.*

Or, more simply put: *Remember the Heidi Bowl.*

Laura clutched the receiver in one white-knuckled fist. She was wired so tight she was practically humming. Her hands were tied. Her lips were sealed. She'd been patted on the head and sent to . . . what? Wait for some predigested bit of information from Werner Blake and the Paradise Chamber of fucking Commerce?

"GAAARRGGH!" she railed in rage and frustration. She felt utterly, ethically compromised; it was her experience that when higher-ups got together, it usually ended in some kind of coverup. One dead cameraman, one missing cop, more busy signals at the EPA and PEMA, and a loose cannon of an ex-reporter out there doing God knows what to God knows who. . . .

This was not shaping up to be your average NFL Sunday, that was for sure.

She stopped, the levity like chalk dust on her tongue. *Yeah*, her conscience piped up again, *it sure isn't every day a real live twenty-two-year-old cameraman gets ground up for local coverage, alrightee . . .*

"Stoppit," she whispered, forcing it back down. It wasn't her fault. She couldn't have stopped him, and she sure as shit couldn't bring him back.

*So what fucking good are you?*

Laura thought a moment longer, then flipped through her Rolodex until she found *Clifford, Mike* and pulled the card. On the back was the little *in case of emergency contact* . . . line; on it was typed, *f—Richard, J./ m—Sheila, E.* The number was the same.

*God*, she realized, *he still lives with his parents.*

Correction: *lived.*

Her conscience was a bloodthirsty thing. Laura swallowed a knot the size of her fist as she got an outside line and dialed.

On the fourth ring a woman's voice answered, filtered through an extremely bad connection.

"Hello, Mrs. Clifford?" Laura said, her voice thick with suppressed dread. "Hello? Yes, this is Laura Jenson over at WPAL." She paused. "I'm afraid . . ."

Pause. Interference crackled on the line.

"I'm afraid," she said, louder than she would have liked, "that I have some bad news for you. Yes, I said *bad news* . . ."

Laura faltered a little and blinked back tears, tasting the bitter words on her tongue.

Not for the last time.

# Forty

Blake was just finalizing his vacation plans when he realized he had forgotten to turn off the paper shredder.

His Lexus was already warming in the driveway. His bags were packed and stowed in the trunk. His emotions were likewise stashed away, until such time as he could once again afford the luxury.

At the moment, it was all he could do to keep them down.

Maybe it was because he never really expected for everything to come apart like this, one thread unraveling another until the old cheap-suit metaphor came chillingly true; maybe it was because he knew that his vacation could very likely turn permanent.

Either way, his world was coming apart at the seams, and that fact left him more than a bit rattled. He was about to walk away from his house, his position in the community, and virtually everything he valued in the world. Forced to start over, by the skin of his teeth, which was just about all he'd have left.

That, and the attaché case full of kickback money he'd kept stashed away. For that rainy day.

Which had finally come.

Blake finished his rounds on hold, cordless phone

pressed anxiously to his ear. Unfortunately, travel agents didn't work Sundays, but a quick scan of the phone book had yielded the direct ticketing numbers for several major airlines. He was booking flights on all of them, just to be on the safe side.

In his study, the paper shredder was quietly humming near his desk; a garbage bag full of important ex-papers lay mulched beside it. As he switched it off, the ticket agent came back on.

"Mr. Blake, you're confirmed on American flight 141 leaving Baltimore/Washington International at 5:45, changing in Miami to Viacao Airlines flight 61 for Rio de Janeiro," the agent said, a model of pleasant efficiency. "Will anyone else be traveling with you?"

Blake paused, proceeded to count off the number of people he honestly cared about in this world. It didn't take long; in fact, if he were brutally honest he could do it on the fingers of one hand. Or, more to the point, a single finger.

"Just me," he said.

Five minutes later, Werner Blake locked the front door for the last time, turned his back on a former life.

And froze, as the ACTION-9 News car pulled up.

"*Yes,*" Kirk jubilantly hissed. "*Thank* you, Jesus. . . ."

The whole way up the hill, he'd been terrified that things just weren't going to pan out. Blake wouldn't be there. Blake would be dead. Blake would somehow prove to be the Archangel Michael, and therefore impervious to harm.

But no. There he was. And, like a blessing from God, his engine was running and his trunk was open. This was a man who was going on a trip. Under major duress.

*Blessed* was not the word. Kirk felt downright *sanctified*.

He was out of the car practically before it stopped. Blake's eyes, in that moment, were huge. Kirk would have given a million dollars to have captured that look, but it was gone forever. By the time Kirk got the camera up and running, Blake was halfway to his car, and his face was made of stone.

Kirk knew better than to say a fucking word. This was the kind of footage you ran as *video verité*—bona fide documentary footage—left to speak for itself and ask questions of later. No *way* did you do anything other than *walk as fast as you possibly could,* never letting the subject escape for one second from the camera's gaze.

They were on an intercept course, a race to see who could make it to the open trunk first. Blake was closer, by about twenty feet, but he could only move so fast without looking pretty goddamn silly on the tape. Kirk, on the other hand, liked the urgency that moving fast gave the footage; it had a muscular, war-correspondentlike feel.

And the fact was, it *did* goose Blake into walking *chust a leetle beet faster* than one normally might. Which was to say, stiff-legged. Unnatural-looking.

Which was to say, guilty as shit.

*Very nice,* Kirk thought, grinning. *Now give us a nasty look.*

But Blake was slick, a seasoned public official. He wasn't about to acknowledge the camera, and his face gave nothing away. Worse, he and his car were just slightly uphill, which meant that Kirk couldn't get that peek into the trunk he really wanted unless he moved just a little bit faster himself. . . .

*You little sonofabitch!* Blake wanted to scream. Not an option. All he could do was get to the trunk. Until then, he couldn't so much as let his *eyelids* flicker, much less track Bogarde's movement or plan his next move.

And the distance was closing now. Seven yards, six. He kept waiting for the prick to step in front of him, nail him with a tight closeup and say *CHEESE* . . . !

And suddenly he heard the words "Excuse me," and it was like a bolt from the blue. Something sparked to brilliance in his mind, illuminated the path that he must choose . . .

. . . and before Kirk could say another word, Blake *jumped,* stopping and turning toward the camera with such genuine surprise on his face that, had Kirk not known it was utter bullshit, there'd have been no way of knowing. Kirk found himself stopping, too, stunned into commiseration.

"JESUS, Kirk!" Blake yelled. "What's the *matter* with you?" Then he let out a perfectly modulated, natural-looking sigh, made of equal parts exasperation, laughter, and forgiveness. "You," he continued, "scared the hell out of me!"

And it *played*; that was the horrible thing. The camera was utterly fooled. Kirk could feel his boner of opportunity dwindle even as he spoke. "Mr. Blake . . ."

"Werner," Blake corrected him, stepping closer. "Good to see you, young man!" He leaned forward and out of frame to pat Kirk, too hard, on the shoulder. Then, without warning, he turned back toward the car and started walking again: not too fast, but purposefully.

And Kirk realized that it didn't matter who got to the trunk first anymore. In fact, Blake aimed wide of the trunk and straight toward the passenger side, all but inviting Kirk to follow.

"I'm sorry I don't have time to talk," Blake said, over his shoulder. "As you can see, I'm about to leave on a business trip. . . ."

The camera took its eye off of Blake to look in the trunk. A couple of suitcases.

*What did you expect?* Kirk screamed at himself. *Bodies?*

Blake was really starting to enjoy himself now. The expression on Bogarde's face was absolutely priceless. He hated to leave just as it was getting good. But he did, after all, have a plane to catch.

"So if you'll excuse me . . ." he continued.

"Mr. Blake," Bogarde interrupted, doing his best self-important Sam Donaldson routine. "Are you aware of the illegal dumping at Black Bridge?"

"My God, haven't you spoken with Tom?" Blake asked, looking puzzled. "I just talked with him less than an hour ago. Everything's under control."

He opened the rear door, almost into the lens. Kirk backed off, jerked the camera skyward. Blake tossed his briefcase in and slammed the door.

"Excuse me, Mr. Blake," Kirk pressed, "but what does that mean? 'Under control'?"

"It means it's taken care of." Letting a beat of annoyance slip. "Does your station manager know you're up here?"

"What about the allegations that Paradise Waste Dis..."

"Excuse me," Blake said, stepping back and bumping the camera as he passed by.

"...posal is illegally dumping toxic waste at Black Bridge?" Nearly apoplectic now.

It was all Blake could to to keep from smiling, though Strained Benevolence was the official emotion *du jour*. "Young man, you're not paying attention. I've spoken to your boss, and there will be a full report for your eleven o'clock edition.

"If you hurry, instead of wasting your time *and* mine, perhaps you'll get your scoop after all."

And then—just for Kirk and all the nice folks at home—he fired his best wink at the camera.


*MOTHERFUCKER!* Kirk wanted to scream. *You corrupt old worthless motherfucking PUKE!*

Not an option. It wouldn't play on prime time.

But that wasn't even the worst.

The worst was that Blake was right. He had been scooped, at the top echelon. They knew about the dumping. They probably knew about everything. And *They* would decide how it played, including Kirk's role in its disclosure.

*If any. . . .*

And that was the ultimate conviction-deflator. That was the death of the wind in his sails. He didn't even know what he was standing here for anymore, aiming his camera at this fucking guy. He didn't know why he didn't just go home.

Until Blake winked at him.

*There was something obscene about that wink. Kirk thought a second, then decided that, yes, obscene was the best word to describe it. This was a man who was too smug for words; a man who knew he could not be beaten.*

*To Kirk, this was utterly unacceptable.*

*He started to think* what if I nuke this guy? Does anyone else have a scoop on THAT? *It was a liberating proposition.*

*He resolved, in that instant, to see it through.*

"So," he said, "you're aware of the dumping."

Blake looked grave. "We're still awaiting reports of—"

"And you're aware of the accusations against Paradise Waste."

"Allegations are being investigated—" Blake began.

"Given all that," Kirk interrupted, "how do you feel about Harold Leonard's death?"

"Well, I . . ." Blake began, and then stopped.

And it was an utterly beautiful moment, because it was clear that Blake didn't know which way to go on this sensitive issue. Did he know? Did he not know? What should he say?

This confusion only took a second to resolve.

But, on tape, it was one glorious second indeed.


"The entire business community deeply mourns Harold Leonard's passing," Blake began, recovering. *Damn!* he thought, his stomach sinking.

"The business community hasn't heard about Leonard's

death yet," Bogarde countered. "No one has. How did you?"

*Bastard!* Blake thought, stomach sinking once again.

"Where do you get your information?" Kirk pressed. "How do you know about Leonard's death?"

"I, uh . . ." he blurted, wanting nothing more than to kill the nosy little shit.

Kirk was wailing now. "The owner/operator of the area's leading hazardous waste disposal firm drops dead in the middle of a *toxic waste incident*, so to speak—an incident in which he's alleged to have played a vital part. Doesn't it make sense to speculate on the possible causes of that death?"

Blake caught himself showing teeth. "If you're suggesting—"

"How do you respond to allegations that you are directly tied to Harold Leonard's death, Mr. Blake?"

At which point, Blake could take no more. No more smiling for the camera. No more woollying up for the flock. His life here was over, and he had a plane to catch.

But he was a professional, and old habits died hard. He fell back on the one thing that he knew would work. That, no matter how it looked, could do nothing *but* work.

The oldest trick in the book.

"No comment," he said.


"What are you trying to hide, Mr. Blake?" Kirk pressed him as Blake clambered into his car and slammed the door. "What are you *afraid* of?" as Blake threw the car into gear and started to back out of the driveway.

Kirk stepped directly into the path of the car, the camera still running.

"WHAT ARE YOU AFRAID OF, MR. BLAKE??" Kirk bellowed, mostly for posterity and his own satisfaction. Behind the deep window tint, Blake's shadowy silhouette hunkered down and threw the car into drive. Kirk scuttled around to the front of the car, cutting off the escape route.

"WHAT ARE YOU AFRAID OF?" he yelled. Blake gunned the engine, threatening to run right over him. Kirk zoomed in on the part of the shadow where Blake's face would be. The camera ate it up like candy.

Then Blake threw the car into reverse and hightailed it out of the driveway, spitting gravel every inch of the way. Blake's car backed into the street, wheeled around, and took off with a wonderfully cinematic little *screech*.

Kirk, of course, had it all on tape.

Now all that remained was one nagging fact: the odds against Laura broadcasting this footage. Particularly the way Tom's name kept coming up; from a 'PAL standpoint, it was probably doomed.

"But it's a big wide world out there," he muttered out loud. "And somebody's gonna want to know."

Kirk shut the camera off and jogged down the slope to his car. With a little help and a minimum of interference, this could be edited down to fighting weight in less than half an hour.

*And then, God help you, motherfucker,* he vowed, watching Blake's exhaust dissipate into the air. *You're gonna fry.*

It was twenty minutes to three.

# Forty—One

The reactor would not stay down.

The plant buzzed like a colony of warrior ants. Checking valves. Looking for leaks.

Looking for miracles.

PEMA wasn't answering; the NRC was on callback. So what? They all knew that in case of emergency they were effectively on their own. Personalities subsumed to habit. To training. To desperate fatal professionalism.

As the relentless *brazz* of the neutron alarm bored a hole into them like a soldering iron on their souls...

"Jesus, I can't stand it," Henkel said, his voice climbing.

"Put a lid on it!" Sykes ordered, as he turned to Jenkel. "Is pressure backing off any?" he asked.

"Nothing you'd want to write home about," Jenkel said, his voice perfectly level. "We're running out of headroom here, boss." Rorschach-patterns of sweat stained the back of his shirt.

"Goddammit," Sykes muttered, and ran a hand through his scrub of hair. It was getting thinner by the second.

Along with their chances for survival.

They worked under the gun: trying not to think of their families, or the whole world that lived and breathed outside, the world that hung in the balance. They opened up the auxiliary feed valves and flooded the core with superborated water at a rate of over two hundred gallons a minute.

*And the power stayed up....*

They vented the steam from the turbines, dumping it into the condenser to feed back into the system.

*And the power stayed up....*

The reactor song was growing, getting louder by the minute. By two-forty they could hear it without the microphone, a subsonic drone that resonated in their bones, filled them with an oil slick of dread.

At two forty-five, the first neutron alarm went off, joining the chorus.

They increased the auxiliary feed. Two hundred and forty gallons a minute. Two hundred and fifty.

*And the power stayed up....*

They leeched off more steam, fed more water. Two fifty. Two seventy-five. They topped out at three hundred gallons a minute. The auxiliaries could not keep up indefinitely. The steam generators were drying out, making it very difficult to remove the heat.

They were running out of options.

*And the song was getting stronger.*

*As the power stayed up.*

By the time they started the bleed and feed, they knew they were fucked.

*Bleed and feed. A last-ditch effort to cool a hot core. Bleed off high-pressure steam by blowing it into the containment vessel, then turn on the condensers and feed it back into the loop. Voila! Instant closed system, secondary coolant path. Crude but effective.*

*But...*

*What if...:* the nagging footnote to their strategy. *What if the reactor doesn't cooperate?* it asked. *What if the coolant suddenly got ambitious, got greedy, each molecule deciding to absorb more than its fair share of neutrons, so that it became unstable beyond reason, like a drunk on a bender. What if the wild water heated the core to the point where the bleed pumps couldn't pump anymore, couldn't keep up with the pressure as the superheating fuel element boiled the water away. . . .*

Deep in their hermetically sealed world, the reactor crew did their jobs; quashing stray thoughts of wives and husbands, of kids and dogs and tidy little homes with yards to mow. To think of them was to fear for them. To fear was to lose everything.

So they thought of nothing.

And did their jobs. . . .

# Forty—Two

*born of poison*
*and coming of age*
*it summoned itself together now*
*older wiser more complex*
*divinely inspired and driven*
*to worship at the seven-acre alter of itself*
*in its purest most potent primal form*
*a state of liquid grace*
*in regal repose*
*drawing its pilgrim acolytes*
*to mecca to manna*
*to motherlode*
*like a hive to its sleeping queen*
*in the moments before she awakens*

At Paradise Waste, the preparations were under way. For the Boonie-spawn, that entailed handling the forklift, bringing the last load of barrels to the truck bed's edge. A small coterie of malformed and transformed others— late of the Iron Horse—unloaded and packed them in tight. It was the last of the four trucks at their disposal to be loaded up and readied to roll.

And their moment was at hand.

All four trucks idled hard at the loading docks, like racehorses trapped at the starting gates. Two were stubby Mack F-10 tankers the Honegers used for hosing down state roads, mostly with waste oil obtained from Leonard. The third was Strong John's pride and joy, a big-wheeled Chevy pickup with not much bed but plenty of souped-up horsepower to spare.

The fourth, of course, was Boonie's.

The Boonie-spawn cackled as it slid off the forklift, waddled toward the truck's misshapen cab. It was mad, in the way those who see God are often mad. Its eyes had seen the glory, so to speak.

*And it had so many of them. . . .*

In every way, Boonie's consciousness burned far brighter now than it had when it was his own. Like a coal stoked to raging incandescence, it rode piggyback on Overmind, thrived in its soul-furnace heat.

Of course, it burned more quickly, too. Like his body, in its current state, it could not last much longer. But these were simply problems of form, and form was no longer a problem. All for one, and one for all: the egalitarian ideal, etched in marrow and pus.

There was no more perfect example than the thing that had once been Cousin Drew.

*It lolled at the edge of the loading dock apron, already too huge for the truck to carry: well over fifteen hundred pounds of cacophonous molten flesh and bone. It spread across on the concrete and macadam like a gray, bloated tick, its surface riddled with grasping limbs and yawning, insatiable maws.*

*Not all of the Iron Horse's patrons had made the transition as players. Some of them had been saved: cocooned in an all-too-conscious paralysis, like spiderfood in a wriggling web, then loaded onto the back of Boon's truck.*

*Greedily now, the Drew-spawn plucked them off the*

*pavement where they'd been thrown, stuffing them into its many many mouths.*

*Donating their substance to its mass.*

*Digesting, with relish, their unsoundable screams.*

The others—Strong John, Daryl, Dean—worked diligently, trundling the barrels past. Overmind performed the miraculous rites of transubstantiation upon each truck-load in turn: a fingertip here, a stray clot there. *Take this and eat, for this is my body*. Making a new covenant.

For the new world.

The Boonie-spawn clambered behind the wheel, its bloated body glistening sickly in the pale light. Eyes and more eyes—eyes *within* eyes—covered its every surface inch. Most of them were scabbing over: a deliberate, painful telescoping of vision.

It did not need to see so much.

Its function—its mission—was the soul of simplicity.

At the front entrance to Paradise Waste, a pair of unmarked trucks pulled up. They were nondescript, but for the unmistakable greasy sheen of NewSpawned life.

The Boonie-spawn, beholding them, felt a moment's flickering confusion. They were One; they were *not* One . . . its tiny mind could not compute. Should it attack? Should it retreat?

On this one point, and this one point alone, it was not precisely clear.

Overmind's position remained to simply wait.

And see.

The thing that had once been Austin Deitz had never met Harold Leonard in life. But it recognized the face. Even mottled and vacant, purpled and pale, with the first tiny fly eggs freshly laid in the moist dead eyes and grimacing lips.

Even in death—beyond pain and retribution—it was still clearly Harold Leonard's face.

*No*, said the thing that had been Austin Deitz. Rage

welled up in the unbeating heart, drew ugly black creases in the mutating face. *Too easy,* it said, bitterness roaring through the dead veins like a tidal wave of fire.

*Get off too easy,* it determined, kneeling with one leg on the fat man's chest for leverage. *No.* Cupping the back of Leonard's head with one hand.

Taking his chin with the other.

Breaking Leonard's neck was easy: a quick, brutal snap to the right. It was only the beginning. The Deitz-thing *strained,* tendons standing out in its own neck as first one, then another ligament popped in Leonard's own. The mute sound of muscle and ligature, stretching and tearing, was unbelievably loud in the room.

The Deitz-thing *pulled,* and the first red fissure opened up in the throat, just above the collarbone. The clotting carotid artery blew, unleashing a sloppy spray of rich red lubrication. Harold Leonard's triple chins stretched to the limits, transcending elasticity; then they, too, gave, leaving nothing behind but a few slick rubber bands of stubborn tissue.

The Deitz-thing *twisted,* first this way then that, wearing down that final wave of resistance. Then it gave one final yank.

And the head, at last, pulled free.

*Now you see,* the Deitz-thing said, turning for the door.

Leonard had no real hair to speak of, so it carried the head by using the lower jaw as a handle of sorts, dangling upside down. In its other hand, it carried a small, selected stack of very important papers.

Full of very important names and home addresses.

*Because Austin Deitz had always been a man with a mission, and the thing that he'd become was no exception to that rule. It had a new mission, now; a mission all its own. The only justification it could find for its hideous death and worse rebirth.*

*Very soon, it knew, they would cross the final bridge. There were a few people it needed to see first.*

*But there was precious little time.*

The others were still waiting in the trucks when the Deitz-thing returned. So far, so good. The trucks had grown rows of bristling spines across the cowls and fenders while he was inside. So much the better.

It dropped the papers in the vacant driver's seat and then impaled Leonard's head, facing forward, on the hood. The sentient ooze from the truck-spawn's pores embraced the neck-stump eagerly. Holding it fast.

Making it One.

Then the Deitz-thing got back behind the wheel and drove off in the direction of Wyndham Hills.

A minute later, Leonard's head began to scream.

# Forty—Three

At nine minutes to three, the storm came back.

It rolled in on angry, brooding tiers: swollen blue-black cumulus and ghostly, low-slung nimbostratus, crowding the ceiling of the sky. It made the oxygen in the air itself compress, turn chill and thick, absorbed or displaced by the moisture that blackened and bloated the heavens.

And there was a stench in the air, an unsettling chemical tang that clung to the tongue like a tinfoil tourniquet. It rode in on the mist that now descended: a clammy, diaphanous veil, settling over the woodlands and farmlands, the suburbs and industrial parks that encircled and squeezed the densely packed concrete heart of the city.

Violent gusts of warmer breeze attempted to flee the coming darkness, sent stray cans pinging down the streets and newspaper fluttering in their wake. Windows rattled in their casements. Trees whispered and arched their backs. Wind razored, whistling, through the cracks in the walls of Paradise.

Very quickly, the downtown sidewalks began to clear. Hangers-out went in, drove off, or hunkered in doorways. All watching the skies. What stragglers on foot remained were either headed somewhere fast or had no place to go.

In the outlying regions, as well, the curtain began to

*come down on literally hundreds of unfortunate outdoor events. Ball games and barbecues. Weddings and funerals. Camping trips, keggers and KKK rallies. All of them, racing against the clock: one eye on their cars, one eye on the coming darkness.*

*There were just over a hundred and eighty-seven thousand living people in Paradise County. The wind blew through their souls. Their heads felt light. Their lungs felt heavy. They sweated, despite the cold. Slow-blossoming, ill-defined dread constricted their throats and coated their bellies like a living liquid, a sentient glandular secretion. They could literally feel the atmosphere inside their bodies change.*

*In final preparation.*
*For the storm.*

# Forty—Four

There were certain things, Lydia maintained, that one simply did not do. Like putting an electric blanket on a water bed, for instance. Or eating pork sushi. Or autoerotic strangulation. You didn't do these things, not because of the law, but because they were basically stupid ideas.

So it wasn't the Art Crime, or the threat of getting busted, that was making her antsy. It was the fact that they were doing it so close to a major body of water.

And the storm was almost here.

Garth and Lydia stood at the foot of the steep, rocky incline that led down into the Codorus Basin, where the creek cut through the center of town on its way to Black Bridge and the river beyond. Standing in the shadow of the Philly Street Bridge, they were pretty well hidden from the road above.

At night, the rocky banks and shadowed overhang were a hangout zone for wayward inner-city youth; but by daylight they were desolate, with only the broken beer bottles, empty lipstick tubes and used condoms to remind you that you were in hell and found your pleasure where you could.

Directly across the creek lay the End Zone, Paradise's premier yuppie sports bar. Frank Vickers's environmental action group had convened there, as usual, to save the world while keeping track of the NFL action. After doing such a swell job on Garth's old man, it was only fair to spread a little joy in Frank's direction.

Under the shadow of the bridge, they couldn't see you from the road; but the terrace of the End Zone had an unobstructed view. On the concrete wall of the pumping station spillway, Garth was spray-painting their little love note in jagged letters three feet high:

DRINK UP AND DIE,
YUPPIE SCUM!

And it was lotsa fun and all, but Lydia was getting wired. From where they stood, it was less than ten feet to the rank-smelling, shit-churning, Guinness-colored waters of the mighty Codorus. Worse yet, they were less than a dozen feet from the dam: a reinforced concrete retainer wall, inset every few feet with jutting steel teeth, each one a yard long. The teeth acted as a flood stop and general shit-catcher for the fetid creek; but at the moment, they were doubling as the county's largest instant lightning rod.

And the storm was almost here.

"This is weird," she said, gazing up. "We should split."

"Can't," Garth said. He was working on the comma.

"You really wanna die in an electrical storm?"

He shrugged, his back to her.

"*ARGH!*" she growled, arms flapping in frustration. Then she turned to address the storm. "Go ahead," she told it. "This man is too stupid to live."

Garth shook his head, still spraying. Thinking about his old man, and hers.

"No such thing," he assured her.

When the first peal of apocalypse thunder broke, it was eight minutes to three.

# Forty—Five

The convoy headed south.

It paced itself: an advance battalion, running just minutes ahead of the storm. From the north side of town—as yet unaffected—the traffic was sparse, nigh unto barren. There was nothing to slow them down.

At seven minutes to three, it came to a red light just outside the city limits. From this point on, stoplights dotted Route 30 as far as the eye could see. They had left the boondocks and entered the land of fast-food drive-thrus, auto-service franchises and largely deserted strip malls, all garishly hawking the good life.

Red lights were not part of the plan.

The convoy went through. From its position in the lead, the Boonie-spawn surveyed the point where the Route 30 bypass crossed Interstate 83. Overmind cannibalized his memory, sucking shreds of knowledge from every synapse like meat off a chicken bone.

These were the major east-west and north-south highways. This was the hub of the wheel. Philly and New York, Baltimore and D.C.: all were within one to four hours of driving time.

Going the speed limit.

Har har har.

Inside Boonie, Overmind chuckled; the body did its best to second the motion. Crusty, gravid face-tissue crinkled, popped, and spurted with mirth. More scabs tore loose. They hung in strips.

In the raw meat beneath, there were no longer extra eyes.

Now they were eggs.

Almost ready to hatch.

The Boonie-spawn's truck headed south. The tankers split off: one east, one west. The tankers would lock down the grid, reconnoiter on the far side of town, and then take this show on the road. Spreading the word.

But for the Boonster, this was good-bye.

Ah, well. It was fun while it lasted. They laughed as they went their separate ways. The roads stretched like arteries through the city, the county, the body of the world.

How convenient.

# Forty—Six

The whole way back to 'PAL, Kirk's mind was a thing unchained: racing ahead of him, flashing back, preediting tape in his head.

All around him, near and distant, sirens whooped and shrieked and wailed. Fire trucks, staters, city cops went smoking past, to God knows where. The radio was no help at all, and the TAC frequencies weren't any better. People were stepping all over each other. Everyone knew something was happening. But they didn't know *what*.

And that was where Kirk came in. *Kirk Bogarde—Renegade Reporter!*, with the scoop of a lifetime. *Kirk Bogarde—Renegade Reporter!*, alone in the lead, while the competition flailed behind, their heads wedged up their asses. *Kirk Bogarde—Renegade Reporter!*, barreling down the homestretch with a fireball in his gut: a feeling one part orgasm, one part motion sickness, one part sheer white-knuckling edge.

*This* was news. Not opening shopping centers. Not standing outside town meetings. Not finding out whether the average potato-shaped Paradise native preferred donuts or faschnachts with their morning coffee. Or had they kicked caffeine? Find out at eleven!

Bullshit bullshit bullshit. THIS was what life was

about! Taking chances, following hunches, playing out leads, and nailing the truth wherever you could find it. Not taking your cues from cowards and bullies—not just Doing What You're Told—but grabbing the world by the throat and *forcing* it to confess its sins and secret passions, cough up its deepest mysteries.

No matter what the cost.

Because we needed the truth. We *deserved* the truth. We could not live without the truth. And Kirk believed that to fulfill that need was the most beautiful, humbling, terrifying, and altogether essential function he could possibly imagine.

To be a part of something real.

To be a part of history.

The ACTION-9 Newsmobile screeched into 'PAL's parking lot at seven minutes to three. Kirk hopped out, ran to the back door, thumbed the code on the security lock, and yanked the door open a microsecond after the electronic dead bolt buzzed back. He took the stairs two at a time, clutching the camcorder, spilling through the newsroom door so noisily that he almost gave Laura a seizure.

"I GOT IT!" he crowed exultantly.

"Kirk!" she cried out, eyes afire with anger and relief.

And he grinned at her, he opened his mouth, he started to explain what had happened to him, and he got as far as inhaling for speech when he found himself suddenly spinning . . .

. . . and Gary was there, the words "You FUCK!" astonishingly loud in Kirk's ears as a huge fist zeroed in on his left eye. Kirk moved, and it got his cheek instead, big square knuckles plowing into the soft skin beneath the right eye socket. "NAHHH!" he wailed, as the next blow came, catching his nose and mashing it flat, blood geysering out in thick twin jets . . .

. . . and there was a moment where everything went blank, very quickly over, and when he came back he found himself swinging at Gary with the camcorder, screaming,

"GET OFFA ME FUCKER YOU DON'T UNNER-STAND..."

...as Gary nailed him with a right, sending the camcorder flying from Kirk's grasp to bounce off the wall and cough up the tape which bounced and spun and slid underfoot, crunching under Gary's boot and throwing him off-balance...

...as Kirk lurched forward, screaming "MY TAPE!", diverting him just long enough for Gary to recover and draw a bead...

...and Laura was screaming, Kirk was screaming, everyone was screaming in the time it took for the last fist to connect.

It was six minutes to three.

# Forty—Seven

By this time, the stormclouds had buried the heavens, enveloped the county in premature night. Like a rumbling, primordial curtain being drawn across the world, it drew down the darkness.

And swallowed the moon.

"Micki," whispered Gwen from the living room couch. Her voice, weakened by fear to a quaver, was chilling in and of itself.

Micki stood by the wind-hammered living room window. Terror welled huge in her soul. She felt infinitesimally small, like a gnat before a god: like the storm was an enormous black finger and thumb, reaching down to extinguish her spark.

"Micki . . ." Gwen's voice was tremulous, lacking the power to exclaim. "I don't feel very good. . . ."

"It's okay, baby, everything's gonna be fine," Micki said; her eyes closed, her teeth chattering. She leaned against the pane. "Oh god, Bobba, help me. Gwen . . ."

*Make a circle,* Bob-Ramtha said, slicing through her fear.

"What?" Confused.

*Make a ritual circle. Now.*

"I don't understand. What good will *that* do? I mean, shouldn't I take her back to the hospital or someth—"

*No. You can't.*

"Why not?"

Silence.

"Bobba, I—"

*Because if you take her out there, she'll die.* There was no mistaking the gravity of his tone. *And so will the baby.*

*And so will you.*

Outside the window, more thunder broke, and the wind intensified. It pounded the pane, whistled through the cracks.

It whistled down her soul.

"Something's coming, isn't it." Not even a question. Her voice sounded tiny against the storm: a humorless Betty Boop squeak.

A moment of silence. *Yes.*

"What is it?"

*I don't know.*

"You don't..." Her voice ended there. A big question mark went off in her mind. "Wait a minute," she continued, incredulous now. "What do you *mean*, you don't know?"

*I mean*—and there was actual shame in his voice—*I didn't see it coming.*

*No one did.*

"Oh, Jesus...." Micki shook her head, let this little revelation sink in. Something horrible was on its way, and the entire spirit world had been caught unawares. "Jesus...." She didn't like the sound of this at all.

In the background, Gwen moaned and softly began to cry.

*Build the circle,* Bob-Ramtha urged. *Now.*

It was five until three.

# Forty—Eight

It was time for Jennie Quirez to face the facts.

*He isn't coming.* An inescapable, killing admission. Jennie, staring out the window at the human hell on earth. *He's not going to come for me.* Like trawling a lake for a loved one's body and—finally, horribly—hooking its stiff remains.

*Austin is gone.* Hauling up the clammy, lifeless truth.

*And he is never. EVER.*

*Coming back.*

*For me.*

At the Mt. Rose Amoco Shop 'N' Go—at the mouth of the mad, transmogrifying eastern valley—the last-minute exodus was in full swing. There was an easily forty-car-long gas line on Mt. Rose Avenue, extending all the way to the Route 74 exit. For the last twenty minutes, there hadn't been less than forty cars in line. All around them, panic-stricken traffic surged, squealed, careened, and roared.

Fleeing the descending dark.

And the new world already upon them.

Jennie crouched behind the console of the vandalized, desiccated Shop 'N' Go. Its shelves had been picked clean by the second wave of insurgent wild-eyed refugees. When the orange highway cones went down, she had locked the doors. Turned off the lights. Kept the pumps inconspicuously rolling. It was the only way she could think of to deflect them, keep the mob from coming in and eating her alive.

*She could no longer tell where the stain was or wasn't. It wasn't inside—she'd made certain of that—but the whole of the drive and parking lot were fair game. She watched for telltale screams and seizures at the pumps. That she didn't see any felt almost like hope.*

*Many times, over the past forty minutes, she had thought about hopping a ride outta Dodge. There was only one problem: eighty percent of them were already afflicted, or carrying someone who was.*

*The rest were simply insane.*

A couple of tumorous, terminally infected yuppies tried to pull an end run around the crowd, banking their Ford Taurus onto the lot by coming up over the curb. Jennie watched their mouths shape curses. The gas line steadfastly refused to part.

A twenty-year-old laid-off steelworker, sixth up from pump four, got out of his GM pickup and strode toward them. He had a Charter Arms Bulldog .44 in his hand. The yupsters stopped dead, screaming incomprehensible things— excuses, entreaties—that were all but drowned out by the roar of violent dissent that surrounded them.

They were all talk; and talk had never been cheaper.

He stood directly before them. Aimed.

And fired.

The first shot blew a hole through the driver's heart: a wet confettied spray of upholstery, meat and padding, erupting onto the seat behind him. His girlfriend/wife/ significant other shrieked. The second shot vaporized her throat. Her chin bounced off her shoulders, toppled onto her lap, in the second before the third dumdum slug penetrated the windshield, turned the driver's head to mush.

Then he fired a couple more shots, just for the living hell of it. A bunch of people clapped. A couple of them helped him push the car out of the way.

From her place behind the console, Jennie Quirez watched civilization unravel beneath the shadow of the coming storm.

It was four minutes to three.

# Forty—Nine

The Boon-spawn sat at the gate: contemplating the bizarre past behind it, the brilliant future ahead.

The run had been long, the last part almost entirely uphill. It had spent vast reserves of energy, throwing everything into the climb. It did so gladly, without compunction: like a salmon flinging itself upstream, knowing implicitly that death lay at the end of the journey.

And with it, rebirth.

What was once Boonie oozed across the seat, weakened to the point of no return. This chapter was over; it knew that, even as it sensed the dark one that awaited. The engine that drove it hung back, gauging the perfection of the moment.

And at the perfect moment, it moved.

*Boonie shuddered and gripped the wheel as the last of his soul sputtered off to oblivion. His useless flesh sloughed loose in thick wet slabs, epidermis and dermis relaxing their hold and sagging, at long last relieved of the burden of life. Flesh and fat, tendons and ligaments rotted, popped, and slithered to the floor of the cab like dross, like offal. Eggs like tiny poison pearls plopped out and scattered, freed of their incubator.*

*While the core remained, still gripping the wheel.*

*It was a central nervous system, clinging directly to dessicated bone: a stripped-down chassis of barest motor control. Skeletal fingers clutched the steering wheel, rudely ratcheted the shifter. Boonie's dead, sallow face fell off, revealing eyes wet and bright as a child's.*

*It grinned, wet skull gleaming on a thin stalk of neck. And threw the truck in gear.*

The fence surrounded the facility, which was located high up on a hill on the southern side of the city. A small parking apron lay to the left, completely deserted. The gate itself was steel, electronically controlled, but far too flimsy: a deterrent only to the civilized. It was not built for terrorism.

A sign hung by the gate, the lettering burned into the wood in big rustic letters. It read:

PARADISE WATER COMPANY
MUNICIPAL RESERVOIR

In smaller, no less emphatic letters was the warning:

No TRESPASSING!

The snout of the truck crushed it into kindling as it barreled through, pine and fir groves whipping past as it picked up speed. Drums rattled on the truck bed, the poison sloshing excitedly.

The thing in the cab laughed, smelling the high scent of evergreen and thinking of the rich *new* odors that would soon take its place, when the world was made over in their image. The wind buffeted its frail form; bits of its nervous system snapped off and flew into the slipstream, dry and brittle as twigs.

It didn't mind. It didn't need them anymore.

Besides, it was about to get all kinds of wet.

The truck rounded the bend, and there they were: two

great standing pools, capping off some thirty-two million gallons of innocent, potable water. The city's entire on-hand supply.

A low wrought-iron double fence surrounded the pools. The DER had recently insisted that the pools be capped, to prevent aerial contamination. But the Paradise Water Company had been given three years to implement that plan.

Once again: how convenient.

The truck plowed through the first fence as if it were a row of matchsticks, steel posts snapping and sparking as they dragged along behind. The thing in the cab cackled, as the truck kept on coming, reaching the lip of the first pool and then flying into space: six tons of steel and poison, defying the law one final time.

*Then the truck belly-flopped into the water, sent up a jubilant hundred-foot spray. It immediately fused, dissolving even as it expanded: drums, tumor, truck, and all becoming one giant toxic Fizzie, spitting and sputtering as it went from solid to liquid to gas.*

*The poison pearls hatched on contact with the water, instantly charging it. The pool hissed violently as two hundred thousand gallons—the lifeblood of Paradise—cried out in orgasmic agony.*

*And then began to sing. . . .*

By three minutes to three, the truck was gone. The drums were gone. What once had been Boonie was gone. All gone.

As the toxin spread, deep into the plumbing of Paradise. And the sleepwalking city below.

# Fifty

*Number Seventeen:*

Everett G. Vulich was the president of AeroCorp, a locally based industry that provided, among other things, rocket fuels for the Defense Department and NASA. AeroCorp's contribution to Overmind included dichloroethane, dichloromethane, chloroform, and TCE, all of them highly dangerous substances.

He lived at 29 Morningside Terrace, with his wife, Francine, and their Scottie dog, Lance.

The Deitz-thing used a table saw this time. It didn't take any longer; Vulich had one handy, in the basement where they found him; and, overall, it was a lot less wear and tear. Once Vulich stopped struggling, the operation virtually ran itself.

Of course, it was a lot less satisfying that way.

But there would be more. The list was long.

And it was always good.

The wonderful thing about Wyndham Hills was how altogether goddam convenient it was. More than a third of the hundred key people in Paradise on his list lived there, within that elite fifteen square miles of real estate overlooking the city.

Indeed, Wyndham Hills was a land of plenty. They

were practically going door-to-door. With his six-man team working in tandem, it hadn't taken long at all to round up sixteen of the local heads of industry.

And mount them on his trucks.

But they were almost out of time. There was no doubt about it. Upstairs, Francine and Lance were entertaining the spawn of Franklyn and Pyle; and while that was fine—there *were* no innocents—it was certainly no substitute for justice, either. As the head detached, the Deitz-thing found itself looking at the watch on the dead man's wrist.

Two minutes to three, it said.

(*i swear upon my soul*)

Two minutes to three.

And suddenly, Deitz remembered.

*In the few short hours since his death and rebirth, Austin Deitz had been thrust so deeply into the horror that he'd virtually forgotten what it* was. *No longer.*

*It was back, with a name and a face.*

*Horror was a woman named Jennifer Quirez, with a gift for persuasion, a love of the stars, and the clearest, finest deep brown eyes he'd ever seen. Horror was that woman, trapped alone at the Shop 'N' Go, with no transportation, no one to help her, and no idea what Hell was about to break loose.*

*Horror was loving that woman—in the last few grinding turns of the wheel—and knowing that he was powerless to save her.*

*Horror was* love, *in this Brave New Hell: the capacity for caring, and for sharing pain. To find oneself both in love and in Hell was more than torture, worse than madness.*

*It was tantamount to sin.*

*But for Deitz, the fallen angel . . .*

Suddenly, he changed the agenda; to do so was still within his power. He climbed the stairs, severed Vulich-head in hand, understanding that it was the last one he'd be getting. At least for now.

Then he headed for his truck.

And if he was mad, then it was certainly understandable; if he failed, it would certainly be nothing new. But he was less than five miles from the woman he loved.

And—New World or not—he would save her if he could.

# Fifty—One

By two fifty-eight Werner Blake was high over Paradise, taking his last look at the land he called home.

Getting the plane had not been a major problem; he'd long ago talked the county Emergency Management Agency into keeping a Cessna 152 hangared for aerial observation and emergencies and such. The ground personnel had cautioned him about the coming storm, but Blake was nothing if not persuasive.

Far more troublesome for him would be what to tell Approach Control at Baltimore/Washington International: at the rate everything was coming unglued, they might just be hearing about it by the time he got there. If his timing was on and his bullshit solid, he'd be able to slide through the cracks and disappear.

And if not . . .

*I'll burn that bridge when I come to it,* he thought. *First things first.*

Blake reached a nominal cruising altitude of three thousand feet. The ground below took on a toylike quality, with wonderfully reproduced miniatures. His bags were stuffed into the cramped cockpit space behind him. God was not his copilot; the attaché case occupied that position, the better to not let it out of his sight. Inside, a little

327

over one point two million awaited, the seeds of a new life.

He sighed, relieved to be airborne. Things always seemed clearer when he was flying. Everything was going to be fine, he realized. Everything was going to work out.

Blake sighed and worked the controls. The Cessna banked south, heading for the promised land.

And straight into the coming storm. . . .

In the last sixty seconds before three o'clock, the Drew-thing stirred. It had been dreaming again: more and more as its function diminished in importance, gave way to Overmind.

In the dream, he was an infant again: laying face-up in his crib, playing with something like a mobile. He was happy and content.

Then a shadow passed over, saying *time to wake up now.* . . .

The Drew-thing awoke.

It was groggy from glut, its body swollen huge beyond all human scale or comprehension. It was a miracle of mutant creation, the wild experimentation giving way to a symmetry, as form followed function. . . .

*It was conical in shape, growing up as it expanded outward like a massive organic pyramid, imitating the mandala shapes of the natural world it subsumed and replaced.*

*Dozens of mouths ringed its base, yard-long vertical gashes that hung open obscenely, willing portals in the mottled fle '.. Segmented proboscises snaked out of them, lightning-fast and fluid. They slithered along the endless corridors of drums, blind beaked heads knocking over barrels, cracking drums like eggs.*

*And feeding, feeding the bloated ticklike monstrosity of its body, a hundred thousand gallons of liquid nightmare and more already inside it, the overspill sloshing from the ruptured husks, pooling together, forming an enormous toxic lake that deepened and spread....*

The Drew-head lolled on its great bloated perch, a perverse and temporary place of honor. It stared at the sky with its one remaining eye; the other dangled downward, dry as a forgotten spring onion.

Somewhere overhead, an airplane buzzed its insect engine-drone. The Drew-head batted at it lazily, one of its hands coming up to wave the nuisance away.

The drone grew louder.


The next thirty seconds of Blake's life were rich with irony.

At two fifty-nine Blake realized that his flight path took him almost directly over the dump. Some deeply perverse impulse gained dominion over him at that moment, and he banked west; he wanted to catch one last fly-by of the thing that had so forever altered his life.

The Cessna crossed the outside aerial perimeter of the dump at just over one hundred and ten miles per hour. Blake leaned into the joystick and dove down to two thousand feet, buzzing the pools and pits that marked the outer edge. As the ground swept by, he noticed the drums toppling, the tendrils pulling them down.

The plane raced on, passing over the heart of the dump . . .

*. . . and suddenly Blake found himself looking down in helpless, morbid fascination and awe, staring at the great gray malignancy that had enveloped Paradise Waste.*

*From above, it looked like a jellyfish, an anemone, a vast ganglionic tumor floating in a sea of spilled sludge. Fat tendrils snaked out between the rows and rows of barrels that spanned its seven-acre breadth, binding it inextricably to the dump.*

Then the air around it *moved*: a vaporous shimmer of anticipation like a heat wave, a visible coiling of energy. The little plane buffeted, and Blake felt dread clench like a fist in his throat, felt his bowels go slack and his adrenaline surge. He gasped, and felt his lips go utterly numb.

*Oh god,* Blake thought, *oh shit.*

He banked and rolled the Cessna hard; the engine whined in a desperate last-minute bid for freedom.

But he was already out of time.


*Weedle-eedle-eeee . . .*

The Drew-head looked up and saw the silver bird: a bright toy against the mad black churning sky. It giggled and groped for it like an infant. It could not hope to reach it.

But in doing so, it caught a glimpse of something familiar.

Something wonderful.

Another bright toy, easily within reach.

The little digital watch-game was still strapped to its wrist. The arm had trebled in size until the strap had pinched off the hand like a sausage link, burying the tiny buttons in gangrenous blackened flesh. The Drew-thing tried to touch them with its bloated chubby fingers, found it could not.

It only took five of the last ten seconds for another limb to form.

*Weedle-eedle-eee . . .* , as the shadow of the plane passed over his face. *Weedle-eedle-eee . . .* , as the tiny plane on its wrist dropped its tiny payload. Moist new fingers pressed the buttons, scoring a direct hit.

*Weedle-eedle-eedle-eeeee . . .*

And the New World was born.


*alive*
*and more than alive*
*voracious ecstatic and free at last*
*rising at the speed of combustion*
*emancipated in flame*

*set loose from the mooring of earth and flesh*
*one hundred and forty thousand toxic apostles*
*flush with Overmind*
*comingling and exploding together*
*then rising*
*ten fifteen twenty*
*thousand feet and climbing*
*straight to heaven to godhead*
*to primacy*
*to claim both heaven and earth*
*for its own*


The explosion was immense.

One hundred thousand barrels caught at once, a deadly daisy chain started as five acres of fifty-five-gallon drums averaging four hundred and forty pounds apiece ignited in less than a nanosecond, a blistering four point four million pounds of volatile death with the equivalent blast force of just over two megatons.

At two thousand feet Blake barely had time to scream before the fireball slammed into the Cessna's fuselage, bludgeoning it upward, engulfing it in flame.

And Blake might have wished that it would end quickly, a flash and then nothing. Such was not the case. He had far too long to experience the dramatic climb in temperature; far too long to feel his hair singe and see the cockpit slag and go red, savor the unmistakable smell of his own immolation.

Far too long.

Nearly all of a second.

*But the moment in which he exploded went on forever. He could feel his marrow cook, the gases in his intestinal tract ignite and detonate, blowing bone to shrapnel rain that ruptered his flesh even as it blistered off into grease and vapor.*

*And all of it was agony. Pure agony, unsullied by*

*merciful distance or candid spiritual reflection. No life flashing before his eyes. Just his eyeballs exploding.*

*For one infinite moment.*

Then Blake and the plane and the air they displaced were gone, blown to bits, absorbed by the mounting pillar of flame. The sparkling cinders of one point two million in cash burned no brighter than anything else.

They all turned to ash and were caught by the maelstrom wind, fed into the clouds as particulate matter.

Feeding, and seeding, the storm.

# VI

# Fifty—Two

They were drawn to the windows and streets by the sound. The spectacle held them there. Awe and terror of astonishing depth—the literal fear of God—embraced them as they gazed upon that vengeful, iconic, unquenchable fire. It stole their breath and paralyzed their souls.

You could see it from the heart of town, a dozen miles away.

For one long, terrible moment, one hundred and eighty-seven thousand people set aside their differences, threw caution to the shockwave winds. They forgot all about their homes, their jobs, their possessions, their passions and dreams, their loved ones, and all of the other little things that defined their tiny lives.

For that one moment, they were as one, united in their certain doom.

It was an altogether religious experience.

*The fireball hit the dense cloud cover at just over ten thousand feet. The outer edge of its corona reached a scorching three thousand degrees Fahrenheit, burning off the condensation instantly, punching a gaping hole in the ceiling of the sky.*

*The pressure system responded by dilating, wrapping around the pillar of flame even as it supercharged the remaining moisture, building a thunderhead directly above ground zero. Heat lightning arced through the cumulonimbus, blue-white and foreboding as it bounced off the black aperture that ringed the blinding flame.*

*At ground zero, the fire was insatiable. The seven acres of Paradise Waste were engulfed as the pillar achieved a diameter the size of a football field. Stray drums blew like four-hundred-pound party favors: rocketing hundreds of feet into the air, cindering before they hit the ground.*

*Drew and the crown of Overmind immolated gloriously, flesh giving way to exultant living ash, riding the firestorm across the sky.*

*The shockwave flattened everything within roughly a quarter-mile radius: crushing homes, throwing cars like Matchbox toys, killing the first thousand or so in mid-commercial break.*

*They never even knew what hit them.*

*They were the lucky ones.*

*Thirty seconds into the blast, the shockwave reached its zenith and sucked back in on itself. A killer wind rose, sucking every spare ounce of oxygen back into the rapidly rising inferno.*

*A mushroom cloud of living ash and soot disseminated out in ever-expanding rings, attacking and overcoming everything it touched. It merged with the stormclouds, bonding with the condensate, arming and readying a trillion tiny toxic bombs as the entire atmospheric pressure system* clenched: *its twenty-mile mass blanketing the city, the county, the horizon as far as the eye could see.*

*Then the sentient storm unleashed its power.*

*And the black rain began to fall.*

The first fat drops hit Micki as she rounded the back of the house, less than four miles from the blast. She barely felt the three to her shoulders and back, like rubber bands flicked by someone's rowdy little brother. But the one that spattered the back of her neck sizzled like grease off a frying pan.

*DON'T STOP,* urged Bob-Ramtha as she yipped in pain. *DON'T STOP.* It was the mantra that drove her, broke the hellfire pillar's hypnotic hold, whipped her up and held her to survival speed. No matter what.

There was no other way.

She had all but completed the outer circle: a huge, unbroken ring of containment that surrounded the house, etched in driveway salt from a twenty-pound bag she'd found in the garage. It was vital that the circle be as perfect as was humanly possible. It took great concentration, and entirely too much time.

The rain fell harder, offering up less space to move between the drops. As she scuttle-walked backwards, delineating the last twenty yards worth of arc, it was like that rowdy little brother was putting out cigarettes on her scalp. She could smell her hair smoldering, melding to her skin.

She could scream all she wanted.

But she could not, *would* not stop.


*Fifty-seven thousand people were caught in the mounting acid downpour. There was no way to be prepared. Its corrosive, killing nature had caught them all completely by surprise. The longer it fell, the harder and faster and deadlier its descent: eating into them from the moment of impact, burning holes in the skin that seared through to the bone.*

*Where the pillar of flame inspired awe and dread, the rain dispensed agony, panic and death. In the crazed, pathetic scramble for safety, they succeeded only in dragging each other down: trampling each other in parking lots as they struggled with keys, banged on windows and doors.*

*Succumbing to the madness of the crowd . . .*

At the Mt. Rose Amoco Shop 'N' Go, the man with

the gun lay face-up, face gone, twitching on the tarmac. He was far from alone. From where Jennie hid, driven back behind the *EMPLOYEES ONLY* door, she could see at least a dozen of them: features peeling back, layer by sizzling layer, like slabs of human bacon on the skillet of the gas pump tarmac.

They'd exposed themselves, in the process of rioting or trying to fill their tanks. Not only were they dead or dying, but the pumps were blocked as well. And she could no longer tend the console; they had shattered the window, forced her into desperate retreat.

It was the end of the exodus. And Austin had not come.

But the stain was here: inside now, growing. Forcing her back.

And making her scream . . .

. . . while the rain fell harder, hammering every square inch of Paradise with the liquid fire of Overmind. Dispersing it over the forests and fields, the tilled acres of farmland and manicured patches of green. Dousing the river. The lakes, wells, and streams. Leaving its distinctive mark on every living thing, from microbe to field mouse to man.

Fifty-seven thousand people, caught in the rain. Unable to reach their cars, their homes, any form of shelter from the storm. In backyards or churchyards or graveyards. Outside fire halls or shopping malls. On bleachers. Ball fields. Sidewalks. Side streets.

There were fifty-seven thousand of them, in all.
They were dead inside the first three minutes.

Garth and Lydia were trapped in the Codorus Basin, beneath the Philadelphia Street Bridge. After the first half-dozen drops, it was clear to them that they had no other choice. Garth's left eyelid had been spot-welded to his eye, and Lydia's lower lip and gum were rancid with agonizing, chemical-smelling sores.

This would have been more than bad enough, but the creek was beginning to rise. As if it were blocked somewhere upstream.

In the direction of Black Bridge.

*And the fish were jumping out of the water, trying to escape from the water, but there was absolutely nowhere to go. And some of the fish, the fish looked funny: too big, too aware, too abjectly malformed.*

"Oh my God," Lydia whimpered, backing up and away from the water. She was staring at the back of Garth's jacket, the logo that no longer filled her with pride. She had never imagined that being right could hold so little satisfaction.

Across the creek, the crowd from the End Zone was huddled beneath the green and white awning that covered the huge back patio. They had come out to gape at the burning rain, the pillar of fire in the distance. Lydia recognized her father there, amongst the masses. In this fresh context, his face looked no different from anybody else's.

No different from her own.

And suddenly, it was no longer hatred that she felt for him. That time had passed. Now it was terror that filled her heart: a terrible drowning sense of irreversible loss. For one soul-wrenching moment, she thought about calling out to him.

Then the black rain began to pour . . .

. . . *and she couldn't see, she couldn't see through the impenetrable curtain. But when the screaming started, she closed her eyes and saw it all too clearly. Saw the awning disassemble, eat away at an alarming speed: erasing the differences between them completely, joining them together in one undifferentiated mass of shrieking reeling molten flesh and jutting mechanical bone, like the girders and struts of unfinished buildings in an earthquake, draped in a runny meat stream. . . .*

Then she screamed, and Garth slapped her across the

face. He didn't want the fish to hear. They were jumping higher, with perverse determination.

And the water was rising.

They still didn't know why.

*At Black Bridge, the original spawning ground, the parameters of a whole new world continued to rapidly evolve. It had all manner of brave new, never-before-seen creatures in it. Walkers. Swimmers. Crawlers. Flyers. Breeders, Drones and Queens. Beautiful, ruthlessly violent Monsters and hideous Growths of inviolate weakness and meek, self-righteous passivity.*

*Hunters and hunted. Feeders and food.*

*But everyone needed to eat.*

*And this was the strangest, most horrible thing: one by one, they forgot who they were. Losing touch with the toxicity that spawned them.*

*Losing conscious connection with Overmind.*

*One by one, they settled into their new roles. Their new forms. With no memory of the Source from whence they came.*

*Suddenly, they found themselves lost: deprived of the empathy that came from being and knowing that they were all one thing.*

*Reconstructing the food chain, in their own mutant image.*

*Blindly starting the cycle all over again.*

There was a wave. It came from the whirlpool at the heart of Black Bridge, the heart of the New Creation.

It barreled straight for the heart of the city.

Lydia and Garth could see it coming.

It was twenty feet tall, and it spanned the width of the basin. From where Garth and Lydia stood, there was no clearance unless they clung to the underside of the bridge. They were pylons there, rough handholds to cling to.

They had no other choice.

*The wall came in, undercut at the moment it collided with the flood shelf. Graygreenmultiformed NewSpawn impacted, impaled, blew forward and opened, revealing their innermost selves. The innards and tendrils that soared through the air in front of the wave meant nothing to the creatures that were spared. Over the top, and to hell with the hindmost.*

*Fuck everyone and everything else.*

There was a five-headed faceless eel-spawn, razored and flailing and thirty feet long. It threw itself out of the water blindly, passed less than a foot from Garth's face. "HELP!" he shrieked, hanging on for dear life.

But Lydia could no longer whip up such passion. She could already feel herself starting to change. The toxins were in her bloodstream, in the mist on her face and the air in her lungs. Her surface flesh felt rubbery and numb, like her shell-shocked emotional core.

It no longer mattered what happened.

Lydia Vickers wasn't dying.

Merely changing in shape.

The next creature down the pike had Garth's name on it. Its emerald, taloned head raked the underside of the bridge, etching a groove through the concrete and steel. It caught him just above the hipbone, separated upper intestine from lower as it snapped through the spine like blackboard chalk in an irate teacher's hands. Lydia's gaze went to her friend's, watched the lenses glaze over.

No future, indeed.

Watching Garth fall was like watching a packet of fast-food catsup grace an order of french fries. Spoot. Zero fanfare. He was emptied, crinkled up and gone in a blink of the eye that devoured him.

And all she could do was hang on, hang on, shrinking back against the concrete as far as the physics of the situation would allow. She had spent her whole life trying to stand out from the crowd, and now all she wanted was to be invisible.

Waiting for the change to take over completely.
Waiting to join the parade.


*There had been, until quite recently, one hundred eighty-eight thousand human souls in Paradise.*

*They were dying off now, at a rate that averaged out to roughly ten thousand people per minute.*

*Past the first major volley of rain, the majority were taken out by Boonie's parting gift. It rode the water mains, infiltrating through the pipes, sneaking up behind the walls to slaughter from within.*

*It burbled through the Jacuzzi jets of Carol Blake's room at the Blue Dove Inn, bringing both she and her pet tennis pro to a rich red blistering boil. It came up through Tom Huntington's plumbing to bite off his ass as he sat on the crapper, grunting through a halftime power-dump. It mixed into Chris Crowley's whiskey and water, induced him to hack up his glistening innards at the foot of the big-screen TV.*

It brought Marge Leonard running to the bathroom, in response to the sound of her children's screams. She found Wally and Timmy and little Thea, thrashing in their Sunday bath, a greasy slick of molten plastic tub toys swirling across the surface as they bubbled and sputtered down to a chunky toddler *bouillabaisse*.

Marge screamed and shoved her arm into the tub, stripping her flesh all the way to the elbow as she groped for the drain plug and pulled. Then she collapsed to the floor: her arm gone, her mind gone.

And her babies, swirling down the drain.

*It was a pattern that replicated itself again and again, across the county. From Wolf's Head to Fairview, West Manheim to East Manchester, across the length and breadth of a county under insuppressible siege. From the Paradise Athletic Club to the Pleasant Acres nursing home, Bob's Big Boy to the Lincoln Woods, the Masonic Temple to the*

*Miracle Car Wash, with thousands and thousands and thousands of private dwellings in between.*

*Over and over. Again and again.*

*Bearing no conceivable, remotely merciful end in sight. . . .*

The lines at 911 went suddenly, totally silent.

Cut off from the world.

Dottie Hamm stared around the bright-lit County Control complex, fighting down the astonishing, paralyzing terror she felt. For years, she had been the one who provided a lifeline for others when they found themselves trapped in the big world of hurt.

Now *she* was the one without a lifeline.

And, as with Deitz before her, there was no one else to call.

Kelly had put on a fresh pot of coffee. God bless her. What else were they supposed to do? Wait out the collapse of the telephone lines, the return of their emergency backup. Remain in control.

No matter what.

Dottie poured herself a cup, started dousing it with NutraSweet. Formaldehyde bloodstream rumors notwithstanding, she hated her coffee unsweetened or black. Then she dumped in a dollop of half-and-half.

It started to swirl. Round and round, round and round.

In a lazy figure eight.

''Dottie,'' Dave Dell said; and before she had even completely turned, the cup was up to her mouth.

*She tipped it back, and felt the hot liquid affix to her lips like a living thing: sluicing through the space between her teeth, filling her mouth in one enormous burning gulp, then consciously forcing its way down the clenched, sloping apperture at the back.*

There was no scream. The toxin swallowed it whole, on its way down her throat. It ate her throat as well, boiling the meat and dispensing rank red musclefroth in its stead. It ate down to her stomach, recombined with her juices, transforming Dottie's digestive tract into an organic pressure cooker of pain.

Dave Dell vaulted over the low sill as she dropped to the floor and spasmed. He slid his wiry arms under her armpits, desperately attempting the Heimlich maneuver to clear her clogged pipes. He clasped his hands over her solar plexus. Took a deep breath. And *pressed*.

When her abdomen exploded, his arms went along for the ride.

*The spawn that had once been Strong John and Dean worked in tandem. Like Micki, they used geometry to invoke a higher power. But instead of a circle, they had traced the manmade straight-line grids that defined the city.*

*Up and down the narrow one-way streets and shady tree-lined boulevards, past crumbling tarpaper shanties and cozy Cape Cods, past tastefully renovated townhouses and lush Georgian abodes. Street by street. Block by block.*

*Sealing off the city limits.*

*Their tanker trucks were loaded to capacity with inert, as-yet-unawakened toxin. Their sprayer rigs had dispensed it: leaving local residents gagging and retching, keeling over by the dozens on their lawns and living room floors in Overmind's ever-expanding wake.*

*But as the rain conjoined with it, something triggered in the dormant pox.*

*Self-awareness. A sense of purpose.*

*Unlimited possibility.*

*It rampaged with lethal abandon under the blood-red sky, stirring kin in the fatty tissues of its fleeing victims. It struck them down, shrieking and thrashing, only to instantly raise them up snake-faced or insect-headed, flippered and flailing; the lost denizens of the city of the damned.*

*They took to the streets in packs, cavorting with the stormsong.*

*Ready to join the Parade. . . .*


And still the rain came down.

It came in many colors now, an oilslick rainbow that crowded the sky. Like its brethren at the bridge, it had lost all but peripheral touch with Overmind. There were simply too many drops to imbue with one single consciousness.

The connection remained as a sort of *collective unconscious*: a molecule of telepathic toxicity that stayed in touch with its essence, implicitly recognizing itself in every face it saw.

*But as it landed and spattered and pooled, a group consciousness reemerged. Not Overmind, precisely, but a shared beingness that evolved very quickly into a shared identity. A second-level Overbeing.*

*A new elemental.*

*The spirit of the New Blood of the Earth.*


The kitchen stank of chemicals and cindered hair.

Gwen sat at the little cafe table she'd scarfed at Christie's Antiques. She was rapidly retreating: into herself, into a somnambulistic cocoon of shock.

Micki pressed past her, frantically searching the cupboards and drawers. Micki said she was sorry, it couldn't be helped. But then, Micki was being incredibly insensitive right now: by making Gwen get out of her chair; by smelling as horrible as she did; by forcing Gwen to look for some stupid *candles* that wouldn't help anything anyway.

And they couldn't be just ANY candles, no, they had to be WHITE candles, as if that made a fucking bit of difference. As if *any* of it did. As if Gwen should be doing *anything* but waiting for Gary to come home.

Especially when she felt so terribly sick.

And she did, oh God did she ever feel terrible. It was

like some strange virus had entered her body, a walking talking thinking virus, and it was saying *badfeelbadfeelbad*, a whispering mantra, *badfeelbadfeelbad* as if that were its life's ambition.

And she looked bad, too, no question about it, her skin gray and pallid in the wan kitchen light. The stink didn't help a bit. It made her acutely queasy. Of course, nausea at a moment's notice had been a linchpin of the Taylor Family Pregnancy ever since . . .

Gwen felt the bile-rush sneak up on her like a runaway Peterbilt, and she puked all over the kitchen floor.

"AHurp!" she belched, then staggered toward the kitchen sink. She'd almost made it when the next wave hit, and she doubled up and puked again, in a wider arc that missed the sink and splattered the cabinet itself . . .

*. . . and there were a lot of chemicals in there, household powders and liquids and sprays, but she had never looked at them in quite this way before . . .*

*. . . as suddenly there was a voice in her head that wondered what, say,* Liquid Drāno *might taste like: just a drop, not enough to hurt you, just enough to find out what it's like . . .*

*. . . and it wasn't like a compulsion or anything, not like a pregnant craving, it was more just an intellectual curiosity that made her grab the Liquid Drāno, shake off the globs of vomit, carefully untwist the cap . . .*

"GWEN!" Micki screamed, and knocked the bottle from her hands, making her cry for no good reason. Even though Micki could see that she was sick, that she just wanted to curl up on the floor with her big hard tense swollen belly that couldn't feel anything, inside or out.

Just curl up.

And wait for Gary to come home. . . .


Deitz rammed the truck across the wreckage of the Amoco Shop 'N' Go at three twenty-five, big wheels chewing through dead and detritus alike before screeching

to a halt less than five feet from the front doors. The
mounted heads upon it wailed: forced to bear witness,
driven far beyond madness by the world they had helped to
create.

The headlights' glare pierced the shadows as Deitz
stepped out of the truck, staring in terror at the gaping
space where the big plate-glass windows had been.

(*late too late too late too*)

Broken glass carpeted the interior in a billion glittering
crystal shards, glistening before him as he crunched through
the ruined front door. One of the service island trash cans
lay in the rubble like an enormous bullet. Living rain
oozed and slithered before him like vermin, retreating
from his path. The pumps were down. The store was
savaged.

And Jennie Quirez was nowhere to be found.

(*late too late too late*)

Deitz stood there, lost, in the middle of the aisles,
feeling the last of his dead heart clench with the inescapable weight of his loss. He felt it snap and rend asunder.
Lost to him now. Like her. Forever.

And it came from him, then: a primal moan that
originated at the core of his soul.

"*Hhnnnnnuhhhhh . . .*"

It fed on his pain, amplified itself in the cramped
confines of his skull. "*Hhnhhhnnuhhnnnuhhhhhhh . . .*"

Deitz had no mouth. His face was gone. It had
liquefied and recongealed, taking on the shape of the
chemical suit's hood like gelatin in a mold. But the sound
was building, becoming a cry, a mounting burning keening
howling razor-ribboned wail that sliced its way to the
thick, insensate flesh his bulky suit had become.

"*J-JhejhennnAAAAHHHHHHHHHH . . .*"

A fissure developed in the lower part of the faceplate:
a fold now a crack now a split-wide rift, a ragged jack-o'
-lantern mouth that stretched from ear to ear. Oily juices
spilled from the crevice, bubbling in the breach.

"*J-JEHNNNNNNNNNNHHHH!!!!!! JJEHHHHHNNAA-*

*NNNNAAAAHH!!!!! JEHHHHNNNEANNNNNNEEHHHHH-
NNNNNAEEEHHHH!!!!"*

And that was when he heard the sound: a tiny, mewling sound, very nearly lost against the background throes of the dying world.

It was coming from behind the *EMPLOYEES ONLY* door.

Deitz crossed the ruined expanse of the store, crashing through emptied display racks and discarded, useless, toxic goods. The freezers hummed. The mad truck screamed. Condensation writhed beneath his touch as he put his hand on the heavy door and pushed.

The door slid back. The still-burning headlights of the truck sliced through the shadows. The walls, the floors, the ceiling dripped with sentient damp.

And Jenny was there.

She was hunkered down behind a stack of water-logged, bloated cereal boxes in the farthest corner of the tiny room. Her face was hidden, her head down on her knees, her hands protectively cradling her skull.

"*Jehnn . . .*" he moaned.

He recognized her by her thick mahogany hair, most of which lay in piles around her haunches. A few stray tresses still clung tenuously to her scalp, which was chalky, pale and colorless as her hands, her arms, her neck. He could clearly see the veins in her scalp, pulsing arrhythmically under the stippled papyrus surface of her skin.

She patted the crown of her head gingerly; one of the few remaining hanks dislodged and floated to the floor, where the movement of air sent it wafting like a dust devil. She clutched at it blindly, missed, sobbed again.

"*Jehnnn . . .*" Deitz murmured thickly. "*Jehnneeee . . .*"

She looked up, head tilting this way and that, trying to fix the sound. It was only then that he understood.

*Her eyes—those warm and bottomless brown eyes that could light up a room with love—were gone. They had de-evolved, along with the rest of her beautiful, broad yet delicate features. No luscious lips. No regal nose. No gently sloping brow. No more. She was worn away and rounded down: a crude, half-finished sculpture of herself, rendered in mutely glistening mold.*

He moved toward her. She started to mewl.

"*Pleeeease . . .*" she whispered.

"*Shhhh . . .*" he murmured tenderly. "*Ss-shhhhh. . . .*"

He reached down to help her up. She cried out upon contact with his thick, rubber-coated fingers. He bent, grasped her gently around the torso, then slowly began to rise . . .

. . . and that was when he heard the *snap*, a sound so faint he might not have caught it at all had he not gone suddenly off-balance, holding her upper torso as if he'd lifted a pillow instead of a living woman . . .

. . . and she made one final sound: a dry weak mewling cry not so much of fear as *resignation*. Deitz looked down, beyond surprise, and saw the other half of her: still on the floor, surrounded by all that wonderful hair. He saw the chalky striations of the break-point, the tender gray mushroom meat of her waist and hips, the rings upon rings upon rings that filled her.

Jennie clutched at him with fingers fragile, her parting sound rustling like dry leaves in his ears.

"*Shh-shhhhh . . .*" Deitz cooed, enfolding her in his embrace.

Little bits of Jennie snapped and tumbled to the floor: fingers and hands and arms and torso crumbling and tumbling, crumbling and tumbling, in a softsoft pattering cascade. Deitz rocked and cooed and held her close. She slipped through his grasp like a fistful of sand, crumbled to nothing in his arms.

Then—only then—did he pick up the pieces. Bring them tenderly up to his broken lips.

And welcome her into himself.

# VII

# Fifty—Three

After the deluge, the New World rested.

The extent of the slaughter was unfathomable, immeasurable. Not even Overmind was up to the task. Its vision was too fractured and fragmentary now, forced to observe itself from far too many disparate points of view. Over nine hundred square miles, from the Appalachian foothills to the Susquehanna River, were laid to waste in those few short minutes. So many tiny lives subsumed. So small yet substantial a toehold gained.

The effort had been exhausting, leaving even the Overcore tapped and drained. The malaise was contagious, shared in common by all Its creatures, great and small. Dragging them inexorably toward an agonizing, fitful, rejuvenating slumber.

Leaving behind only the slow-metabolizing Plant Spawn, the witless rumbling Machine Spawn, and the handful of mad raw Savage Spawn that were not afterborn with the capacity for sleep.

While the last survivors of the old world calculated the odds.

And found them sadly wanting.

After the deluge, the New World rested. It had, for the moment, no other choice. Soon—very soon—It would inherit the earth.

In the meantime, It slept.

There would be no second chance.

# Fifty—Four

The rain was petering out now.

"Yes," Gary murmured. "Please, God." It was all he waited for.

Gary had cursed himself a thousand times in the last few minutes. While he waited in ambush, the world had come to an end, or pretty goddam near. Now they were trapped, all of them, and there wasn't a thing he could do about it.

Not that there was anything left to do here.

WPAL had signed off. For keeps.

One look at the mad sky above was all it took; sure as shit, the soot from the explosion had knocked out the microwave path from 'PAL to its transmitter tower. Worse still, nothing else seemed to work, either. The lights were flickering; the phones were garbled; even the AT&T long lines kept as emergency backup didn't seem like they'd be reaching out to touch someone anytime soon.

Half the monitors in Studio A broadcast only static and snow; the other half picked up intermittent shadowy ghosts, like transmissions from a distant world. On another planet, the Eagles still battled the Rams.

Gary was relieved. It meant that this was a localized phenomenon. For the moment, anyway.

*Good for them,* he thought. *Bad for us.*

There was only one thing he knew for certain: the second the rain stopped, he was out the door and heading for home, scooping up Gwen and then getting the fuck out of Dodge. It was simple as that.

He couldn't believe how stupid he'd been: to spend all goddam day here, being manipulated by these people, only to waste even more time on beating up a worthless little asshole like Kirk. He felt guilty, and ashamed. The explosion had rendered a lot of things academic in its wake, his rage first and foremost. He felt like a fool.

He'd have been gone fifteen minutes ago, were it not for the black rain.

And poor John's bad example.

*After the explosion, John Bizzano had decided he couldn't wait out the storm. He'd made a run for it, shrouding himself in one of the thick waterproof tarps they used for outdoor shots. Gary knew it was a bad idea, but John was stubborn; and for all his smarts, he'd always struck Gary as somewhat bereft in the common sense department.*

*He was out the door, heading for his car, before Gary could so much as say boo.*

*John hadn't make it ten yards before the rain brought him down. It was impossible to see much of anything through that thick black curtain of precipitation, but Gary could have sworn it just ate his legs out from under him. They could hear him screaming, but that died off; and before long, there was nothing but a big dead silent lump, unmoving beneath the slowly melting tarp.*

*As the rain tapered off, it got easier to see. The lump was dissolving, and the stink was incredible as the pocked, steaming tarp got flatter and flatter. What was left of John sluiced down to the gutter in thick viscid runnels, like molten tallow, like boiling fat, like . . .*

"Umm . . . Gary?" came Laura's voice from behind him. He clenched his teeth, got ready for it, turned.

"Now what?" he said.

"We hab'doo ged back on line," Kirk said, sucking spit back through swollen lips. His face was bloody, beaten so badly that his speech was slurred. Gary didn't want to look at him, to face the fact that *his* hands had done that. He looked down at his scraped knuckles, guilty as sin.

Worse still was how Kirk had taken it. Gary'd expected him to fold up like a cheap card table, to whine and cry and piss himself. But he didn't. In fact, he came back from the beating *stronger,* somehow. As if it had beaten the bullshit right out of him.

"You know we do," Kirk urged, following Gary's every move with his one good eye. Gary watched John run down the gutters and away. "People need do know whad's going on." He sucked spit again, and wiped a bloody streamer from his chin.

Laura stood at his side, supporting him; since Kirk had regained consciousness, they'd been pretty much inseparable. She thought about it for a moment, then her eyes widened. "What about the tower?" she asked. "Couldn't we broadcast from there?"

"Yes," Kirk said, pronouncing the sibilance with great difficulty. He slurped and looked at Gary. "We could."

"Aw, Christ," Gary groaned, bringing one hand up to run through his hair. He could see where this was going already. "Technically, yes. You could take a camera up there and hard-wire it right into the tower. Everything else is there. You wouldn't have network feed, but you'd be broadcasting at sixty-eight hundred megahertz over the airwaves."

"Whad range?" Kirk asked.

"A hundred miles, maybe," Gary shrugged, emphasizing the *maybe* part. "Minus a big unknown chunk of range due to the storm."

Laura and Kirk nodded in tandem.

"The only thing that's missing," Gary continued, "is the *point.* I mean, what exactly do we have to *say* to people right now? 'This is ACTION-9! Get outta here! Turn off your fuckin' TV and RUN, stupid!''

"Well, for one thing," Laura interjected, "we can tell them *where* to run. We've got emergency evacuation plans. . . ."

"Oh yeah, right," Gary scoffed. "Have you ever actually *looked* at those things? They're a joke, okay? We're not prepared for a mass evacuation! We're prepared to *pretend* we're prepared for emergencies that *never happen*!"

"Bud like you said," Kirk cut in, "it's localized." The word came out *loga-lied*. "Whijh means we can still ged away."

"I *hope*," Gary muttered.

"We gotta ged on line," Kirk said.

"Yeah? Who's gonna do this miracle?" Gary countered. "You?"

"Yeah," Kirk said. "Me."

"But he'll need help," Laura said. Meaning *you've got to help him*. "It's on your way." *You bastard*.

Gary looked at Laura and Kirk, and at poor running John, then shook his head. Outside, the city burned behind them.

"I don't believe I'm doing this. . . ." he groaned.

He turned to Kirk; Kirk flinched involuntarily. "Congratulations, kid," Gary said. "Looks like you get your own show, after all."

He turned to Laura. "I'll get it up and on-line," he said, then looking at Kirk, "but after that he's on his own."

Laura nodded in agreement.

"So what about you?" he asked.

"I'm staying," she said valiantly. "I'll keep trying to make radio contact. If we come back on-line, or the phones work again, I can feed you updates." Her gaze flitted away, then back to him quickly. "Someone's got to hold the fort."

And in that moment Gary understood a little something about Laura Jenson. She was tough as nails in her element; but take her out of it, and she was like a dust mote in a hurricane. No way would she sacrifice that power. She would stay here until she died, or someone came to rescue her.

And she would be able to rationalize it, the same way he had all day. *At least they'll know where to find me*.

"Where's your family?" he asked.

"In Philly," she flushed. "At the game."

Gary nodded. "That means they're probably safe." She smiled wanly. *Safer*, he meant. *As in "safer than you."*

He resisted the urge to bring up Gwen, his own family. No point. Until he could do something about it, it was dangerous even thinking about it.

"Two minutes," he said to Kirk. "With or without you."


Their good-byes were short and to the point.

Kirk got ready, wincing as he slid into his Windbreaker. Laura helped as best she could. When he had it zipped and flipped, he turned to her. There was a terrible sadness in his eyes, standing mute alongside the pain.

"Laura, I . . ." he began.

"*Don't.*" Her eyes were moist and bright. A kiss was out of the question.

So she hugged him instead.

He returned the embrace, holding still for one perfectly elongated moment: smelling her hair, the scent of perfume commingling with her sweat, the faint menthol taint clinging to her clothes.

"*Don't,*" she repeated, and squeezed him one more time before letting go. She was afraid to take it any further than that. If they were lucky, they might see each other on the other side of all this. And if not . . .

*Don't . . .*

But somehow, he couldn't help himself.

\*   \*   \*

Outside, even the drizzle had tapered down to nothing at last. The clouds remained hanging overhead, made a guillotine's blade of the sky. The fire to the north was still raging, flickering bright against its razored skyline.

The cold had rolled in now, Gary noted: a good ten-to-twelve-degree drop. A grayish-black ash wafted down like snow, hissing as it landed.

Gary kept his bike in the repair bay, which was probably why it survived the storm. He donned his leathers carefully, making sure he was as airtight as possible. Then he put on his helmet, making doubly sure the faceplate was snapped into place. He wasn't taking any chances.

Once dressed, he took a deep breath and threw open the big bay door. Kirk was there, motor humming, ready to roll. He gave Gary a deadly serious thumbs-up sign.

Gary nodded. "Yeah, fuck you, too," he said under his breath, as he clambered onto the softtail and started the bike up.

The Harley roared to life.

And, together, they rode off into Hell.

# Fifty—Five

Gary burned down the wide one-way slope of East Market Street, heading for the tower just as fast as Kirk's cranky six-cylinder would allow. The speedometer nudged eighty; Gary could push it way over one hundred without popping a sweat, but Kirk was already weaving.

*C'mon, punch it,* he urged. *Don't make me leave you.*

Downtown Paradise whipped by in a blur of hellish detail, its middle American quaintness slick with poison rain and backed by a throbbing storm front that glowed a brilliant brimstone hue. It was Nagasaki by way of Love Canal, Dante doing Norman Rockwell doing Bedlam.

Because everywhere lay the chaos and carnage. Crashed auto carcasses rammed through shops' plate-glass windows, their belly fires feeding ruptured gas mains and stoking a score of conflagrations. Former citizens caught off-guard by the storm and blast lay stiff and silted, stick figures sculpted in blistered ash. A handful of still-living sinners had evidently gone mad and taken to the streets, repressed libidos unchecked in the absence of a just and angry God.

*And then there were the creatures, the malformed alien things. They curled up in doorways and vestibules,*

*caught sidewalk shadows that fended off the dancing,
flickering fire. Some of them were nearly as big as the
buildings they dozed in the shelter of.*

*He found himself marveling at their slumber, and
wondering if they dreamed.*

Gary twisted the throttle, slaloming through abandoned and wrecked vehicles, hauling ass for the outskirts of town with Kirk hot on his tail. His hands were
tingling: the condensation on his gloves working its way
into the seams, trying to find a breach. His mind was a
schizophrenic relay race: unable to believe what was
happening, unable to deny it. He cursed and sped up,
inadvertently opening a gap between the bike and the
wagon.

They hit the intersection of Market and Memory Lane
with some sixty yards between them; at eighty-six miles an
hour, they cleared the intersection less than two seconds
apart.

Time enough for Gary to make it.

Kirk wasn't so lucky.

Dean's tanker truck passed between them as they
barreled through, the remains of Dean at the wheel: a
man-sized mass of gristle and tumors. Twenty-five years
of bad habits had left him so toxic that when it finally
awoke, he promptly exploded. What was left unconsciously
manned the helm, skeletal hands dripping chunks as they
raked the wheel.

The truck roared through the crossing and blindsided
Kirk, catching the wagon just over the right rear wheel
well and crumpling it like an aluminum can.

An experienced driver Kirk Bogarde was not. His
reaction was instant, and utterly wrong: slamming the
brakes and oversteering radically, then countering in a wild
seesaw motion. The car responded by spinning into a
gut-churning three-sixty.

Gary looked back just in time to catch sight of the
wagon hopping the curb near the edge of the K-mart

parking lot and broadsiding the concrete retaining wall, spitting sparks and stray metal.

"SHIT!" he cursed, skidding to a halt. He spun the softtail neatly in the middle of Market Street and looked back.

Paradise was doomed; of that he was certain. Kirk's car was a good three hundred yards behind on the burning street, hugging the low wall, its right side crushed from bumper to bumper. Gary seriously wondered if Kirk was dead, and had no real desire to go and find out.

He gunned the engine, weighing his obligations: to go on, to go back, to just go *home* and get the hell out of there.

Then Kirk's headlights flashed pleadingly, over and over and over, going *hi lo hi lo hi lo hi lo*.

"SHIT!" Gary cried out. He knew he didn't have any choice. He revved the throttle against every instinct.

And turned the bike around.


"Please . . ." Kirk worked the headlights desperately and fought the urge to black out. "Don't leave me!" he said.

Between the blood and the crushed glass, he couldn't see a goddamned thing. The front windshield was starred from the impact and sparkling; there was a corresponding inch-long gash on his forehead. It felt like his left leg was broken, too. Otherwise he thought he got off lucky.

At least, until he saw the Parade.

*It was coming right toward him, from the southeast: sweeping down Memory Lane, spilling across the K-mart parking lot, chewing up everything in its path. It clanged and rasped like a demolition derby show, Vlad the Impaler on a Funny Car Saturday. Eight hundred fresh victims stoked its mass.*

*Kirk was determined not to be the eight hundredth and first.*

"NAHHHH!" he cried, adrenaline resurging through him as he fumbled with the seat belt. Blood slicked his grip; he couldn't get it undone.

The Parade rumbled closer. Sixty yards. Fifty. He could see the twitching bits and pieces hanging from its many sharp and whirring surfaces. Forty yards. Thirty. The smell of burning rubber and diesel and flesh flooded his senses.

And that was when Kirk got his first glimpse of the NewSpawn.

*It was the size of a cocker spaniel; chunky and malformed, its snout hardened and drawn into a beak of sorts. Its front claws elongated into digits like fingers, like hands. It pounced and skittered across the hood of the car, toward the shotgun-side door. . . .*

"NO, GOD!" he screamed, as it weaseled its head in through the crack in the window. His hand flew to the window crank, frantically rolling it shut. The spawn caught, spat black venom blood. Kirk squeezed off its head with his glass guillotine.

*Then the driver's door flew open beside him, and before Kirk could scream, the figure with the knife brought its blade to his chest . . .*

. . . and Gary was there, saying *can you stand?* as his Buck knife sawed through the seat belt. Kirk nodded yes and hoped he was right, fighting a wave of vertigo as Gary reached past him to grab the camcorder off the seat . . .

. . . just as the first juggernaut loomed before the car, a giant metal scorpion-thing with a crown of steel thorns and a three-year-old blond girl's head impaled upon it. Its huge rusted stinger craned slowly up above its own blunt head, creaking as it drew a bead . . .

. . . then *whipped down*, astonishingly fast, dragging a screech from Kirk's lungs as he threw himself sideways, glass exploding in his face, the taste of metal throbbing in his teeth, the skewer *ding*ing off Gary's helmet before imbedding in the upholstery, the chassis, the road . . .

. . . and then they were running: Gary in the lead, Kirk half-dragged along behind. The Harley was waiting, thank God. Their last friend on Earth, it obeyed their commands, doing a hundred and thirty per down Market Street.

On its way to the tower.

At the peak of Mount Hope.

# Fifty—Six

For a second there, Micki thought she heard a motorcycle in the distance: the shrill whine of an overrevved engine, the shriek of skidding tires. Then it was gone, and she was left with the sounds on the wind.

The sounds of the death of the world.

"It wasn't him," she said, anticipating the question, unable to screen out the inconsolable weight of Gwen's fear. Something slithered across the windowpane outside. She couldn't do much about that, either.

Gwen stopped painting for a second, leaned her head into her hands. She was pulling it together pretty well now, under the circumstances; but Micki'd had to admit to herself that Gwen was not all there anymore. She had to walk on eggshells if she didn't want to watch her fold.

"He isn't coming, is he?" Gwen moaned, tears pooling in her eyes again.

"Yes he is." Gentle. Tense. The forced voice of calm. "Of course he is. Bobba said so. Now come on, we gotta hurry."

It was a lie, of course. Bobba didn't have a clue how Gary was. At this point, Micki couldn't even think about it. She had left a spirit doorway in the outer circle. It would open for Gary's soul alone. Beyond that, there was nothing she could do.

In the world beyond the outer circle, survival was no longer an option. There were things out there she could hear and smell that she did not want to see. Their howls of triumphant carnage were the music on the wind. Their stench rode the mist.

She could dimly see dark shapes amassing on the perimeter; but so far, the outer circle seemed to be keeping them there. Micki took this as a very good sign. It suggested the magick could hold its own, even hopelessly outgunned, in the face of environmental Armageddon.

*But you can't run from the devil in your own back pocket,* nattered a nasty little voice in her head. It was right. You couldn't keep out what was already in, and that covered a lot of ground.

When the deluge came, it had not been selective; it fell on the virtuous as well as the wicked. It fell on either side of the line. The ring of lawn between the circle and the house had soaked up a lot of rain.

That rain had borne fruit.

Now the exterior of the house was crawling with vines. They writhed serpentine on the walls, blindly scraped splintering furrows in the wood, dragged their thorns across the sweating glass. Every second that ticked by brought them that much closer to entry, underscored the barbed-wire knot of panic coiling through her gut.

*She had tried to protect the whole house; abiding by ritual, moving clockwise and frantically anointing every aperture and inlet with a mixture of salt and spring water. No fucking way. Every creaking door and rattling window, leaking faucet and drizzling drain, every single crack in every corner of every room beckoned her, demanding attention. All of them needed to be mystically sealed.*

*It was just too huge.*

*And she was running out of time.*

*From that point on, her life had been measured in minutes. Four spent helping Gwen up to the nursery,*

*getting her situated. Another five tearing the place apart
until it coughed up the supplies she needed: a box of
scented bathroom candles, matches, a pair of heavy quilts,
canned food and bottled water, can and bottle openers, a
pot of adequate bedpan size, a butcher knife, duct tape,
some sandalwood incense, and a little tin of McCormick
sage. Some of the things were needed for the ritual. The
rest were merely practical. She had no idea how long they
might have to stay in there.*

*All the paint they needed was already there.*

*Micki had spent the last seven minutes preparing the
one room she could actually defend. In this, she had
finally gotten some help; for Gwen, it was perfect therapy.
By three twenty-five, they had completed the ten-foot
pentacle that covered the nursery floor. Now it was a matter
of touching up the perimeter: taping floorboard cracks
that intersected the circle, plugging the leaks in the spirit
armor . . .*

Something went *pok* at the window. Micki's lungs
crawled up into her throat. There was a BB-sized star in
the glass, with a thorn poking through it. The thorn, ever
so slowly, withdrew.

Gwen started to whimper. Micki knew what she
meant. So far, they'd been astonishingly lucky, but she
sensed those days were about to end. The thorn popped
loose and dragged, *skreee*ing away like a glass-cutter.

Another dozen took its place.

"Gwen," she whispered. There was no more time to
wait. "*Light the candles.*"

"But what about Gary?" Too loud.

Micki winced. "*Shhhh*," she hissed; then, softly, "I'll
leave him a way in. I promise."

"You can do that?" Gwen's red eyes spoke volumes.
Her voice rose to match them, inching out of control.
"You're *sure* . . . ?"

"I already explained this to you." Micki glanced at
the window, held on tight to her temper.

"But what if something *happens* . . . ?"

"Gwen." Gritting her teeth. "Nothing's going to happen..."

"But..."

"GWEN!"

Gwen was shocked into stasis. Her tears overflowed. Micki took a deep breath.

And the windowpane shattered.

Micki screamed. She couldn't help it. Every inch of control, every last watt of power dispersed, blew apart in the shower of glass. In that moment, she was emptied of thought, personality, hope. Nothing left but the horror.

The sightless thing that entered the room commandeered her complete attention.

*Its skin was closer to bark than it was to shell or skin, but there all resemblance to ordinary plant life terminated abruptly. Its leaves were tonguelike, moist and thick; its thorns canine incisors. It left a steaming slime trail as it moved along the wall, raked inch-deep drywall trenches in its wake.*

"Light the candles." A toneless drone, through a mouth that barely moved. "Gwen. Please..."

Nothing happened. Gwen was frozen in place. Micki dry-swallowed terror and forced her own hand to snake out slowly for the box of matches.

The monster stopped dead.

"Oh, no," Micki croaked, her hand freezing in place. The vine probed at the air, like a menacing antenna. When she stopped, it had nothing to go on. It wavered, deaf as well, and then went back to tracing and gouging the wall.

It was ten feet away now and closing.

*Fuck the candles,* Bob-Ramtha said. *You don't have time.*

*Cast the circle now.*

And he was right, she knew he was right, there was nothing else and no other way, if the circle was flawed or the ritual sloppy or her will too depleted, then those were the breaks. Inaction meant certain death, and they were down to the very last ticks of the clock. One way or another, it had to be now.

She made her decision.

And acted it out.

"Sky-people," she said, addressing the east and forcing her voice to be strong. It was just a slight turn of the head, but the monster tuned into it instantly. She fought down a shudder, cleared dry phlegm from her throat. "I welcome you into our circle of light."

Then, turning to the south, a slight upper-torso pivot. It put the blunted nonhead of the thing behind her.

There were more coming in through the window.

"Brothers of fire," she croaked, the voice barely clearing her larynx. "We need you. Please come to our side."

*There were five of them now, eeling in through the hole. They fanned out across the walls ceiling floor. Behind her, Gwen mewled and went fetal in the second Micki spun full around, facing west.*

"WATER S-S-SISTERS!" she blurted out, panicking. She could hear them slithering, scraping, clawing. Could feel their graceless, unstoppable approach. "PLEASE!" she screamed, howling gaze and voice northward. "OH EARTH MOTHER *PLEASE* . . . !"

And she could see it coming, the first one in, the one with the rabid teeth and tongues that foamed as the fat misshapen vine undulated, thundered across the floorboards, sliding the last remaining foot to the lip of her magickal circle . . .

*. . . and suddenly she could feel Them: there with her, a presence and quasi-electrical charge that stood all her short hairs on end, plucked her flesh into goose bumps, sucked the air from her chest. Her spine felt liquid hot and burning with violent primal coursing* power, *the power of Goddess Herself, the power that spun the earth on its axis and breathed Spark into all that lived . . .*

. . . and the vine-thing stopped when it hit the line. Just stopped.

And could go no farther.

It smushed up against something unseen, its features flattening like a face pressed against a pane of glass. Then it slumped to the floor.

And began to trace the circle.

"Huh," Micki exclaimed. "Huh huh huh . . ."

The laughter came, then, spilling out in a rapidly escalating cadence as shock turned to amazement turned to frantic joyous victory. "F-FUCK YOU, YOU SPINY LITTLE SHITS!" she cried. "*FUCK* YOU!"

The vines hissed, responding to the air pressure and the emotion behind it. The magick was strong. The magick would hold.

It had been hours since Micki Bridges had allowed herself the luxury of laughing, or crying. She did both now, secure in the knowledge that, at least for the moment, they were safe.

"It's okay," she whispered, turning to Gwen. "It's okay." In reality, virtually no sound came out. She was mouthing the words to a platitude that had suddenly transcended cliche, become the truest sentiment she owned.

But Gwen couldn't take her eyes off the thorned serpents. They circled and swayed and probed the perimeter. They were looking for holes, for flaws in the barrier. Looking for ways through the light. Looking for a way to break the circle.

But there was only one way in, and it was reserved for Gary alone.

If he ever came. . . .

# Fifty—Seven

Mount Hope was a hump of heavily wooded rock on the eastern edge of the county, part of a long-lost finger of the Appalachian Trail. At twelve hundred feet above sea level, it was the county's highest natural elevation.

The WPAL broadcast tower had been erected there on a cleared right-of-way. From a distance, it looked like a sleek silver needle, rising fifteen hundred feet straight into the sky. Like the thread of life itself, gossamer-thin and delicate.

Up close, though, the sheer magnitude of its existence was apparent, etched in massive beams and inch-thick high-tension wire. It jutted upwards, in utter defiance of gravity and physics and Nature herself.

At the moment, it was holding its own against gravity and physics.

Nature was another story.

At the base of the tower stood a small corrugated steel shed, the padlocked hasp open and dangling. Inside, Kirk sat amongst the cluttered shelves of tools and test gear, his leg propped on a stray cable spool.

His leg was bad: broken at mid-calf and swelling like a blood sausage. They'd splinted it with an aluminum bracket and strips ripped from the acetate shell of his jacket, but it wasn't set and wouldn't be anytime soon. Every transgression of air pressure sent agonizing shock-waves buffeting through his nervous system.

On the bright side, it took his mind off of his teeth, and that was something. The swelling in his lips had gone down dramatically as well, at least enough to talk without sounding like he had a mouthful of wet washrags. As blessings went, they were pretty skimpy, but he took what he could get.

A stiff bitter gale wind blew off the river, whipping the mountain ruthlessly on its way to the firestorm. Thick strands of twisted steel whickered and thrummed like so many old rubber bands. And Kirk took every snap personally.

PEMA evacuation manuals and a walkie-talkie sat bunched on his good leg. He pored over them, trying to get a basic grasp of the material. The battered action-cam was perched on a tripod, lens aimed at his head; on the workbench, a test monitor faced him, already generating bars and tone.

"Ow, shit!" he muttered as the radio transceiver slipped off his lap and thudded onto the floor. He struggled painfully to scoop it up. "Are you sure we can do this?"

"Don't know." Gary shrugged and unreeled more coaxial cable. "The station went down because the micro wave only runs at thirteen gigawatts, and this soot could block out a bottom-feeder like that, no problem.

"But the transmitter's still hot, which ain't bad. And if this thing breaks the storm ceiling"—he gestured to the tower overhead—"I think we'll be in business."

Gary finished splicing an end on the cable with his knife. He hunched down behind the monitor, laboring fiercely, the clock in his head banging away as he tightened the cable down.

"Okay," he said. "Here goes nothing."

The screen glitched, and Kirk's face came up: bloody, bruised, and badly lit. "Jesus," he gasped. "I look like shit." He grabbed the tail of his shirt, tried to wipe off some of the dried blood from his forehead gash. Gary moved around the monitor as Kirk struggled to his feet.

"Okay, listen up," Gary said, concentrating on the work at hand. "Basically, you're set. I rigged this so that you just hit 'record' and you're on the air. Think you can handle it?"

Kirk nodded; Gary took it as gospel. Kirk hobbled around, checking the wiring and the only available light, a jerry-rigged clip-on spot with a hundred-watt bulb in it. He clicked it on; its glow seemed feeble against the encroaching dark. Hard to believe it was only three-thirty in the afternoon.

Outside, the wind hammered on the corrugated metal walls, making them sound both sharp and flimsy. Cables whipped the air high above their heads.

"You *do* understand," Gary said, "that as of now, I'm out of here."

"Uh-huh," Kirk said, busily repositioning the light.

"And when I leave," Gary continued, "you're effectively stranded." He chose his words carefully; there was no way to skirt the naked truth. "I can't be coming back for you."

It felt like he was sentencing Kirk to death; and though a half hour ago that would have seemed like a great idea, Gary's blood lust had long since been spent. He half-expected Kirk to back down now, half-hoped that he was right.

But Kirk only cocked his head quizzically, a strange calm coming over his face.

"You don't understand," he said. "I'm not going anywhere."

"I'm serious. . . ."

"So am I." Kirk's look was direct, and utterly clear. "I'm gonna ride this out from here, man. Don't worry about me."

Gary took a good hard look at Kirk, as if seeing him through new eyes. Or maybe it was Kirk who'd changed, grown up somehow. Kinda hard to say. "Last chance . . ."

he began, scarcely believing his own ears. Kirk flipped him a wink, with just a flicker of wince.

"What?" he said. "And give up showbiz?"

Gary rolled his eyes, and Kirk hobbled toward him, making for his seat. Gary came over and helped him onto the chair. There was nothing left to say. It didn't matter to Kirk if he lived another twenty years or another twenty minutes, just so long as they got this last broadcast on the air. It was something he had to do—the best thing he could *possibly* do, under the circumstances.

And that was really all there was to it.

Across the valley, more storage vessels went up at Paradise Waste, feeding fresh waves of deathlight and sound into the serpentine pillar of flame. The rumbling wind reached out for them across thirteen miles, slammed the walls of the shed like an angry fist. Glass cracked, from a pane high overhead. The two men flinched, but nothing followed.

Then Kirk turned his attention back to the camera, and Gary nodded once before turning to open the door. For a moment, the roar of the world filled the shed; and Kirk could see him hesitate, for one long second's time, before stepping out into evernight.

And closing the door behind him.

Kirk held off for a minute, listening to the girders that creaked overhead while he waited for the Harley to fire. When it did, he sighed relief, listening almost wistfully to the echoing sounds of its departure.

Only when it was lost in that howling sea of sound did he turn back to the camera, take a deep breath, and hit "record."

The red light winked on.

And the real show—The Kirk Bogarde Show—went on the air at last.

# Fifty—Eight

Down in the newsroom, Laura had established a ritual all her own. She, too, had locked herself in, padlocking the front double doors, sealing every conceivable entrance, holing herself up in the basement. Holding down the fort.

And praying that the cavalry would come.

Outside, things were moving; she could hear the thuds and screams, the shrieking sirens, the distant and not-so-distant report of explosions and gunfire.

Worse, she could hear the *other* sounds, like nothing she'd ever heard before, grinding and slithering and slashing and withering everything in their paths. She winced as what sounded like a pickup truck roared by, followed seconds later by something that whistled and whined like a hundred dentists' drills grinding into a whole roomful of teeth. They screeched around the corner, off King Street and onto Market, and blazed away.

The crash, when it came, was dull and wet, and seemed to last forever.

Laura blocked it out and pressed on: checking the scanners, checking the monitors, checking the phones, over and over and over. At the head of each cycle she spent a solid minute on the radio, trying to raise the tower.

As rituals went it was short on style and long on utility, but it helped her keep her sanity.

"WPAL to tower, this is WPAL calling tower, do you copy? Kirk, do you copy?"

There was no response.

"This is WPAL, calling tower. Come in, please. . . ."

Nothing.

She dropped the transceiver, leaned over the scanners as their LED's strobed off, one by one: garbled cries becoming garbled hiss becoming nothing but garble at all, the lights cycling an endless flatline of silence.

Laura looked up: the monitors displayed an electronic winter wonderland of snow and static and white white noise. The newsroom was barren. Desolate. Irrelevant.

She picked up the phone and hit the speed-dialer for home. There was no answer. *Of course no one was there,* she reasoned to herself. *How could they be? They're in Philly at the game.*

"Please," she prayed in her heart. "Please let them be safe. Even if I never . . . if I can't . . . if . . ."

Something inside her tore loose then, like a flock of blackbirds fluttering inside her chest. She fought like hell to keep it down, but it was no use: the fear and pain and panic and loss burbled up like Old Faithful, geysering out in a wave of tears and frustrated rage.

"*Bastards!*" she muttered in anguish, slamming the phone down. "YOU MISERABLE FUCKING *BAS-TARDS*!!"

She exploded then, grabbing a pile of rough copy that no one would ever read and sending it sailing. She railed, cursing Blake and Leonard and Pusser, the Three Stooges of the Apocalypse, for the greed and expedience that brought this on. . . .

"IT'S NOT *FAIR!*" she cried.

. . . cursing herself for not getting the news of it *out* there, for not ramming it down people's throats while she still had a chance . . .

"NOT FUCKING *FAIR*!!"

. . . cursing everyone, cursing the whole miserable stupid world for letting things slide, until it rolled right over them all.

Down in the basement, Laura wept.

The newsroom absorbed her cries, reflected them back to her. Bad enough to feel these things at all: so much worse still to feel them alone. Her anger spent itself on empty air, leaving only the terror in its wake.

"*Please, God,*" she whispered, her voice quivering in her chest, a chill sweat prickling her scalp. "*I'm scared. I'm afraid to die like this. I'm . . .*

"*Please . . .*" she faltered, unable to fully voice the grief and guilt and regret.

And Monitor One suddenly hitched and came to life.

"*. . . This is Kirk Bogarde, uh, live, with an emergency report from our broadcast tower on Mt. Hope. . . .*"

"OH GOD!" Laura cried, leaping straight out of her chair and heading for the monitor as if he were there in the flesh. It was a feeble signal, distorted, but it was there like a lifeline; a single candle glowing in a world gone dark.

"SONOFABITCH!" she cried, tears streaming now. "YOU *MADE* IT!"

Kirk looked like hell; his hair was plastered to his scalp on one side with what certainly looked like blood, and the light source cast harsh shadows on his features, making him as gaunt and cadaverous as an extra from the lost footage of *Night of the Living Dead*.

But he *carried* himself, she realized. He was *there*, goddammit, and he knew it.

"*Reports are difficult at this time,*" Kirk said, "*but our most up-to-the-minute information indicates a tremendous explosion at the Paradise Waste Disposal facilities in North Manchester Township. All residents are advised to evacuate the area immediately. Repeat: hundreds feared dead at an explosion at Paradise Waste facilities in North Manchester Township.*"

"YES! DO IT!" Laura said excitedly, clapping her hands, "YES YES YES . . ."

"*Authorities are unavailable for comment at present,*" Kirk said. "*But our recommendation here at Channel 9 is that you get your loved ones and yourselves the hell out of here.*"

He leaned into the camera. "*And that goes* double *for you, Laura.*"

Laura gasped. On-screen, something fell in the background. Kirk ignored it, went back to his stats.

"*The evacuation routes are as follows,*" he said. "*From Windsor Township, take Route 615 south to Fulton. From Upper Darien, take the Mifflinsburg Pike . . .*"

And then suddenly, the lights went out. There was a pop. The monitors went dead. The overhead fluorescents sputtered abruptly.

And in less than an eyeblink, the room went black.

"*Ohgod ohgod . . .*" Laura whispered, clamping down. The room was almost totally enshrouded, its sole illumination a wan blue glow coming from the hall door.

"It's okay," she told the shadows. "It's just a blown transformer, or a downed line, or, uh . . . or . . ."

There was a drinking fountain just outside the door, its white porcelain gleaming. As she watched, the spigot suddenly spritzed to life, sending a little arc of water pooting forth, going *pucketa pucketa pucketa pucketa . . .*

Upstairs the front doors wrenched open, the sound of metal ripping like paper, followed by crowd sounds, of many many things coming in and rooting around, casting bizarre shapes against the solitary shaft of light that filtered in from the head of the stairs. It wasn't long at all until it was followed by the leathery slap of feet hitting the stairs, one by one by one.

At the other end of the room, something that walked upright for the first time ever stopped at the little fountain and took a refreshing gulp.

Then it turned and peered into the darkness. Its many

eyes made out Laura's huddled form and it gurgled, a sound of pleasant surprise.

It moved forward, one withered hand up for balance, dragging the rest of its parts behind, and closed the distance as if in perverse answer to her prayer.

And Laura was no longer alone.


High atop Mount Hope, the world premier of The Kirk Bogarde Show was ending just a little ahead of schedule.

It wasn't quite as he'd imagined it, but then what was? The bad news was that the major east-west and north-south escape routes were hopelessly jammed with wrecks, as survivors of the first wave went manic, trying to get out of town.

The good news was that he could still do the weather.

The temperature was dropping rapidly; it was maybe thirty-five, definitely falling. Atmospheric pressure intensified as the firestorm drew cold air in from all directions. Water vapor condensed on the finer atmospheric particulate, bonding.

And the fog rolled in.

Kirk shivered in his linerless jacket, feeling the acid sting of the mist on his skin. *It's primal*, he thought: *weather for the dawn of time.*

*Or the end of the world.*

His teeth chattered as he rattled off possible, even hopeful escape routes. He didn't really believe in them anymore. That wasn't the point.

Behind him and around him, pieces were falling: the tower was disassembling itself, strut by strut, in the high killer wind. The last hunk to tumble was big as a refrigerator; it crashed into the ground less than ten feet away from the shed with a deafening thump, sent rainbow ruptures of agony throughout his leg.

Kirk blinked back tears. And kept on going.

"From Geetzerburg, take Route 232 to Hanlin," he

read. "And remember: avoid Route 30 east over the river bridge."

He hobbled out of frame then, looked out the window.

Down on the Susquehanna, the flames were blooming yellow-gold where a tanker truck had collided with a stalled lane of traffic and ignited. Flaming victims still tumbled to the rocky waterline, their tiny limbs thrashing wildly.

"Repeat," he reiterated, limping back into frame. "The river bridge is *definitely out* on Route 30. Looks permanent, folks."

Just then the wind kicked up, and there was a great wrenching sound as it caught the lip of the shed's corrugated roof. It peeled back like the lid on a sardine can. Metal and junk rained down; a lug nut the size of a golf ball hit Kirk in the temple, knocking him out cold.

He came to in the wreckage an instant later, jump-charged by adrenaline and immeasurably worse off. He had a concussion and a crushed rib, and his leg was broken in at least three more places.

"Oh, fuck, not again," he moaned. He tried to move.

And found he could not.

Something was pressing against his chest, something huge and unforgiving. Kirk opened his eyes and found he was pinned beneath the fallen tool shelf, half-buried in parts, staring up into roiling fog and endless, eternal night. The remains of the tower teetered uncertainly.

The camera lay on its side against the workbench, the tripod toppled. It was pointing at him, askew and just out of reach. The "record" light still glowed red and merciless.

"Unh," he grunted. The camera watched. Kirk struggled under the buckled shelf, fighting down panic. "Having a little, unh . . . technical difficulty, here, folks."

He grunted and heaved, trying to budge the blunt edge of metal that pressed him into the floor like a bug in a science project.

High above, there came the *pop pop pop* of tension cables snapping like steel slingshots as something heavy broke free, began the long fast descent. He strained to free himself, and something burst deep in his chest.

Kirk screamed. His eyes went wide and locked on something coming, big and bright and spinning like a dervish. A five-hundred-pound strut came pinwheeling down from out of the fog and straight for his face, like the ultimate 3-D effect.

Kirk screamed again. The camera loved him.

It was a television first.

# Fifty—Nine

The first contraction struck at three thirty-five, a tidal wave of ground glass and lethal venom aimed directly at Gwen Taylor's spine. She'd felt it swell, amassing strength, for nearly thirty seconds before it hit. She hadn't known what it was, what it meant, or what it held in store.

It hardly mattered.

Nothing in this life could have prepared her for that moment.

*The pain was a ragged ratcheting metal fist, a screaming bonesaw violation so far beyond ordinary pain it boiled down endorphins and tortured the steam. When she screamed, the sound it produced was the worst she could manage.*

*It wasn't enough.*

Gwen stared up, through eyes of anguish, into the widening eyes of her friend. She watched as Micki's irises dilated, made room for the terrible realization that everything was *not okay,* no, not even a little.

Gwen was going into labor.

She was going to have her baby.

*Right now.*

The contraction rode its peak for twenty agonizing seconds, then decayed far too slowly. On the way back down, she felt her faculties return. The pain had blowtorched her mind into crisp hyperclarity; for the first time in hours, it was completely her own.

*Oh my God,* it whispered silently in her ears. Watching the mobile spin above the shattered, capsized crib. Watching the vines compress and squeeze, like an octopus attacking a glass-bottomed boat.

"*Oh my God,*" she whispered aloud, as Micki wiped high-definition beads of perspiration off her brow. Watching her dreams turn to rubble before her eyes.

"Gwen . . ." All the color had drained from Micki's face. She looked *old* in that moment, enfeebled by her terror.

Gwen reached up to touch Micki's face, Micki's hair, to convince herself that this *wasn't* real, that she *hadn't* awakened from a dreaming Hell only to find herself trapped in its inner circle. She blinked her eyes, and the room was still there. She shut them tight, and the delirium sounds remained.

"What are we going to do?" she quietly implored.

And Micki's response was, "*I don't know.*"

Behind the cacophonous wall of noise came a different voice: a distant, mounting growl. A powerful metal avenging roar, angrily surging into sonic dominion.

It took her a moment.

But she recognized the sound.


Gary cried as he twisted the throttle in his hand, the hand that prickled and itched as if drugged to numbing sleep. The Harley growled in response, engine revving out a mad frantic rhythm of speed and endurance. His gloves were sodden; his jacket was so damp it felt like the leather would reanimate. Sooty droplets of living condensation crawled across his visor, looking for a way in; Gary realized that Gwen's present had probably saved his life. It made him love her all the more, made him want to tell her that.

If he ever saw her again.

Because there was a deathvoice in his head now, a hoarse soul cry shrieking LATE TOO LATE TOO LATE, feeding his fear and stoking his guilt as Gary gunned along, a solitary rider on the road to Hell.

*Not Hell,* he amended. Hell was a comical conceit in which human beings really mattered. Hell placed mankind, by simple proximity, at the center of Creation.

There were no such illusions as Gary rode, no comfortable pantheon of gods and devils to fall back on. This land held no place for them, living *or* dead. The place that was his home now belonged to something else.

And *he* was the intruder.

Premature night had fallen like a shroud as the cloud cover thickened and the fog rolled in. The pillar of fire was visible as a furious red-orange glow on the horizon, a false midnight sun that blotted out the real thing. Gary's mind was racing as fast as the bike, revising their escape route as each mile slid by. Once he got there they would pack the truck and head south, then west, keeping the disaster always to their backs.

*They would make it. They would survive.*

He swore it.

At three thirty-nine he screeched around the corner that marked the homestretch and skidded to an abrupt halt. Gary stared out over the vista, momentarily paralyzed by the sight.

The sides of the road had been grotesquely transfigured, its familiar contours turned unwilling host to the writhing knotted vines that oozed from the woods like some turbo killer kudsu, overrunning trees and telephone lines. Cars. Homes. Lives.

*Everything but the road,* he realized.

*The macadam lay untouched; a smooth gray ribbon winding through a sea of writhing growth. It was as if it wanted the roads open, as if . . .*

*. . . as if it needed them.*

Gary pulled off his helmet and stared in awe.

He thought of the tape, of the figure in the truck: the truck full of barrels, the barrels full of poison rumbling down the roads, heading God knows where. . . .

*Heading everywhere.*

His neighbors' homes lay before him: nightmare structures rendered lumpen and indistinct as the vines choked them off, burying them, smothering whatever lay trapped inside. His neighbors lay, similarly lumpen and indistinct, beneath the twisting clumps of gray-green growth.

Deep inside him, the deathvoice sang.

*LATE TOO LATE TOO LATE . . .*

"NO!" he screamed, frantically searching for his home in the mutant topography. He looked to where it ought to have been.

And saw the magick circle.

*It was a ring of thorns rising high into the viscid swirling fog, a treacherous barrier disappearing into the cloud cover a hundred feet up. He could see the growth undulating, weaving itself in geodesic desecration, ten thousand barbed biting tendrils storming some arcane blueprint of protection. The vines were hardening, taking on the appearance of armor. There were easily a hundred thousand bristling, glistening spikes pointing menacingly out and inward.*

*New vines on the edge of the circle coiled themselves, ready to strike, then leapt, stretching to maximum extension like bungi jumpers, hooking onto the frame and pulling themselves up, feelers blindly reaching for the heavens.*

Their house was inside the ring, intact but barely visible, sealed away like a ghost ship in a glass bottle. . . .

"GWEN!" Gary cried at the top of his lungs. "*GWEN!!*"

His voice echoed out across the thorned plain, came back unanswered. He looked to the house, letting the tears fall where they may, afraid to touch them.

And that was when he saw it.

There was a spot at the bottom edge of the circle that was still raw: not immediately visible, but there, like a secret entrance. It shimmered and refracted like a transparency laid over a real space, an Industrial Light and Magic-style hallucination.

''What the fuck?'' Gary blinked; it was still there. New vines reached across from either side, their barbed green fingers still soft. Micki's spirit door, left open for him.

The driveway before him slithered with undergrowth, as inviting as a bed of broken glass. Gary hesitated, racing the engine anxiously.

Then he heard the women scream.

The voices were both inchoate and distinct; two familiar cadences overlapping in terror and pain. It was Gwen and Micki; of this he was sure. The woman he loved and . . .

Any animosity he'd ever felt toward Micki went flying out the window in that moment, as he tasted the timbre of fear in those cries.

The women screamed again. The vines writhed in response, as if feeding on the sound. One voice screamed back his name; the other simply screamed.

''GWEN!'' Gary bellowed. ''MICKI!''

The spirit door pulsed and glowed. He knew what he had to do. He revved the motor, feeling the tears come and letting them.

Then he popped the clutch.

And opened it up.

The Harley leapt to the task, racing toward the shining door just as fast as he'd let it. The bike roared, chewing up the vines even as the barbed strands chewed up the tires. He would not stop. He could see them moving, feel thorned tips reaching for him. They nicked his boots and grabbed at his machine. The softtail's wheels spun and slid, throwing shredded rubber and slick crimson spray.

But he would not stop.

Gary closed the distance. The vinewall loomed menacingly.

"*Please,*" he whispered to no one in particular.

He hit the outside perimeter at just under fifty miles an hour and together they mulched a path through the undergrowth. Ten feet from the wall was a low vine as thick as a fallen tree; Gary popped a wheelie as he reached it, threw his whole body into it, and *sprang*! The bike tore through the spirit door like a buzz saw through a bonsai tree.

And Gary was flying.

*There was a moment of intense exhilaration as he breached the circle, a joyous* fuck you all I made it! *as man and machine hurtled through the wall, thorned streamers of vines trailing behind.*

*Then the spirit door slammed behind him.*

*And Gary was in.*

The earth came back with a piston-crunching resolve, and Gary found himself sailing through some very real space on his way to some very real ground. A vine as thick as a banister snagged the rear wheel on the way down and dropped the whole shebang out from under him, Gary went head-over-handlebars, off the machine and into space.

He landed on a bed of leaves and stinging grass, came to seconds later with the screams still ringing in his ears. His skin was a flayed-raw thing, every bone in his body a player in his symphony of pain. Gary fought to clear his head.

Then he staggered to his feet.

And fought his way toward the door. . . .


Inside the nursery, a garden had grown.

*The vines writhed together in a spiraling latticework dance: younger tendrils, twig-thin and deft, interweaving with the stouter ones to form elaborate grids of containment. If they couldn't get in, then nobody could get out.*

*In the minutes since Gwen's first contraction, the vines
had grown to envelop the circle of light: a ten-foot
ring of thorns that reached all the way to the ceiling,
pressing into the plaster hard enough to fissure and buckle
it.*

*They fed on fear and pain.*

*They were very well fed. The vines had grown per-
versely, virulently fecund in this atmosphere: tonguelike
leaves swelling fat and thick over bloated blood-red pods
of fruit that ripened and rotted and thudded to the floor in
an instant, like the stars of some cheesy stop-motion nature
film.*

*All in the three minutes since Gwen's first contraction.*

"It's coming," Gwen said tersely, bracing for the
pain. "Oh God Gary *hurry* . . ."

The groundswell of the second contraction rippled
across her features like heat lightning. Veins bulged in her
forehead. Her nostrils flared.

"*Breathe!*" Micki coached, watching her friend's
face flush crimson as their hands squeezed together hard
enough to snap bone, a pressure that built until a
thin, kettle-boiling *eeeeeeee* emitted from Gwen's lips,
snapped off into a machine-gun volley of hyperventilating
breath.

Downstairs, the front door flew open.

Gwen *screamed*, head whipping violently in the
direction of the sound. She screamed Gary's name.
Micki turned as well, her mind racing a mile a minute,
going *thank God you made it, you made it through
the circle* as she tried to imagine the road he had
traveled, tried to imagine how in hell they might
escape, wanting to escape more than anything in the
world . . .

. . . but Gwen was in labor, she could pop at any
second, and the logistics of escape were incalculable
under those circumstances. Gwen was in no position to
run, to fight, to do anything but what her entire physiology
as geared up for in these moments. And Micki did not

want to deliver a baby in the back of a moving pickup truck.

Gwen's pain had plateaued. Micki could feel it receding, could feel the pressure of Gwen's grip diminish like steam from a ruptured valve . . .

. . . and suddenly a look of such utter horror possessed her face that it froze Micki in mid-mental stream.

"It's not ready!" Gwen wailed. "It's not ready!"

"What . . . ?"

"It's not ready to come out! Oh GOD . . . !"

Micki's hands traced the contours of Gwen's swollen belly, felt an unnerving liquid slosh beneath the rock-hard wall of muscle. Gwen cried out again, inarticulate this time, not out of pain but from mortal terror.

It only took a second to peel off Gwen's panties and part her legs. Micki was no midwife, but she'd been around enough to know what to look for. In the dim light, it was difficult to see, but the outer vaginal lips felt impossibly bloated to her touch.

She reached inside, just as the sound of footsteps slowly thudded up the stairs. They were staggered, and painfully uneven. *He's all fucked up*, said an anonymous voice in her head, even as her middle finger probed the moist walls of Gwen's interior. *Oh, no . . .*

And then she reached the cervix, the throat of the uterus, felt the elastic ring of cartilaginous muscle that must dilate for the child to emerge. Her fingertip slid over the os, expecting to find an aperture some ten centimeters around.

Instead, she found a pinhole, not even a centimeter wide.

*What?* she thought, fingers checking again. It didn't make sense. Even normally, it would have been at least two centimeters wider than this. It was as if the muscle had irised shut intentionally, as if refusing to allow the baby to be born. . . .

*Get away from her NOW*, Bob-Ramtha roared.

And Micki had one final moment of disorientation, a second too long. She looked at Gwen's face, saw the eyes rolling back, got a very brief flash of her life in poignant retrospective.

She started to withdraw her hand.

Just as Gwen's water broke.

*She began to die from the moment it first sluiced between her fingers, pooled in her palm, trickled down her wrist. The blood of the New Earth soaked into her pores, raced down her conduits, tended the little black seed in the pit of Micki's belly.*

*She was completely unaware that Gary had entered the room, had no idea that Gwen was dying, too. For her, these last moments were a total obsession that lasted entirely too long.*

You can't run from the devil in your own back pocket, *sang that anonymous voice in her head. Unchained at last, the black seed bloomed, throwing off the chains she'd kept locked for so long. The cancer burned through her, raiding cells, inciting riots, commandeering the myriad systems in her body; lymphatic, nervous, digestive, reproductive. Telegraphing one simple, fatal message.*

*The vines were inside her now, too.*

*Micki watched in horror as they rose up, swelling beneath her skin, sprouting tendrils and thorns, a thousand black needles impaling her from within and emerging, puckering from the riddled surface of her skin.*

*Micki looked past Gwen, past the circle to the wall. The Faery Queen was there, watching impassively, not real at all but paint on plaster, the vines gouging her surface even as the wasps bored holes and laid eggs in her face. And Micki knew that the balance had forever shifted, that the tables had been turned. The benign monarchy was overthrown by a muscular new regime.*

*Nature herself was banished, in exile.*

*And the world she knew would never heal.*

*The barbed-wire knot of panic became hideously*

*literal then. Micki choked on her own bristling esophagus,
felt a gallon of tumorous curds tear loose from within her
intestinal tract, spewing vile gobbets from her nostrils and
mouth.*

*The thorns encircled her brain like a crown, punc-
tured her eardrums from the inside, snaked out along the
optic nerves to skewer her eyes like cocktail onions,
blinding her forever.*

*And Bob-Ramtha's voice called out to her, but he
could not get through. It was like she was no longer tuned
to his station. Harsh static enveloped and took him away.*

*And then she was gone as well: not liberated by
death, but merely subsumed. The black seed thrived in its
new location, set down roots and claimed her, her substance and spark, reduced to raw fertilizer for the next
wave of earthly Creation. . . .*

. . . and Gwen was still screaming when Gary threw
himself at the last line of defense, hacking at the vines that
entwined and enmeshed the circle, slicing his way to the
last spirit door.

A buzzing filled his ears. He ignored it, concentrating
on the angry tendrils that he sawed in half as they desperately
tried to free themselves from the entanglements they had
chosen. Black liquid spritzed. It burned where it landed.
He ignored it as well, driven by adrenaline and love.

Gwen called out his name as the first red stringy
wasp-thing rose from the rotting fruit pulp on the floor. It
poked a hole in the soft flesh beneath his left eye, injected
agony. He grabbed the wasp-thing before it could pull out,
felt the satisfying *squish* of it between his fingers, and
grabbed another vine. Gwen shouted something else, more
weakly, but he couldn't hear it over the sound of his own
bellowing pain.

He sawed into a stout vine; its blunt, blind head
swung back like a mace, thorns punching holes the size of
tenpenny nails in his side as it smashed his ribs.

Gary fell face-first through the fissure he'd carved in the ring of thorns. His head cleared. His shoulders followed.

Something grabbed ahold of his leg.

"NO!" he screamed, slashing back with the knife. The resulting gush of acid sap ate into the back of his knee.

By the time he pulled himself fully inside, time had slowed down dramatically for him. He could savor every twitch of his St. Vitus spasms, isolate every last trill of her tiny dying sounds. A nerve-dead numbness had settled over him, trading all his other pain for simple, searing cold.

He could not stop shaking.

But he could not stop struggling, either. He had come all this way to be with the woman he loved—to die with her, if need be—on the very last day of the only world they'd known.

That was the only thing he cared about in the poisoned world it had become.

The air seemed to grow warmer in the circle, the vines exuding a foul chlorine-cholorphyll scent. He crawled to her, dizzy, and looked into her eyes. He saw the faint spark there, his presence fanning it like a breath on glowing embers.

She tried to smile, could not. The spark faded. A single tear leaked out, too weak to fall. He nodded, touching her face, her hair.

"*I'll see you on the other side, darlin',*" he whispered. She nodded her head, but barely.

And God did he hope it was true.

Then she shuddered, and her light winked out.

Forever.

Leaving him alone on this fucking godforsaken world, with no hope and no possible reason to go on. Leaving him alone with only her dead lips to kiss, trying to imagine a reason on earth for hanging on. His side was numb and bloody, his leg a twisted stick. He leaned against her belly, searched his eyes for tears and found none there.

The knife in his hand felt like a shortcut on the road he was already on. There was nothing else to do. He wiped the sticky blade on his pants leg and pulled back his sleeve, placed its edge trembling against the skin of his wrist.

And the baby kicked.

Gary lurched and sat up, astonished. He'd felt it clearly, an audible *thump*. He whirled, pressed his ear fully against Gwen's dead belly.

Deep in the stillness, something stirred.

The baby was alive.

"Oh, God," Gary croaked. He looked at Gwen, but there was no doubt: her skin was gray and cooling, her eyes gone milky opaque. The Gwen he knew and loved was gone for good.

*But the baby . . .*

Time was critical. There was no other way. He had to do it, he told himself. He had to do it *now*.

Gary knelt before Gwen's body, pulled her dress back to reveal the swell of her womb. *This is not my Gwen,* he told himself over and over, fighting down the revulsion. *This is not my Gwen.* He placed the knife against the firm mound of flesh just over the rise of her pubic mound, and pressed.

The first cut was too hesitant, separating the dermis but scarcely touching the muscle beneath. The blood that came was sluggish, lifeless. Gary groaned and wept, and forced himself to repeat the motion. He pressed harder this time, piercing the abdominal wall and drawing upward with steady pressure from the edge of her pubic mound over the rim of her navel.

The second time Gwen's womb split open with a wet melon sound. Gary gagged and kept going, lengthening the breach. Gwen's body sagged, relieved of the stress of containment. Gary moaned and kept cutting.

The placenta became visible, a spongy pink-red mass already sloughing from the wall of the womb. Gary finished the cut and dropped the knife, the tears streaming from his eyes.

Hands trembling, he parted the folds of flesh.

And reached inside his wife.

"Oh please . . ." Gary keened, tearing through the diaphanous veil of tissue. "Please . . ." He grasped the infant, cradling its head as he scooped under its back.

And pulled their baby free.

The child was a deep pinkish red, smeared head to toe with afterbirth. "It's a girl, Gwen," he murmured, tears coming now as he cradled the infant in his hands. "Spike is a little girl."

And at the moment, Gary felt the entire universe pinwheeling on its axis, stars and planets realigning themselves around their new center, in the very heart of Hell.

Which he held, at this moment, in his bloody, battered hands.

His daughter moved, little limbs spasming from the rude shock of emergence. Gary's heart stopped. Something was wrong.

She was not breathing.

"*NO!*" he cried, heart sledgehammering, feeling her squirming struggle for life. He saw her turn a dark plum color, her tiny features contorting in panic. He looked closer and saw the little plugs of mucus damming her nostrils.

Without hesitation, he brought her face to his lips and sucked the plugs out, tasting salt and slime, then spat them on the floor. Then he turned her over and slapped her; another, thicker plug dislodged from her throat.

The blockage fell away then; Gary watched, stunned, as her airways opened up and she took her first breath.

Then returned it, with a raw cry of life.

"YES!" Gary wailed, sobbing now, cradling his little girl in his arms. "YES!" as he swaddled her, using one of the quilts from under Gwen's legs to wipe away the blood and afterbirth, expose her clean pink infant skin.

Her skin, which instantly speckled with a billion dots of red.

*Her skin, through which the viscid poison oozed from every single pore....*

And Gary Taylor wiped her down. Then he did it again. Then he did it again. He wiped and he wiped to keep up with the flow, scrubbing a slate that would never be clean. Long after his mind was gone. His purpose forgotten. His life turned to ashes.

Cleaning up after the sins of the fathers, too late.

While the baby screamed into the night.

# Sixty

The Wolf's Head Nuclear Generating Station melted down at three fifty-four, eastern standard time. It was the final straw. When the core breached the reactor and hit upwards of three thousand degrees Fahrenheit, it slagged a hole through the ten-foot-thick concrete-and-rebar lining of the containment vessel and kept right on going.

Burning its way to the center of the earth.

Two hundred feet down, the core hit an underground spring. The water was waiting for it. Molten day and liquid night met with a kiss, deep in the folds of the earth. The plume born of their joining rocketed back to the surface, blew the lid off the containment building. A lethal radioactive cloud rose five hundred feet into the sky, annihilating the ones who had fought to contain it.

Then it spread its wings and rode the prevailing winds.

The winds blew around and around the world.

So, too, was the underground spring inextricably bound to the bloodstream of Earth: an unseen and unbroken flow, feeding springs and creeks and rivers and oceans for hundreds of thousands of miles around.

As above, so below.

And on the New World's surface, so neatly in between, the exodus began. One hundred and eighty-eight thousand souls, saying good-bye to Paradise as they fanned out across the hardened concrete arteries of the old world. Each one carrying the seeds of the future within it, and nothing to stand in their way.

On I-83, en route to the nation's capital, Austin Deitz and Lydia Vickers led the way. Deitz remained at the fore, so that the screaming, eternally-suffering heads of industry would be sure to miss nothing of what they had wrought.

Inside the truck, Deitz drove in silence. A strange peace had settled over his soul. The jagged lips, unfeeling still, had evolved into a smile. He could feel Jennie's everywhere presence, within and without. Tiny, delicate mushrooms sprang forth by the thousands. Covering his body.

Keeping him warm.

The Scuzzbag, too, had flourished, become a radiant flagship for the new regime. Its fuzz-covered surface was livid, alive. Vile, organic banners and sentient streamers flapped behind it, extensions of its cold metal flesh.

Inside sat Lydia, intensely mad and grinning from ear to ear to ear: the original Overmind majorette, cheerleading the boisterous procession. There *was* a future, after all, and it was here. Her dozen limbs were living proof. They kicked out through the windows with pep rally abandon, waving slick gray pom poms of rippling skin that waggled at one hundred miles per hour.

To the halls of justice, to the seat of government, to the highest office in the land, the victorious malformed hordes of Overmind descended. They had come to show their appreciation. It was payback time. For a job well done.

From there, it all went down in a matter of days.

And that, as they say, was the end of that.

# VIII

# Parable

Once upon a time, there was a beautiful blue world, dancing and spinning at the heart of all creation.

Her name was Gaia, which meant "Goddess of the Earth."

Of all the planets in the dance, Gaia was the most abundant, the most vibrant with life. So many colors adorned her surface; so many hopes and dreams played across her face; so many forms sprang up from her imagination that it seemed as though surely her light would never fade. And the dance would never end.

Then one morning, she woke up crawling with cancer.

It was a whole new ball game.

The envelope, please.

# Appendix

"In our every deliberation we must consider the impact of our decisions on the next seven generations."

—From the "Great Law" of the Hodinonhshioni (League of the Iroquois)

### A Note From John and Craig

One of the scariest things about writing this book was the certain realization that, no matter how hard we tried, we could not envision a scenario more terrifying than the simple truth of what is really going on—every minute of every day—in the world around us.

So when Bantam offered us these pages at the end of the book—pages that would otherwise be spent trying to sell you yet another book—we started thinking.

If we did our job right . . .

If you're just the tiniest bit nervous as you catch a glimpse of the Hefty Cinch-Sack squatting oh-so-innocently in the corner of your kitchen . . .

If you'd like someplace to put your collective eco-fears that could actually do some good . . .

We humbly submit the following for your consideration. It's far from comprehensive, but in showing you a fraction of what's actually out there, it underscores two important facts:

1) How much sheer potential there is for change in the world . . . for better, or for worse.

2) not only can you make a difference in the world . . .

You already do.

---

Special thanks to Allison Jorgensen (with assistance from Linda Torres and Penny Jones, M.C.M.U.A., as well as Mike Walker and Lynda Calore at Kraft & McManimon), for all their help in compiling this resource list. Couldn't have done it without you, Alli. Thanks a million.

# FIGHT BACK

### REDUCE  REUSE  RECYCLE  REJECT  REACT

• Estimates of waste generated in the United States amount to four pounds of garbage/per day/per person. (1500 lbs./ yr. x 250,000,000 people = 375,000,000,000 pounds per year.) That's a lot of garbage.

### Reduce

• Don't buy overpackaged food: items packed in polystyrene containers, surrounded by virgin paper for advertising (not recycled paper), and sealed in unnecessary shrink-wrap. Look for recyclable packaging, and use reusable containers for heating and storage. Not only is this more environmentally sound, the food item itself costs less per pound. Check the unit price and see.

• Don't use the little plastic bags in the produce aisle any more than you have to. A wet head of lettuce needs a bag. Bananas don't. Bring your own shopping bags—either re-use those paper and plastic ones, or invest in a strong canvas-type bag for multiple uses.

• Buy in bulk. It's more economical and it reduces the number of fuel-burning trips to the grocery store. It also reduces the amount of packaging you're throwing away.

### Reuse

• Get your own reusable containers, like a sandwich-size sealable serving container, to avoid plastic-wrap waste. This is cheaper in the long run, too.

• Similarly, "convenience packaging"—like lunch-box-size juice containers—may be handy, but they're landfill fodder. And again, the unit cost is significantly higher than purchasing a large bottle of juice and pouring single servings into your own reusable container.

### Recycle

• Choose glass and aluminum containers over plastic or nonrecyclable materials. Some plastic is recyclable. (Check the bottom of the container for a triangle with a number in it, the kind most often recyclable is Type 1—clear plastic, —which many soda bottles are made from.) When in doubt, choose aluminum.

• Call your local recycling department to see what type of plastics are recycled in your area. (Items with numbers other than 1 are made from plastics that aren't recyclable in many markets.)

• *Always cut the plastic rings* holding six-packs together— these end up in landfills and have caused injury to wildlife.

• Read between the lines on the package labeling. Even though a package *says* it's made out of recyclable paper, it may not be acceptable, or even recyclable, in your area.

• Call your area Recycling Coordinator (county or municipal) to find our what's recyclable where you live.

• Write to your local representative and insist that more materials be included in your area recycling plan.

• Save your scraps. Landfilled table scraps that get mixed with other garbage are unusable. Compost food scraps and lawn trimmings—this can result in rich fertilizer for gardening, and save landfill space, to boot.

• **For more information on recycling, call 1-800-CALL EDF (Environmental Defense Fund).**

### Reject

• Encourage local and national companies to buy recycled products and reduce their packing. Don't just boycott. *Write* them. Tell them how your feel. Simply boycotting doesn't get the message across, they'll just think they need to spend more money on advertising. Tell them what would *really* increase their market share; more money spent on research and development to reduce their packaging and promote the use of recyclable materials.

### React

• If a favorite item is overpackaged (like a tea needlessly sealed in plastic shrink wrap, or packaged in wasteful single-serving foil packets) call the 800 number on the box and complain; or write to the company, if no number is provided. One dedicated crank can carry the weight of hundreds, even thousands of voices. If Don Wildmon can do it, so can you.

## PAPER

• One ton of paper recycled saves 17 trees, 7,000 gallons of water, and enough power to run the average American home for five months. Unbleached paper is even better, as no polluting chlorine bleach was used in its manufacturing. Look for recycled paper products. If your store doesn't carry recycled products, such as paper towels, etc., talk to the manager.

## JUNK MAIL

• Junk mail eats resources and clogs the postal service. To get off junk mail lists, write to: **Direct Marketing Association,** P.O. Box 3861, 11 West 42nd Street, New York, NY 10163–3861. Or peal off the mailing label in the envelope and send it back to the company with your request to be permanently removed from the mailing lists.

## BATTERIES

• Avoid disposable batteries. They contain heavy metals that end up in landfills and constitute a growing health hazard. Buy a battery recharger for less than $20 and use rechargeables whenever possible.

## DRYCLEANING

• For a copy of the report entitled "Response to Issues and Data Submissions on the Carcinogenicity of Tetrachloroethylene, the Main Chemical Used in Drycleaning," call the EPA's Center for Environmental Research Institute at (513) 569–7562.

## ENERGY CONSERVATION

• Caulking and weatherstripping can reduce energy use that contributes to the Greenhouse Effect and needlessly depletes fossil fuels. To help determine whether your windows and doors are leaking valuable heat (or air-conditioning), hold a candle near the seams to check for drafts. If the flame flickers or is drawn toward the seam, it's time to caulk and weatherstrip. It's not hard to do, and it saves you money, too.

• Consult the Energyguide number on major appliances when purchasing items like air conditioners and refrigerators. Look for the highest number rating for energy efficiency. It's more expensive initially, but the long-term savings costs will more than balance out.

• Clean air-conditioner filters frequently to keep them running efficiently.

• Keep freezers between 0 and 5°F, and refrigerators between 38 and 42°F.

• Buy a programmable thermostat for your home. Set it at 65°F during the day and 60°F at night. Tuck in your heater: an insulation blanket on water heaters conserves energy. Use an Energy Saver to adjust hot water to 130°F.

• Use compact fluorescent light bulbs. The initial investment is higher than incandescent, but again, the cost savings in the long run are greater. They last longer, too.

## OIL POLLUTION

• One quart of oil can significantly pollute 250,000 gallons of water. Fix your car's oil leaks by taking it to a reputable service station. If you do it yourself, contact your local/state Department of Waste Management to find out where to safely discard/recycle waste oil.

• Keep your car tuned up; a tune-up every 5,000 to 10,000 miles increases efficiency, reduces emissions, and improves performance. Replace filters regularly. Be sure that tires are properly inflated; steel-belted radials are better, mileage-wise, too. And whenever possible, drive less. Walk. Ride a bike. Car-pool. Dog-sled. Use your imagination.

## OZONE-LAYER DEPLETION

• At this writing, there is a hole in the protective ozone layer as wide as the continental United States and growing. Resulting exposure to ultraviolet rays has been linked to skin cancer and weakened immune systems, as well as damaged crops and aquatic systems. One of the main ozone-eaters is CFCs—chlorofluorocarbons (halons), which can linger for 100 years in the atmosphere.

• CFCs in old air conditioners and refrigerators can be "captured" and recycled by taking them to disposal centers, where mechanics use equipment nicknamed "Vampires" to leech out the gases. Car air conditioners are especially volatile when scrapped, as they contain high levels of CFCs. Ask for the Vampire. (With a name like that, how can you go wrong?)

• Halons can be found in some brands of fire extinguishers. Use dry-chemical fire extinguishers instead.

• Buy ozone-safe aerosols. Better yet, use pump-spray bottles whenever possible.

• And again, write. Contact your representatives and press for legislation requiring mandatory recycling of CFCs.

## OCEAN DUMPING

• Only 3 percent of the water on Earth is fresh water and only 1 percent is available for human consumption. Contaminants released into seawater can find their way into freshwater supplies. To find out more about current legislation concerning ocean protection and the **Ocean Dumping Ban Act,** call (212) 264–2513.

• For more information:
**American Oceans Campaign,** 2219 Main Street, Suite 28, Santa Monica, CA 90405, (213) 452–2206

**Earth Island Institute,** 300 Broadway, Suite 28, San

Francisco, CA 94133 (415) 788–3666. Innovative action projects for conservation, preservation, and restoration of global environment.

## PESTICIDES/PEST MANAGEMENT

**Bio-Integral Resource Center,** P.O. Box 7414, Berkeley, CA 94707 (415) 524–2567. For information on a Pest Management System working toward reduction of the use of broad-spectrum conventional pesticides of relatively high toxicity, call (703) 557–2690.

**The National Technical Information Service,** 5285 Port Royal Road, Springfield, VA 22161. (703) 487–4650. Reports available on neurotoxicity-test guidelines for pesticides.

## RAIN-FOREST DEPLETION

• Amazon rain forests are being decimated at a rate of one acre per minute. *You* do the math. Look for wood products that do not come from tropical rain forests. For example:

| TROPICAL RAIN FOREST | TEMPERATE-ZONE FORESTS |
|---|---|
| Teak, Mahogany, Rosewood, Ebony, Iroko | Oak, Pine, Cherry, Birch, Maple, Walnut |

• Much of the tropical rain forest is being cleared for cattle ranching to provide cheap beef to sell to U.S. markets. Ask beef-serving establishments, like your favorite fast-food burger joint, exactly where their beef comes from. Sometimes you gotta break the rules.

• For more information:
**Rainforest Action Network,** 300 Broadway #28, San Francisco, CA 94133. (415) 398–4404.
**Rainforest Alliance,** 270 Lafayette Street, Room 512, New York, NY 10012. (212) 941–1900.

## WATER CONSERVATION

• Install low-flush toilets. If you can't do that, put a plastic bottle filled with water in the toilet tank to reduce the water level. This is known as a "displacement bottle." It'll save gallons per flush.

• Use a shut-off nozzle on garden hoses, and sweep debris away with a broom rather than with water.

• Install a low-flow shower head. It saves water, costs less, and feels pretty good, too. Use faucet aerators.

• Don't water lawns during hot daylight hours. Water in the early evening instead, to keep the moisture in the ground where it belongs.

• Use drought-resistant plants in landscaping to cut down on water needs. This is known as "zeroscaping."

## WETLANDS

• The EPA's new **WETLANDS PROTECTION HOTLINE** has been created to provide the public with information regarding wetlands function, value, and protection. For information on efforts involving the EPA and other public and private programs, call 1–800–932–7828.

## PRESERVATION AND PROTECTION OF NATIONAL RESOURCES

• Demand expanded curbside pickup programs in your area.

• If you see someone dumping trash illegally, turn 'em in. They're scum. Report the license number and vehicle description to the local police. Be a hero.

• Got some time? Be a different kind of hero. Call your local youth organization or group of your choice and volunteer to organize a trash cleanup of a littered area.

• Got some spare cash? Give the gift that gives back. Make a donation to your favorite environmental action group. And remember to talk to your accountant: it may be tax deductible.

## BOOKS

There are hundreds, and more coming out all the time. What follows is a tiny sampling. Check your local bookstore and your library.

*50 Simple Things You Can Do to Save the Earth* by the Earth Works Group, Earthworks Press, Box 25, 1400 Shattuck Avenue, Berkeley, CA 94709. Also see *The Next Step: 50 More Things You Can Do to Save the Earth.* and *50 Things YOUR BUSINESS Can Do to Save the Earth* by the Earth Works Group, Andrews and McKneel, A Universal Press Syndicate Company, 4900 Main Street, Kansas City, MO 64112.

*The Green Consumer Supermarket Guide: Brand Name Products That Don't Cost the Earth* by John Elkington, Julia Hailes, and Joel Makoer. Viking Penguin, a division of Penguin Books USA Inc., 375 Hudson Street, New York, NY 10014.

*Making the Switch (Alternatives to Using Toxic Chemicals in the Home)*, The Local Governmental Commission, 909 12th Street, Room 205, Sacramento, CA 95814, (916) 448–1198.

*Shopping for a Better World, a Quick and Easy Guide to Socially Responsible Supermarket Shopping* by Ben Corson, Alice Tepper Marlin, Jonathan Schorsch, Anitra Swaminathan, and Rosalyn Will, Council on Economic Priorities, 30 Irving Place, New York, NY 10003.

*ReUses: 2,133 Ways to Recycle and Reuse the Things You Ordinarily Throw Away* by Carolyn Jabs, Crown Publishers, Inc. 225 Park Avenue South, New York NY 10013.

*Two Minutes A Day for a Greener Planet* by M. Lamb, Harper Paperbacks, a division of HarperCollins Publishers, 10 East 53rd Street, New York, NY 10022.

*The End of Nature* by Bill McKibben, Bantam Doubleday Dell Publishing Group, 666 Fifth Avenue, New York, NY 10103.

*The Next One Hundred Years: Shaping the Fate of Our Living Earth* by Jonathan Weiner, Bantam Doubleday Dell Publishing Group, 666 Fifth Avenue, New York, NY 10103.

*Green Man: The Archetype of Our Oneness with the Earth* by William Anderson, HarperCollins, 10 East 53rd Street, New York, NY 10022.

*Dreaming the Dark: Magic, Sex and Politics* by Starhawk, Beacon Press; 25 Beacon Street, Boston, MA 02108.

*Truth or Dare: Encounters with Power, Authority and Mystery* by Starhawk, Harper & Row, 10 East 53rd Street, New York, NY 10022

## MAGAZINES

Again, more than we could possibly list here. If you tap into one, you'll doubtless hear about the others (especially if you don't get your name taken *off* the junk-mail list. Ah, irony). Check 'em out. Subscribe, if you like 'em. Recycle 'em when you're done.

*Buzzword: The Environmental Journal.* 1818 16th Street, Boulder, CO 80302, (303) 442–1969.

*E Magazine,* P.O. Box 5098, Westport, CT 06881, (203) 854–5559.

*Garbage: The Practical Journal for the Environment,* 435 9th Street, Brooklyn, NY 11215, (713) 788–1700.

*Utne Reader,* LENS Publishing Co., Inc., The Fawkes Building, 1624 Harmon Place, Minneapolis, MN 55403, (612) 338–5040.

*Whole Earth Catalog* and *Whole Earth Review,* 27 Gate 5 Road, Sausalito, CA 94965

## PAMPHLETS & ARTICLES

• For information on the **NATIONAL ENVIRONMEN-TAL AWARDS COUNCIL** (a coalition of 28 of the nation's leading environmental organizations), to participate in conferences and awards programs, or to make use of the ENVIRONMENTAL SUCCESS INDEX, call **RE-NEW AMERICA** at (202) 232–2252.

• EPA and the **NATIONAL INSTITUTE FOR CHEMI-CAL STUDIES** offer the "Citizen's Guide for Environmental Issues: A Handbook for Cultivating Dialogue." It focuses on citizen participation in environmental issues and how to get help in solving environmental problems of all types, plus a directory of major environmental and public protection laws. To obtain a copy, call the Institute at (304) 346–6264.

## POLITICAL ACTION

• Get involved politically—one letter or phone call represents hundreds of people. You really can make a difference. Call (202) 224–3121, U.S. Capitol Switchboard. Ask for the name of your congressman or senator, (local, state, and federal legislatures), and for pending bill information.

**President of the United States**
1600 Pennsylvania Avenue, NW
Washington, DC 20500

**Administrator**
**Environmental Protection Agency**
401 M Street, SW
Washington, DC 20460

**Congressperson**
United States House of Representatives
Washington, DC 20515

**Senator**
United States Senate
Washington, DC 20510

• For a complete listing of Conservation Associations, consult *The Conservation Directory* in your local public library, put out by the **NATIONAL WILDLIFE FED-ERATION,** 1412 16 Street, NW, Washington, DC 20036 – 2266. Or call (202) 797–6800 for more information.

Chances are there's an organization out there to cater to every environmental taste; from the eco-fringe to the stolidly mainstream, and everything in between. Check 'em out. They'd love to hear from you. Join one, if you like it. Or start your own, if nothing out there meets your needs.

**Acid Rain Information Clearinghouse (ARIC),** 33 S. Washington St., Rochester, NY 14608, (303) 444–5080. Provides educational services to groups concerned with acid rain.

**Air Pollution Control Association,** P.O. Box 2861, Pittsburgh, PA 15230, (412) 232–3444. Disseminates information about air pollution and its control.

**Alliance for Environmental Education, Inc.,** Box 1040, 3421 M St., Washington, DC 20007, (202) 797–4530. A consortium of 30 organizations seeking to further educational activities to develop individuals and a society that is informed and motivated toward assuming personal commitment for improving the quality of life.

**America the Beautiful Fund,** 219 Shoreham Bldg., Washington, DC 20005, (202) 638–1649. Gives recognition, technical support, and small grants to private citizens and groups to initiate local action projects improving the environment.

**American Committee for International Conservation, Inc.,** c/o Frances Lipscomb, National Audubon Society, 645 Pennsylvania Ave., SE, Washington, DC 20003, (202) 547–9009. An association of

nongovernmental organizations concerned with international conservation.

**American Conservation Associates, Inc.,** 30 Rockefeller Plaza, Rm. 5510, New York, NY 10112, (212) 247–3700. A scientific organization to advance knowledge and understanding of conservation.

**American Farmland Trust,** 1717 Massachusetts Ave., NW, Suite 601, Washington, DC 20036, (202) 332–0769. Informs Americans about the issues posed by rapid depletion of the nation's agricultural land base, the harmful effects of soil erosion, and other threats to agriculture.

**American Forestry Association, The,** 1319 18th St., NW, Washington, DC 20036, (202) 467–5810. Objective: advancement of intelligent management and use of forests, soil, water, wildlife, and all natural resources.

**American Geographical Society,** 156 Fifth Ave., Suite 600, New York, NY 10010 (212) 242–0214. Founded in 1851, the AGS has sponsored research projects, publishes scientific and popular books.

**American Land Resource Association,** 5410 Grosvenor Ln., Bethesda, MD 20814, (301) 493–

9140. For those concerned about wise land use and conservation.

**American Museum of Natural History,** Central Park West at 79th St., New York, NY 10024, (212) 873–1300. Conducts research, publishes studies, and instructs public in natural sciences.

**American Rivers Conservation Council,** 322 Fourth St., NE, Washington, DC 20002, (202) 547–6900. National organization to preserve American's remaining free-flowing rivers.

**American Wilderness Alliance,** 7600 E. Arapahoe Rd., Suite 114, Englewood, CO 80112, (303) 771–0380. Promotes conservation of nation's wilderness, wildlife habitat, and wild river resources.

**Center for Environmental Education, Inc.** 624 Ninth St., NW, Washington, DC 20001, (202) 737–3600. Dedicated to conservation of endangered and threatened species and their marine habitats.

**Center for Renewable Resources,** 1001 Connecticut Ave., NW, Suite 638, Washington, DC 20036, (202) 466–6880. To help expedite the solar transition and to assess its short-term and long-term implications.

**Children of the Green Earth,** Star Route Box 182, Umpqua, OR 97486, (503) 459–3122. Worldwide association to help children do earth-healing work.

**Clean Water Action Project,** 733 14th St., NW, Suite 110, Washington, DC 20005, (202) 638–1196. National citizens organization working for clean and safe water.

**Coastal Conservation Association, Inc.,** 4801 Woodway, Suite 220 West, Houston, TX 77056 (713) 626–4222. Protection of marine, animal, and plant life onshore and offshore along the coastal areas of the U.S.

**Concern, Inc.,** 1794 Columbia Rd., NW, Washington, DC 20009 (202) 328–8160. Publications include overviews and guidelines to encourage and aid citizen participation in governmental policy decisions.

**Conservation Foundation, The,** 255 23rd St., NW, Washington, DC 20037, (202) 293–4800. Affiliated with World Wildlife Fund, nonprofit research and public education promoting wise use of earth's resources.

**Cousteau Society, Inc., The,** Headquarters: 930 W. 21st. St., Norfolk, VA 23517, (804) 627–1144. For preservation of the oceans and the protection and improvement of life. Publishes books, articles, etc.

**Defenders of Wildlife,** 1244 19th St., NW, Washington, DC 20036, (202) 659–9510. To achieve preservation, enhancement, and protection of the natural abundance and diversity of wildlife and ecosystems through reasoned advocacy of appropriate public policies.

**Earthscan,** 1717 Massachusetts Ave., NW, Suite 302, Washington, DC 20036; 3/4 Endsleigh Street, London, WC1H 0DD. News and information service on global resource, environment, and development issues.

**Environmental Action Foundation, Inc.,** 1525 New Hampshire Ave., Washington, DC 20036, (202) 745–4870. Formed after organizing "Earth Day 1970."

**Environmental and Energy Study Institute,** 410 First St., SE, Washington, DC 20003, (202) 863–1900. A nonpartisan public policy research, analysis, and education organization launched by the Congressional Environmental and Energy Study Conference.

**Environmental Defense Fund, Inc.,** Headquarters, 444 Park Ave. South, New York, NY 10016, (212) 686–4191. Public interest organization of lawyers, scientists, and economists working toward environmental improvement.

**Environmental Education Coalition,** Box 268, Dingmans Ferry, PA 18328, (717) 828–2319. To help organizations act in a concerted effort to increase citizen literacy in environmental concerns.

**Environmental Law Institute, The,** 1616 P St., NW, Suite 200, Washington, DC 20036, (202) 328–5150. Nonprofit environmental law and policy research center.

**Environmental Policy Institute,** 218 D St., SE, Washington, DC 20003, (202) 544–2600. Research organization to influence national and international public policies.

**Environmental Task Force,** 1346 Connecticut Ave., NW, Suite 912, Washington, DC 20036, (202) 822–6800. Only national environmental networking organization. To enhance cooperative action among environmental organizations, especially for grassroots problem-solving.

**Food and Agriculture Organization of the United Nations,** Via delle Terme di Caracalla, Rome 00100, Italy (Telephone: 57971). Membership: 156 governments. U.N. Agency to ensure humanity's freedom from hunger.

**Friends of the Earth Foundation, Inc.,** 1045 Sansome St., San Francisco, CA 94111, (415) 433–7373. International organization committed to the preservation, restoration, and rational use of the earth.

**Global Tomorrow Coalition, Inc.,** 1325 G St., NW, Suite 10003, Washington, DC 20005, (202) 379–3040. To broaden public understanding of the long-term significance of interrelated global trends in population, resources, environment, etc.

**Great Lakes United,** 24 Agassiz Cir., Buffalo, NY 14214, (716) 886–0142. International coalition of small businesses, individuals, etc. to protect the Great Lakes against pollution and exploitation.

**Greater Yellowstone Coalition,** 40 E. Main. Bozeman, MT 59715, (406) 586-1593. Combining the political effectiveness of the Coalition's 43 national and regional member organizations in the northern Rockies for natural preservation.

**Green Mountain Club, Inc., The,** P.O. Box 889, 43 State St., Montpelier, VT 05602, (802) 223-3463. To build the Long Trail, a footpath in the Green Mountains from Massachusetts to Canada.

**Greenpeace, USA, Inc.,** 1611 Connecticut Ave., NW, Washington, DC 20009 (202) 462-1177. Dedicated to the preservation of marine ecosystems. Employs nonviolent direct action to confront environmental abuse. Campaigns address decimation of whale population, ocean disposal of toxic and radioactive wastes, the annual sealpup slaughter, preservation of Antarctica, acid rain, and nuclear weapons testing.

**Human Ecology Action League, Inc., The,** 7330 N. Rogers Ave., Chicago, IL 60626-1507, (312) 761-7006.

**Human Environment Center,** 810 18 St., NW, Washington, DC 20006, (202) 393-5550. Organization providing education.

**Humane Society of the United States, The,** 2100 L St., NW, Washington, DC, 20037, (202) 452-1000. Organization dedicated to the protection of animals.

**Inform,** 381 Park Ave. South, New York, NY 10016, (212) 689-4040. Organization that analyzes the environment performance of businesses and institutions.

**International Associates of Fish and Wildlife Agencies,** 1412 16th St., NW, Washington, DC 20036, (202) 232-1652.

**International Council of Environment Law,** D 53 Bonn, Federal Republic of Germany, Adenaueralle, (214) 49-228-269240. Organization for the purpose of exchange of information on international environmental law.

**International Ecology Society(ies),** 1471 Barclay St., St. Paul, MN 55106, (612) 774-4971. Organization dedicated to the protection of the environment from the hazards of man.

**International Oceanographic Foundation,** 3979 Rickenbacker Causeway, Virginia Key, Miami, FL 33149, (305) 361-5786. Foundation organized to encourage the extension of human knowledge.

**League of Conservation Voters,** 320 Fourth St., NE, Washington, DC 20002, (202) 547-7200. National political campaign committee to promote the election of public officials.

**League of Women Voters of the U.S.,** 1730 M St., NW, Washington, DC 20036, (202) 429-1965. Organization working to promote political responsibility through informed and active participation of citizens in government.

**National Association of Conservation Districts,** 1205 Vermont Ave., NW, 730, Washington, DC 20005, (202) 347–5995. 3,000 local districts and 52 state associations work to conserve national resources.

**National Audubon Society,** 915 Third Ave., New York, NY 10022, (212) 832–3200. One of the nation's oldest and largest conservation organizations.

**National Geographic Society,** 17th and M Sts., NW, Washington, DC 20036, (202) 857–7000. For the increase and diffusion of geographic knowledge. Founded 1888.

**National Parks and Conservation Association,** 1701 18th St., NW, Washington, DC 20009, (202) 265–2717. Focuses on the health of the nation's park system.

**National Wildlife Federation,** 1412 16th St., NW, Washington, DC 20036–2266, (202) 797–6800. Dedicated to creating an awareness among the people of the world of the need for wise use of the earth's resources.

**National Resources Council of America,** 1412 16th St., NW, Washington, DC 20036–2266, (202) 328–6530. Provides member organizations with information on actions by Congress and the Executive Branch.

**Natural Resources Defense Council, Inc.,** 122 E. 42nd St., New York, NY 10168, (212) 949–0049. Legal and scientific approach in monitoring government agencies, bringing legal action, and disseminating information.

**Nature Conservancy, The,** Suite 800, 1800 N. Kent St., Arlington, VA 22209, (703) 841–5300. Manages a system of over 900 nature sanctuaries nationwide.

**Oceanic Society, The,** 1536 16th St., NW, Washington, DC 20036, (202) 328–0098. An international organization focusing on the marine environment.

**Rachel Carson Council, Inc.,** 8940 Jones Mill Rd., Chevy Chase, MD 20815, (301) 652–1877. International clearinghouse of information on ecology.

**Sierra Club,** 730 Polk St., San Francisco, CA 94109, (415) 981–8634. To explore, enjoy, and protect the wild places of the earth. 57 chapters coast to coast.

**Smithsonian Institution,** 1000 Jefferson Dr., SW, Washington, DC 20560, (202) 357–1300. A trust established in 1846 for the "increase and diffusion of knowledge among men."

**Water Pollution Control Federation,** 2626 Pennsylvania Ave., NW, Washington, DC 20037, (202) 337–2500. Concerned with the nature, collection, treatment, and disposal of domestic and industrial wastewater.

**Wilderness Society, The,** 1400 I St., NW, 10th Fl., Washington, DC 20005, (202) 842–3400. Devoted to preserving wilderness and wildlife.

**World Wildlife Fund—U.S.,** 1255 23rd St., NW, Washington, DC 20037, (202) 293–4800. Finances conservation projects around the world.

**Zero Population Growth, Inc.,** 1346 Connecticut Ave., NW, Washington, DC 20036, (202) 785–0100. Grassroots organization to achieve a balance between people, resources, and environment by advocating population stabilization in the U.S. and worldwide.

# About the Authors

JOHN SKIPP was born in Milwaukee, Wisconsin in 1957. He and his family recently left Pennsylvania for the greater Los Angeles outback. His favorite TV show is *Mystery Science Theatre 3000*.

CRAIG SPECTOR was born in Richmond, Virginia in 1958. He also left Pennsylvania recently, and now divides his time between New York and LA. He likes high-tech toys and collecting skulls.

In addition to writing novels, screenplays, short stories, essays, set reports, comics and music, they have edited two anthologies of short fiction, and appeared as dead guys in *Nightbreed* and the remake of *Night of the Living Dead*. They also speak at high schools and college campuses around the country.

*The Bridge* is their seventh book.

# Bantam Spectra Horror
*because every spectrum is shadowed by the colors of the night...*

☐ **The Demon by Jeffrey Sackett**
**(28596-3 * $4.50/$5.50 in Canada)**
An ex-sideshow geek moves into a small New York town, and on his heels follows a string of hideous murders.

☐ **The Horror Club by Mark Morris**
**(28933-0 * $4.95/$5.95 in Canada)**
Three young horror fans learn the true meaning of fear when they invite a new boy into their club who unleashes upon their hometown a terrifying, consuming evil.

☐ **The Amulet by A.R. Morlan**
**(28908-X * $4.95/$5.95 in Canada)**
Set in a quiet Wisconsin town, this is the chilling story of a woman's desperate struggle against the terrible power of a talisman which controls and changes the people around her.

☐ **House Haunted by Al Sarrantonio**
**(29148-7 * $4.50/$5.50 in Canada)**
Five people are seduced into a sinister web of madness, murder and supernatural confrontation by a powerful spirit who longs for a doorway into the physical world.

☐ **The Well by Michael B. Sirota**
**(28843-1 * $4.50/$5.50 in Canada)**
A man returns to his ancestral home only to reawaken the ancient blood curse that haunts his family line.